Tales & Transformations

Stories by

MELISSA MEAD

Edited by David Stokes

GUARDBRIDGE BOOKS
ST ANDREWS, SCOTLAND

Published by Guardbridge Books,
St Andrews, Fife, United Kingdom.

http://guardbridgebooks.co.uk

Tales & Transformations: Stories by Melissa Mead

Edited by David Stokes.

Cover art © Melissa Mead.

ISBN: 978-1-911486-90-9

Contents

"It is not often that someone comes along who
is a true friend and a good writer."
—E.B. White, *Charlotte's Web*

Introduction

Melissa Mead was a bright soul. Despite challenges, she faced the world with joy, and brought friendship to many who were blessed to make her acquaintance. Her writing brought enjoyment to many more. She wrote many short stories and was working on a novel at the time of her death too young in February 2022. Her stories were published across a variety of publications, so this collection brings some of them under one cover so that her writing is better remembered.

Melissa—Missy to her friends—had Cerebral Palsy, which left her legs atrophied. She used a wheelchair for mobility. She lived independently in a house Loudonville, NY, near Albany, that was fitted with ramps for wheelchair accessibility. She was especially proud of her garden; I recall her showing off her vegetable plants when I visited.

Missy loved her job working for New York State as a Disabilities Analyst. She was admired by her colleagues and the many people she helped. She also assisted several charities—a particular favorite of hers was Toys For Tots; she collected toys year round in order to have them ready for the holiday season. Royalties from this collection will go into a fund set up by her sisters to support good works by her favorite charities.

One small example of her positive approach to life was her weekly Grocery Gratitude. Each week she would go shopping, and as she used a wheelchair sometimes had to ask for help getting things from high shelves or other awkward locations. After, she would post on social media Grocery Gratitude thanking the people who had helped her. Sometimes when she knew it she thanked them by name, but often it was anonymous strangers who did a simple good deed—"Thank you to the man who helped me get bread from the top shelf, etc…"—but she made sure they received public recognition for their kindness. She believed in sharing and recognizing kindness to make the world a better place.

My own relationship with Melissa started when I ran a small webzine, *Parageography*, in the early 2000s. I was just getting started and so far had received a bunch of unusable slush. Her submission, 'Sacrifice' (included in this volume), thrilled me with its clear language, its sly twist, and the connection I felt with the main character driven by grief into a devastating deal—all packaged in brief tale. It made me feel confident that I would find good stories worth publishing, I just had to look for them. Hers was one of the first stories I bought for the 'zine, and I was one of her first paying publications.

We remained friends after, mostly online but we did see each other occasionally. I bought two more of her stories for the webzine, 'The Mighty Quill' and its sequel 'Second Judgment'. The later did not see publication before the 'zine shut down, so I am pleased to present them here together at last. Then, when I opened Guardbridge Books with the anthology *Myriad Lands*, I commissioned a story from her. The result was 'God Daughter', and when I read it I immediately knew it would conclude the anthology—ending with a pun like an after dinner mint following some rather dark stories. And I end with the same story here. "Always leave them laughing," the classic advice goes, and Missy did just that.

Melissa's joy and empathy shines through her writing. That's not to say they are all happy stories—some are filled with heartbreaking sadness, and even the 'happily ever afters' often come with a price. But she brings readers to the emotional core of the story and reveals the inner strengths of her protagonists.

She was a member of the Carpe Libris writers' group. She was a frequent contributor to *Swords & Sorceress* and *Daily Science Fiction*, as well as appearing in the magazines *Intergalactic Medicine Show*, *Bull Spec*, and a bunch of anthologies.

While she explored several genres, her favorite was the fantastic. The clear tropes, especially of classic fairy tales, gave her a starting point where she could develop ideas by how she altered those tropes. She had themes which appear repeatedly in her work, and I've used these as the framework for organizing this collection. Of course, many stories could contain elements of multiple themes, and I've organized them to highlight some of each of the topics that she wrote frequently.

FAIRY TALES were her favorite form. She wrote a series of stories taking classic fairy tales and retelling, or twisting, or subverting them in various ways. They were a shorthand to communicate with an audience familiar with the traditional story so she could present them with new ideas. Her fairy tale characters are often aware of the tropes of the genre, and she uses this for comic and philosophical effect.

Many of her stories feature TRANSFORMATION of some form. Much like Ovid's *Metamorphoses*, her characters transform: between human and animals, between gods and humans, and even between mechanical and living. Many of the fairy tales and stories in other categories also feature shape-shifting—it is a common feature of her writing—but these are some showcasing transformation is an essential component.

HUMOR is an important element in her work. Again, she wrote funny stories in all categories, but here are a few where the joke is prominent. (Even if she makes fun of Editors...) Some of her jokes are silly, others are dark. But her sense of humor was never far away.

DRABBLES are a form of short fiction that is exactly 100 words long. They condense a story idea down to its essence, often with a surprise twist. Melissa enjoyed this format and wrote a bunch of these. She often used them to combat writer's block—when she felt unable to work on a longer work she would write a drabble to keep productive. A sampling is collected here.

DISABILITY AND ACCESSIBILITY were obviously a major part of her life, and a theme she explored in her fiction. She wrote an essay on how to write about disability which I include here because her insights are important. She found it important to portray people living with disabilities not as objects of pity but as fully realized characters, and to promote that accessibility for all makes for better societies.

Many of her stories deal with WOMEN'S ISSUES. Most of Melissa's stories have female protagonists—though not always human. For instance, her fairy tales have princesses, who often rebel against their assigned roles. Here I collect a few stories that specifically feature women dealing with problems of abuse and grief, or grappling with jobs viewed as traditionally male, or with women's friendships.

Another theme Melissa wrote about was the AFTERLIFE. She did not try to present a unified metaphysics—rather she sampled from Classical Mythology, Christian/Dantean Heaven and Hell, parapsychology, reincarnation, and invented mythologies of her own. She was fascinated with exploring the ideas of what lies beyond death with her stories. While editing this posthumous collection, I can't help wondering what she found—I hope it is somewhere happy.

Finally she wrote about FAMILY. It is appropriate to conclude the collection with this theme as family was a major part of her life. She was particularly close to her two sisters. It is only with their help that this collection has been possible.

Missy left us too soon; I am saddened by the stories that will never be told. She was in the process of writing a novel, the first of a planned series which will never be finished, when she died. But she left us with remarkable stories that brought joy to many readers. I hope this collection will keep her memory alive and allow new readers to discover the wonder of her imagination.

—David Stokes
Guardbridge Books, 2024.

Inside Things

Over her years of guarding her unseen Mistress, the she-beast had learned things:

Strangers with swords were dangerous. Strangers with books were even more so.

Books were inside things, Inside things belonged to the Mistress, not to her guard-beast.

The she-beast struggled for years to puzzle out the mystery of books. Intruders who carried them seldom blundered about the way the ones with swords did. It looked as though the paper told strangers the way through the maze, how to avoid the traps, and even about the she-beast herself.

The she-beast could read the clouds overhead and the tracks that smaller creatures left in the sandy earth, but paper and ink refused to speak to her. The she-beast thought about asking the Mistress to unlock the magic symbols for her, but the Mistress had stopped answering her silent questions long ago. The invisible perimeter confining the she-beast had contracted, taking away the slice of grassy meadow and scrap of shady woodland that used to be part of the she-beast's territory. The grass and trees seemed farther away each day. The she-beast feared she had angered the Mistress somehow.

But she still longed to know how to make paper speak.

Every day the she-beast prowled around the edge of her territory, sniffing for intruders. Intruders left the smell of their wrongness on the dark stones and warm pale sand. Sometimes they got through the beginning of the maze and past the traps, into the she-beast's territory. They wanted to kill the Mistress and steal her treasures, but the she-beast killed them first. Even the ones with books.

❧

From behind a pile of rocks, the she-beast watched the latest stranger. One of the ones with books, obviously. He'd bypassed the sunny meadow with flowers that absorbed nutrients from human flesh, and ignored the fragrant, toxic fruits that grew all around the edge of the forest. Although he must have been thirsty, he didn't drink from the spring, with its icy waters that turned humans to stone. He did pause before the petrified shapes ringing it as though guessing what they used to be. He stopped at the edge of the perimeter, as though he could see it, or feel its burning cold touch, and called.

"She-beast! Are you there? See: I'm not on your land. Come out and talk to me."

Her ears shot erect. An invader, calling to her? Perhaps he'd gone insane from resisting the illusions that surround him.

There were no illusions in the she-beast's territory. Sand was sand, stone was stone, bones were bones. The she-beast didn't believe that this stranger had journeyed from the lands of men and struggled through the maze just to talk to her, but this was something new. Something to make this day different from all the others. The she-beast decided to prolong her treat. When the stranger called again she slipped out from behind the rocks, her venomous tail lying flat across her back, her ruff smooth, her teeth hidden. The stranger didn't see her at first, and when he did, he smiled. His body said No-Fear. Not-Hostile.

The stranger's body said something else, too. It was female, and young. The she-beast had never had to deal with a female intruder before. She listened for commands from the Mistress, but heard only silence.

The newcomer extended her hands toward the she-beast, stopping just short of the invisible barrier. She was dusty and battered from long travel, but a smile lit her dark eyes.

"Hello! I know the rules: Once I cross over I won't be able to get out alone. May I cross?"

The she-beast growled. The stranger took a step backward.

"No? All right; I suppose that was a bit abrupt of me. My name is Suha."

The stranger waited. The she-beast had once seen two intruders meet at the edge of the maze, and she knew that Suha was waiting for her to speak her name. But names and speech were both inside things, and the she-beast had neither.

"Well, this is awkward. You see, Levasarion—he was my tutor, way back, and he's practically immortal and knows everything but common sense, my nurse used to say—he said to seek out the Guardian. According to everything I've read, that's you, but we don't seem to be hitting it off."

The she-beast watched while the intruder sat crosslegged on the sparse grass and took out a book—a dusty, crackling, ancient thing. The intruder handled it with the tenderness the Mistress had once shown, stroking her newly-animated guard-beast.

"Nope, nothing in here about your name. I didn't think so. I've got most of the book up here." Suha tapped her head with a finger. "It's better not to have to open it too often, but I thought I'd check, just to be certain."

The she-beast ignored the chatter, all her attention on the book, lying tantalizingly open on the grass.

"You want to see? Here."

She held up the book. The she-beast strained forward, bringing her muzzle as close to the barrier as she dared, and yelped in surprise. The meaningless tracks of words covered one page, but the other had a picture of the she-beast herself.

How wonderfully fierce she looked! Her teeth and claws shone bright, even on the yellowed page. Her ruff bristled, and her eyes glowed green as the venom dripping from her tail. The Mistress would be so pleased with this picture of her servant, so brave and loyal.

The girl, Suha, laughed. "Look at you! All proud of yourself, are you? You're wiggling like a happy dog."

The she-beast froze, and the girl turned solemn. "But you're not a dog, and I won't forget that. You're a Guardian. I know. Don't worry. I'm not here to hurt the Lady of Promises. I'm here to help her."

Lady of Promises. The she-beast hadn't heard that name since long ago, before the maze, when the Mistress had a face, and a voice heard with the ears, not in the head, and gentle hands. The she-beast studied the girl more closely. She remembered the Mistress as tall and golden. Suha was small and dark. Behind her quick smile lay the gravity of someone who has traveled for a long, long time in hard places and seen things that shatter less resilient hearts.

"They're calling her the Lady of Broken Promises now, because of the storms," said Suha. The girl's cheerful face turned solemn. "There's been flooding and sickness. People are saying it's because the Lady has abandoned the land, but Levasarion said it's a sign that the Lady herself is in danger."

The she-beast's hackles rose. The Mistress couldn't be in danger, not with her Guardian always here to protect her.

"She's not in danger from me." Suha's voice was gentle, reassuring, the way the she-beast remembered the Mistress' being. "But maybe she's in danger from something like an illness. Something you can't see or fight. The book says she'll need a…well, 'helper' was the best translation we could come up with."

Inside things again. The she-beast stood trembling. Her duty was to keep the Mistress safe by killing intruders who made it this far, and she had never failed in it. This intruder had no black-glass sword. She wore no copper ring to protect her neck from the she-beast's teeth. The she-beast could kill her as soon as she crossed the barrier. But if she did, if the Mistress was truly in danger from some inside thing, the she-beast would have killed the only one who might have saved her.

And she was carrying a book with the image of the she-beast in it.

Suha packed up the book and studied the she-beast. She took a deep breath and stepped over the boundary. The she-beast stilled her teeth and claws, but her tail lashed out in instinctive defense. The tip just grazed Suha's arm.

"Ow!" Suha looked down at the green-coated scratch, then at the penitent she-beast.

"You didn't mean to do that, did you? If you wanted to kill

me I'd be dead now instead of later. Maybe it's not deep enough to kill me after all, then."

The she-beast knew better. There were no illusions in her territory. She licked Suha's wounded arm in apology. The poison burned her tongue. She didn't care, as long as it kept Suha alive long enough to save the Mistress.

ॐ

Suha seemed unchanged at first. Eyes wide, she followed the she-beast along the unseen path among the stones and bones. Her eyes got even wider when she rounded an outcropping and noticed the she-beast's secret treasure.

"A pile of books? What's a pile of books doing here?"

The she-beast meant to growl, but only whimpered.

"Are they yours? Can you read?" Suha didn't touch the pile the she-beast had so carefully collected, but she shook her head. "Nobody could read those. They're all crumbling and moldy."

The she-beast moaned. She'd killed the books. Books were inside things, and she just didn't know how to guard them properly.

"Don't look so sad, she… oh, this is ridiculous! I have to call you something more than "she-beast". Haven't you got a name?"

The she-beast shook her head.

"Let's think of one. Something you can say. Something growly. Can you say "Ru?"

She tried. "Rooh."

"Close enough! Where I come from, that means Scholar. Someone who learns from books. Do you like it?"

The she-beast squirmed. She'd tried to learn from the books, but now they were dead. She'd killed them. She didn't deserve this name.

"If you don't like it, that's all right. I can keep calling you she-beast."

A name. An inside thing, freely given, just for her. No one would ever offer her such a thing again. Not even the Mistress.

"Rooh!"

"All right then. Let's go, Ru. No, wait." A mischievous smile crossed Suha's face. She picked up a stick and carved lines in the sand.

"Can you copy that?"

The she-beast had clever paws, but the toes were too broad to make thin lines. She brought her tail forward. Suha only flinched a little. The venomous stinger traced shaky lines in the dirt. Two straight, one slanting across them. The she-beast looked at Suha, expectant. The girl broke into a grin that almost hid her pallor.

"Very good! That's the symbol for Ru. You just wrote your name."

The world spun. She, the Mistress' she-beast, had written her name. She had spoken it. These inside things were hers now.

❧

Ru blinked. With her head still full of the sound of her newborn name, she didn't remember walking the last few yards to the center of the maze: a pale, polished stone dome like an egg half-sunk into the earth, with the dark arch of a doorway facing them. Ru had never come this close to Inside before. She didn't realize she was trembling until she felt Suha's hand on her shoulder.

"It's all right, Ru. You don't have to come with me."

Her voice was weary. The stung arm was swollen and mottled. The other hand, on Ru's shoulder, felt warm and comforting. The Mistress once had gentle hands like that, long, long ago.

Of course Ru would go with her.

❧

The hallways glowed pale blue from something growing on the walls. Ru hoped that was the only reason Suha looked so sickly. The girl's hand was getting heavier on her shoulder.

"The book says the Lady of Promises possesses knowledge greater than any library." Suha's breathing was heavy in the near-dark. "They say so many people came to her for help that her heart broke from pity, and she hid herself away at the ends of the earth."

They took a few more heavy, dragging steps. "I hope her knowledge includes healing," said Suha in a whisper.

The air got colder, pressing down like a weight. Ru didn't realize she'd been walking with her eyes closed until Suha's gasp made her open them.

They were Inside. They were at the very heart of Inside. The round, domed room glowed with warm light, illuminating books and bottles, scrolls and skeletons. Dust danced around their feet. Even in this light, Suha looked wan and shadowed.

"My Guardian," said a voice as warm as the light. "You've brought me a Holder."

The Mistress! Ru's ears perked up, and she looked around the room. Suha was looking around too, but Ru couldn't tell if she'd heard the voice or not.

"But it's too late." The voice laughed—a sad, brittle laugh. "Oh, I got what I wanted! I wanted them all to leave me in peace, and they did. So completely. I'm not certain I have the strength to make the transfer now."

Ru knew outside things, like bones. She found the Mistress first. No kind smile now, no gentle hands, just bones and a voice.

Bones were bones. They should not have a voice. Ru whined. Suha came to her side, holding on to furniture and shelves for balance.

"Oh my." Suha looked at things other than the bones—sparkling jewels and scraps of moldered cloth lay mixed in. "This was the Lady, wasn't it? Your Lady of Promises. Oh Ru, I'm so sorry."

"Ru?" said the Mistress' voice. She sounded puzzled and amused, not angry.

Ru longed to tell her everything—about her name, about

writing, about Suha. "Rooh!" she said, wishing that she had more words. She wished that the Mistress was the way she was supposed to be. She wished that she hadn't stung Suha, who was now sitting on the floor with her eyes closed.

"My she-beast," said the voice of the Mistress.

Didn't she understand? Names were inside things. The Mistress had to understand about them. Ru tried again, louder. "Rooh!"

"Yes, my good Guardian, I know. You brought the Holder to me. But she's dying. I doubt you meant to harm her, but if she can't hold onto her own spirit, how could she hold mine?"

Ru struggled to understand. "Spirit" must be the thing that made the bones speak to her with the Mistress' voice. The thing that left intruders when Ru killed them. The thing that was leaving Suha now.

The Mistress sighed; a faint wisp of sound. "I suppose there's only one alternative. Come here, my she-beast."

Ru left off nosing Suha and crouched before the bones. The golden light wrapped around her like a memory of caressing hands. It flowed inside of Ru and showed her new things.

Words. Thousands of words, like leaves on trees. The Mistress would share all these words with her. Ru would know everything the Mistress had learned from books: how to study the stars, how to work miracles on the most secret parts of the body, how to make the wind and rain dance to her pattern. All she had to do was let this remnant of the Mistress inside her. It would have a body again. Ru's body. Ru would sit inside and watch, and learn more inside things than she could ever imagine.

The light flowed through Ru, illuminated her, left her feeling transparent, empty, like a cup waiting to be filled. The Mistress was straining to fill her. All it would take was a touch. Ru's body trembled. Her tail stabbed into a table, holding her like an anchor.

There were no illusions for Ru. Bones were bones. Bones

were dead. Suha was alive, however little. Because of Suha, the she-beast had become Ru. Ru was not hollow inside.

One last time, Ru killed. She didn't touch the bones that had held her Mistress. Instead, she yanked her tail free, turned away, and went to Suha.

"My she-beast!" the Mistress' voice wailed, and faded away. The bones were just bones now. A last trace of the golden light lingered within Ru. Ru lay next to Suha, pressing against her, letting the golden light embrace her.

"Ru?" said Suha's voice inside her. Ru felt a moment's violent shock, and then a busy whirring as Suha took in her situation. Ru caught glimpses of the girl's thoughts as they picked up scraps of ideas the Mistress had left behind.

Oh, but Suha was clever! Ru tingled with joy as she felt the last golden motes blend with Suha's mind and everything that Suha had read from the book. Suha was thinking of a way to revive that cooling body on the floor. A way that might even work. One paw lifted, flexed like a human hand. Ru startled.

"Sorry, Ru. I suppose that was a bit abrupt of me," said Suha's voice inside her. "Levasarion was right. I do need the Guardian's help. Will you work with me? Please?"

Please. The old Mistress had never said 'Please' to her she-beast. Suha had given Ru another gift. Together, they walked to a nearby table. Suha opened a book, and they began their work.

FAIRY TALES

Charming

Only a few turns into the dance, Ella could tell how the prince had earned his nickname. Those sapphire eyes met hers with such warmth. His smile kindled as though he'd been waiting for her all evening. His touch, while perfectly respectful, felt like a caress. His steps matched hers as though they'd danced together at a thousand balls, even though Ella hadn't danced since her father's remarriage. And his voice, after her stepsisters' scorn and taunts and Stepmother's cold commands, felt like a warm blanket enfolding her.

He brought her sparkling drinks and dainty treats from the loaded tables. She did her best to savor them slowly rather than gobbling them down, marveling at their flavor and freshness after months of crusts and scraps. If her bliss over a simple hot croquette puzzled Charming, he didn't show it.

She savored all these things, the attention and kindness as much as the food. The closer midnight came, the more she allowed her imagination to wander. Everyone knew that the Queen had thrown this ball in hopes of finding her son a wife. Why shouldn't she be the one? After all, he'd picked her out of the swirl of silk-clad ladies. He'd danced three dances in a row with her, and Ella was fairly certain, seeing Her Majesty's thoughtful frown as she surveyed the dancers, that this was neither usual nor polite.

Perhaps it didn't all have to end at midnight. Perhaps, despite her godmother's warning, there was something—a kiss, maybe, or some sort of Royal proclamation—that could keep her here in this bright, dreamlike castle forever, with that strong hand on hers, that intent gaze, those brilliant smiles for her alone. Perhaps…

Behind her, a servant dropped a tray, the crash making a cacophony out of the music. The Prince dropped Ella's arm and stormed over to where a young girl cowered amid a wreckage of shattered china and splattered cream.

"Stupid girl! What are you even doing in this room? Clean up this mess and get back to the scullery where you belong."

He slapped the girl, and both she and Ella cried out.

"Don't, please! It was just an accident. There's no need to hit her."

Charming frowned.

"You're too kind, my tender-hearted beauty." He glared at the girl's back as she scurried away, and gestured for the music to resume. "Once they know you'll tolerate laxness, you'll never get an honest day's work out of them."

Ella was still staring toward the door where the girl had vanished. She turned back to the Prince. He was scowling now, displeased with what he saw in her face. His grip on her hand as he whirled her back into the dance felt tight, impatient. Ella reminded herself that this was a prince, a man who could have her executed with a word, and only said "I've heard my stepmother say the same thing, Your Highness."

"A wise woman, your stepmother. Is she here tonight?"

"I haven't seen her, Your Highness," said Ella. Truthfully, since she'd been careful to avoid her stepmother and stepsisters since arriving.

"And your father?" That dazzling smile was back, holding Ella in the center of a world where nothing existed but herself and the Prince. "I'd like to speak to him before the night's out."

Ella missed a dance step, and the Prince frowned again.

"My father? He…I'm afraid he passed away shortly after marrying my stepmother, Your Highness.

"My condolences," he said, looking as though she'd presented him with a thorny problem. "To whom would I speak about asking for your hand?"

Now that the dream was possible, Ella found herself trembling. "My…my stepmother would be more than happy to speak with you, Your Highness."

"Very well. Take me to her."

Ella tried to imagine which would be worse: his reaction if she refused, or her stepmother's, once she realized that Ella had gone to the ball against her wishes and captured the Prince's attention. The clock struck.

"Midnight! Oh, your Highness, let me go, please. I have to get home."

"Nonsense. I'll speak to anyone who objects if you arrive home later than expected. Or perhaps it would be better for you to simply stay at the palace. One moment."

He released her hand and went to talk to an official-looking man in livery.

She ran.

Halfway down the stairs she stumbled, losing one glass shoe. People were shouting behind her. She picked herself up and ran on, leaving the shoe behind.

The last chime faded. She stood by the side of the path, wearing the stained apron she'd had on when her fairy godmother showed up. One bare foot felt bruised from the pebbled path. The other foot still wore a glittering shoe. She took it off and turned it slowly, watching the moonlight swirl over the glass. Created just for her, her fairy godmother had said.

And she realized the real gift that her godmother had given her. Clarity. And a choice. She hid the shoe deep in an apron pocket, and joined the babbling throng outside the palace doors.

It was like another sort of dance, winging her way through the silken crowd, not too directly, as though she'd just happened to stumble through the doorway. And of course, Charming was at its head, shouting orders, pointing, sending servants in all directions, searching for her.

So she came to him, barefoot, ragged, with the other shoe hidden deep in her pocket, and curtsied, the same as she had in the ballroom.

"What are you doing, girl? Get out of here."

"Beg pardon, Your Highness. Might they be giving away the bits of the feast down to the scullery?"

"Who let her inside the gates? Out! I'll have no beggars on the palace grounds."

She looked him straight in the eye and saw frustration bordering on fury. No recognition at all. The last of her sweet illusions shattered like glass.

"Out!" He didn't strike her, just turned on his heel and strode away to direct the search for "That stunning beauty I intend to wed."

A footman ran up, breathless, holding Ella's dropped shoe. "Your Highness! We found this on the steps."

He turned. "So find me the girl that goes with it! Try it on every female in the kingdom, if you have to!"

Ella didn't wait to see if the footman would offer to try it on her. She scurried down the steps like the miserable wretch he supposed her to be, and rounded the side of the palace.

"Miss!"

Ella turned, her heart hammering in her chest. But the person beckoning to her wore an apron, not a uniform. Ella recognized her as the girl from the ballroom, holding the scullery door open. Ella lost no time in darting through, ignoring the damp cold of the stone floor on her bare feet.

"I thought it was you. Though how you changed your dress so fast, I'll never know."

"It's… Well, it's a long story."

"And none of my business, I'm sure. But you're the first who's spoke up for me, and one good turn deserves another, they say."

"The first?"

"Why do you think Her Majesty had to resort to this fancy ball to find a bride for her son, when most princes—and an only son, yet!—have young ladies lined up after them near from the moment they're born? Anyone who's spent time with him knows what he's like. Her Majesty's been sending ambassadors, holding parties, anything to get him properly wed. To invite every girl in the kingdom? Even commoners? She must really be scraping the barrel."

"He really is that bad?"

"Oh, you just got a taste of it. Some of us girls try to warn off the strangers. But none of them ever spoke up for one of us before. I'm Coral, by the way."

"Ella. Thank you. I never would have guessed. He seemed so, well, charming!"

"He does. Charms any girl he wants to, until the dross shows through. Which doesn't take long. But it sounds like things are quieting down. You should be getting home."

"Oh. Yes. Yes I should. Thank you again, Coral. Unless… Unless there's a place open for more kitchen staff? I'm a fairly good cook."

"Let me see your hands."

Ella held them up.

"Calluses! On a girl who talks like a lady. You *are* a puzzle! If you really can cook, and if it were up to me, I'd hire you on the spot, but you can't stay around here. Her Majesty will do everything in her power to track down this mystery girl. Otherwise she'll lose face. And not everyone's as blind as His Highness. There'll be a reward, and plenty of folks willing to turn you in. But if you head east a few miles to Stonebridge, across the river, they might have a spot for you in the kitchen of The Flying Fox. Ask for Louisa."

❧

Ella thanked her and headed out into the dark. A full moon made light dance on the nearby river. The shoe made a weight in her pocket. The hand the Prince had gripped started to throb.

He really would try that shoe on every girl in the kingdom, rather than "lose face." And dozens, even hundreds would try to make it fit. Her stepsisters, for instance.

Ella considered leaving the shoe on the front steps. She chuckled for a moment, imagining her stepsisters fighting over the shoe like it was the last breakfast muffin.

But it wouldn't fit, because her fairy godmother had said the shoes were "just for her." And when a fairy made something for one person, no one else would do.

They might try to make it fit. They'd crammed their feet into "fashionable" shoes before. Ella shuddered to think what it might take to make a magical shoe stay on someone it wasn't meant for.

And now that she knew what Charming was really like, she couldn't knowingly send anyone into his arms. Not even them.

She flung the shoe into the river, and watched the moonlight on the rings it made as it sank. Then she turned east. With luck, she'd reach Stonebridge by morning.

Changelings

<u>**Part 1**</u>

The woodcutter and his wife didn't recognize the changelings, at first. The creatures looked just like their own children, down to the freckles across Gretel's nose and the tiny scar on Hansel's forehead.

"Only… Hansel's fingers were never so long and crooked," said the mother. "His nails were never so sharp. And Gretel's teeth never looked so pointed."

The woodcutter studied the children, sleeping curled together on the bed.

"They've been sick for a long time, Marta," he said at last. "They've gotten thin—but now that the fever's broken they'll get their appetites back, and be their old lively selves in no time."

ఈ

He was right about one thing. The creatures woke ravenous, greedy for anything that could be remotely called food. All the cakes and fruit that the neighbors had brought vanished within an hour. Within a day, they'd eaten all the bread, meat and milk in the house. The next day they'd found the cellar and devoured all the store of cheeses. By the end of the week the wretched things were still pale and scrawny, but they'd managed to scramble onto the roof and find the eggs in the dove's nest under the eves. These they sucked dry, then crunched on the shells. Marta, frantic, called up to them from below.

"Don't be afraid! I'll get you down. Just sit still."

ఈ

Hours later the woodcutter came home to find his wife sobbing hysterically and the wretched wraiths still scrabbling about on the roof, pausing to chew on bits of thatch and spit them out again.

"They're just children, Conrad. I don't know how they got up there… it's impossible!" She clung to her incredulous husband's arm, while two fierce tiny faces grinned down from the roof.

"Unnatural, more like," croaked a voice from behind them. They turned to see an old woman sitting on the rain barrel, watching the ravenous creatures with interest. Beneath her hood, dark eyes glittered in a shadowed face.

"My children are not unnatural!"

"No doubt. But these aren't your children."

"They look like our children," the woodcutter protested.

"They're changelings," the old woman pronounced. She creaked to a standing position, leaning on her cane, and hobbled to stare up at the roof. The children shied away from her, and hissed. When she poked at them, Hansel sank his teeth into the end of the stick.

"Changelings, all right." The old woman nodded sagely. "Older ones, too. And two at once… that's a first for me, and I've seen a lot of 'em."

"You've seen this before?" Marta looked pleadingly at the stranger. "Can you tell us what's happened to our children?"

"First of all, I told you, these aren't your children. They're Faerie wights, or maybe even logs, enchanted to look and act alive. Your own children will be in Faerie by now."

"But why? What will happen to them?"

The old woman shrugged. "Some are pampered and cosseted, I hear. Others are made servants of. I suspect they're well fed, at least. Others…" She shook her head. "Well, if you're going to do anything, you'd best do it quickly. The Faerie hold on mortal children gets stronger by the minute. If you ever want to see yours again, you have to get rid of these monsters first."

"What should we do?"

"I'm no Mother of Charity," the old woman grumbled. "I know more about changelings than anyone living, and I don't give away my secrets for free." She began to stump off into the woods.

"But…" the woodcutter protested.

"What could we give you?" Marta interrupted.

The hooded figure paused.

"Sugar." Wet smacking sounds came from the depths of the hood. "Sugar, honey, molasses… enough to fill a house, and some over. All the sweets you can find. If this turns out as difficult as I expect it will, we'll need every grain."

"But the childr… changelings… have eaten everything in the house!" Marta looked ready to cry.

The hag shrugged. "That's your affair."

"We could call the wight-hunters," Conrad remarked. "They'd have silver arrows, or whatever they use on unseelie monsters."

The old woman froze, turned, and looked toward the roof, where the changelings growled and wrestled like a pair of puppies.

"I never could resist a challenge," she said. "Send your man to town, to get whatever sweets he can. Meanwhile, I'll show you some of the simpler tricks."

"Oh, thank you!"

"First off, try the basics." The old woman turned to Conrad. "Take them both with you, on your way to town, and leave them in the woods. I doubt you could just lose them, but it can't hurt to try."

"We'd have to get them down first…" Conrad began, but at one look from the strange visitor, the changelings scrabbled to the ground and huddled at her feet.

"How did you do that? Are you sure you can't just take them yourself?"

The old woman, busy weaving a rope of vines and what looked like strands of her own hair, didn't reply. When she was finished, she went to each changeling and knotted a loop of cord around one skinny wrist. The creatures never moved. When she handed the rope to Conrad, however, the changelings circled him, sniffing and baring their teeth. Conrad edged backward.

"Afraid of the little tykes?" the old woman cackled. "They won't harm anyone while the cord's on them. Get along, now—your children can't wait forever."

Part 2

Conrad kissed his wife and left, with the leashed changelings pulling and tugging behind him. "Hansel" watched a white pigeon fly back to its ruined nest and smacked his lips. Marta shuddered.

"Eggs," said the old woman. "And beer."

"What?"

"Eggs. And beer," the crone repeated slowly, as though to a stupid child. "Borrow some from your neighbors. We'll need both come morning, I'm sure."

Sure enough, at first light the changelings came scrabbling at the cottage door. Each one still had a loop of vine around one scrawny wrist, and gnawing on it had stained their teeth green.

"Now what do we do?" Marta looked up from a mat by the hearth. The crone, lounging in the depths of Marta and Conrad's featherbed, snorted and sat up.

"What? Oh...back already, are they? Do like I told you—break the eggs and boil beer in the shells. They'll declare they've never seen such a thing in a hundred years, and vanish. Don't waste those eggs! I like them fried, and mind you don't break the yolks."

Swallowing her protests, Marta cracked two eggs into an earthenware bowl. She poured beer into the shells, propped each shell in a framework of twigs, and lit the twigs. When the precariously balanced eggshells began to steam, she opened the door and hurried to stir the eggs from behind the safety of the table.

The changelings rushed toward the hearth, and then stopped, sniffing. Marta and the wisewoman froze. Each changeling seized a beer-filled eggshell...

...swallowed down the whole thing, belched, and came sniffing toward Marta. Marta flattened herself against the wall, holding the bowl above her head. The changelings clawed at her stockings.

"Well," rasped the crone, "that didn't work. You could try… You devils! Those are *MY* eggs!"

Hansel stopped trying to climb Marta's leg, and kicked her in the shin instead. Marta dropped the bowl, splattering both changelings with egg. They lapped it up before a drop had time to hit the floor. Next, the creatures drained the rest of the beer bottles, staggered about for a few moments, and collapsed in a snoring heap.

❧

They were still snoring when Conrad came home—aching, exhausted, and laden with jugs of honey and bags of dried fruit and other sweets.

"Oh. They're back." He began piling sacks on the table. "Stuff's a little old, but there's plenty of it. Fair's just ending, and when folks heard what was happening, they gave me their leavings."

The old woman nibbled a dry cake. Her nose wrinkled. "It'll have to do," she said.

Under her direction, the woodcutter and his wife found an abandoned charcoal-burner's hut and set about transforming it. Slices of dried apple dangled from the roof. Day-old gingerbread men danced along the walls. Daubs of honey caught the last rays of sunlight, bathing the rickety structure in a sugary golden glow. Inside, they set up a plank table and piled it with slightly stale cakes, raisins, and crumbling barley sugar. Their benefactor sniffed each item, nibbled, tasted, and sighed.

"Now," she said, "we wait outside."

❧

They waited for hours, joints stiffening, fingers chilled. Marta dozed on Conrad's shoulder, and jerked awake when the old woman whispered, "There!"

The changelings came lurching along the path to the hut, sniffing like underfed hounds. They caught sight of the dangling fruit and rushed forward, ignoring the humans in the underbrush. They gnawed their way along the walls until they reached the door, and then rushed inside.

"Now!" Faster than Marta would have thought possible, the old woman bolted forward and slammed the door.

"Give me the torch!" In the flickering light, her gnarled face looked nothing short of demonic.

"What?" Conrad and Marta recoiled in horror.

"Burn the hut! Now, while the changelings are distracted." When the pair still hesitated, she wrenched the torch from Conrad's grip and flung it into the thatch. It kindled at once, filling the clearing with red light and the stink of burnt sugar.

"But they're children!" Marta shrieked.

"Your own children will be waiting for you at home," the old woman snapped. "The Fair Folk will abandon them there and come to rescue their young. Get out of here before they arrive!"

❧

The woodcutter and his wife stumbled blindly along the path toward home. Predawn light began to filter through the trees. Exhausted, Marta fell behind. A shriek tore through the forest.

"Gretel!" Marta called. "Conrad, our baby…" But Conrad was too far ahead. Marta turned and rushed back to the clearing.

Part 3

The hut was a pile of glowing embers. Three bulky shapes skulked away from it, lumbering toward the forest. As Marta watched, one reached out a scrawny arm and pinched its companion. Someone screamed, high and piercing.

"Gretel?" Marta ran forward. All three specters turned and flung themselves on her, alarmingly solid and heavy. Something bit her arm. Something else clawed her leg. Marta wrapped her arms around a wriggling, kicking body, and held on.

"Let go!" bellowed a deep voice. "Curse you, Peg Powler—you said the humans would be gone!"

"If you two hadn't been drunk…" The voice stopped short.

Marta stared. The creature in her arms looked like Hansel—but he was swearing like a demon in a tub of holy water. And he was swearing at the "wisewoman." Sacks lay at their feet, spilling cakes and candies. "Gretel" shrieked and wailed. Only the old woman's grip on her arm kept her from bolting into the forest. The crone turned to Marta with a contorted attempt at a smile.

"Marta, my dear. If you could just let go of my boy, there? We were just on our way to your house when…"

"Your boy?" Marta gripped the male changeling until it yelped. "What about my children? Where are Hansel and Gretel?"

"Your children. Ah. Yes. We were just cleaning up this mess before bringing them back to you. Sugar attracts ants, you see, and…"

"Where are my children?" Marta shook the changeling until its pointed teeth clicked together. It had Hansel's cherubic face, but an ogre's voice.

"Cave…" it grunted. "Not hurt…we swore off Human—ask Peg. Go fetch 'em, Fionn."

The female changeling looked to the old woman for confirmation, then scrabbled off. Marta bound her captive's wrist to hers with the silver chain Conrad had given her at their wedding. Changeling and old woman both groaned.

"You'll go free when I have both my babies back safe, not before," Marta snapped. "Now, what did the other one mean about 'Swore off human'?"

"We're Drowners." A grin spread over Peg' green-tinged face at Marta's involuntary start. "Or were. Got tired of living in swamps, waiting for careless travelers."

"Thought we'd join the Seelie," the changeling growled. "Arrogant sons of…"

"They wanted nothing to do with us," Peg Powler interrupted. "But they laid a geas on us all the same. We can't eat human flesh now. Makes us sick."

"But nothing else is that sweet," the changeling groaned.

"Except the fine sugar you humans make. That's all we wanted. Peg would've brought your younglings back, once we were safe away."

"See?" The old woman pointed. "There they are, safe and sound."

Marta looked. The female changeling crept through the woods, holding a toddler by each hand.

"Gretel! Hansel! Are you hurt?" Marta dropped the chain and scooped the children in her arms. The male changeling bolted for the woods, but the female—Fionn—lingered, watching the scene with a look that, on a less sinister little face, Marta would have called wistful.

"They ain't hurt," she rasped. "Near fell in the river, but I put the Gift on 'em."

Peg Powler froze halfway to the safety of the trees. "You did what?"

"They can't drown now," the changeling explained to Marta. "Boiling water won't hurt them, nor ice neither."

"I… thank you."

Marta had meant to send wight-hunters after the trio the instant she got home. Now she hesitated.

"Why did you do that?"

"You didn't want to burn us. You said 'Stop'." The creature edged toward the woods.

"Wait," said Marta.

Fionn stopped. Peg Powler froze. Marta saw the other changeling crouched in the shadows of the trees.

"Take your sweets. You did keep my children safe."

Fionn's face lit in a smile. The wights gathered up their sacks and crept into the forest. Marta watched them until Hansel whimpered, calling her back to herself. She sighed, hoisted her children into a more secure carrying position, and started for home.

Return To Sender

Hiya, Little Brother! How're you and the missus liking the new place? I still don't get why you'd build on clouds, but whatever floats your castle. What do you do during thunderstorms? Anyway, thanks for the wedding invite. You guys really know how to throw a party. The roast kid was delicious, and I haven't had baby back ribs that tender in ages. You two should come visit me sometime. I've got plenty of room on the Carabas estate. Maybe this summer?

Your big brother,

Barney

✿

Hey, BB. We'd like *our* place better if it didn't stink of human. We'd just got all settled in when this beanstalk popped up near Cloudbank. One of the little parasites must've climbed up it, 'cause the smell's all over the kitchen, and now there's a bag of gold missing. And Nellie let the stinker get away! Said it was "cute." Seriously? Good thing that woman's the world's best cook.

Later,

Bert

✿

Hey, Bert! Still got humans coming up that beanstalk? Wasn't getting away from the little buggers one of the reasons you moved to Cloudbank? I've got to admit, I'm surprised one of them made it all the way up there. Sorry to hear that one of the little stinkers got away with some of your gold. Maybe you can hire that piper guy who catered your wedding banquet to get rid of them.

Best of luck.

Barney

✿

Yes. Yes, we still do. And this time it made off with Mrs. Scramble. Nellie was crushed. We can make do without the gold eggs, but she raised that hen from a chick. The human isn't looking so cute now. If it comes back I swear I'll stew it in its own beans. And grind its bones for bread. Great source of calcium, bones. Darn it, now I'm hungry.

Your frustrated baby bro,
Bert

⇢

You've got to be kidding! I was only joking, you know. It climbed all the way up that beanstalk again? You should uproot the thing. And what on Earth (or cloud) would a human want your hen for? I mean yeah, gold eggs, but the critters can't eat gold (I know. I keep a herd of the tough older ones to farm my lands, and the little buggers always need feeding.) They just play with it. And try to steal it from each other. If your thief shows up in town with a gold egg, all the rest of the pack will start fighting over it. That's why our Grandma Yaga moved out into the boonies, you know. The humans were too aggressive. Especially the ones with tender young.

The humans say "Bad luck comes in threes," so if you really think it's the same thief, maybe you should watch out. And set a few traps. I hear chocolate makes great human bait.

Your loving brother,
Barney

⇢

Hey, Bert, what's up? Forgot how to write back? That harp I gave you for a wedding present put you to sleep? I know you're newlyweds and all, but drop your big brother a line sometime.

Hoping to hear from you soon,
Barney

⇢

Bert? Nellie? Are you guys even getting my letters? You're starting to worry me here. Write back, ok?

Your concerned brother,
Barney

Guys, just a quick note to let you know I'm on my way. Baba says she hasn't heard from you in ages either, so I know something's up. I'll be heading out just as soon as I deal with an unexpected visitor. You won't believe this, but it's a cat! And it's wearing boots!

Seriously. I'll tell you all about it when I get there. Or maybe I'll bring it along. Sounds like you guys could use a good mouser.

See you soon,
Barney

Frog/Prince

The frog basked in the sun. Settled in the soft muck of his pond, he didn't notice the princess until she scooped him up and pressed her hot mouth to his skin.

He kicked out with his strong back legs and tumbled into the water again. Safe!

But he wasn't. Something was wrong. His body twisted and writhed. At first he thought he was shedding his skin, but the change went deeper. Something stretched and pulled him, warped and reshaped him. This body sitting in the mud wasn't his. It was large and hairy, and far too dry.

The frog blinked at the mammals watching him. He couldn't see properly. The black and white world changed. Distances and depths shifted. There were predators all around, maybe even above him, where his vision no longer reached. He couldn't see where to leap. The one who had touched the frog twittered and pointed a hand at him. Its pale skin changed to match the setting sun. The frog tried to burrow into the mud.

More mammals, with what looked like heron beaks at the ends of their arms, surrounded the frog. They grabbed hold of him. He struggled and kicked, but they dug their claws in harder. His legs wouldn't work right, wouldn't fold for a jump. In a frog's last defense, he emptied his bladder. They bellowed, but didn't let go.

The mammals didn't eat him. They wrapped him in some sort of net and carried him away from his pond, to a stone place that smelled of dust. A thin gray man in a sparkling skin pressed his hand down on the frog's head and spoke. The frog's head throbbed. The heron-beak men carried him to a smaller stone place and left him there.

Predators were watching him—the first mammal and another, wrinkled like a toad. The first mammal was pale again. Perhaps it had sipped some of his blood before and wanted more. The frog held perfectly still while the mammals twittered. The throbbing faded from his head, and words slipped in.

જી

"But he's supposed to be a prince!"

"And perhaps he is among frogs, my lamb. Right now he's just a frightened wild critter." The toad-woman came closer to him. "You poor thing. Not an idea in your head about what's happened to you, I'll wager."

The frog tried to leap away from her. His misshapen body sprawled on the stones. He gathered himself up and crawled into a corner, panting.

"What's the matter with him?"

"He doesn't know how to move in a man's body." The toad-woman shook her head. "You know I love you, child, but this is wrong. You're tormenting the poor creature."

"I didn't mean to." The young one came to look at him. Water leaked from her eyes. The frog wondered if she felt as parched as he did, trapped in this dry skin.

"I'm sorry. I thought it would be like in the stories. I thought you'd be glad to be human, and we'd fall in love… Don't look so frightened, Mr. Frog. I don't want to hurt you. I'll ask Cato Magus to change you back."

"No," said the old woman, shaking her head. "Changing twice so soon would kill him—if he were lucky. Besides, Cato Magus won't want to admit that his experiment turned out less than perfectly."

"But what can we do for him?" The young one sounded distressed. The frog wished he could communicate with her, but air wouldn't stay in his transformed throat. It went down inside and hurt him.

"Can you talk, Mr. Frog? I'm Princess Laura. Do you have a name?"

The frog opened his mouth. The sound that came out wasn't a proper croak, but it was reassuringly loud, and his insides felt better afterward.

"Oh dear," said Princess Laura.

The old woman, chuckling, pulled on a dangling cord. More

people came. They brought a round wooden thing and filled it with water to make an artificial pond. The frog's interest perked up, and when the old woman shooed away all the strangers he crawled over to investigate. The sides were half the mammals' height. Half his size, now. This strange, big body could jump that far, if he could only make it work.

"Wait," said the princess. "Put your hands on the edge. Hands. Here. Now stand. Like this. See?"

The frog pulled away from her touch, climbing, stretching out his hind legs.

"Very good!" said the princess. The frog lurched over the side of the tub and into the water, where he hunkered on the bottom until he had to come up for air. The mammals sat watching him.

They didn't hurt him. When his belly rumbled, speaking more eloquently than he could, they brought him bits of meat and watched him lick them from the plate.

"You really are still a frog inside, aren't you?" said the princess. "I'm sorry, Mr. Frog."

The frog blinked at her, watching the movements of her mouth as intently as he'd watch a flying insect.

"Rrrogg," he said.

⚜

Princess Laura looked happy when he spoke. The frog liked to make Laura happy. Laura was gentle and moved slowly around him. Her laugh sounded like the ripple of water. Her eyes sparkled when she smiled, and she smiled whenever he learned something new, so he learned everything he could. Words. How to drink water through his mouth, not his skin. How to wear extra skins. How to walk on two legs. How to smile back. He couldn't tell if the older woman, whom Laura called Nurse, was happy when he acted like a man or not.

Laura was always supposed to be "Princess Laura," but "princess" was very difficult for a frog to say. The mammals called him Prince Robert. "Rob" wasn't too different from Frog, not too hard to say. He rather liked having a name.

&

"Ora!" he called when the princess entered his room. "'Lo, Ora! Thwim me? Eyde day."

She laughed, but Robert could see that she was distracted. "No, Robert, I'm not going swimming with you, even if it is a nice day. I need to tell you something serious."

He dropped into a squat at once, all his attention on her. "Tell, Ora."

"Cato Magus says that it's been long enough that he can try changing you back."

Robert caught his breath. He could have his right shape back, sleek and strong. He could return to his pond and sing in the warm spring evenings. Sing to the females…

The sound he made was neither a frog's croak nor a human's sob. "No."

Laura looked startled, almost afraid. "Why not?"

"No Ora," he said.

Laura's eyes filled with tears. "Robert, I'm so sorry."

He reached out to touch the water that spilled down her cheek. "Don' gry, Ora."

"I was afraid of this," said a dry voice. Robert turned to see Nurse and a wrinkled gray man in glittering robes standing in the doorway. The man looked toward Robert, not quite at him. "He's too far gone."

"Stop talking about Robert as though he were spoiled meat, Cato Magus!" snapped Nurse. "You're the one who got him into this fix to begin with."

The gray man looked affronted. "I merely followed Their Majesties' commands."

Nurse snorted and bustled into the room to pat Robert on the arm. "You poor boy. You can't stay stuck between one thing and the other all your life."

"I'll concur with you on that," said the Court Wizard,

somewhat sulkily. "If he's to fulfill the purpose for which he was summoned, his interior transformation must keep pace with the exterior. It will be a challenge, but I'd be more than willing to assist."

Robert stood in front of Cato Magus, his feet planted wide apart and his hands on his hips. Cato Magus liked to puff himself up with words but Robert was bigger in body, and not about to back down. "What you thay?"

The wizard chuckled. "If you won't let me make you into a frog again, I'll make a man of you."

❧

Not just a man, a prince. Robert soon learned that the second was much harder. It wasn't enough to speak in full sentences and use silverware at the table. Cato Magus, in every one of his endless, demanding lessons, made that clear.

"Princes, by virtue of their God-given status, have responsibilities beyond those of ordinary men," the wizard intoned.

"You make me prince, Magus," Robert retorted. "That make you God?"

For once, the wizard was speechless. When he spoke again it was with poisonous words, as though Robert had bitten him.

"I'm a man who knows my duty to Their Majesties. Perhaps you just can't grasp such abstract concepts."

Robert shook his head. "Frog has duty. Live. Not get eaten. Make tads. More frogs live. You stop me doing that."

The wizard looked amused, not angry. "At least you understand the importance of begetting heirs. That's a start."

Robert sat up straight, feeling like he'd been pithed. "Ora want to make tads… with me?"

Cato Magus smiled one of his dry smiles. "In some ways, the duties of royalty and frogs are not dissimilar. But in this case, Her Highness is genuinely fond of you. My duty is to make you an acceptable heir to the kingdom as well."

"Ging and Gween?" Robert had been presented to Their

Majesties—an unsettling experience for all concerned. He hadn't seen them since.

"And the people of the kingdom. You have much to learn."

"I learn," said Robert. "If Ora teach, I will learn."

❧

"'Thee thells shee sells…' Laura, you know I hate these, don't you?"

She smiled. "Say that one perfectly and I'll go swimming with you."

Robert groaned. "And it's not fair that the word for a thing as wonderful as swimming is sho hard to shay!"

Laura just laughed that wonderful, musical laugh of hers. Nurse, who had been singing tunelessly while she dusted the furniture, smiled. Robert looked her way, and grinned.

"Ora," he said, trying to look beseeching, "the way I say it, does it matter?"

"What do you mean?"

Robert took a deep breath and sang, in a bass that shook the flagstones, "She sells… sea shells… by the sea shorrre!"

This time Nurse laughed too, as they ran for the promised swim.

❧

He practiced, and when the wedding came he said his vows perfectly. And a few months later, when Nurse explained why Laura was ill in the mornings, he could give full vent to his shock and enthusiasm.

"We're going to have tads, my Ora?" he said, bouncing in place. "Lots and lots of little tads?"

She laughed. "Just one, I hope. That will be plenty."

"Only one?" he said, perturbed. "What if something eats it?"

Nurse answered, since Laura was laughing too hard to speak. "It's different for humans, Robert. Nothing's going to eat the baby. And you're not going to swim off and leave my lamb once it's born, either."

Robert took his wife's hand in his. "Never," he said. "Not my Ora."

It was different for humans. There was only one baby. It came too soon. And there was blood. Too much blood. Laura was screaming. Then she was crying quietly in his arms. Then she was silent and still, and for once Robert didn't worry that she felt too warm, because she was too cool. As cold as a frog. As cold as the half-made little creature with webbed fingers and a human face who had taken her life.

"Ora!" Robert sobbed, words slipping away in his grief. "Stay. I stay for you. Shtay."

He looked to Nurse for comfort, but the old woman's face was a mask. She gathered up the bundle by Laura's side, hiding the tiny webbed hands.

"They'll blame you," she said. "The king and queen, the people." One tear slid down the old woman's face. "Go."

Laura had taught him to kiss. He kissed her still, cold face, and ran to Cato Magus' suite."

"Change me back," he demanded. "Now."

The wizard turned, and looked him up and down. "It's far too late. You're a prince now."

"I'm not a prince! I'm a frog. You changed me, and Laura died. Change me back. Now."

The wizard went pale. "It's not that simple. You have duties. The kingdom expects you to be more than a dumb beast."

"You expect. You want to say 'Look what I made!' You didn't make me, Cato Magus. You changed me. You call me prince? I order you: Take your words. Take it all. Change me back before I hurt more."

The old man muttered and grumbled. Robert couldn't make out the words. Candlelight dazzled his eyes, filled his vision. Spicy powder made him sneeze. He was falling, and the world was growing, colors fading…

Then he was crawling out of a pile of clothing, blinking at the man who towered over him.

&

Cato Magus left him at an unfamiliar pond, in another kingdom. "I wouldn't want to be a local frog for the next few months," he muttered as he left.

And Robert understood him. The words were still in his head. He hadn't forgotten, couldn't forget, even if he could no longer shape words with his frog's mouth. Most words.

"Ora."

&

"You're still a man inside, aren't you? I'm sorry."

Robert woke from his dream with a start, and fell off the log. He thrashed for a moment, then stopped and laughed inwardly at himself.

A frog, afraid of drowning? He wasn't a frog any more. Frogs didn't dream—in color, yet! They didn't choke down flies while remembering an apple split in two and shared. They didn't grieve. They didn't talk to the rushes for hours, forcing their mouths to form words that frogs didn't even understand.

"I'm sorry, my Ora," the frog rumbled in his throat.

Nurse had been right. He couldn't stay stuck between one thing and another. But he could no longer be a frog, and he knew only one way to become a man.

&

He swam against the current to a hidden garden, and watched its occupant. A girl, soon to be no longer a child. Today she was playing with a golden ball, tossing and catching it with clumsy hands.

He'd watched this girl, this princess, before. Yes, she was clumsy—and rather spoiled, too. But from the games she made up he could see that she was clever, and resourceful, and determined.

He'd been clumsy himself. He could hardly hold that against her. And spoiled—well, the Queen here had died. He could see loneliness in her eyes. He understood lonely. Any frog grown to adulthood understood about surviving when the others were gone. A frog's duty was to survive. A Prince's duty was to marry a Princess. He could no longer be a frog. He had to become a prince—to shed his frog-self, both inside and out, so as to not endanger this girl. A princess might be able to change his outside, if he could be a prince inside.

He hoped Laura would want that.

He heard a cry, and looked up just as the golden ball splashed into the water beside him and sank. The princess stumbled through the trees in search of it, sounding more and more distressed.

Robert shaped his words as carefully as he could.

"Princess," he said, "I'll get the ball for you, but you must promise to take me home."

Promises And Pastry

I'd just taken a loaf of rosemary bread out of the oven when the old woman appeared in the kitchen.

She looked like an old woman, like the kindest pink-cheeked, white-haired granny possible, but her eyes gave her away. They always do. All the Good Folk of our land have silver eyes, like mirrors with a fathomless hole in the middle, taking everything in and giving nothing back. All their magic can't change that.

Besides, benevolent grannies don't just appear from empty air.

"I'm your fairy godmother, Ella dear," she said.

I stood there with the bread peel in my hands and a smile pasted onto my face, wondering what I'd done to attract her attention.

"I know how you've yearned to go to the prince's ball tomorrow night, and I'm here to help you do just that." Her smile shone brighter than the copper I'd spent hours polishing.

My heart sank. Yes, my plans had involved going to that ball. Through the servant's entrance, the way I'd been sneaking out to do for months. Cook was expecting me. I'd slowly earned her respect through hard work and more skill with spices than she'd expected from 'gentry'. For weeks, my yearnings had involved getting away from my stepmother and stepsisters and doing what I loved best in the gloriously-equipped royal kitchens. Had I really been foolish enough to speak them aloud? I was sure that my ostensible benefactor's plans didn't involve kitchens.

"I don't want to be disrespectful, but I thought that the Good Folk didn't like the word 'fairy'," I said, playing for time.

She didn't. I saw her wince when I spoke the word, but her smile replaced it almost instantly.

"Merely a word, my dear. What do names matter? And I am

your godmother. Your dear mother swore this when you were born."

Worse and worse. What had Mother done? And names didn't matter? To a fairy? Something strange was going on.

"Mother never told me about you, Godmother," I said, careful to keep any hint of skepticism or reproach out of my voice. Saying "Where were you when she died? Or when Father did? Or when Stepmother decided to use me to replace the entire household staff?" could end not only my plans, but my life. If the rumors were true, it might even do worse than that.

I hadn't been careful enough. Those mirror eyes glittered.

"You're refusing my gifts?"

I didn't know what happened to people who refused a fairy's gifts, but I'd seen what happened to people who accepted them. Ida, the Squire's milkmaid, had worn a real silk dress to marry her sweetheart, just like she'd wished. Then her husband was hanged for stealing the dress. The next day, they found Ida's body five miles downriver. She'd barely begun showing.

"I'm overwhelmed," I said, which was true. "I mean—to have someone as powerful as you just show up—I really don't deserve this."

"It's your destiny," the fairy godmother assured me. "You were born to marry the prince."

"Born to?" I had a horrible feeling that now I knew what Mother had done. And why she had died so young.

"Enough talk. This wish has been a long time waiting. Put down that bread, child! Your hands—what have you been doing with them? Such dark circles under your eyes—haven't you been sleeping? And young ladies shouldn't have muscular limbs, like some common laborer."

I was proud of my strong arms and legs. Of my ability to heft full cast-iron kettles and churn cream until the butter came, and make the old iron stove heat evenly. My stepmother and stepsisters, who'd never cleaned a stove in their lives, turned up their noses at the sight of my sooty clothing. I didn't care. I wasn't the sheltered, ornamental thing I'd been before Father's ruin. I had a real skill, one that stopped the neighbors from pitying my scorched and flour-spotted dresses and had them swooning over my baking instead. It didn't excuse Stepmother's cruelty or her daughters' scorn, but it was a consolation I didn't want to give up.

"Perhaps some other young lady would be more worthy of your gifts," I suggested.

This time I had gone too far. The air of the kitchen crackled. I felt a pressure on my mouth, like a shushing finger held to my lips. "What happened?" I exclaimed. My voice sounded oddly muted and flat.

"Take your hands away from your mouth, girl. I can't see your lips. That's better. Don't worry; the spell will wear off in time for you to say 'I do.' And I haven't done anything to you directly, my darling saucy godchild. I've just stopped your voice from traveling further than an inch from your lips. Now; be a good girl and let me make you happy. You'll want a pretty dress, of course. Something pale pink. No, you've let your complexion go too much for such a dainty color. Blue, then. Trimmed with blush roses. And more for your hair. Look into my eyes!"

Startled, I did. Those otherworldly mirrors reflected back my astonished face, crowned with a pink wreath that prickled my forehead. A sudden weight of satin dragged against my body.

"Beautiful! A full-length mirror appeared next to the icebox, displaying the whole frothy, lace-trimmed creation, complete with slippers the color of my godmother's eyes gleaming beneath the hem.

"The slippers are my own creation." She beamed. "Windows, as it were. No, not for peeking up your dress. Don't look like that. They simply show me the area around you. The palace is such a big, imposing place, I can't have you wandering off. And if you do, the thorns in your headdress will give you a little reminder to get back on track."

I shuddered.

"Now, I have to go arrange suitable transport for tomorrow night. I suggest you get to work on your hair. It's a disaster. You'll have to arrange it more becomingly. I've laid a little extra enchantment on your washtub to keep the water hot, and left you some much better soap than that harsh yellow lump you were using. Until tomorrow, my little flower!"

And she was gone, leaving me in that absurd froth of a dress. My carefully-baked loaf lay cold on the counter, and Stepmother's summoning bell was jangling at a furious volume. I stripped off the ball dress, wreath, and slippers, hurried into my other work dress, and ran to answer it.

Not being able to talk had one benefit. Once I convinced Stepmother and her daughters that I was ill with a sore throat, they left me alone for the night rather than risk getting sick. I scrubbed with my fairy godmother's rose-scented soap (no sense wasting it), slipped out the back way, and ran the mile to the palace. The sun hadn't quite set, and I hoped that Cook would be far too busy to notice my tardiness.

I was right. The other kitchenmaids teased me for smelling like a fine lady's rose garden, but Cook waved me in without my having to say a word. The ovens roared at full blast, pouring forth roasted beef and fowl, and loaves of bread enough to build a wall. Two girls were pushing thick soup through a stretched tammy. Others stirred pots, chopped vegetables, and minced forcemeat.

I went to work on a batch of salmon pastries, without joining in the usual chatter. The others commented on my silence, but I just grinned and turned my attention back to the intricacies of working with puff pastry. My stepsisters would have berated me for ignoring them, but these girls, my friends, just shrugged and let me work.

I worked all night and stumbled home to collapse on my cot and sleep like a stone. Fortunately, when Stepmother stormed downstairs to harangue me for ignoring her summons, she took my heat-flushed cheeks as a sign of fever and declared that no one was to enter the kitchen.

My fairy godmother entered anyway, of course. As soon as Stepmother's carriage had rattled off to the ball, she appeared.

"Up, lazy child!" she exclaimed with false gaiety. "Get dressed! You only have until midnight!"

To do what? I managed to convey the question with a look of silent bewilderment.

"To win over the prince, of course! Your destiny demands that you both fall in love before midnight, or all my hard work will be for nothing. Your dear mother would be appalled."

While she bustled me into that bouquet of a ballgown, I pondered. She wasn't granting my wish; she was granting my mother's. Her dearest wish had been for her daughter to marry a prince.

I wish she'd told me. Mine had been, for the longest time, to have my mother back. Now it was to get away. Away from this house, from Stepmother and her endless demands, from her whining, mocking daughters. And from the fairy godmother I'd never wished for.

I have to admit, her magic was impressive—and reminded me that despite her taste in dresses, my godmother was one of the Fae, older than mankind and more powerful than the prince, king, and queen combined. She led me outside (and when I quietly tried balking, a thorn jabbed me in the forehead, hard enough to draw a bead of blood).

At her command, a pumpkin growing near the house tore itself from its vine and rolled to her feet like a dog coming to heel. There it swelled and grew, becoming as large as a coach. While it was growing, my godmother called fieldmice from their burrows and began an odious transformation. The poor things squealed and shrieked as their bodies re-formed, their tiny substance stretching to fill an illusion of horse-ness. I turned away, nauseated, to see that the coach-sized pumpkin had become a coach in truth. My godmother, smiling beatifically the whole time, manhandled me into it. I felt as manipulated as the poor mice.

But as the coach rolled away, guided by unseen hands, I

had time to think. The fairy hadn't come with me. Something was restraining her. And what happened at midnight? If I could keep away from the prince until after twelve o' clock, I hoped I might just get free of whatever curse my mother had unwittingly set in motion.

❧

The bewitched coach stopped in front of the palace. I tried to steal around to the servant's entrance. My crown of roses drew more blood. And this time, the crown wouldn't come off. Nor would the gloves, or those treacherous, spying shoes. Or that overblown dress. Before anyone could catch me trying to strip off my clothing on the palace lawn, I steeled myself and entered by the front way.

A trumpet blast startled me. (Not, alas, right out of my shoes.) The major domo looked expectantly at me. His silence attracted more attention than a shout would have.

Of course. He was waiting to announce my name. But the fairy's prohibition was still in effect, and I wasn't about to press my mouth to his ear in order to be heard. I smiled and inclined my head, and tried not to blush as I descended the staircase into the gaslit ballroom.

After an entrance like that, I had no hope of retreating to a quiet corner, much less the kitchen. Young gallants swarmed from all sides, begging the honor of signing my dance card.

"Gentlemen."

That one quiet word, delivered in a matter-of-fact voice, parted the whole crowd. The speaker strode past the men surrounding me and studied me with frank curiosity. I studied him back. Yes, I stared at the prince. In this ballroom, in this dress, washed ghostly by the gaslight, deprived of my voice and name, I felt unreal. This other girl, this Not-Ella, didn't quite exist, and could stare at royalty with impunity.

The prince's mouth quirked up at my scrutiny. He had a nice face. Brown eyes—warm brown, like cinnamon. A quick smile. He wore the formal crimson and gold uniform of the royal family easily, as easily as I wore my baking apron. A silvery coronet circled his wavy hair. I thought it would have looked better in gold, to match the uniform, but overall he made a fine picture.

"May I have the honor of this dance, Miss?" He extended his hand.

I hesitated. Dancing with the prince only put me one step closer to completing whatever my godless godmother had planned. But my crown of roses dug its thorny claws into my forehead, and the prince looked hurt and baffled by my silence. I had no real excuse to refuse him and no way to leave. I relented and allowed myself to be swept onto the dance floor.

"I'm Prince Theodore," he said, unnecessarily. Everyone knew about the prince, and story of Their Majesties' long, barren years of praying for an heir. Of their rumored meetings of sorcerers and astrologers.

And their longed-for heir was now wearing a coronet that shone like my enchanted shoes.

I stumbled. Officially, the Royal Family had nothing to do with the Fae. Fairy bargains were the stuff of peasants' tales and nursery warnings. Officially, making deals with the Fae was a crime. A sin. The Church claimed that it involved selling one's soul. Officially, no respectable person would do such a thing.

But my mother, a respectable merchant's wife, had made one. I suspected I knew how Their Majesties had gotten their heir.

"Are you all right?" said Prince Theodore.

I nodded, hoping that no trace of my treacherous thoughts showed on my face.

The prince's silver coronet winked in the light of the chandeliers. No, not silver. Glass. Mirrored. Like the shoes I wore.

The prince noticed my gaze. "Darn thing pinches horribly," he said, guiding me through a turn. "But it's expected." He looked at me sidelong, as though about to divulge a great secret. "Sometimes, when I'm in a temper, I could swear it burns. Ridiculous, no? If I'm stubborn enough, it leaves blisters. Father says I'm just not used to wearing it."

I shook my head, laid a hand on his arm to guide him away from the worst of the crowd, and signaled for him to watch. Then I turned my back on him and walked away.

The thorns dug in at once. I kept walking. They clawed harder. One more step. Two. Three. A drop of blood trickled down my forehead. Hiding it with my hand, I walked back to the puzzled prince.

"What was that all about?"

I moved my hand. He gasped. I motioned for him to be quiet.

He produced a spotless white handkerchief from his pocket. Gently, apologetically, he wiped away the blood. "Fae curse?"

I nodded.

"And your voice, too?"

I motioned him closer. I could feel myself blushing, but after all, he'd touched my face. I was only whispering in his ear. "Until I obey."

"What do they want you to do?"

I blushed even harder.

He looked grim and waltzed me back to my seat as the song ended. "Mother and Father won't admit it, but the Fae really rule this kingdom. Even people who won't bargain with them are afraid of them. They're everywhere."

I started to nod. Then I grabbed my dance card, with its stub of pencil, and wrote *"None here."*

"You're right. It's as though they can't set foot in the castle. Miss…?" He bent his head again for my name.

"Miss Ella, will you violate every rule of courtesy and dance with me some more? We seem to have much in common."

I pointed to his coronet and gave him a cheerful "You're the prince!" grin. And though plenty of young gentlemen looked disgruntled when we danced off again, none objected.

"Tell me truthfully, Miss Ella," he said, the music of a rousing quadrille drowning out his voice. "Did you bargain with the Fae to wed me?"

Of course he would assume that. He was the prince, after all. And not bad-looking, either. Most girls would jump at the chance just to dance with him. I responded with a firm headshake. He chuckled.

"You don't have to be so adamant about not wanting me. Was the wish your own?"

If he thought my other reply was decisive, this one nearly snapped my neck.

"Neither was mine. So, someone else made bargains with your life. Can they be summoned to court?"

I was surprised to find tears stinging my eyes. Mother had cared for me, sang silly songs with me, told me she loved me with nearly her last breath. Despite her foolish bargain, I still missed her.

"Someone you cared for. And they're gone?" he asked, more gently than I ever would have expected from a prince.

I nodded.

"Yet the bargain stands. And you're tied to me." He looked grim. "I think the Fae may have found their way into the palace. Through you. You may not be looking to marry me, but someone expects you to, right? And those thorns will hurt you badly if you don't. Possibly even kill you."

Nod.

"I suppose marrying wouldn't be too terrible. We seem to be getting along well enough."

I remembered poor Ida's waterlogged body, the catcalls and jeers from the streets on the day of her husband's hanging. What fate would they inflict upon the prince? And his family. Whatever the Fae had planned, it would leave the kingdom without an heir, leaving an opening for whatever the Fae convinced the desperate townspeople to accept. This kind, gentle young man didn't deserve to be their pawn.

I laughed a silent, bitter laugh, tears of anger and frustration pouring down my face.

"It would kill you, your Highness," I whispered in his ear.

Prince Theodore glared at the roses in my hair. "And it

wouldn't be pleasant for you either, I suspect. But how do they know? This castle is warded against all supernatural beings. We'd know if one got in here. How do they know when you walk away from me?"

I held out a mirror-shod foot.

"Ah. I've heard that the Fae use mirrors and crystals to spy on people. They… Wait, the set's ending. May I escort you for refreshments? It will be easier for us to talk sitting than dancing."

The salmon puffs I'd helped make had come out perfectly. The prince had three.

"You're examining those pastries as though you'd made them yourself and were waiting for someone to judge them," he said.

I blushed, and at his encouragement, whispered my secret aspirations.

"Now I'll have to try all your creations," he said. "These are wonderful—and I don't even like salmon! Here, have some."

It felt strange to be eating the ball supper instead of preparing it, and even stranger to have the prince approving of both my cooking and my secret wish. Even with thoughts of fairy plots filling my mind, I savored each taste, making notes to myself of tricks I wanted to learn after I got out of this bargain.

If I could. This was about more than one mother's romantic wish for her daughter. Official declarations or no, people believed in fairy godmothers. A thousand seemingly innocent wishes granted, with consequences coming years or months later, so no one connected the wish to the tragedy…

"Can you take the shoes off?" Prince Theodore asked.

I shook my head. Thorns prickled my forehead, as though they'd been listening.

"May I try?"

The shoe felt glued on. But glued, not nailed. I gestured for him to pull harder.

"I don't want to hurt you."

If I'd spoken to the prince in the commanding tone my gesture implied, I'd have been jailed for treason. He pulled. The shoe moved ever so slightly. He pulled harder. I thanked the fates that my forced muteness kept me from screaming aloud.

Silk stockings tore, and took a layer of my sole with them. One shoe slid free. Theodore looked up at me and grinned.

"One more, and then you can help me with this cursed coronet." He tugged at it. "It looks made of the same stuff as your shoes, and it won't come off either. I may have to shave myself bald. Your other foot, please."

Just as he took hold of the second shoe, the palace clock began to chime midnight.

What had my fairy godmother said about midnight? I was hardly falling upon Theodore and declaring him my one true love. Surely thwarting the fae's plan couldn't be as simple as not getting betrothed tonight?

Then the pain started. Not one thorn. Dozens, digging deeper by the second. Blood trickled down my forehead. The prince dropped my foot.

"Good God! Ella!"

I clawed at the wreath. Petals flew, but the thorns clamped down. They were going to kill me unless I begged Theodore to marry me right that instant. I'd be able to speak those words, I knew.

I ran. If the thorns were going to impale me, better somewhere far from here, where I couldn't succumb to the curse. And where Theodore wouldn't have to watch my punishment.

I've scalded myself with boiling fat and burnt myself on red-hot iron, but nothing hurt as badly as those thorns, unless it was my flayed foot. Half blinded from blood and the sudden change from bright ballroom to night, I stumbled from the castle's paved paths onto cooler grass. My head and foot were both on fire. Surely thorns couldn't pierce my skull?

The last chime faded away. I'd done it. I might bleed to death now, but I was free of my fairy godmother.

"Look at you, you naughty girl. You've gotten blood all over your pretty dress."

My godmother's voice dripped poisoned honey. Her hands gripped my arm, pulled me forward.

"Most girls dream of marrying a prince. Of course, you're not most girls. You're the seventh generation of a hopelessly romantic family. Wishes right down the family tree, in every generation. Everything was going so well, until your mother died before her wish came true. Do you know what happens when you leave a wish unfulfilled?"

I didn't know, and I didn't care. My head spun. My body felt too heavy to carry, and wintery cold. And it had all been for nothing.

I expected my fairy godmother to strike me dead, or at least turn me into something slimy and easily squashed. Instead, she led me to a cottage and pushed an overstuffed chair under me before I collapsed.

"This will never do," she said. I felt both revulsion and dizzying relief as the thorns slipped from my skin and the crown of roses crumbled to dust. The remaining shoe dropped from my stinging foot.

"Playing hard to get? That really isn't necessary. Oh, don't expect me to believe that you were really running away! You two were getting along so well, dancing so close, whispering sweet nothings to each other. You're really quite fond of the boy, I can tell. You'll have just enough time to get yourself prettied up before he arrives. The washroom's in there. I'll take care of the dress. Go on now."

I didn't move. Some part of me took satisfaction from the small defiance. Most of me was just plain exhausted.

My fairy godmother's lips thinned. Her mirrored eyes tried to lock onto me. I closed mine.

"Very well."

She didn't touch me, but the air around me might as well have grown hands. Something swept through my hair, combing out the tangles and sticky blood, and leaving it smooth. I felt bathed in air, cleansed and once again rose-scented. I sighed and opened my eyes.

That fluffy cloud of a dress was back, and infuriatingly spotless. The shoes were gone, thank goodness. So was the flowery crown, but I had a horrible suspicion that the invisible hands would find some other way of making me obey. Something that wouldn't leave bloodstains on the dress.

Despite my godmother's glare, I actually started drifting off. I woke at the pounding on the door.

My godmother didn't move to open it. She just stood there smiling while a royal guardsman kicked it open and Prince Theodore rushed in, my discarded slipper in his hand.

"How nice of you to return my property, your Highness," she said.

"Ella! You're as pale as paper. And there's blood in this shoe. Are you all right?"

I smiled, tried to stand to greet him, and fell back into the chair.

"Poor thing." My fairy godmother sighed. "It's every girl's dream to dance with a prince. She must be overwhelmed from awe."

"From blood loss, more likely." Theodore caught my hands in his. His were so warm. "Let her go."

My fairy godmother laughed. "I'm not keeping her!" The door slammed shut. The bolt slid home. Outside, I could hear frantic guardsmen pounding on oak. "I'm keeping both of you. Just until you agree to marry each other."

Now I sprang up. Rage can work wonders for blood loss. Theodore's hand went to his hip—he'd clearly rushed out without a sword and was regretting it.

"Two families making wishes for generation after generation… Your Highness, haven't you wished for a girl unlike the court beauties? And what girl wouldn't wish to have you for a husband? Would it would be so dreadful to grant my goddaughter's wish? If you offer, I'll grant her leave to say I Do."

"What would be dreadful, Madam, would be to grant your wish. Dreadful for the entire kingdom."

The coronet flared. Theodore gasped. His hands flew instinctively to pull off the burning circlet and jerked away, blistered. The smell of burnt hair overpowered the scent of roses. I stamped my foot.

"What is it, my dear? You want this charming young man to marry you? To grant your wish?"

I didn't look at her. I looked at Theodore, willing him to understand what I was trying to tell him. At the word "wish," I nodded vigorously.

You don't grow up to be a successful prince without being able to pick up on nuances. Prince Theodore went down on one knee before me.

"Miss Ella," he said, as charmingly as he could manage despite the pain, "would you give me the honor of granting your greatest wish?"

My fairy godmother looked ready to burst with triumph. The band on my throat loosened.

"I do!" I shouted.

Prince Theodore ripped off the coronet—now dull—and flung it away. The frilly gown became my old brown dress and apron. The cottage door crashed open, and the guardsmen grabbed hold of my fairy godmother. She twisted in their grip, looking incredulous.

"So that's what happens when a wish goes unfulfilled," I said. It felt so good to speak aloud again! "It limits your power. That's why you wanted me back before midnight. And when your victims actually say no to you… well, I doubt you have the power to turn a pumpkin into pie right now."

"But… you said I Do! I granted your wish!"

"My late mother's wish, not mine. My wish is to become the prince's chef, not his wife. No offense meant, your Highness."

"None taken. I do hope that you are capable of turning pumpkins into pies?"

"Absolutely."

"Then I'll officially welcome you to my staff tomorrow." He

gestured to the guardsmen to take the fuming fairy godmother away.

"You look better in the apron," said the Prince. "More like yourself. I don't mean that disrespectfully…"

"I understand, Your Highness. And you're right. I feel more like myself."

We looked anywhere but at each other.

"It might not have been so bad, granting your mother's wish," he said.

"Maybe not. But I suppose there are alliances and things to be considered."

"There always are. Miss Ella?"

"Yes, Your Highness?"

"Please, call me Theodore. I give you official permission."

"Thank you… Theodore."

No, it wouldn't have been so bad, if it hadn't been for the fairy's machinations. Perhaps in a few years…

I bowed, and Theodore and I headed back to the castle. Home. I smiled.

One wish at a time.

The Fairest Of Them All

Of course Snow White was an alias. My real name is Bethanie. It's all right to name a guard dog or a milk cow something like Red Fang or Old Brownie, but no mother would label her daughter with a set of adjectives instead of giving her a proper name. A good queen just wouldn't do that to her people, give them a princess with a name chosen out of a paint box, just because the girl had "skin as white as snow, lips as red as blood, and hair as black as ebony wood." It's terribly undignified, and superficial too. My mother understood how important it was to take her responsibilities seriously, and that included not naming her daughter after her complexion.

That's what the whole business was all about, really. Being a responsible queen. Being fair to the kingdom. That's what they called my mother—Constance the Fair. I try to be. I know I haven't had as much experience in ruling as I might have had, but you've got to admit that things were pretty awful under…*her*, and I plan to make them better.

Sure I'll tell you the whole story. Go ahead and cover the mirror; it would be wrong to break it, but that doesn't mean we have to have that face looking down on us while we talk.

The minstrels have gotten so many things wrong already. They like to claim that my mother died when I was born. It sounds so dramatic and touching, and I'm sure the minstrels mean well, but really I was old enough that I remember my mother quite well. She didn't die in childbirth. She had been trying to negotiate with a dragon who lived in the Sooty Mountains. The dragon had been stealing sheep from the local villagers. My mother had heard the villager's side of the story, (which would have ended, if they had their way, with the dragon's severed head hanging over the doorway of the village hall), and she felt it was only right to hear the dragon's side too. So she rode out to the Sooty Mountains and announced herself as an emissary from our kingdom. Unfortunately, in the

Dragon language, the word for "emissary" is the same as the word for "hors d'oeuvre."

I missed her terribly. She used to read to me when I was little, and teach me how to dance and sing and draft legal documents in a fair hand, and all those things that a princess is supposed to know. I cried for a while, and then I decided that I'd make her proud by being a splendid Queen someday, and make this kingdom into the sort that gets written into the Happily Ever After Listings.

Father missed her too, but he dealt with it differently. The way he saw it, Mother had gotten herself killed because she insisted on dealing with the dragon herself, rather than delegating the task to one of the members of the court.

"Talking to monsters. In my day we whacked their heads off. My sainted mother, Lady Aletheia… she never tried talking to dragons! Proper lady, she was. Embroidered, dressed well… none of this 'justice and diplomacy' nonsense. My poor Constance. Crisped by a dragon. Such a lovely woman, too."

He gave me a regretful look. I wished I wasn't wearing my oldest dress, pitted with holes from experimenting with my Little Enchantress alchemy set.

"Proper feminine role models. That's what's lacking. Can't go on like this. Place needs a woman's touch."

"Mrs. Kettleburn's a woman, Daddy," I pointed out, naming the castle's housekeeper. "And Jayel from the Huntmaster's stables, and Sophy, Tracy, Christina and Jenny in the kitchen."

"A gentlewoman, child! Someone refined. With that certain Jeanie Sayquoy."

"Je ne sais quoi," I corrected, unheard. "Don't do it, Daddy! I read in *Enchantress Weekly* that any stepmother in a kingdom with an Enchanted Forest just outside the gate and dragons within a 50-mile radius has a 93.7% chance of turning evil."

But he didn't listen.

❧

Lady Sable arrived within a month. I'd barely changed my muddy clothes—when her carriage arrived at the castle I was out in my garden, trying to improve the growth rate of my beans—before Father summoned me to meet her. He wore a disturbing expression, equal parts awe, glee, confusion, and terror. The strange woman stood before him, straight as a waxwork. She had no more expression than a hatmaker's mannequin. The newcomer ran to me and caught my chin in her hand.

"Such perfect bone structure!" she gasped. "Those cheekbones, that glorious black hair, that snow-white complexion…which face powder do you use, child?"

She turned my face back and forth, scrutinizing me from under eyelids painted like storm clouds. I felt like a bug pinned inside a collector's box.

"None, Ma'am," I said when she released my bruised chin.

"What?" Her eyes narrowed. Her scarlet mouth thinned. That carefully-painted face looked about to crack.

"Lady Sable, this is my daughter…" Father began.

"It's natural? No powder, no rouge?"

"Bethanie takes after her mother," said my father. "Quite the fair young lady."

Lady Sable glared at me. "Indeed."

❧

Lady Sable's squadron of servants included a dancing-master, a lady's maid, and teachers in elocution and deportment. To my horror, I learned that these last were for my benefit.

"Your education's been lopsided," my father said. "Sable will set you right. Quite the beauty, Sable. Knows all that feminine fol-de-rol. Answer to a prayer." The besotted look faded for a moment. "Not that she's Constance. But as Constance herself used to say, 'For the greater good,' hey?"

The besotted look returned. Lady Sable's army descended with tapes and shears, and strapped me into a whalebone restraint called a "fashionable corset." They wrapped me in gilded crimson velvet, and braided my hair into a Medusa's tangle. Then Sable painted me with white lead and crushed beetles. My cheeks swelled. My eyes watered. I scrubbed the stuff off while Lady Sable cackled.

"It really is natural. Pray it lasts, young lady. Once age sinks its claws into you you'll be a mummified crone, with no way to lessen the blow."

"Lady Sable," I wheezed.

"You look like you've been stung by a wasp…"

"Lady Sable…"

"Like someone's blacked your eyes…"

"Lady Sable, I can't breathe!" I staggered against the cosmetics box, spattering everyone with eyeliner and clots of rouge. Powder billowed in choking clouds. The hairdresser cut the corset strings just before I blacked out. Lady Sable threw a tirade and banished me to my room until after the wedding. Looking back, I wonder if she arranged the whole fiasco so I couldn't disrupt the wedding.

She dragged me out to show off her favorite wedding present—a full-length mirror, the frame beautifully carved with leaves and vines. While Sable preened before it, I examined the back.

"It's by the WNDFTFT!" I exclaimed.

"The what?" said Queen Sable.

"The Homunculi Brothers. WNDFTFT stands for 'We're Not Dwarves, for the Fortieth Time!'" I explained. "People call them the Eight Dwarves. They make the best enchanted products."

"My mirror's enchanted? Make it work!"

She shook the mirror. I flipped the switch on the back.

A starburst of light radiated from the glass. I blinked away the pink afterimage, and a worried spectral face peered from the frame.

"Too melodramatic? Sorry, I'll tone it down. Ahem. I am Fred, the Servant in the Mirror, bound in this vitreous state to serve the owner of this mirror…"

"Fred?" I said. "Just Fred?"

"Just Fred, fair maiden."

"I'm your owner, slave!" Queen Sable interrupted. "Address me as Your Majesty."

The spirit's face fell. "Well, technically you own the mirror, not me."

"I also own a large, heavy scepter."

The glass was sweating now. "Yes Ma'am. Your Majesty. Um, I'm required to state that the owner of this mirror shall agree to hold the crafters blameless in the event of malfunction, breakage…"

"Enough! What are you enchanted to do?"

"Er, talk," said the mirror-spirit. Sable frowned.

"That is, I can praise Your Majesty's charms in fulsome and extravagant terms…"

She leaned forward. "Go on."

I left poor Fred stammering odes to Sable's every feature from earlobes to toenails. I wanted to find my father. No one had seen him since the ceremony.

He was in bed, feverish. I ran back to the hall. Poor Fred looked relieved to be interrupted. Queen Sable, furious, banished me from the hall. I set to work with my alchemy set.

I developed a floor wax, six varieties of hot sauce, and a lotion that de-warted toads, but no fever cures. I spent every moment that I wasn't with him with that alchemy set, trying in vain to find something to save him. Father got steadily worse. Lady Sable discovered my experiments and confiscated the set.

❧

After Father died, Queen Sable kept me running after ingredients for new beauty potions. When I objected, she threatened me with a loaded blush-brush. Fortunately, she never noticed my substitutions: well water for dragon tears, or crushed eggshells for powdered unicorn horn.

I was pondering a plausible substitute for fairy gold when Fred hailed me from his mirror.

"Fred? You look glassy-eyed."

"I'm inside a mirror! I always look glassy eyed!" he shouted. "Sorry… Princess, I tried to object, but the sadist has a glass-cutter—"

"Object to what?"

The tapping of Queen Sable's six-inch stilettos echoed through the marble hallways. "Find the Speaking Oak," Fred whispered.

Lady Sable spotted me and beamed. "Ah, there you are! I've splendid news. I've discovered the Elixir of Youth! It just needs the heart's blood of a fair maiden."

I started to protest that I wouldn't murder some poor girl just so she could make wrinkle cream. When she summoned our Master Huntsman, I realized she meant me.

Wulfgar had faced charging boars, but he would've preferred rabid wolverines to Queen Sable. If he'd had a tail, it would've been tucked between his legs.

"Remove her heart, Huntsman," said Queen Sable. "But not over the carpet! Outside."

"Woooods…" Fred moaned. "Harness the power of the Wooooods!"

With no idea what Fred was doing, I played along. "Not the Enchanted Forest!"

Queen Sable's face lit up. "Perfect! That infuses the elixir with Arcane Mystical Forces. Wonderful exfoliant. Do it there."

Poor Wolfie looked nauseated. I acted like he was forcing me out the door. Once we'd crossed the bridge, he cried "I won't kill you, Princess! Even if that witch has me tortured. Which she'd enjoy."

I could've hugged him. "Trick her. I do it all the time. Just point me toward the Speaking Oak, please."

Wolfie obliged, looking savagely gleeful about hunting something edible instead. I ran the other way.

The Enchanted Forest unfolded around me as I passed. Twittering birds landed on my shoulders. Wide-eyed rabbits hopped around my feet. Graceful deer stepped out into the path in front of me. I really wished they'd all get out of the way so I could stop tripping over them. Despite their crowding, I managed to get to the Speaking Oak. It stood alone in a small clearing, golden sunlight raining down on its mighty branches. When I approached, the limbs waved as though storm-tossed. Verdant eyes opened below the crown. A mouth-like crack split the bark.

"Yoohoo, boys!" the tree bellowed. "Company!"

Wizened faces peered from behind trunks. I'd never seen anyone like those people—stick-thin, their skin patterned like wood grain. The tallest was barely my height, yet they weren't children. They glanced toward the tree, green eyes wide.

"Oh, for sap's sake, don't be bashful! She's that nice princess Fred talks about. Come say hello."

"You know Fred?" Compared to talking trees and silent tree-men, the disembodied mirror-spirit seemed comfortingly familiar.

"Honey, they *made* Fred!" the Speaking Oak boomed. "I'm Donna. These are my boys: Orrery, Astrolabe, Ratchet, Kerf, Mortise, Bevel, and Chris. The best crafters in the Enchanted Forest."

"Chris?"

The smallest crafter blushed, looking polished.

Recognition dawned. "You're the WNDFTFT! Aren't there eight of you?"

Mortise looked at his feet. "Tenon got sick of people calling us dwarves, when we lived in town. Said he wanted to move back to the Forest and put down roots," he said. "So he did. Deep ones. Now we can't dig him up."

"Tenon always was a stick in the mud," said Donna, unperturbed.

My head spun. "Donna? The Homunculi Brothers are your children?"

"All branched from the same family tree," said Donna proudly. "Had a crafter's knack since they were little sprouts. The whole Forest respects them, because they never cut living wood and give new life to dead wood with their work. You'll be safe with them."

The little men led me deeper into the woods. No one spoke but Chris, who talked enough for all seven.

"You're the meat people's princess? Shouldn't you be Queen? You know we're not dwarves, right? Dwarves are meat people. We're not. Why does the Queen want you chopped down? Because Fred says you're pretty? Fred says you know Alchemy. Do you know LaVerre's Transformation? I think…"

"Chris, stuff a knot in it," said Orrery, and the smallest Crafter fell silent.

❧

We reached a clearing. Orrery stumped over to a nearby thicket to argue with a sapling.

"Tenon says she's to stay in the workshop," he reported. "And Fred's so upset he's about to crack."

"Fred? Fred's in the castle!" I said.

"I thought you knew alchemy!" Chris chided. "Fred's a mirror-spirit, not a mirror. C'mon." He wrapped twiggy fingers around my hand and pulled me through the thicket into an open space. Towering trees formed a living fence around us, branches twining overhead. The dirt floor had been planed smooth. I turned in slow circles, awed. The place melded an alchemist's laboratory, woodworker's shop, forge, and greenhouse. The forge had its own stone-shielded corner. Workbenches lined one wall. Plants sprouted from tabletops. Flasks and beakers dangled from branches growing through walls. A spring bubbled through a hole in the floor and streamed out between the tree trunks. There was only one true door in the workshop, flanked by pines.

"Flesh people aren't supposed to see this," said Chris. "But Tenon says you'll need a roof and a fire, and the forge is the only fire we allow near the living trees. You won't tell, will you, Princess?"

"Of course not."

"Tenon, we've got a crisis here!" shouted a familiar voice from behind the door.

"Fred!"

Chris nodded. On the other side of the door was a gatehouse, lit with alchemical lamps that switched on and off like Fred's mirror.

"Tenon?" said Fred's voice from behind a curtain on the opposite wall.

"Don't crack yourself. We're here," said Chris.

The curtain hid a mirror, plainer than Sable's, with Fred's anxious face peering from it. If color could've rushed back to his face when he saw me, it would've. I'd considered him a sort of two-dimensional court jester. He wasn't joking now.

"Princess! Thank goodness. Wolfie brought back this dripping… anyway, you're alive!"

"Did Queen Paintbox really eat something's heart?" said Chris, with nauseated glee.

"Yes, you twisted little rootstock. Raw. She couldn't bully anyone into cooking it."

"Ewww!"

"Enough of that," said Orrery from behind us. "Fred, what's up?"

"Everyone's mourning the princess. Sable's bought a black mink cloak for the occasion and created a new Blush Tax to pay for it." Fred flickered nervously. "And Wolfie wants out. I don't blame him. Anyway, he wants you to perform LaVerre's Transformation on him."

Orrery frowned. "I'll consider it."

"I think we should Transform *you*, Fred!" Chris piped up. "Then you could—"

"Chris," said the mirror-spirit, "Shut up. Go find the nice lady some food. Like fruit and nuts. No dirt. And something soft to sleep on."

"Flesh people are so delicate!" Chris scampered off, shedding leaves.

"It's so good to see you, Princess!" Fred was beaming, but I was too bewildered to be polite.

"Start explaining or I'll soap you."

"Er, yes. I suppose I should introduce myself properly: Alfred Glass, Homunculi Brothers Prints and Images Division, mirror-spirit and W and D FTFP agent. At your service, Princess."

"WNDFTFT agent?"

He smiled, and spelled it out properly. "Wild and Domestic Faerie-Tale Forest Protectors," he explained. "Although the mixed-up version's wonderful for our cover."

"Cover? You're a spy?"

He shook his head. "A counselor to the Royal Family. I was with your lady mother when she faced the dragon. Reflected in her shield. But the smoke dulled the polish… there was nothing to hold. I failed her. I'm sorry, Princess."

I swallowed. "Then why do you serve…*her?*"

He winced. "I watch Sable. We need eyes in the castle, and I can go places Wolfie can't. A mirror, a basin of water, polished silver—all windows, to me."

"Peeping Tom."

"Princess! I swear by my silver backing, I'm a gentleman. And mirrors don't lie."

I believed him. I realized that he could've been spying for Queen Sable, but I doubted it. Sable was too unpredictable to win the loyalty of someone she could shatter in a fit of temper.

"Anyway, what's this LaVerre's Transformation that Wolfie wants? Why does Chris think you should do it too?"

He grimaced. "A shapechanging spell. Excruciatingly painful, but effective. You did know that Wulfgar's a werewolf, right?"

"No, I did not!"

"Oh shards. I assumed all the Royal Family knew. Well, he is. You're all perfectly safe; he has a weak stomach and only eats beef tea and lamb chops. But he wants wants the Brothers to change him into a real wolf, so Sable can't find him. "

"Why does Chris want you to transform?"

"The little troublemaker thinks it would be funny to turn

me into a human man," said Fred shortly. "Never mind that it would hurt worse than cracking one of my mirrors would. Ah—the Royal Face-Powder Keg is calling me to tell her she's the 'fairest of all' again. Fortunately, since 'fair' can mean 'light-complexioned' and she's wearing inch-thick white talc, I'm safe. Pardon me…"

He vanished. Over time I grew accustomed to that, living in the gatehouse. Fred and I talked a lot. He was wiser than I'd given him credit for.

"I've had a lot of time to reflect," he said.

The brothers were uncomfortable with having me around while they worked at first, but I made myself useful, first by keeping the place clean and washing the glassware, and eventually by helping with experiments. Chris appointed himself my teacher. Fred's latest news gave me an incentive to learn everything I could: Queen Sable had started experimenting with my old alchemy kit and was fast becoming a competent alchemisorceress.

So was I. Turning lead into gold was easy. Wolfie's Transformation was hard both to assist with and to watch. By the end the poor wolf was panting and exhausted, hoarse from howling. I could see why Fred didn't want to put himself through such an ordeal.

Within a year I was a full-fledged sorceress and member of the W+DSFTFP, with "Snow White" as my alias. The kingdom was in chaos. Queen Sable passed sumptuary laws banning cosmetics for commoners. Her Vanity Police flogged anyone wearing so much as lipstick. Three bears caught eating their breakfast porridge were accused of making oatmeal scrub and shaved bald. The rumors grew worse and worse… every week we heard of girls locked in towers or having their hair shorn off, or men sticking sausages to their wives' noses in order to avoid the Vanity Police.

"We have to distract Sable." I told the W+DFTFP. We'd all crowded into the gatehouse for Fred's latest report. "Get her attention off the people long enough for them to rebel."

"And onto what?" said Ratchet.

I grinned. "Snow White."

"No!" said Fred. "I'll have no part in it." He vanished, but I was a certified Alchemisorceress now. I knew how his mirrors worked. I flicked the switch on and off, turning the lights on and off with it, until he returned.

"Stop! You're making me dizzy."

"Will you help?"

"No."

"You owe it to the kingdom."

"No."

"You owe it to my mother."

He looked like I'd threatened him with a sledgehammer. "Not fair!"

"What do you want Fred to do?" Chris piped up.

"I want him to help me make the Queen so jealous of 'Snow White' that she'll forget everything else," I said, still staring down Fred. "All he has to do, the next time Queen Sable comes to him for reassurance, is to say that Snow White is the fairest woman in the kingdom, not her."

"So why won't he? 'Snow White's' just a made-up name. Or does that mean that Fred would have to lie? 'Cause he can't."

"Because Sable will look for her, you knothead!" For an image, Fred looked quite solidly stubborn. Snow White's a fiction, but Bethanie is a real person. A person that I… that I'm sworn to protect."

"Fine," I said. "I'll distract her myself. In person."

"*NO!* I'll do it. But promise me that you won't leave the workshop alone. Please."

I sighed. "Fair enough."

"I don't think it'll work," said Chris. "Because you said the princess wasn't being fair. So you can't say she's the fairest of all."

"Oh, she is," said Fred, with a look that made me forget how to breathe. The glass of the mirror fairly glowed. "She is."

❧

Fred did his work well. Soon Queen Sable was spending days at her mirror, skeletal and hollow-eyed from forgetting to eat and sleep.

"You're a genius, Princess," said Orrery. "Half the Queen's Guard's quit because she forgets to pay them. She doesn't ride around the kingdom scrubbing pretty girls' faces with cold cream any more. No one's hiding their daughters behind briar hedges or sending them to live with monstrous but possessive beasts just to keep them away from the Vanity Police. Snow White's becoming a legend."

"Snow White's becoming an obsession," said Fred. He didn't sleep, but he was developing a nervous flicker in his reflection. "Sable knows, Princess! She talks to her reflection. She knows you're alive. It's driving her mad that she doesn't know where or how."

I'd never seen Fred so terrified. "It's not like she knows where I am," I pointed out.

"You don't understand!" Fred wailed. "I can't lie! If she asks me how to find you, straight out with no room for misinterpretation, I'll have to tell her. I've told her where to find the Fairest of Awls, the Forest of Owls, and the Failed List of Ales. Soon she'll realize that I can't be hard of hearing, because I don't have ears!"

The little room was suddenly full of the sound of eight mortals not breathing. (Plus Fred, who never breathed.)

"She'll remember eventually," said Orrery.

"She'll realize that Fred's been toying with her," said Astrolabe.

"She'll be furious," said Ratchet.

"She'll probably break Fred's mirror," said Kerf.

"Which would be excruciating for him," said Mortise.

"And then she'll come here," said Bevel.

"I don't want her to come here!" Chris wailed. "I don't want her to break Fred. Stop her, Princess!"

"She'll do worse than break Fred," said Tenon from the doorway, his voice like wind in branches. "She'll chop down

Mother and burn the Forest. The W+DFTFP will have nothing left to protect."

"If she'll find me eventually, let's make it on our terms," I said. "Fred, tell the Queen that she'll find Snow White at the Speaking Oak."

"And what will she find?" said Fred, immediately suspicious.

"Me. With Donna. Nothing short of an axe can break Donna's grip."

Fred objected, but the Brothers were confident that Donna could easily overpower the Queen. After all, she was solid oak.

❧

Sable showed up with an axe. Fortunately, Donna's a quick thinker. Acorns rained down. Queen Sable screamed.

"I knew it was… Ow!… you all along. I… Ow! Ouch! Stop that! You'll give me bruises! Stop at once!"

She grabbed hold of me and tried to truss me with a corset lace, but the barrage of falling acorns and a few unladylike kicks from me forced her to retreat, stumbling over nuts.

"You look beautiful, Princess!" said Chris when I went to conjure up some ice.

"I do?"

"Yeah! You've got all these pretty knots and burls on your head. And you're turning more colors than Autumn."

I gave him a pained smile and went to talk to Fred. Well, first to get yelled at by Fred for endangering myself. Eventually he agreed that since the queen knew roughly where I was, we had to try again.

"A Reflective Reversal!" Fred said. "I'll goad her into trying an enchantment on you, but reverse it with my mirror. The boys will be in the workshop if anything goes wrong. We'll control the place, the spell, everything."

"Except the queen," I pointed out.

Chris peeked in from the workshop. "Let's make 'Crabby's Deadly Apples'! They put flesh people asleep until they die or a prince kisses 'em, and they smell like cinnamon."

"Chris, you're one warped little man. Go back to work," said Fred.

"A sleep spell's not a bad idea, though. Sandalwood Slumber would make her drowsy and suggestible."

"Plus it sounds like an eyeshadow. Brilliant." Fred grinned. "Want to watch?"

"How?"

"Second switch on the back up, others down. Sable won't see or hear you. Go ahead."

It was unnerving to have Queen Sable staring at me, through Fred, close enough to see every crack in her pancake makeup. I had to remind myself that she couldn't see me.

"Mirror, mirror, on the wall, who's the fairest of them all?" she demanded.

"Lousy poet, isn't she?" I muttered.

"Ready for worse?" Fred whispered back.

"Stop mumbling, Mirror!" Queen Sable shouted. "Answer me!"

"My humblest apologies, your Majesty. Um…My Queen/ I'm sworn to tell the truth/It cannot be ignored, thus/Upon my oath, I have to say/'Snow White' is drop-dead gorgeous!"

I giggled. Then I remembered that Fred couldn't lie, and blushed.

Queen Sable hefted a heavy jewelry box.

"Seven years bad luck!" Fred shouted. "Your Majesty, if I might suggest something less drastic…"

With admirable calm, Fred mollified her and talked her through creating a sandalwood comb that would induce sleep upon contact with the wearer's head. Then, looking innocent, he proposed a costume that would make Queen Sable look as gnarled, ugly, and ancient as possible. "What better way to ensure that 'Snow White' won't recognize you, O Queen?"

Fred couldn't lie, but he could act.

❧

Queen Sable arrived at the gatehouse looking crone-like and disgruntled. I welcomed her with the enthusiasm of someone desperate for company and offered her tea. She refused, although she eyed the teapot with the look of someone parched from a long and thirsty hike through the Enchanted Forest. I admired the comb, holding it up as though to study it better. Really, I wanted it in Fred's line of sight. I slid it into my hair—and heard a click and Fred's anguished cry as the lights went out.

I came partially awake in cinnamon-scented darkness.

"Smells like pie," I mumbled.

"Apple pie, princess," said a voice I really should've recognized. "The best you'll ever taste. Take a bite."

I did. Crabby's Deadly Apples really do taste like cinnamon.

&

The next thing I knew, something was pressing on my lips. I slapped whatever-it-was.

"Ow! I think it worked," said a familiar voice. "Princess? Wake up, please. Mind the broken glass."

I opened my eyes and sat up. That seemed to please the young man beside me. He was remarkably pale, except for my handprint on his cheek. His white-blond hair looked like he'd survived a hurricane, but he radiated joy.

"Pardon me, Princess, but there's only one cure for Crabby's Deadly Apples. I was prepared for the comb, but not those."

"Fred? But you're not a prince."

"Prints and Images Division," he reminded me. "I was an image. Now..." He shrugged.

"But..." I took in the shattered glass, the empty mirror-frame on the wall, him. "LaVerre's Transformation?"

He nodded. "You can't kiss if you don't have a mouth."

"And boy does he!" put in Chris, sticking his head through the door. "Screaming, swearing..."

"Chris," Fred and I said in unison, "Shut up."

"Aw." He closed the door again.

"Sable?" I asked Fred.

"You were right. Once you were unconscious, she drank the tea. She's out cold."

"We tied her up really good!" said Chris, popping in again. "Come see!"

Fred insisted on carrying me into the next room. He didn't drop me, although the commotion he made tripping over his new feet would've woken Sable if I hadn't used extra-strength tea.

The Brothers had bound Sable in roots and were watching, rapt, as squirrels made a nest in her hair.

Orrery scowled. "Princess, she tried to kill you. She threatened the Royal Family, and by extension, the Forest. The W+DFTFP has authority over her now."

Chris twisted his twiggy fingers together. "Let's put red-hot iron shoes on her feet and make her dance until she falls down dead!"

Everyone stared at him. "No!"

"Stuff her in a spiked barrel and roll it downhill?"

"No! Honestly, Chris! Where do you get these ideas?"

He shrugged. "Fairy tales."

"She does deserve a harsh punishment, though," said Fred. "I know just the thing."

❧

You guessed right. LaVerre's Transformation, reversed. Sometimes the people who suffered the most under Queen Sable beg us to let them break one of her mirrors. We just point out that they'd get seven years of bad luck.

Which just wouldn't be fair.

Little Red

There once was a girl who always wore a little red hood and cape, so everyone called her Little Red Riding Hood.

She would have preferred Red the Bloody Blade, but her mother wouldn't trust her with anything larger than a bread knife and refused to give Red fighting lessons. Instead, once a week she sent Red off to her grandmother's to learn witchery.

"But Mother, sorcery is for old women! Old ugly women, who like pottering about with smelly leaves and bat guano. There is nothing glamorous about bat guano. You're turning me into a Crone, Mother! I'm much better suited to be a warrior. Bruno the Blacksmith said he'd give me lessons, and the Amazons are always hiring. You're ruining my career aspirations."

"Ethelberta Smith, we're fairy-tale peasants. We don't have career aspirations. Crone is a perfectly respectable occupation. Now take this basket of hearty, nourishing goodies to your grandmother. Don't even think about calling her an ugly crone, and please, try to learn something besides Introductory Candle Lighting."

When Red's mother used her given name, Red knew she'd better obey. She took the basket and set off through the woods.

Red knew that her mother and grandmother expected her to study magical plants along the way, but instead she practiced swordplay with the butter knife from the basket. Absorbed in her footwork, she paid no attention to the enormous wolf pacing beside her.

"Ahem. This is the part where you scream and flee in terror," said the wolf in a voice like a dog gnawing on a bone. "Oh… and it's also the part where you drop that basket."

Red whirled and pointed the knife at it. "Stand back! I know how to use this!"

It sniffed the end of the blunt utensil. "So do I. You Humans grease your bread with it. Bizarre habit. Do I smell sausage?"

"Yes, and you're not getting any of it. It's for my sweet, beloved and wise Granny, who lives just down that path."

"Please?" the wolf whined.

"No."

"Just one little link?"

"No."

"Half of one?"

"No. Shoo."

The wolf growled, showing startlingly white, sharp teeth. It bristled and charged—past Red, down the path toward Granny's house. As soon as her heart restarted and she realized she was still alive, and not wolf kibble, Red charged after it.

&

Granny's door handle had wolf slobber on it. Not good. Red knocked on a non-slobbery part of the door.

"Who is it?" called a voice that sounded like a mastiff trying to sing soprano.

Red winced, but decided to play along for now. "It's Ethelberta, Granny!"

Long pause. "Who?"

"Ethelberta Smith! Your beloved granddaughter. You held me at my christening. You cleared up that misunderstanding with those porridge-eating bears last year. You raised me until I was three. That Ethelberta!"

Another pause. "Sorry, not ringing any bells."

"Red hood and cape? That you made for me?"

"Oh, *that* Ethelburger! My dear, sweet granddaughter. Of course. Come in, my darling child. You don't know how much I've missed you."

Red shouldered the door open, dreading a scene of bloody carnage. She'd never seen Granny do anything impressive like shoot lightning bolts at people, and she could never fight off a wolf.

The room looked pretty much like it always did: red-and-white checked cloth and a vase of flowers on the table, copper kettle hanging over the fire in the fireplace, the scent of Granny's latest potion hanging in the air. In the bedroom, the only things out of the ordinary were the flannel-nightgowned wolf in Granny's bed and a notable absence of Granny.

"You brought me sausage, you sweet child!" said the wolf. "I could just eat you up."

Red's heart was pounding. This could get ugly. She wished in vain for a sword and tried to remember the spells that Granny had taught her. None of them dealt with talking wolves in nightcaps. Paralysis required certain mushrooms—or a stout club and good aim, none of which Red had. Besides, the last time she'd had a lesson in mushrooms… well, thank goodness Granny knew her antidotes.

"What big eyes you have, Granny!" she exclaimed, stalling.

"The better to see you with, my dear." The wolf watched her, seeming amused.

Blindness! If the wolf couldn't see her, it couldn't eat her. But that took six ounces of crushed fireflies and a phoenix egg—way beyond any fairy-tale peasant's budget. Even Granny wouldn't have that on hand. "What big ears you have!"

"The better to hear you with." The wolf licked its chops.

Ears. Red listened. Granny's thatch-roofed cottage housed generations of skittering mice. A sudden influx of plump, spell-dazzled rodents should be enough to distract any sane predator.

Trying to look casual, Red approached the bed—and the wall—and started whistling a tune she'd learned from a boy across the river in Hamlin. Enthralled mice crept out onto the cottage floor, but the wolf didn't even glance at them.

"Why, what big teeth you have, Granny!" Red said, pointing at the mice and willing the wolf to take the hint.

It didn't. "The better to eat you with!" The wolf sprang. Red screamed and cast her Introductory Candle Lighting spell.

The wolf's tail burst into flame. It howled—and transformed into Granny, beating at the back of her nightgown.

"Ethelberta Smith, that was the most ham-handed mishandling of a crisis I've ever seen. Didn't you wonder how a wolf could talk, or why it was wearing my nightgown? A simple Perception spell… and did you never notice the Wolfsbane in the vase on the table?"

Red sat quietly under the tirade, the picture of chastised penitence. "But Granny," she said, "don't you always say, 'Any spell is the right one if everyone gets out alive in the end'?"

Granny stopped in mid-scold, and sighed. "I do. Very well; get those mice out of here and get lunch ready while I fix this gown. Candle-lighting… you'll be the death of me yet, Ethelberta!"

"Oh, I hope not, Granny dear!" said Red earnestly. She busied herself with setting the table in order to hide her triumphant grin.

If she could manage a few more months of this "incompetence," Mother just might reconsider giving Red those sword lessons after all.

The Velveteen Rabbit Says Goodbye

There once was a rabbit who had been made of velveteen. For many years now he'd been real—not just real in the eyes of the Boy who loved him, but real to the world of grown-ups and rabbits with twitching noses and springy hind legs.

The Rabbit's hind legs weren't as springy as they'd once been. They ached in the wintertime, and he hopped more slowly. He liked nothing better than to lie in a sunny patch by the thicket of overgrown raspberry canes and dream of the days when the Boy had held him close and warm beneath soft blankets.

He was drowsing like this when he felt someone stroke the fur between his ears. He opened his eyes to see a dainty figure in a dress of pearls and dewdrops. Her face would have been quite the loveliest thing the Rabbit had ever seen, if it weren't all wet with tears.

"I know you," said the Rabbit. "You made me Real."

"I gave you flesh and fur, long ago," said the Nursery Magic Fairy. "Your Boy made you Real."

"But you're crying! Whatever is wrong, dear Fairy?"

A new tear trickled down her dainty nose. "Do you remember your Boy?"

"Of course! He got tall and strong, and went off to a place called War."

"War isn't a place, little Rabbit. It's a terrible thing that grown-ups do when they forget that others are Real."

"And my Boy is there?"

"He calls for you in his sleep."

"Oh please, bring him back!"

"I can't do that, little Rabbit. Fairies, especially nursery fairies, have no place in the middle of a war."

"Then take me to him, please, so he won't be alone."

"I can send you to him, but only the Boy will know that you're Real."

"But I thought that that once you become Real it lasts for always," the Rabbit protested.

"And so it does, but one of the dark magics of war is that it blinds people to Realness in others, even those who are right before their eyes."

The rabbit shuddered. "I can't leave my Boy alone like that. Please, send me there."

The fairy kissed him between the ears. The raspberry canes vanished. He was in a dark place that smelt of damp and mildew, surrounded by hard lumpy objects that jostled and poked him.

Light poured in above him, the way it had when the Boy used to pull back the covers. And it was the Boy who looked at him now, although his face was a young man's, filthy and stubbled, and his eyes looked like he'd just woken from a nightmare.

"Is this a joke?" The Boy reached down and lifted the rabbit gently. "Bunny? But you disappeared a long time ago."

His hand stroked the rabbit's head where the fairy had kissed him. It felt different, and the rabbit realized that he was once again made of velveteen, all in one piece. He sighed a little for his strong hind legs and long twitching ears, but the Boy was holding him again, and that was all that really mattered.

The rabbit tried to snuggle up under the Boy's chin the way he used to, but he'd forgotten how to wear his old velveteen body. But the Boy smiled anyway.

"It must be the gas. I'm seeing things. But I don't care. I'm glad you're here, old buddy."

The rabbit wasn't glad to be in that place. Even stuffed down in the knapsack, he heard cries like a rabbit being caught by a fox, and the air smelt sharp and rusty. But his Boy was smiling. That was what mattered.

The Boy kept him out of sight in the knapsack most of the time. "You don't want to see what's out there, Bunny," he said, his young face looking pained and old. But sometimes the rabbit saw, through a hole in the canvas, glimpses of torn-up earth, and still bodies, and glints of light on metal.

One day the Boy snuggled him under his jacket, for warmth, and the rabbit saw another face. Someone else's Boy, he thought.

But the other young man looked at his Boy, and the rabbit realized that he wasn't seeing them at all. To that other Boy, they weren't Real. The other Boy raised a stick and pointed it at them. It flashed and thundered. Something tore through velveteen and stuffing, and into his Boy. The rabbit felt something warm and wet, like tears.

The other Boys made a great fuss when they found the rabbit. They sewed up the holes and washed away the blood. They called him Hero, and the Boys in the other beds all asked to hold him. They pinned shiny things on his spotted velveteen front, and touched the sewn-up place, and a bit of light came back into their too-old eyes. The rabbit was glad for that, because his Boy lay with his eyes closed, his skin burning with fever. He didn't speak or respond when anyone else spoke to him, but when they put the rabbit back in his arms, he held tight and wouldn't let go.

The rabbit lay close against his Boy's chest and trembled. In his sawdust heart, he called out for the Nursery Magic Fairy, but she didn't come. All around him, Boys-grown-old moaned with pain, or cried out in the long, lonely hours of the night.

Toys don't sleep, or dream. The rabbit no longer slept, but he lay throughout the night on his Boy's thin pillow, dreaming of the day when his Boy should be well again and take him home to the old dear house. How he wanted to see the house again, and the bright cheerful gardens, and the late afternoon sunlight slanting golden through the trees.

"You see it too, don't you, old buddy?" said the Boy.

The rabbit startled, for although the Boy had talked to him many times, he'd never really waited for an answer. Now he sat on the edge of the bed, looking faintly shimmery at the edges, with everything around him washed in shadow, so that the rabbit could only see his pale, wistful face.

"You're well again!" the rabbit cried and snuggled fiercely up against him. "Now we can go home, and have picnics in the raspberries, and play hide-and-seek in the woods…"

The boy chuckled. He picked up the rabbit and stroked him. "You sound just like I imagined, Bunny. I always wished you could talk."

"I'll talk all you'd like," said the rabbit, quite breathless with excitement. "Maybe… maybe I'll even learn to sing!"

The Boy laughed out loud, but none of the sleepers around them stirred. "Oh, Bunny, I wish we could go home and play in the garden. But people are different from toys. You can't just patch 'em up with a bit of fabric. We've got blood and bones and things, and sometimes nobody can fix them."

The rabbit remembered running, and a glimpse of sharp teeth. "Like when a fox catches a rabbit?" he said in a very small voice.

The Boy looked startled and held him even closer. "The fox got me, little friend. I have to go."

"I want to come with you!"

"I don't think toys can go on this trip," said his Boy.

"I'm not a toy! I'm Real!"

Once again, the Boy looked startled. He looked into the rabbit's boot-button eyes, and nodded.

"You are, aren't you, Bunny?"

"Yes!"

"Would you do something for me?"

"Yes!"

"Look around. See all those other fellows, sleeping? They're hurting. They're scared. They need a friend. Would you be their friend?"

"But… but you're my Boy."

"Now you'll have dozens. Aw, don't look so droopy. It's not like I could ever forget you, you know. Perk up those whiskers. There you go."

"But…"

"But you're not just a toy, remember. This isn't make-believe. This is real."

"And Real is for always," said the rabbit. "Only War makes people forget."

His Boy just looked at him. "You're a very wise little Bunny, you know that? Will you help them remember?"

"I promise. And I won't forget, either."

"That's my Bunny!" His Boy smiled: a real, bright, joyful smile, and was gone.

The rabbit never forgot that smile, or his Boy, or any of the others. And many of the boys who did go home never forgot the velveteen rabbit who reminded them, in a corner of their hearts, that they were all Real.

TRANSFORMATION

The Blackbird Maiden

Centuries ago, when the kingdoms of Men and Birds were closer than they are now, the Blackbird Maiden lived in the Jade Tower, filling it with light and song. Birds came from all the lands, bringing treasures and news to their Lady.

Dearest to her was the young handmaiden Robin. Sometimes the two would fly together in bird-form. In those days, Robin's feathers were snowy white. As they flew overhead, Robin cloud-pale and her Lady midnight-dark, people in the fields below looked up and smiled at the perfect contrast they made.

One day they flew over a palace overgrown with untended gardens. A child laughed somewhere below. Curious, the Blackbird Maiden descended. Robin followed.

Sheltered in the branches of a willow, the Blackbird Maiden looked out and saw a young man in black velvet, playing with a little boy.

"Who is that, Robin?" she whispered.

"A human king, Lady." Robin scoffed. "His mate died birthing the fledgling. Now he does nothing but mourn."

The Blackbird Maiden studied the king. Handsome, for a human. Gentle with his son. Only… grief and pain shadowed his eyes. He moved slowly, as though under a great weight. The Blackbird Maiden longed to see him smile, or at least to lift some of the shadow from him. She sang.

At the first crystal notes the King looked up, wonder dawning on his face. He rose, hunting for the singer. The birds fled.

Back in the Tower, Robin laughed.

"Well done, Lady! That clumsy human never saw us. Though why you even let him hear your song, I'll confess I don't understand."

The Blackbird Maiden did not smile. "He's lonely, Robin,"

she replied. "Alone in that palace, with only the servants and the child for company…"

Robin stared, alarmed at look in her mistress' eyes.

"Don't go back, Lady! He's only a mortal, and you're Queen of the Air. It's wrong."

➚

She did go back. Each day the Blackbird Maiden perched in the willow and sang. Each day something of the darkness lifted from the king. The Blackbird Maiden grew hopeful—and frightened. How could she, so long apart from men, care so much now for this one?

Robin, indignant, scolded her Lady. Forget that wretched man, she begged. Remember her duty and tend to the Tower. She, Robin, was better company than any human.

The Blackbird Maiden wouldn't listen. And one day, as she sang, the shadow of grief lifted from the king for just a moment. He smiled. The smile transformed his face, lighting his dark eyes, filling the Blackbird Maiden with joy. She resolved to return with a ring that would allow her to remain human outside of the Jade Tower and show herself to the King.

"Lady, you can't!" Robin cried. "The Jade Tower needs its mistress."

"I'll bring them here, then." The Blackbird Maiden lifted the jade ring from its box and smiled. "The child will like the gardens."

"It's desertion, my Lady!" Robin protested. "It's… betrayal."

The Blackbird Maiden wasn't listening.

The next day Robin followed her mistress, staying just out of sight. She watched as the Blackbird Maiden sang, the jade ring resting on the branch beside her. The King looked up, smiling.

"Show your face, fair singer," he called.

Before the Blackbird Maiden could move, Robin swooped low and snatched the ring onto her own claw.

A maiden appeared before the king, all in purest white, bright-haired, with a jade ring on her finger.

"Surely you can't be my little singer!" he exclaimed.

"I was," said Robin. She took a step toward the king, tottering on bare human feet. "I was Queen of the Birds, but I took this form for love of you."

The Blackbird Maiden flew at her treacherous friend, her cries anything but musical. The king caught her, and she trembled in his hands.

"Poor creature!" Robin cooed. The Blackbird Maiden could only glare at her. "Let's keep it to amuse the young Prince—in an iron cage, safe from the cats." For Robin knew that, surrounded by iron, the Blackbird Maiden could work no magic to free herself.

It was done. The Blackbird Maiden brooded in the cage, near to despair. No birds sang in the gardens—they were all keeping vigil over the empty Tower. The king never noticed. So completely did Robin keep his attention, he never even came to his son's nursery, never heard the Blackbird Maiden sing. Instead, the Prince was left to the care of servants, who wondered aloud how besotted the king seemed with his new love. Some whispered of witchcraft.

"She hardly speaks, and will never sing, though His Majesty entreats her. He says she used to sing most wonderfully," they said. The Blackbird Maiden's heart leapt when she heard this, but nothing came of it. Soon word came that the King planned to marry the strange, silent girl.

❧

On the day of the wedding, the prince's nurse stole off to watch the festivities. To cheer the boy, the Blackbird Maiden whistled a sprightly tune. The child laughed and clapped his hands. Encouraged, she sang again. The Prince toddled up and grabbed at the cage, trying to get at the pretty creature inside. The Blackbird Maiden whistled and coaxed until he managed to catch hold and pull the door ajar.

The Blackbird Maiden circled the delighted Prince,

caroling her gratitude, and then flew to the chapel, where Robin and the King knelt.

Before the priest could begin the ceremony, the Blackbird Maiden poured forth her most impassioned song.

The King looked up in wonderment. "I know that song!"

Robin blanched.

The Blackbird Maiden landed on the ringbearer's cushion, taking the bride's ring into her claw.

Instantly she stood before them, tall and regal, her dark hair flowing down her back. The parishioners crossed themselves. The Blackbird Maiden didn't notice. She saw only the king.

"Your Majesty." she said and bent one knee before him. At the sight of the Lady of the Tower kneeling before a human, Robin's face flushed red.

"Who are you?" said the King sternly. "Why do you disrupt my wedding?"

"Majesty," she said. "I am the Blackbird Maiden, Lady of the Birds. My song comforted you in your grief. I would stand beside you today, had not one I once trusted usurped my place." She spoke without rancor, for Robin was weeping, and the Blackbird Maiden felt only pity for her.

"Is this true?" said the King to Robin with utmost gentleness. Robin turned and fled the chapel.

The King had come to care for Robin, and the Blackbird Maiden's heart ached both for her beloved and her lost friend. Gently they comforted each other with shared silence, with soft, caring words. They played with the young Prince and rejoiced to see him smile and laugh. As joy returned they would sing together, and the King knew that here indeed was the one who had been his true joy and comfort.

❧

So they were wed, with much celebration and merriment. The birds thronged the air above their Lady, and the people lined the roads below. Among these was Robin, clad in ragged brown, her pale face pinched and thin. The hearts of the King and Queen broke when they saw her, and they summoned her to the palace.

"Leave me be, Mistress." she said to the Blackbird Maiden. "I understand loneliness now. I understand pity, and I want no more of it."

"And I understand responsibility, now that I am a wife, mother, and Queen. I had a duty to the Tower, you were right in that. Ask what you wish. I will give it, if I may."

Robin's face flushed, and she bowed her head. "I would return to my bird-form." she said. "But the others will despise me, for daring to cage the Lady."

"Not so." said the Blackbird Maiden. "You reminded me of my duty to the Jade Tower. Here in the presence of all the birds I declare you its Mistress. Your song shall herald the Spring, and all will rejoice to hear it." She kissed Robin tenderly on one cheek, and the King did likewise on the other. The Blackbird Maiden drew the jade ring from the girl's finger, and Robin became a bird, brown as her peasant's garb, with a blush of red in front. She gave a hesitant trill, and all watching smiled. Emboldened, she took to the air, singing. The young Prince laughed aloud in delight.

And every spring thereafter, Robin would come first to the Palace, to sing for the Prince and his siblings, children of the King and the Blackbird Maiden.

Banjooli

Yama stood outside the thorn fence that circled the banjooli pen and called "Banjooli! Come, Banjooli-Yama!"

All around the dusty compound, what had looked like lumps of dark earth sprouted long necks with ostrich-like heads. All the heads turned toward Yama, watching her with identical blank expressions.

Yama sighed. With a mischievous smile, she called more softly, "Naa, Dara!" *Come, Nothing!*

One of the smaller messenger-birds rose, shook red dust from its shaggy feathers, and loped to the fence.

"Kee-ya," said the bird. When Yama didn't produce any food, the other birds went back to their napping and became lumps again.

"Kee-ya-ya-ya," the small banjooli said.

"That's my smart boy! You understand me, don't you?" She twined one slender braid around a finger, and the banjooli pecked at the brown beads on the end.

"No, silly! You can't eat my Rider's beads," said Yama, laughing, and the banjooli backed off, clucking.

"Did you just call that runt by name, farm-girl?" said a human voice. "And did it answer you?"

Yama whirled to face the older Rider. "I called it nothing, Keela Safara!"

Safara looked her up and down, elegant as always and stiff with disapproval. Her dark braids, with their yellow beads, swung with the movement. The banjooli at her side didn't react. "That thing's not a pet. It's a banjooli. It used to be an enemy warrior. If it were still human it would kill you, or worse. Your job is to control it, not coddle it. Are you trying to draw the Soul-Sweepers' attention?" She glanced toward the forbidden corner of the compound where the sorcerers lived, and her expression soured further.

"We can't have that, can we, Keela Safara?" said Banjooli-

Mistress Binata, hobbling up. "Such concern for discipline! Under your supervision, Keela Yama just might earn the Yellow Rank after all."

Safara looked as dismayed as Yama felt. "That's how you expect me to earn the Red Rank, Mistress? By minding Farm Girl and the runt all the way across the Drylands to New Town? Why not one of the other girls?"

"If Yama's capable of becoming a full-fledged Keela, she won't need minding, just observing," said Binata, grunting as she shifted her weight off her bad leg, lamed by a long-ago banjooli kick.

Yama knew better than to protest. If she disobeyed the Banjooli-Mistress, she'd be sent home in disgrace. Instead of bringing honor to father, she'd be adding to his burden. She fetched her travel bundle without complaint. Dara, though, refused to cooperate, sidestepping away from the leather saddle pad and crying "Kee-ya! Kee-ya!"

"Sit down, you silly bird! Of all days to be naughty!"

Mistress Binata watched without comment. Safara rolled her eyes. "You've indulged that runt too much. Now it's spoiled and undisciplined, and you'll have to resort to Command Words."

Yama set her lips tight and gave a hand signal for Down. Her bird obediently folded its long legs and sat.

"Actually, it's so clever it doesn't even need regular words to understand me."

Safara snorted and kicked her own mount into a walk, not waiting for Yama to catch up.

* * *

Yama felt Safara's disapproving presence even while she slept. The Yellow Rider criticized Yama's posture, her riding speed, the way she cared for her banjooli, even her snoring. But that was better than the second day, when Safara rode alongside all morning, telling Yama horrific tales about how the Soul-Sweepers created the banjooli.

"…after they strip you they paint white stripes on your body, for cowardice. Then they beat the heart-drum…"

"Keela Safara, stop! You're making the banjooli nervous."

"It's not the banjooli that's losing her nerve. If you can't face me, how will you face a pack of thorn-dogs, or worse, enemy raiders?" Safara's messenger-bird loped along smoothly, never swerving to peck at insects or shiny rocks the way Dara did. Safara didn't look stiff and sore, just smug. Yama's stomach growled, and Safara laughed.

"You need to stop for dinner already, farm-girl?"

Yama surveyed the hills and thorn-trees and broke into a smile. "Not yet. I'm heading for that village just ahead."

Safara raised an eyebrow. "I didn't think you'd take advantage of Rider's Right to make the farmers feed you, Keela Yama."

Yama just smiled and kept riding.

❧

"Yama! Yama's come home!" Yama's father and three brothers came running from the groundnut field. The twins, Baaku and Baayu, tried to grab her banjooli's harness.

Yama gasped. "Taxa!" she shouted—the Command-word for Stop. The banjooli froze in mid-kick, and the twins gaped at its clawed foot.

"Boys! Are your heads cracked? Never run up to a Rider like that," said their father, his face ashen. "Show respect."

"It's just Yama," Baaku pouted.

"But the banjooli could still kick you to death," Yama pointed out. She released Dara from the spell and walked the stunned banjooli in circles until it calmed down. Safara looked on in consternation.

"I wish I could be a Rider," said Abdou.

"You're a boy. You'd get too big and heavy," Yama teased.

"Your banjooli just stood there until you let it move," said Baayu in awe.

Yama grinned. "Keela trick. I wonder if it works on little

brothers?" Her grin vanished when she saw her father's expression; the courteous, formal expression he always showed to visiting messengers. She wasn't his little daughter now. She was Keela Yama, riding to prove herself worthy to be trusted with the Sweepers' correspondence. And Safara was watching.

Her father bowed to them both, more mindful of Yama's position than she was. "May I offer you food for your journey, Keelas?" he asked, and Yama felt tears sting her eyes. "Yes, please," she said.

Had she been anyone but a Keela, even a stranger, she would have been welcomed with warm greetings and embraces, and invited into her childhood home for groundnut stew and tea. For the first time she felt like she shared her messenger-bird's punishment.

"Can't you come inside?" said Abdou. Yama shook her head.

"Tell her it's all right, Keela," said Baayu to Safara, pleading.

"It's not, little boy. Keela Yama's jeopardizing her chance at the Yellow Rank with this familiarity. A Keela's duty is to the Soul Sweepers."

"A Keela doesn't have to be stone-hearted," Yama retorted. "Don't worry, Baayu. My banjooli and I are fast. This isn't slowing us down much."

Still, she got back into the saddle before she accepted her father's offered bread, plus hot stew and tea in travelers' gourds.

"You have fine sons," she said. That was an acceptable compliment in return for hospitality, and the closest a Keela could come to expressing affection for anyone outside of the Riders' Compound.

"I have a fine daughter too," her father said softly. Yama blinked hard and rode on, urging Dara to the fastest pace possible without using Command Words. Only when she was out of sight of her family, her home and even her village did she stop for her meal.

"Even a Keela-in-training should know better than to associate with villagers," Safara chided her, reluctantly accepting a share of the food. She wrinkled her nose as though the rich aromas of cumin and roasted goat were toxic.

"They're not just any villagers. They're my family."

"A Keela's only family are her fellow Riders. Why are you doing this, Yama? Why not stay home with the other farmers and raise babies?"

"Someone has to raise the future Riders and Sweepers, and if it weren't for us farmers, everyone else would starve," Yama retorted. "Why are you doing this, Keela Safara? A grand lady like you could be a headman's wife, or even a Sweeper's…"

"Sweepers don't marry!" Safara's disdain flared into anger. "If you don't stop this fraternizing and devote yourself to the Riders, you'll learn what the Sweepers are like when…"

A cry from the banjooli made them both turn. A lean thorn-dog was sniffing around the remnants of their dinner.

"Don't be afraid, banjooli," Yama said. "It's just a thorn-dog. Hello there, boy! Are you hungry?"

The wild dog gave her a long, appraising look, and turned to Safara.

"Keela Yama, get on your banjooli and run," she said. Her voice shook.

"Why? It's just a dog, and I don't think it's rabid. Although it might have fleas."

"Rrrrun," said the dog. Yama's jaw dropped. She scrambled into the saddle. Safara was already mounted and fleeing toward New Town.

Dara needed no urging to break into a long-legged run, but the thorn-dog kept pace beside them, white teeth showing in a canine grin.

"Aca!" Yama shouted. The Command Word spurred the banjooli into magically enhanced, muscle-straining effort. Hot wind blew past Yama's face, scouring her with dust. She rode with her head down and her eyes half-closed, and when Dara came to an abrupt halt she looked around dazed and blinking.

They'd reached the outskirts of New Town. The Drylands had given way to irrigated fields of groundnuts, beans and millet surrounding whitewashed buildings like the ones back at the Riders' compound. Keela Safara stood with her back against one wall, disheveled and haggard, without her banjooli. And the thorn-dog stood in front of Yama, still showing those bright teeth.

"Thorn-dogs just don't run that fast," Yama panted.

The dog growled and stood on its hind legs. Yama watched in horror as it stretched and lengthened, fur changing to skin, canine muzzle changing to human face. The air around the figure reddened and clung, becoming a Sweeper's scarlet robe.

"Astute observation, Keela Yama," said the man.

"Sweeper…" Yama breathed again. "We made it!"

"Eventually." The Sweeper turned to Safara. "Did you enjoy your little picnic, my beauty? I would have thought you'd be in more of a hurry to get here."

"Kee-ya-ya-ya!" shrieked Dara. The messenger-bird was drooping from its ensorcelled run, but backed away as the Soul-Sweeper approached.

"Don't take Dara!" Yama exclaimed, and at the shapechanger's sharp glance she added "I'm sorry, Sweeper. But this banjooli and I work well together. If it needs to rest before we go back to Mistress Binata, I'll wait."

"What did you call him?" the Sweeper demanded.

"Dara. I meant no disrespect. I wanted to give my banjooli a name, but Mistress Binata said we must call the banjooli nothing…"

"So you did. Literally." Some of the sternness in the Sweeper's face dissipated, and he chuckled. "I am Sweeper Suluwo. You came closer than you knew, Keela Yama. His name is Daraja. Dignity, not Nothing."

Safara gasped. "The runt? But you told me my banjooli…"

"Be quiet, Safara," said the man in the red robe. He spoke in a normal voice, but Yama felt a strange echo to the words. Safara didn't speak again. A tear rolled down her cheek, and a chill whispered over Yama's skin. That had been a Command.

The Sweeper was giving her a suspicious look. "I thought

the banjooli weren't allowed to have names or gender, sir," she stammered.

"Ah, that's what's bothering you. You've all had a hard ride, and need to refresh yourselves. Come; I'll explain. Bring the banjooli with you."

❧

Sweeper Suluwo's house felt like Paradise after the hot, dusty Drylands. Although she was still wary of a Sweeper who would use Command Words on a human being, Yama couldn't help appreciating the chance to rinse the dust from her face and hands and enjoy a drink of cool hibiscus punch. Dara followed her into the tiled inner courtyard and sat pressed against her side. Sweeper Suluwo didn't object to the ungainly messenger-bird's presence. He just watched them with both an intensity that made Yama want to squirm. Safara knelt on the cushion beside him, expressionless, her drink untouched.

"Daraja seems quite attached to you, Keela Yama."

"He was hurt when I found him, Sweeper. He wouldn't go to the Compound without me."

"Surely the wise Mistress Binata has given you her lecture on Duty Before All Else?" said the Sweeper, without correcting Yama for calling the banjooli "he" instead of "it." "Before family, before friends or lovers, before anything that can divide a Rider's heart—even one's banjooli?"

"If I'm a Rider, then he is my duty, Sweeper."

"And have you never wondered who he used to be? What he did to deserve his current state?"

Safara was shaking and sobbing now. Dara squawked and tried to hide his head in the crook of Yama's elbow.

"He did nothing," the Sweeper went on. "Absolutely nothing—except to be an embarrassment to a Soul-Sweeper. Which is unforgivable."

"I don't understand," said Yama, bewildered, trying to calm the agitated banjooli.

"Watch."

Sweeper Suluwo called, and Dara came, standing before him and meeping plaintively. Seemingly without a thought for the power of the banjooli's deadly kicks, the Sweeper ran a hand along one wing and plucked out a feather.

"You're about to witness something that usually takes a heart-drum and multiple Sweepers to do, Keela Yama. Now, the faster I do this, the harder it will be on him, but the less distressing it will be for you to watch. I would hate to distress a guest…"

He spoke a string of Command Words, and Dara screamed. Yama ran to the bird's side. The scream turned to harsh cawing cries. Sweeper Suluwo raised his voice just slightly to carry over the sound.

"Many years ago, perhaps twelve or so, lived a Rider not much older than you, Keela Yama. She was a pretty girl, and praise turned her head."

Safara turned away, still mute. Dara hunched in on himself, seeming to shrink. Yama put her arms around the bird's skinny neck.

"Shh, it's all right. There's a good boy."

"Kee-ya. Kee-ya-ya-ya."

Sweeper Suluwo looked startled, but went on. "She found a young man as foolish as herself and neglected her duty."

Safara glared at him. Suluwo ignored her. Yama's attention was all on Dara. The banjooli was writhing as though he'd gone boneless, shrinking, his neck and legs shortening…

"The Rider produced a child, which might have been convenient if the boy had been willing to put the skills he'd learned as a Sweeper's… apprentice… to good use. Alas, he was not."

Dara's head enlarged. His cries became sobs. He was smaller than Yama now, shedding feathers. He clutched Yama's arm with a wing that looked more and more like a hand streaked with white paint…

"A banjooli is more useful than a disobedient boy," Sweeper

Suluwo declared. Yama stared, aghast, at the child weeping in her lap.

"Dara? Are you all right? Does it hurt?"

"Kee-ya-ya-ya," he whimpered.

Yama choked, but kept her voice steady. "I think you could say it the right way now if you tried, Dara. Yama. See? Yaa-mmmma. Yama.

"Eeyaa-mmaa. YaaMmaa. Mama." He tipped his head to one side and repeated the word. "Mama?"

Safara cried out and reached for the boy. He screamed and clutched at Yama, nearly knocking her over. "Kee-ya! "Kee-ya Yama!"

"Give him back to me," Safara wailed. The boy shrank from her reaching hands.

"Daraja's old enough to make his own choices now, don't you think?" said Suluwo. Daraja's head snapped toward that calm voice. He'd looked at Safara without recognition, just bewilderment. Now his expression combined terror and remembered awe.

"You turned him into a mindless messenger-bird! He can't even talk, let alone make choices," said Safara.

"The way he's clinging to Keela Yama speaks clearly enough," said Suluwo. He draped his scarlet outer robe over the shivering child. "Say something," he Commanded.

Daraja looked about to panic. "Kee-ya Yama!" he shrieked.

Sweeper Suluwo frowned. "Say something else."

Daraja's face contorted with effort, but no other words came out. He shrugged off the robe, leapt up and started pacing in circles.

"So; that's all he can say," said Suluwo, his voice flat.

Yama halted Daraja's agitated circling and draped the robe over him.

"Let's go outside and walk, Daraja. In straight lines."

"Don't wander off!" Suluwo warned. "Any other thorn-dogs around here are not Sweepers."

❧

A fountain played a short distance from the house. Daraja ran straight to the basin and scrubbed the paint from his arms.

"I'm sorry," said Yama softly. "I didn't know who my banjooli was."

He stopped, turned to her with a puzzled expression, and said, "You the only sorry one, Keeya Yama."

"You really can talk, besides my name? But Sweeper Suluwo Commanded you!"

Daraja scowled. "I am not doing anything Papa says, not after he make me banjooli. He teached me how that works, so I not listen. But it hurts!"

"Papa? Sweeper Suluwo is your father? And he did this to you? I thought all the Sweepers had to vote to condemn someone—and for things like murder! What was he thinking?"

Daraja shrugged. "Papa says I serve Sweepers one way or other, and I will not make more banjooli for him, so…" He searched for words and paced, frustrated, in a tight circle. "Sorry, Keey… *Keela* Yama. Things are still crooked in my head."

Things felt crooked in Yama's head too. And the sight she found behind the house gave her already-unsettled thoughts a cruel twist.

Banjooli. At least a dozen of them, smaller than Daraja had been, milled about inside a thorny pen, pecking bugs from the red dirt. Daraja gave a cry of dismay.

"He do it anyway, without me. And so many!"

"Daraja, who were those banjooli?" she asked, dreading the answer.

"Boys and girls," he said in a near-whisper. "With no Mama or Papa. The alone ones, the hungry ones. So Papa will outrun Riders. Let them out, Keela Yama!"

She longed to, but she remembered Dara the banjooli, torn and bleeding in her father's beanfield. "No. They'd panic and get lost, and starve or be killed. Unless… Could you make them human again?"

"I could!" His face fell. "But would take very long time, and Papa would catch us."

Yama edged away from the corral, back toward the courtyard. "Mistress Binata could stop this, but we'll never get back without a banjooli. One who can handle a rider. I don't think these can." She eyed the Sweeper's son, thinking.

"Please, Keela Yama, don't make me be banjooli again!"

"I wouldn't do that, Daraja! Besides, I haven't trained as a Sweeper. I wouldn't even know how. But you do, don't you?"

He looked away.

"Daraja?"

"I won't do that to you, Keela Yama!"

They'd reached the house. Sounds of conversation carried from inside.

"Why, Safara!" Sweeper Suluwo was saying. "I never realized you were so sentimental. Or do you just need something to keep you occupied once you get too old to ride?"

"He's my son! Give him to me. Take Yama instead."

Yama stiffened. Daraja clutched her hand.

"It's a poor trade." said Suluwo. "She's a puny, undersized thing, no substitute for a Sweeper's offspring."

"An offspring you've damaged with your bullying! She has three brothers. I know where to find them. You could have them too."

"Four for one? The flock would rival Binata's. I'll consider it."

"Daraja," Yama whispered, "You have to do this. Change me now, as quickly as you can."

"I don't want to, Keela Yama! And it hurt you terrible."

"Then silence me with a Command Word, like Suluwo did to Safara, so I don't scream and bring them running. But hurry up and do it!"

❧

Yama was running. There had been pain behind her. She was running away from the pain. She could run faster if there weren't a weight on her back…

"Keela Yama!" said a voice behind her head. The voice spoke a Word, and something in her throat relaxed. "Talk to me."

She hissed at the voice, and then remembered. Daraja. She tried to answer him, but produced only inarticulate squawks.

"Talk anyway. I need practice, and you must remember Yama, not banjooli. If you were not always talking to me I would forgot."

Yama remembered why she'd started running, and twisted her neck to look behind her. Two thorn-dogs were chasing them, running low to the ground. "Awgs!" she croaked.

Daraja looked, and whimpered. "Papa only becomes dog when he is angry. So he can bite and kill."

"Fasssher!" Yama cried.

"The Fast word! I forget it. Help me, Keela Yama."

"Aca," she croaked, focusing the Command Word on herself. It spurred her muscles into effort she would have thought impossible. Red dust flew, obscuring the pursuing dogs. The walls of the Riders' compound rose up ahead of her. She halted outside the gates and screamed—the scream of a wounded banjooli.

Girls came running. The dogs backed away from the gate. Mistress Binata, moving faster than Yama had ever seen her, swept through the crowd, smacking any obstructing bodies with her cane. She hauled open the gates and glared at Daraja.

"What in the name of the Lady of Swiftness is a boy doing on a banjooli, at my very gates?"

Daraja slid to the ground and stammered "Keela Yama!"

The Banjooli-Mistress' eyes narrowed. "You're saying that this is Yama's banjooli?"

"No, is her! Sweeper Suluwo…"

The thorn-dogs stretched and reformed into Sweeper Suluwo and Keela Safara. Safara looked disheveled and drained and cried without a sound. The young Riders screamed.

"Hush, boy," Suluwo muttered and smiled when Daraja fell silent.

"You know every banjooli here as though it were your own

child, O Binata the Wise, but not this one. This boy's trying to destroy my chance to get back into your good graces."

"That would take a lot, considering that you almost ruined Safara with your disgraceful behavior."

"What if I told you that this banjooli was once the man responsible for Safara's… distraction?"

"I'd laugh in your face," said Binata, not laughing. But she allowed Suluwo through the gate, shutting out the curious girls and putting a protective arm around Safara. "Come on, all of you."

⁂

Yama walked close to Daraja's side, trying to look mindless and harmless whenever a Sweeper glanced her way. It was disturbingly easy. She found herself drawn to shiny bits of rock or a dangling tassel.

Even as a banjooli, Yama felt a sense of awe at entering into the forbidden territory of the Sweepers. At first she thought it looked disappointingly like the girls' dormitory: low whitewashed buildings with thatched roofs, patches of corn, groundnuts and beans, and a convenient well. Then they entered a small, innocuous-looking building. Smoke obscured the ceiling, but not the vast round object that squatted near one wall like an earthbound moon.

The heart-drum. It drew her eyes even before she noticed the half-dozen Soul-Sweepers staring at her little group.

"Do you want that banjooli turned into something that takes up less room, Binata?" said one.

"Suluwo, what are you doing here?" demanded another.

"He claims that this banjooli used to be Safara's real seducer, and that this boy stole it," said Binata with a sniff.

"Simple enough to prove," said the eldest Sweeper. "Link the bird and the young thief, and switch their bodies. You can have the thief for your flock, and we'll question the former banjooli."

Suluwo looked aghast. "You'd restore a dangerous criminal?

Right here, where he could kill every Sweeper in the district at once?"

"What; you thought they'd believe everything you said just because you used to be one of them?" said Binata with a smirk. Yama chuckled to herself at his dismay, but then the Sweepers laid hold of Daraja. The boy's mouth opened in a voiceless scream. He thrashed and kicked until one Sweeper said "Don't bother with the paint. He's unnerved enough already."

Yama went stiff with anger but didn't dare kick when they bound Daraja next to her. The sight of Binata leaning ever more heavily on her cane reminded her of what her kicks could do now. She held perfectly still so they wouldn't bother to hobble or enchant her.

The oldest Sweeper, muttering something about "maintaining standards around here," took his place behind the heart-drum and began to beat a steady, pulsing rhythm. Another Speaker stroked Yama's wing, and she felt a twinge. He spoke Words that her ears didn't hear, but her body did. It shrank and twisted, pulling, contorting, slowly reforming. Beside her, Daraja writhed on the floor. Fine down sprouted along his arms, and tears ran down his face.

Yama turned away, unable to watch, and caught sight of Suluwo.

He was smiling, a fierce, cruel smile. Whatever his fellow Sweepers might do to him afterward, for now he was enjoying his disobedient son's anguish.

Rage flared through Yama, burning away the pain of transformation. Still mostly banjooli, she strode forward and kicked with all her strength. The Sweepers screamed.

Everyone stared at the gaping hole in the heart-drum.

"Nah shange Darazha!" she shouted.

Binata peered at her more closely. "Yama, is that you?"

She nodded—and hissed as Suluwo transformed himself into a thorn-dog and hurled himself at her.

"Taxa!" Daraja shouted.

The thorn-dog froze in place. Daraja smiled sheepishly at her and rubbed his throat with a feathery hand. "I learn that Word from you, Keela Yama."

Mistress Binata was surveying the broken drum with a look of dismay. "Yama, you've trapped yourself in this shape. None of us knows how to do a singlehanded transformation like Suluwo did."

Yama poked her beak at Daraja. "Ee duz."

"If Keela Yama helps me remember words, I can," said the boy.

❧

This transformation hurt less, with the Sweepers assisting Daraja. When both Yama and Daraja were fully human again and the Sweepers had gone to free Suluwo's banjooli herd, Mistress Binata asked the question Yama had been dreading.

"Keela Yama, who is this boy?"

Yama looked at Safara. The Yellow Rider hadn't spoken up when the other Sweepers negated Suluwo's powers, trapping him in dog form. Now she shook her head and turned away.

Yama sighed and put an arm around Daraja. "He's one of my brothers, Mistress."

"You don't say. He's remarkably talented. The Sweepers will be overjoyed to have him."

"Please no, Mistress!" Daraja said in a panic. "I not want anything to do with magic now, ever!"

"What matters is what the Sweepers want."

"Mistress Binata, I don't think Daraja can do magic any more," Yama said. "I think that extraordinary feat burned it out of him."

"You don't say," said the Banjooli Mistress again, with a wry twist to her mouth. "Your duty is to the Sweepers, Keela Yama."

"I'm not a Keela without a banjooli, Mistress."

An expression crossed Binata's face too quickly for Yama to read. "You're a Keela until I release you from service. Which I will do, once you've done one last thing."

Yama cast a wistful glance toward the Riders' dormitory. "What's that, Mistress?"

"The Sweepers are going to be returning with a dozen or so frightened, confused children. I suspect the Sweepers wouldn't think twice about giving them a scrap of food and abandoning them to fend for themselves. And only the least self-absorbed would remember the scrap. You're going to convince your father that he needs several more pairs of hands around the house. Those hands should be conveniently showing up at his door any day now."

"A dozen? That would take a lot of convincing, Mistress."

Mistress Binata motioned for Yama to hold out her hands, and poured what looked like kernels of corn into them.

"I think a Rider of the Yellow Rank is up to the challenge. And consider: if Daraja looks like just another of a dozen farmboys, any persistent Sweepers will be less likely to pick him out of the crowd. Now close your mouth and put those beads in your hair."

Yama did. "I don't think this is the message the Sweepers expected me to carry. Come on, Daraja." She bowed to the Banjooli-Mistress, turned her back on the Riders' Compound, and took her new brother home.

The Salt Man

When a widow weeps, the Salt Man comes to her.

When the surgeon's knife has bitten deep, the Salt Man is waiting.

He takes the tears of grief and agony and despair, and of joy so sharp and fleeting it feels like pain. The salt drops, from prisoner and penitent alike, collect on his thin pale palm and nourish him. Only the first tears of a newborn are forbidden to him, for it is said that one taste of them will unmake him.

His cadaverous face and long black coat, half-glimpsed in moments of despair, haunted the people of Volkburg. Mourners saw, briefly, bottomless dark eyes looking into theirs from a salt-white face and felt a cold hand touch their cheek. Then the Salt Man vanished, to become part of the shadows and frost until human pain called him forth again. Those he'd touched gasped, felt their hearts resume beating, and life went on.

&s;

Gisela felt him stalking her even before her husband died. She wouldn't cry in front of Hartwin, who'd given her a white-faced smile after the surgeon left and assured her in a whisper that he still had another perfectly good leg. She only allowed herself to cry in the other room of their little cottage. That was when she first sensed the cold presence in the room with her. A dark shadow, half-glimpsed. A scent of stone and sea. She dried her tears before they could fall and hurried back to Hartwin's side.

She held back her tears while Hartwin thrashed and moaned, while she sponged fever-sweat from his forehead, while his loving eyes stared through her as though she were a stranger. But when those eyes lost all expression and his damp, hot hand turned as cold as clay, she knelt by the bed and sobbed. When something colder still touched her face, she screamed. The touch withdrew.

From that point until the funeral, Gisela kept silent and dry-eyed, working until last light on what visitors assumed was a piece of delicate crocheting. The ignored visitors shook their heads, murmuring sympathetically about Gisela's youth, the cruel brevity of her marriage, and the fragile state of her nerves. Gisela pressed her lips tight and kept working.

Snow lingered farther up the mountain on the day of Hartwin's funeral. The chilled mourners didn't stay long at the graveside. Soon only Gisela remained, fingering her delicate work with one hand while she steeled her courage.

"Hartwin, mein Geliebter," she said and let her tears fall.

She felt the icy touch on her cheek at once, the haunting presence made briefly solid, and turned to confront her stalker. Her hand clamped onto a bony wrist. Untaken tears slid down her cheeks. She glared into bottomless black eyes. "Give him back."

The Salt Man tried to pull away, but Gisela held him fast.

"Release me," he said in a voice that rasped like the hinge of a long-unopened door.

"Give me back Hartwin."

"I have not that power. I am not Death."

"Oh no? You stand by deathbeds and open graves, shrouded in black. I've seen you. I've seen people cross the road to avoid you, even though they say they don't know why they do it. What can you be but Death by another name?"

"I do not take lives. Only tears. I do what I must to live."

"You live on other people's pain. If you're not Death, you're his dog." Her lips curved in a bitter, heartbroken expression that wasn't really a smile. "And a dog that preys on people needs to be chained."

Now she removed her hand from his, revealing a mesh of silver, gold, and white embedded in his wrist.

"Made of silver wire, my hair, and a thread from Hartwin's shroud. The book says it will vanish once you give me what I wish." She took a deep breath. "Take time from my life to bring Hartwin back. Years, if you need to. Just leave us a few together, please."

"I cannot."

"Please. Just a few weeks. A few days."

"I have not that power."

Gisela's heart sank. She'd been prepared for rage. Inhuman fury. Treachery. Anything but this impassive refusal.

"If you won't let him go, I won't let you go either."

The Salt Man just watched Gisela's untaken tears dry on her cheeks. When she walked away, he followed.

People turned as they passed, whispering behind their hands. The young goatherd who took Hartwin's flock to and from the upper pasture stared outright.

"Frau Solberg, your shadow is wrong," said the boy in a worried voice.

Gisela kept walking, ramrod straight, determined not to show fear or despair to the creature behind her. When they reached the cottage, she turned to find the Salt Man paused on the threshold.

"I must not wear flesh for long," he said.

Gisela remembered Hartwin's body lying cold and empty on their bed. "Some of us have no choice about how long we 'wear flesh.' Or don't. Get inside."

He strode past her into the main room. In the little house, he loomed all the larger. Gisela braced herself, remembering stories of his bone-chilling touch, his merciless gaze. But the Salt Man just stood on the rag rug before the hearth, shifting from foot to foot as though the soles were tender as an infant's. "I feel pain," he said.

He sounded more like a child with a bellyache than a creature of nightmares. "Sit down, then," she said, taken aback.

He sat, clumsily, as though he'd never tried to sit before. On the rug, although there was a chair just steps away.

Gisela stirred up the fire. In its familiar light, she studied her prisoner's inhumanly white face without flinching. "The stories say that you drink tears."

"Yes."

"The stories say you bring sickness and suffering to cause more pain."

"I do not. I cannot. The Law forbids it."

"Will you bring back Hartwin?"

"I cannot. I have no power over death."

"I don't believe you. I still think you are Death. No matter what you call yourself, that chain will hold you. I won't let you stalk anyone else."

The Salt Man fingered the mesh that bound him. It had sunk within the skin. He pulled on the skin as though it were clothing that he could remove. When that did no good, he turned and thrust his arm into the fire.

Gisela screamed. The Salt Man howled in astonished pain. Gisela knocked him to the ground and threw a blanket over his smoldering arm. When she took the blanket away his charred coat-sleeve fell to ash. The skin beneath it was red and blistered, but the mesh shone undamaged.

The Salt Man stared at his burned arm with a look of disbelief. He held it to his chest, rocking and moaning, but dry-eyed.

Gisela rushed outside and returned with a pan of cold water. "Sit in the chair. Give me your arm."

To her astonishment, he obeyed. She soaked clean rags in the water and wrapped the cool bandages around the burn. Relief flooded his face.

"Kindness for kindness is the first Law. I will repay this kindness, Gisela."

She couldn't meet his eyes. "Don't call me that. Ever. And I'd have done the same for a dog."

"Is that not your name?"

"My name that friends use. If you must call me something, call me Frau Solberg."

❧

Someone knocked on the door. A gentle voice called "Gisela? Are you there, dear?"

She ran to open the door. "Oma Solberg!"

Hartwin's grandmother hobbled into the room and set a stoneware bowl on the table. "I brought you some einbrennsuppe."

"How can you both be Frau Solberg?" said the Salt Man.

Hartwin's grandmother froze with the fragrant steam from the soup swirling about her, and stared at the chair where the Salt Man sat. Her vision seemed to change focus. "Der Salzmann? Oh dear."

"You can see him, Oma? Really see him, not just a shadow?"

She nodded. "Gisela, child, what is he doing here?"

Tears stung Gisela's eyes. The Salt Man leaned forward in trembling anticipation. Oma Solberg frowned, and he leaned back.

"I want him to give back Hartwin."

Oma Solberg dropped into a chair. "Oh, child, don't you think I'd have asked for my Heinrich back, if such things could be done? I loved my grandson, but this… No. And this poor creature can hardly help you."

The Salt Man's indignant look at being called a "poor creature" would have made Gisela laugh, if she weren't so near tears.

"But isn't he Death, Oma?"

"No, Gisela dear. Just a child of the mountain and the sea." She sniffed. "What have you been burning? Old clothes? Sausages?"

The Salt Man held out his arm. Oma Solberg looked horrified.

"I've bound him with the Undying Link," said Gisela. "I learned it from one of your books, Oma."

"Oh, Gisela! Herr Salzmann, I ask forgiveness for my granddaughter's foolishness."

The stern pale figure inclined its head. "Forgiveness in

return for young Frau Solberg's relief from pain. Kindness for kindness is part of the Law. Perhaps this is a good way to end."

"End? What are you talking about?" said Gisela.

"I cannot do what you ask, but no mortal can break the Undying Link. Therefore I must serve you until the child is born."

Gisela went cold. "What child?"

"The one you carry, of course, Frau Solberg. The one who will be my end."

The room spun. But Gisela hadn't fainted at her first sight of Hartwin's mangled leg, and now she managed to stand straight and reply with only the slightest tremor in her voice. "Nonsense. Why would you know something like that before I would?"

"I see lives. The one inside you shines both like you and like the man."

"His name is—was Hartwin." Gisela's tears spilled over. The Salt Man stood up. He loomed over her by at least a foot.

"Don't touch me!"

He stopped and bowed. "As you command, Frau Solberg. Perhaps this is another kindness. The child's first tears will taste all the sweeter, after I go without any for so long."

Gisela stood with her hand pressed to her stomach. She couldn't feel any life stirring there. To have Hartwin's child, with Hartwin gone…

The Salt Man had to be lying. Could he lie? Her plan had seemed so simple: detaining Death long enough to plead for Hartwin's return, offering as much as her own life in exchange as he demanded.

But Oma Solberg, who'd welcomed her when the rest of Hartwin's family had eyed her askance, said that the Salt Man wasn't Death. If that were true, she'd trapped a creature from one of the Marchen told to children, no more threatening than a kobold or an elf. The pale stranger's look of confusion as Oma Solberg pushed the soup bowl toward him only strengthened the impression. Surely the End of All Things wouldn't look so bewildered when confronted by a spoon?

"Eat, Herr Salzmann," said Oma Solberg. "Nothing with a belly can go long without food in it."

"But this is not tears."

Gisela hesitated, then stirred a heaping spoonful of salt into the broth. "Now try."

He stuck a finger into the bowl. Gisela had to demonstrate how to use the spoon. She caught Oma Solberg's amused look and guessed what the old woman was thinking: If the Salt Man's prediction was true, she'd welcome the practice in teaching helpless beings how to eat.

A tear slid down Gisela's cheek. The Salt Man, intent upon his task, didn't look up when Oma Solberg led her from the room.

❧

Gisela woke convinced that the events of the previous day had been a nightmare. She opened the door to find the Salt Man still sitting in the same chair.

"Oh. Have you been sitting there all night?"

He stood up. "No, Frau Solberg. The weise alte Frau said that you would need a fire. She showed me how to keep it alive."

Sure enough, a rejuvenated fire crackled on the hearth. Gisela's cast-iron skillet sat amid the flames. Gisela stared at the blackened lump inside it.

"Ah… what is that?"

"A sausage, Frau Solberg. For you to eat."

Gisela rescued the pan. "No one's going to be eating this. Unless you like charcoal?"

"I would not know. The weise alte Frau called it a sausage."

"Oh dear." Gisela went to the stone crock in the corner of the kitchen and scooped up a bowlful of sauerkraut. "Try that. It's salty."

"I cannot drink that."

"You don't drink sauerkraut. You eat it." She ate a spoonful herself by way of demonstration. He followed suit. His eyes widened, and he dug in with relish.

Gisela, on the other hand, left the room when her stomach gave a sudden twist of revulsion. Not at the Salt Man. At the smell of sauerkraut, which she'd always loved. Her stomach knew what her heart denied. The Salt Man was right.

❧

Every time Gisela coaxed her unwanted prisoner into trying a new food, or dressing himself in Oma Solberg's late husband's clothing (Gisela wouldn't let him touch Hartwin's), she saw herself doing the same for her child. Sometimes it was a girl, sometimes a boy, but it always had Hartwin's loving eyes. And soon she couldn't help but think of it daily. Her breasts ached. Her body thickened. People soon noticed that she was with child.

They noticed the Salt Man, too. Every day he became more solid, more visible. Oma Solberg commented on it first.

"You have color in your face, Herr Salzmann! And you look like there's a body in those old clothes of Heinrich's now."

At first, when he followed Gisela to market, carrying cheeses and charms for her to sell, people had made comments about her odd shadow while looking straight through him, not even seeing the items that he carried. Now Volkburg knew him as Menno, Gisela's simple-minded cousin, come to help the young widow during her pregnancy.

Oma Solberg had scolded her for calling him simple-minded. "He's older than either of us, older than the mountain itself. He's not the village idiot, Gisela! He knows things we can't begin to understand."

"He doesn't know how to tie his own shoes, Oma,"

"I do now," said the Salt Man, holding out a shod foot as evidence.

"But they're on the wrong feet," Gisela pointed out. "Oma, how else would you explain the strange man in my house? You know the things some people said when Hartwin married me and not a local girl. A simpleminded cousin is, well, innocent."

"He is that," said Oma Solberg, and Gisela felt another pang of guilt.

"Fourteen," said the Salt Man from his place by the window.

"Fourteen what?" said Gisela, puzzled.

"People crying outside in the street today. Yesterday it was twelve."

"Children?"

"Not all. Frau Muller, Herr Hoffman, Herr Schmidt"

"The blacksmith? Crying in front of everyone? I can't believe that."

"I have worn flesh for too long. Tears fall with no one to gather them and make them part of the earth and sea again. There are too many tears in the world."

"Nonsense." Gisela shook her head. "You're telling me that your stalking people like a carrion crow makes the world a happier place? I don't believe that."

"Someone must gather the tears."

"I don't believe that either."

Oma Solberg said nothing.

❧

Summer turned to autumn. Gisela's step got heavier. She sat down more often to rest and stretch her aching back, letting "Menno" do the actual marketing instead of just carrying her purchases. She had to admit: now that he'd learned the concept of money, he did it well. No one cheated him. Not out of fear, though. No one crossed the street to avoid him now. In fact, it looked like people sought him out, greeting him with a handshake or a hug. Gisela was forced to realize two things: The people of Volkburg, who'd always borne injuries, bitter winters and hunger with grim determination, now cried at burnt porridge. The butcher wept while slaughtering cattle. The minister sniffled over his sermons.

And the Salt Man's touch lessened that sadness, however briefly.

❧

The somber pall over Volkburg deepened, and Gisela's time drew near. Oma Solberg explained the concept of birth to the Salt Man. His look of shocked incomprehension made the old woman smile for the first time in weeks.

The baby arrived with the first snow: a perfect, healthy girl with her father's eyes. When her first cry rang through the little cottage everyone, even the Salt Man, smiled.

But little Ruth didn't stop crying. Gisela's heart broke to hear her, but no amount of rocking, soothing or songs from either her or Oma Solberg could quiet her. Gisela cried too, in sympathy.

"Give her to me," said the Salt Man.

Gisela held her sobbing daughter closer. "No. You said that her tears would mean the end of you. I've done enough wrong to you already."

"Frau Solberg, as long as I wear flesh, people will grieve without stopping. This is part of the Law, like giving kindness for kindness."

"It's not kindness to kill you!" Gisela had to shout to be heard over her child's heartbroken screams.

"Your child will cry forever."

"Take my tears, then. A mother's tears must mean something."

He shook his head. "You may hold her, Frau Solberg, but let me take the child's tears."

"Gisela," she said.

"Your pardon, Frau Solberg?"

"Call me Gisela. Please. Will it… Will it hurt?"

"I don't think so, Gisela." Gently, the Salt Man touched the newborn's cheek. The tip of his finger glistened with tears. Little Ruth stopped crying at once.

"No, it didn't hurt her at all. I think she's happy, Gisela."

"I meant you…" Gisela protested, but the Salt Man had already touched the finger to his lips. Gisela held her breath.

And the Salt Man stood there, staring at his finger as though he'd never seen it before.

"You're, ah, still here," said Gisela at last.

"Yes," he said, sounding puzzled. He held out his wrist.

"The Undying Link is gone. But you're still here," said Gisela. She knew she should feel relieved, but instead an overwhelming gloom swept over her. Ruth's cries started up again, and redoubled.

"No he's not," said Oma Solberg over the din. She, too, was crying. "The Salt Man is gone. That's just Menno."

"But…" said Gisela.

"I wore flesh for too long. I broke the Law. Forgive me." Menno, who had been the Salt Man, trembled. Gisela had never seen him cry, but now tears streaked his face.

Gisela kissed her daughter, handed her to Oma Solberg, and kissed the old woman's cheek. "Danke," she said, and went to stand before the former Salt Man.

"You had no choice. I didn't mean to trap you. I only wanted Hartwin back. Can you ever forgive me?"

"You have shown me nothing but kindness, Gisela. If giving you my forgiveness is kindness in return, I give it."

Gently, as she would have for Ruth, Gisela wiped the tears from his cheeks with her thumb. She saw the look of shock on his face, then on Oma Solberg's as the tears touched her lips.

Then all was salt and darkness.

ð

A salt-white, black clad figure haunts the town of Volkberg. Mourners see her face briefly, feel her touch on their cheeks before she vanishes and life goes on. Some call her the Ruthless Widow, although her touch is gentle. Only one person now living, an old man with a grown daughter, knows the reason for the name. When asked to tell the story, he turns away, his eyes bright with tears.

And when the Salt Man weeps, the widow comes to him.

On Her Own Two Feet

I perched atop the oversized tire, switching my tail in anticipation of the overture. I suppose every actress gets the first night jitters. I don't know how many shed from sheer panic. All I knew was that if this run of Cats didn't work out, I'd be back on the street. Back to scrounging in alleys for scraps. Back to sleeping curled up under newspapers, in boxes. My family would sniff in disdain. None of them had the urge to dance, to sing. They'd never understood what drew me to the stage month after month. None of them appreciated the magic of theater, the wonder of music, the camaraderie among the actors.

The house lights dropped. The curtain rose. The first number went perfectly. I danced with as much grace as anything on two legs could. Still, I couldn't ignore the nervous tingling in my toes.

Waiting offstage for my next entrance, I actually felt glad that I only had a minor part. It gave me a chance to soothe my ruffled nerves. A hand touched my shoulder, and I nearly jumped out of my costume.

"Easy there," whispered John. "Stay loose."

I nodded. I liked John. He wore his costume well, almost as though it were his own skin. Almost leonine, John, with his mane of red-gold hair. Sleek and muscled, graceful, with such a powerful voice…

"Looking good tonight," he added. "You'd think that was a real tail, the way you carry it."

"Thanks," I said, not trusting myself to say more. I bounced on my toes, ready for my cue. The tingling spread over my ankles. Still, as the saying goes, "the show must go on," and so did I. With every twist and leap, the tingling got worse and worse.

And my dancing got better and better.

I could feel their eyes on me. All of them. The eyes of the audience, rapt, under the spell of the show. The eyes of my castmates, casting surreptitious glances my way. The other eyes, moonlit outside the windows of the tiny theater. These watched me, knowingly, while the tingling crept over my knees and hummed up my spine. My joints loosened. Still I danced.

Someone in the audience had smuggled in a packet of jerky. I could smell it. Rich, salty… the aroma made me dizzy.

More eyes shone in the moonlight outside. The whole family. What were they doing here, tonight of all nights? None of them could tell Andrew Lloyd Webber's music from traffic noise. Why did they have to come? I ignored them and concentrated on the music, the thrumming of the stage beneath dancing feet, the energy flowing through us all in warm counterpoint to the sharp, deceptive current crackling through my body. So much harmony and light, such wonderful, glowing color…

Terpsichore, please. Let me hold on, just a little longer. Keep the world from twisting away. Keep this power at bay. If it gets to my throat I'll never make it. I only have to finish this one show. Let it work, just once. Please.

Almost there. Just the last chorus! I opened my mouth to sing…

…And a true cat's cry wailed from my throat. Too late! I bolted from the stage, the rest of the cast covering my escape as best they could. I'm just grateful no one saw me leap through the open window.

By the time I'd fled halfway down the block the change was complete. I leapt on top of a stack of crates and sat down to wash traces of greasepaint from my fur. Thick, oily… the stuff clogged my tongue. I wanted to spit, but I couldn't. I couldn't cry, couldn't curse, so I washed with fierce disdain. Greasepaint. Human stuff. Stupid human stuff. Like giant pretend tires. Silly. All fake, pretending to be something they're not. Real tires stink of rubber, and they're always full of sludgy water when you want to sleep in them.

The theater emptied. I crept back up the alley and watched

the humans spill onto the street, chattering and laughing. The door thudded closed, trapping the warm light inside. I sat with my tail wrapped around me, waiting.

The door creaked open again. I recognized John's shadow, his scent, even before he spoke.

"Um, Victoria? You out here? Are you OK?" He took a gulp of soda from the can he carried and stepped into the alley.

I ran to press against his legs. He'd changed out of his costume. Now he wore those wonderful old jeans of his, heavy with the odors of backdrop paint and dust from the recesses of Wardrobe, and his own clean, masculine scent. I purred. He stiffened, and then pushed me away.

"Go away, cat. I'm busy. Victoria! Where are you?"

He stalked off. I followed. I tried to call his name, but all that came out was a meow.

"I said get out of here!"

I recognized that tone, the raised, half-clenched hand. It said: "Run!" But this wasn't just some human. This was John.

"Get!"

The can hit me alongside the head, splattering me with cola. The blow stung. The look in John's eyes...*that* hurt. I stared at him for one long moment, remembering, before I ran.

Slowly, the rest of my family crept out of hiding, purring sympathy, washing soda from my matted fur. I should have realized—they may not understand the arts, but they all recognize the family curse. It takes different forms in each of us, but the pull is always there. The urge to change never dies.

I felt their purring caressing my skin, soothing my heart. I purred back. But deep inside, I still heard music like no cat ever made.

That's the blessing of lycanthropy, such as it is. Three things are certain: The cycle will always come around again. When it strikes hardest, the others will always be there, ready to offer comfort. And when the time comes, I'll get another chance to stand on my own two feet.

Sacrifice

Robert Masterson propped his elbows on the sun-warmed table, squinting at the hotel's tiny outdoor stage. An actor in a feathered headdress posed in front of a garish flowered curtain. Bob shook his head. Against the living backdrop of real palm trees and serrated volcanic cliffs that surrounded the hotel, the whole setup looked as fake as the cardboard-box theater that Aunt Tillie had made for Bob and his sisters, long ago.

The actor struck a gong. All around the vine-draped courtyard, diners turned to face the show. Waiters began circulating among the tables, trading empty glasses for deceptively sweet concoctions in bright primary colors.

"In the First days, the gods created this island," the actor intoned. "A paradise on earth. But the Eldest god decreed that for such beauty, there must be a sacrifice. He touched the mountain with his burning finger, claiming it for his own. And where the Eldest god touches, there can never be Paradise…"

Bob groaned and leaned back in his tiny chair. This was the tropical wonderland that Aunt Tillie always talked about? Some flyspeck island, off the main tourist trail… He felt like he was back in kindergarten, hunched behind a minuscule desk, watching some puppet show. And the place had more flowers than a funeral. The scent of plumeria, so thick he could taste it, was giving him a headache.

Aunt Tillie would have scolded him for sulking, he knew. She would've loved this place. But then, if Aunt Tillie had been there, he might've liked it too…

The couple at the next table giggled, oblivious to anything but each other.

"Humma-himma-nutta…" babbled the woman.

"No, Sugarlips, it's hoomi-himmu-nupu." her mate corrected.

"It's humuhumunukunukuapua'a," muttered Bob's waiter, setting another drink in front of him. "Idiots."

"Um, do you know what they're talking about?"

"Trying to pronounce the State Fish of Hawaii." He snorted.

"Island-hopping honeymooners. Will there be anything else, Mr. Masterson?"

"A refill sounds good… er…"

"Rex."

"Rex? Like a dog?" Bob struggled to focus on the waiter. All that registered was an impression of very black eyes and very white teeth. He'd had too many of those green drinks with the pineapple wedges on them. Or maybe it was the red ones, with the little umbrellas… "Fetch me another drink, then."

"No, like Oedipus. Sir." The last word sounded like an afterthought. "And no drink I can bring you will solve your problem."

Bob sighed. "And you know what's causing all my problems, Fido?"

"Rex. Sir. Yes, I do. It's because you're mortal. And so was your Aunt Matilda."

That focused Bob's blurred mind. "What do you know about Aunt Tillie?"

"I know that she wanted to bring you here. Thought you were getting jaded, needed cheering up." He shook his head. "Such a pity about the stroke. Nice that she left you enough to come here on your own, though. Next best thing, I suppose." He took a swig from Bob's untouched drink, paused, as though searching for the flavor, and set down the glass with a look of disappointment.

Bob ground his teeth. "If this is a joke, it isn't funny."

"I would never joke about your aunt, Mr. Masterson. I know you'd have done anything for her."

"Play dead, Rex."

"Can't bring her back, though. Pity. Too bad you're only human."

Bob choked on a laugh. "I suppose you're not?"

"Of course not!" Rex looked affronted. "I am *the* god of this island."

Definitely too many drinks. "What, like Maui and Pele and all those guys? And you're waiting tables?"

"Upstarts." The waiter snorted. "No, this island was here long before Hawaii, or any of Polynesia. And so was I."

"Yeah, right."

Rex set down his tray, leaned back in a chair, and waved a hand at the billing, cooing honeymooners. "Tell me those two aren't getting on your nerves."

"Well, yeah, but..."

Rex snapped his fingers, and the couple was gone. Bob stared.

"What did you do to them?"

"Nothing painful."

"You... you're..."

"A god. I told you. Now, if you were a god, your aunt would still be..."

"Shut up!" Bob thundered. The other diners—and the waiters, and the actors—turned to stare at him. He buried his head in his hands. Rex chuckled.

"You're attracting attention, my boy. Meet me at the top of the hill if you want to talk."

After a moment, Bob lifted his head. Rex was gone. The diners avoided Bob's questioning looks. He shoved back the table and sprinted toward the hill.

৵

The hill was steeper than Bob expected. The climb sweated some of the fogginess out of his head. Rex lounged against a palm tree, watching him gasp his way up. Even in the coat and long trousers of his waiter's uniform, he looked enviably cool.

"Hill? This is a volcano!" Bob wheezed. "What's so darned important up here?"

"One of my old altars." Rex sprang lightly over a rotting stump. "It used to be quite magnificent—all obsidian and bloodstains. Now—well, see for yourself." He shrugged. "Times change."

Bob looked. Stared. At an ebony block, draped with a clean white cloth and set with dishes of fruit and lavender taro cakes.

"Nice. No ambrosia?"

"Hmph. Cigar?" Rex produced a case from his jacket pocket. "I got them from a friend in Haiti." He held out the case, and Bob saw that his fingernails were long and sharp.

Bob's skin crawled. "No, thanks."

"Suit yourself." Rex sprawled in the crotch of a tree. "Let's get straight to business, then. You want to be a god? We'll swap."

"Swap what?"

"Bodies. Well, your body. My avatar. Nice-looking, isn't it?"

"Oh, no. No, no, no. I know this game. You heard the play, down there. The Eldest god always gets his sacrifice. Even if you are some kind of 'god', or genie, or demon, you'll have some way of tricking me out of ever getting my body back."

Rex smiled, showing all his very white teeth.

"Mr. Masterson, think about it! Once the trade is made, *you'll* be the god. How could I possibly stop you from doing whatever you wanted?"

Bob tried to think about it. He really did. But all that came to mind was Aunt Tillie's face, alight with childlike wonder, admiring every flower and bird and tree. She'd think the tourist shows were magical. If, by some miracle, he could bring her here…

"Do it."

"You're certain, Mr. Masterson? I can't stop the change once it's begun."

If he were a god—gods didn't have regrets, or guilt, or hangovers—did they?

"Do it!"

"As you wish."

Bob closed his eyes, and felt…nothing. He opened them again. The slender shape of Rex had vanished. A hungry-eyed doppelganger of himself crouched where the god had been.

Bob staggered, dizzy. His new body adjusted its balance with perfect, mechanical grace. A tropical breeze caressed Bob's cheek. Instantly he knew: Wind, 5 mph, 77 degrees Fahrenheit, carrying pollen from 5 species of nearby plant—but it didn't feel warm, or gentle, or fragrant. The world was growing. He could see more of it every second—the hillside, the hotel courtyard, with the actors taking bows, the tourists applauding. Thirty-seven people, twenty-nine speaking English, two French, the rest dialects of…

"Stop it! Stop it!" cried Bob.

"Why, whatever is the matter, Mr. Masterson?" asked the thing with his face.

"Everything's out there…but nothing's real!" Even as he spoke, the relentless tally in his mind recorded the pitch and decibel level of his new voice. Bob grabbed half a pineapple off the table and buried his face in it, trying to suck out any trace of sweetness. His mind droned on: Contents: fructose, citric acid… Bob looked up, sticky juice dribbling down his chin.

"But it has no taste!" Bob wailed. "I don't understand. Help me!"

Ever so gently, Rex took the fruit from the new god's shaking hands. Then, he tore off a sweet mouthful and chewed, closing his eyes in ecstasy. Bob Masterson groaned, shuddered—and tore into smoky fragments.

❧

Rex opened his eyes and watched impassively as the shredded avatar thinned and dissipated. He strolled to the table, picked up the smoldering cigar, and pressed it to the soft underside of what had been Bob Masterson's wrist. Pain shivered along every nerve.

The Eldest god smelled the burning and smiled. "Ah!" he breathed. Such intense sensations! He considered. The human's ravaged spirit wouldn't be able to form even the beginnings of an avatar for at least a century. It would be far longer before he could hope to ask for his body back.

In the meantime, there was so much to try. Drinks with umbrellas in them. Motorcycles. Fire walking. Cliff diving.

He wondered how long this body would last.

Wingless

Leaftips Fourthplant Thirdrow undulated toward the pearlbud field at the center of the compound. She'd never been so late to duty. The torches at the corners of the inner fence had guttered out long ago. Tips could just make out the shape of her egg-sister, Midrib Fourthplant Thirdrow, swaying upright on her balance-legs to peer above the crowd of Larvals outside the gate. In the trees surrounding the field, the glittering strings of milkstones dangling from the Protectors' colorful nests shivered as their owners stirred inside. She caught an acidic whiff of Middy's warning scent.

"Hurry, Tips! The Protectors will land soon. Hurry!"

Tips inched faster, all eight stout walking-legs pumping. Leaf-hunger was enough to hurry her along, even without the spur of fear. Her skin felt tight, near to molting, and her body just wouldn't move as easily as usual.

"The Protectors are not true birds. The Protectors care for us," she chanted under her breath. "They keep us safe from real birds and Wingless. They make the pearlbuds grow."

Nevertheless, every segment of her body contracted in instinctive fear as the avian shapes dropped from above. The Protectors perched on the inner fence surrounding the pearlbud field, cocking beady eyes at the assembled Larvals. Tips looked away, turning her attention to the iridescent green of the tender pearlbud plants. The nearest Protector squawked, grasped the gate in his beak, and swung it open.

"Eat."

The Larvals surged forward. Tips dived into the nearest row of plants and tore off a mouthful. The tangy-sweet taste sent a ripple of pleasure through her body. She fell into her usual rhythm of tearing and chewing, tearing and chewing. All around her, Middy and her other egg-siblings were doing the same. Warmth and well-being flooded through Tips with every bite. She stopped hearing the harsh calls of the Protectors. In fact, she felt sorry for the poor things, standing lonely guard on their fence posts instead of basking in the sun with egg-siblings and feasting on pearlbud leaves.

A butterfly landed on the plant she was eating. Tips stopped, rose swaying onto her balance-legs, and extended her grasping-arms. "Greetings, Ancestor," she said, wondering if the stories were true, if transformed Larvals really had wings so graceful and delicately shaded.

"Mouth is for eating, not talking," the nearest Protector croaked. Sunlight glinted off the edge of its beak. Tips dropped back onto her walking-legs, feeling vaguely troubled. She wrenched off another mouthful of pearlbud leaves, and soon the feeling went away.

Middy eyed her from farther down the row and bent her body into a questioning shape. Tips glanced toward the Protector and responded in the silent field-language of ripples and body movements while her mouth went on chewing:

"&cestor. U C?"

"Yes."

Tips dreamed of wings while the glands along her sides filled and swelled. Even when they grew uncomfortably tight she forced herself to swallow one more mouthful. Every bite made her more productive, and everyone knew that productive Larvals grew faster and got their wings sooner. Middy was already waiting for her. The egg-sisters joined the others inching toward the collection area, moving as quickly as their bulging sides would allow. A few Larvals already swayed upright in their places, their hind segments submerged in cold water.

Tips hurried to her water-filled collection pan, rose up, and compressed her segments one by one. Milky fluid wept from slits in her sides, burning, hardening into opalescent drops as it hit the water.

"Shiny," croaked a watching Protector, cocking its head to count the shimmering jewels in the pan. Although Tips knew that its hungry look was only meant for the treasure she produced, she fled as soon as the pain in her sides faded. Middy wasn't far behind.

"Brr, I hate watching the Protectors count!" said Tips. Her shiver went deeper than the usual after-giving chill. "The way they clack their beaks… Oh."

"Come on; let's get back to the field. I'm cold. I need… Tips? What is that?"

"Something on the far-fence. I think a Wingless," Tips replied in field-language, staring at the outer fence that surrounded the entire compound.

"Looks like a stick with spindly legs," said Middy in horrified fascination.

The stiff, spotted creature had climbed nearly to the top bars of the outer fence when a Protector swooped down and snapped it up. The Wingless gave a shrill cry as the Protector flew out of sight. Middy cringed. Tips stared at the spot where the Wingless had been. It left behind a scent of terror, not unlike a Larval's.

"It almost got in," said Middy.

"That's a Wingless? How dangerous can a stick be?" said Tips. "And it could have just gone under the fence. I wonder what it was doing up there?"

"Come on, Tips. Let's get back to the field. I'm hungry."

Tips inched forward for a closer look.

"Not the outer fence! Don't go over there! It might've contaminated the wood, and if you touch it your wings'll never grow. Tips!"

Tips ignored her egg-sister. A frisson of excitement tingled through her, overriding the craving for pearlbud. She'd actually seen a Wingless. It hadn't looked as terrifying as the whispered tales made them sound. There'd been no reek of poison, no fangs, no tearing spines. The Protector who'd grabbed it hadn't fallen from the sky.

She touched the fence. It didn't burn her. She sticky-footed up a post and looked around. From here she could see three sides of the pearlbud field. To her right, Larvals crawled to the collection area and back. She had a hazy memory that the unseen far side held the hatching trays. On her left, farthest from the collection area, was the forested side where Larvals never went, where the Protectors nested. Tips turned away from that sight and looked out. The land rolled away from the fence in gentle green waves. She'd never seen so much unguarded space.

"Middy, come look!" she called, but her egg-sister had already hurried back to the pearlbud field.

Tips leaned farther and farther out until her front segments hung over empty air. Just as she felt herself beginning to slip, a Protector swept down and caught her in its beak.

"Thank you! Ow… Protector, you're hurting me."

The Protector flew higher. Tips squirmed, releasing the last bitter drops of pearlmilk, and the Protector dropped her.

The plant she landed on wasn't pearlbud, but something bitter. She couldn't smell any pearlbud at all, and her body ached with wanting it as much as from the fall.

"Come back! Protector…"

"Shut up, you stupid worm!" The shrill voice came from under one of the not-pearlbud plants. Tips peered more closely—then writhed in terror as a Wingless crawled out from under the leaves.

"Don't touch me! Go away!" Tips tried to get away without turning her back on the dreadful stick-like creature, but her legs wouldn't go backward, and her skin felt like it was splitting.

"Fine. I'll leave you to be eaten." The Wingless turned away, showing a scrap of crimson protruding from its side.

"No you won't, Red," said a second, gentler voice. "Can't you see she's about to change?"

Despite herself, Tips inched closer to this new Wingless. "Change? You mean grow wings?"

"Yes, dear."

"I have to get home! Middy and I need to change together. I'll miss the celebration."

"Celebration?" said Red. "What are the Takers telling the little worms these days?"

"The Protectors said there'd be one. With a feast. Maybe there'll be pearlbud flowers. I have to hurry!" Tips climbed down from the plant and inched toward the fence. Spindly legs grabbed hold of her. She screamed. Before she could scream a second time, the first Wingless stuffed a bitter leaf into her mouth.

"Red!" said the second Wingless.

"You want her bringing the Takers down on us?" The Wingless's stiff body quivered with terrified rage. He started pushing, trying to roll Tips across the lumpy ground.

"Red, for flight's sake, be gentle!"

"Help me get her out of sight, Dreamer. Then you can coddle her all you want."

The other Wingless picked up one end of a leaf underneath Tips and motioned to Red to lift the other. Tips swayed just above the ground between them. Her head spun. She wanted to wriggle free and find Middy, to escape from these bizarre Wingless, but the swaying and a strange dizzy lethargy pushed her into unconsciousness.

❧

Tips woke and fought her way through a sticky wall of entangling threads. Disoriented and off-balance, she clung to a leaf. Nothing smelled right. The world looked like she was seeing it through a million dewdrops. A glance down made the world spin—but confirmed that both Wingless were watching her from below. Possibly more than two. She couldn't be sure.

"You tied me up," she said. Her voice sounded strange, hollow and higher.

Red chuckled. "You tied yourself up. In a cocoon, that is. I would've thought you were too far gone to manage it."

"Now you need a name," said Clouddreamer.

"I have a name. Leaftips Fourthplant Thirdrow."

Red laughed outright. "That's not a name. That's a label the killers stuck on you so they could locate you among their chattel."

"I am not chattel! Whatever that is."

"It means they own you. You and all the other Larvals they milk for nectar."

"The Protectors do not own me! They protect us until we grow our wings. The milkstones are how we show our gratitude. And Tips is a better name than Red. At least I'm not named after some useless scrap that's not even a real wing."

Red's antennae trembled. "Listen. That scrap isn't a real wing because…"

"Red, don't," said Clouddreamer.

"No. Listen to me, you sap-addled idiot. I had wings. Scarlet and gold, broad and strong. And your "Protectors" ripped them off, like they do to all their kept Larvals just before they eat them. I have this scrap because I fought. I made them drop me. I lived. And I'm proud to have a name that I earned!"

"No. You're lying!" Blood pounded through Tips. She felt like she was expanding with rage.

"Have you ever seen a winged Larval? Not the small, mute, underdeveloped Ancestors. One of your own kind, transformed. Have you ever seen even one?"

"No." Tips looked to Clouddreamer, but saw only sadness.

"That's because the Takers rip our wings off for trade, just like they trade the milkstones. Anything shiny or colorful," said Red.

"But the Larvals…"

"If they're lucky, left to die. A few escape. Right, Dreamer?"

The gentle Wingless' antennae drooped with grief. "My wings were gold, with fine black webbing. And little dots of blue. No, not quite blue. Violet? I thought I could never forget."

"Deeper still," said Red with a gentleness Tips wouldn't have believed possible. "Underblue, rich and glowing."

"Like that," said Clouddreamer in awe. She was looking at Tips.

Tips managed to focus some of her fractured vision behind her. Silken color swayed with her movements, bluer than the sky, shot through with streaks of white.

"They're lovely, dear," said Clouddreamer.

Tips balanced on the leaf, feeling the breeze push at her, urging, coaxing.

"Well, go ahead, use the things," said Red.

Tips let go. The breeze caught her up and tumbled her around, tickling her wings until she laughed.

"They're real! Real wings! I have to show Middy."

Red and Clouddreamer shouted protests, but Tips ignored them. The pearlbud field, so far away when she was crawling on the ground, looked tantalizingly close from the air. Spots of white dotted the emerald plants.

"The pearlbuds are blooming!" Tips shivered with delight and flew over the field. The scent of pearlbud blossoms rose up to her, sweet and intoxicating. Tips didn't even notice the fading light, or the torches blazing at each corner of the empty field. Still unsteady on her new wings, she drifted downward. Before she could land and taste the heady nectar, she heard a Larval scream.

Middy. From the Protectors' side of the compound, where Larvals never went.

Her wings weren't made for swift flight, but Tips flew toward the sound as quickly as she could. She passed under the Protectors' hanging nests. For the first time, she realized that the colorful structures were made of shredded wings.

Middy lay on the ground below, surrounded by Protectors, held in place by a scaly foot. She had transformed. Her wings were green as new grass, speckled with black.

The Protectors were trying to pull them off.

Middy screamed again. Tips screamed even more loudly.

"Let go of my friend!"

The Protectors paused long enough to laugh until they lost their balance and croak "You next. Wait."

While they were laughing, Middy wriggled out from her captor's raised foot. She'd barely left the ground before they brought her down again. Tips used the distraction to flee the other way, toward the pearlbud field.

"Tips! Don't leave me!"

Tips steeled herself and kept flying toward the field.

"Tips, please!"

Tips kept flying away from her.

Toward the torches.

Without stopping to think, Tips dipped one wing, then the other, into the flames. Wings ablaze, she flew through the pearlbud field. The plants kindled, paper-thin blossoms blazing. The Protectors abandoned Middy and arrowed toward Tips, only to be driven back by the fire. Tips heard them screeching as she plowed, smoldering, into the sandy earth.

Tips hurt. Soot clogged her spiracles, making it hard to breathe. The only thing that didn't hurt was her wings. She couldn't feel them at all.

"Tips?" said Middy's voice from above her. "Are you all right? You saved me. Tell the Wingless I'm your friend, please. They don't believe me."

Middy hung in the air above her, bobbing with every passing breeze. The sight made Tips nauseous.

"Yes. My friend. Now leave me 'lone."

"Figures. Pair of brainless fools," said Red's voice, oddly subdued. "But at least they gave the Takers' beaks a good twisting. What a mess!"

"The poor Larvals. They won't know where to turn." Clouddreamer came forward to touch Tips gently with her antennae. "Some will end up here, I suppose. You'll have company while you recuperate, dear."

"If they aren't all afraid of Wingless," Middy put in, fluttering into view again. Tips couldn't see Red's reaction, but Middy protested "Well, I'm not! I mean, Tips is a Wingless now, and I'm not scared of her."

There. Middy had said it. The beautiful wings, darker than night but brighter than summer sky, had burnt to ash. Tips tried to turn away.

"Oh no you don't!" said Red. The Wingless stood before her, fierce in his intensity. "You don't quit now. Not when you've torched that treacherous pearlbud and given those poor miserable worms a chance at lives of their own. Don't you dare quit now." Red rounded on Middy. "And stop calling her Tips! She's not just a spot on a Taker's grid."

Middy dropped onto a leaf, baffled. "But what else would I call her?"

The Wingless who had been the Larval Leaftips Fourthplant Thirdrow remembered wings, heavenly and briefly hers, No Takers could take that memory from her, and she had a way to make sure she would never forget.

"Call me Underblue."

Lilly

The sign over the door read "Thirteenth Annual Mechanifeline Fancier's Competition". Inside the hall, the ladies of the Society opened baskets and carriers, releasing their prized mechanicats onto the tables. Gears clicked and whirred. (Purred, their owners would insist, although some purists declared that a true purring effect could be achieved only through the bubbling of a precisely-controlled steam engine, an as-yet-unmastered technique.)

"What a pity about Abigail Fields," said Lady Staffordshire, with a simper that turned into kissing sounds directed at her latest creation. "She wasn't as old as she looked, really. The competition just won't be the same without her. Will it, Plushikins?"

She stroked her mechanicat's back, and, with a faint pinging of springs, it arched into her hand. The watching ladies oohed and ahhed.

"Response to light touch!" Mrs. Fitzmorris exclaimed, her usual critical façade shaken. "*Very* well done! I don't think even Abigail ever managed that."

"I hear she was working on self-sustaining motion before the accident," said another Society member. "But no one could find her notes, either. They suspect she had them with her when…" The speaker broke off and turned away. The Ladies fell silent and busied themselves with their creations, brushing fur and oiling joints. Lady Staffordshire appeared not to notice.

"Plushikins is the most advanced mechanikitty I've ever known. Aren't you, Sweetums?" she cooed. "Poor Abby, rest her soul, would be green with envy. Look."

Lady Staffordshire held up her little machine. The tail ratcheted back and forth. The hinged jaws opened and emitted a tinny mew.

"It doesn't like being picked up!" giggled one of the younger ladies.

"Nonsense," said Mrs Fitzmorris, all the more sternly for her earlier lapse of decorum. "Clockwork can't like or dislike anything. This exhibition is about craftsmanship. These creations, however elegant, are simply machines. They are to be admired, not fawned over."

"Then admire my Plushikins for the work of art that she is," said Lady Staffordshire, undaunted. "Look. Ermine fur with realistic markings on all exposed surfaces, retractable claws, fully articulated joints. She only needs winding once a week, and only a master craftswoman would spot the keyhole. And when she DOES need winding, she curls up in a natural sleeping posture. And look at this!"

Lady Staffordshire flipped her mechanicat over and unbuttoned a seam hidden in the thick fur. Ignoring its waving legs and intermittent steam-driven hisses, she pointed into the opening. "There, below the vocal bellows. Tiny hot water bottles, connected to a boiler. A network of them beneath the skin keeps Plushikins at near a live cat's natural temperature. So…"

"She's cuddly!" squealed the youngest Fancier.

"You've achieved steam control," said Mrs. Fitzmorris with more subdued admiration as the mechanicat started up a steady, bubbling purr.

"Exactly." Lady Staffordshire buttoned up her mechanicat and set it upright, regarding her fellow Fanciers with an expression that said that she knew perfectly well that her Plushikins surpassed every other clockwork beast there, although she certainly wasn't about to be so rude as to say so herself. In fact, there was really no reason not to just give her the Best In Show ribbon on the spot…

"My Lilly is cuddly too," said a soft voice. The Fanciers turned to see a middle-aged woman in half-mourning in the doorway, holding a small grey tabby.

"I'm certain she is, Madam," said Mrs. Fitzmorris—gently, because the stranger appeared somewhat disoriented. "But this is a private exhibition for crafters of mechanicats. Clockwork cats. And your pet looks quite…biological." Indeed, Lilly had leapt from her owner's arms, sniffed Plushikins over from upholstered head to jointed tail, and was now washing the mechanicat, to Lady Staffordshire's consternation. "Perhaps you were looking for the Benevolent Society across the street?"

"No, I'm in exactly the right place," said the strange woman, with a stiff smile. "And I know the purpose of this Society as well as any of you." Her voice changed, sounding like a gramophone recording as she recited: "To honor Nature, and celebrate Mankind's mastery of Her secrets by perfecting the craft of Natural Engineering." She turned that odd smile on Mrs. Fitzmorris. "Is that correct, Emily?"

The Ladies all stared. The stranger removed her grey bonnet, allowing them all to get a better look at her face. The gaslight shone in blue glass eyes. White silken hair almost hid the stitches along her scalp. In the near-perfect silence, the sigh of her breathing echoed the mechanicats'. For once, Emily Fitzmorris looked shaken.

"Abigail? Abigail Fields?"

"More or less. I thought more, at first. Now I'm thinking perhaps less. Do you mind if I sit, ladies?"

The ladies nodded, dumbfounded, and Abigail took a seat, her clockwork joints clicking. "Ah. Much better. Thank you." The gray cat jumped onto her lap, and she stroked it rhythmically, while studying Lady Staffordshire's creation. "Plushikins really is quite impressive, Ethel. Were I still on the Committee, I'd award you the ribbon."

"But of course you are!" said half the Society in unison. "This is beyond craft."

Abigail Fields shook her head, with a sound like the ticking of a clock. "I've had enough of trying to master Nature. I know now that it's impossible. I can only hope to work with Her for a time."

"You reworked yourself," said Emily Fitzmorris in tones of awe. "This is nothing short of miraculous. You're not just a crafter. You're a magician,"

That metronome ticking echoed softly in the hall as the reanimated woman shook her head. "I'm someone who couldn't bear to lose, even to Death. I'm someone who couldn't tell the difference between life and mere animation."

The Ladies fell silent, except for one.

"But surely you agree that craftsmanship should be rewarded," said Lady Staffordshire with an unctuous smile. "And you're clearly the greatest craft here. I mean, crafter, of course!"

&

And so the Thirteenth and last Annual Mechanifeline Fancier's Competition came to an end. Its members parted with uneasy smiles and glances at their remade former idol. Some made warding signs. Abigail sighed and removed the coveted blue ribbon from around her arm.

"They missed the point entirely, Lilly," she said. "As though you need to be 'perfected'. Or could be." She tied the prize around the neck of the small grey alley cat, who curled contentedly in her owner's wooden arms and purred herself to sleep.

HUMOR

Bronze Bras and More!

As they had every morning for the past three months, the women of the King's Royal Guardiennes woke not to sunlight, but to the sudden flash of a magic mirror coming to life.

"Bronze Bras, 50% off!" proclaimed the banner behind the glass, followed by images of buxom, scantily-clad Valkyries modeling said bras. The Guards groaned.

"50% off? They probably have only one cup," Bellatrix LaRouge muttered. A snicker ran through the barracks.

Since the mirror took up most of the wall, the constantly-shifting images were impossible to ignore.

"At least it doesn't have sound," said another guard.

"Oh, the King wants it to, believe me! But the royal wizards haven't found a sound-spell that won't shatter glass."

By the time Bella finished dressing, the mirror had touted not only bronze bras, but dragon-burn ointment, eight-league boots (A Step Beyond The Rest!), Genuine "Unikorn" Horn, and dates with half a dozen Prince Charmings.

The dining hall had a mirror too, of course. So did the armory, the training rooms, and even the privy. Bella had heard rumors that the infirmary was still mirror-free. She'd briefly considered breaking a bone, just to get a few days away from the glass menaces.

It was bad enough that the King required all his Guards to keep these mirrors in their quarters for "strategic purposes." Bella would've liked to break a mirror over the head of whoever'd suggested renting them out for advertising.

According to His Majesty, the whole point of the magic mirrors was to give him a way to contact all his guards instantly in an emergency.

"Wars are emergencies," Bella muttered, planting a throwing knife in the eye of a target carefully painted to look nothing like the king whatsoever. "Or earthquakes, or fires, or floods. Or the barbarian horde camped less than a mile from our gates at this very moment. *Not* cheap armor or—she glanced at the mirror—'Potions to double your bodice size'."

Bella yanked her knives out of the target and headed for the stables. Ravenheart *did* need exercising, and not even His Majesty could expect her to carry a full-length mirror while riding a galloping horse.

Just as she was about to leave, Lady Hyacinth ran up, smiling and waving. Bella sighed inwardly and smiled back.

"Have you got your compact yet, Bella?" Lady Hyacinth held up a little round powder box of painted ivory. She flipped it open to show the mirror inside—complete with advertisements. Bella groaned.

"Guards don't have much call for makeup on while on duty, My Lady. And a pretty little mirror like that would only get lost or broken in battle. So no, I don't."

"Oh, what a shame! I'm going to ask the wizards to make one that you can carry into battle."

"No! I mean, don't trouble yourself, Lady Hyacinth. You shouldn't go to all that bother on my account."

"Oh, it's no bother at all! I'll go ask them right now, while you go for your horse ride. Toodles!"

Bella spurred her startled horse into a gallop, wishing she could leave all this nonsense behind her for good. Makeup boxes, when Bronzefist the Bloody and his men were waiting to storm the city! Mirrors in battle. Mirrors with stupid advertisements for bronze…

Bella reined her poor baffled horse to a halt and rode back to the castle. She rubbed Ravenheart down, gave him an apple by way of apology, and hurried to talk to the wizards herself.

❧

The King's Royal Guardiennes rode up to the barbarian camp. Every woman carried a shining new shield.

"Glass shields!" Bronzefist the Bloody guffawed. "Very pretty, girlies. Sparkly, even. But you'll cut your lovely faces when we shatter all that glass. What a shame."

"Ah, but these shields are magic," Bella retorted.

"So they won't cut you all to shreds? So much the better. My men always appreciate good-looking…"

He stopped. His jaw dropped. Yep, thought Bella. This is the real audience for those bronze bra ads.

Every barbarian stood mesmerized. The wizards had programmed all their shields with a special set of advertisements for custom-fitted armor, Rapunzel brand hair conditioner, belly-dancing lessons, and more. The barbarians didn't even notice when the woman laid their shields on the ground and began a slow retreat.

"She's talking to me! What's she saying? I wanna hear!" shouted one barbarian.

–The lipstick ad. Get ready to run– Bella signaled.

"Hey, lookit! It says, 'For sound, touch the center of the shield'."

The Horde bent over to touch the glass shields. For just a moment, a squadron of sultry voices echoed across the field. "…luscious cherry flavor…"

The shields exploded.

❧

Those barbarians still in a condition to surrender did so unconditionally. The king, elated, promised the Guards anything they wanted as a reward.

"Get rid of those mirrors!" they chorused.

His Majesty pouted and sulked, but kept his word. He had the mirrors taken down and re-spelled for the wizards to use for scrying. Bella and company breathed a sigh of relief.

"You're smiling!" said Lady Hyacinth the next time Bella encountered her. "I'm so glad. I thought you'd be miserable over losing those beautiful shields."

"Not at all, Lady Hyacynth. I haven't felt this well for months. If you'll excuse me, I'm just about to go riding."

Bella jogged up to the stables, whistling. Just before she reached Ravenheart's stall, the whistle died in her throat.

Ravenheart turned a forlorn eye on her while Bella stared in at the cheery pink fabric draped over the warhorse's back. Bold purple script read "Buy Stagshome's Hot Breads and Pies!"

"His Majesty says he'll dock three months' pay of anybody who refuses to use 'em," the frowning stablemaster warned her.

"How's Ravenheart supposed to maneuver with that thing on him?"

"His Majesty swears they're all enchanted so the horses won't even notice. Sorry, Bella. But it's my head if I let you take it off."

Bella scowled and thumped her fist on a beam. "Galloping into battle with that's like announcing…" She stopped. "Are we allowed to adjust them a bit? So as to show them off more effectively?"

"I don't see why not. His Majesty just said it has to stay on the horse whenever somebody's riding him."

Bella went to work with needle and thread. She folded and crimped, covering a letter here, an apostrophe there. When she finished, the stablemaster nodded approval.

"Yup, those're some fine alterations. All your ladies'll be wanting something like that. But I doubt His Majesty'll appreciate your needlework. You'd better get to thinking."

Bella grinned. "I do my best thinking in the saddle," she said, and rode away. The pink banners on Ravenheart's sides fluttered proudly. They read: BuSt some Heads!

Paper Tigers

"Here's our newest exhibit, on interplanetary loan from Earth." Our guide flourished a pseudopod. Several visitors twittered and cooed, admiring the skillfully recreated Urban Earth habitat. Glass windows. Fluorescent lighting. Synthetic carpeting. Blocky furniture, clearly designed for bipedal vertebrates. Dispensers in each corner, labeled "Coffee," released a bitter, stimulating scent. The sign in front, scrolling through thirty-seven dialects, read: "EDITORS".

"This is the most extensive collection of Editors in the Thetan Arm." Our guide flushed turquoise with pride. "We have several species, from Novel to Small Press—even the smaller, elusive 'Zine."

"All mainstream, no doubt," one visitor snorted.

"Oh no, sir! We have plenty of Speculative Fiction editors as well. No collection is really complete without them."

We stared. Behind viewscreens, Editors of both sexes prowled and paced. Some sprawled on chairs, while others jostled each other at the coffee dispensers.

"What's the big one with the black coat playing with?"

"A 'cell phone'. We provide plenty of stimulating materials for all our exhibits. Blue pencils are popular with this group—these fellows are amazingly dexterous and will mark up anything. Recent studies hypothesize that they have a quasi-symbiotic relationship with the Authors in the next exhibit. Authors produce 'manuscript', which they…"

"Look—look at the little one in yellow stripes!" gushed a wrinkled dowager. "She's smiling!"

"Don't let that mislead you." Our guide closed three of his eyes tight in a frown. "Never forget—these creatures are born professionals. Their keepers can tell you: you can spend a lifetime working with Editors, building a trusting relationship… and they can still reject you!"

The dowager swooned, oozing across the floor. We turned

away while she reconstituted herself, and watched as assistants trundled paper-piled carts along the corridor.

"You're in luck, folks—it's feeding time! Watch-these fellows can devour a ream of manuscript in a sitting!"

Wall slots snapped open. The Editors roused, fingers twitching. Such powerful hands! The assistants eased manuscripts through the slots. Each Editor seized a teetering stack and carried it off to devour.

A child flattened himself against the glass for a closer look.

"What's wrong with that one? See—he's shaking his head and snapping pencils in half."

Our guide scowled. "Looks like that poor fellow was fed too much slush back on Earth. Makes them lethargic and irritable. We only give our Editors high-quality, double-spaced, professionally formatted manuscript. Keeps 'em much happier." He flicked a switch. "Listen!"

We listened. From inside came contented murmurs of "Hm!" and "Aha!" Our guide beamed.

"That's what we like to hear," he said. "We have a great medical department too, just to keep an eye on their circulation. This batch is doing wonderfully. They've already produced a few new contracts."

One Editor had already finished his manuscript and come looking for more. Our guide searched his pockets.

"I may have a treat here... yes! A tasty bit of flash fiction. A little over its word limit, but, well..."

He dropped the paper into the slot. The Editor pounced on it, teeth bared in a grin. He marked it enthusiastically with the nearest blue pencil... then stopped. He scanned the tidbit once, and again. He sniffed, shredded the tiny manuscript and flung away the scraps. Then, growling something unintelligible, he stalked away. Our sheepish guide turned back to us and shrugged.

"Professionals to the bone, folks! Never forget it!"

Melonheads and Squashers

Yuka was certain of one thing. She was not going to be a sex worker her whole life. She told Hana so, when they both left the rows of sweating, aching women for a drink of water. Hana looked exasperated.

"We're pollinators, not 'sex workers', Yuka. Must you make everything to do with the Art sound degrading?"

Yuka shrugged and waved a hand at the watermelon field, the Pollinators' Barracks, and the workers in their cantaloupe-colored coveralls. "Fruit sex, people sex, what does it matter? I don't want to spend my life hunched over melon-blossoms in some field, diddling at them with a paintbrush in hopes of creating the Pearl of Melons." She returned to her row and picked up her paintbrush. "There has to be more to life than tallying how many melons you impregnated today."

"It's for the greater good," said Hana. Hana kept working as she talked, leaving Yuka behind in her trek down the row. "Creating the Pearl of Melons is the true quest of all Melon Valley. What more do you want?"

"Something. Anything! I mean, suppose one of us does create the Pearl of Melons. Then what? It's just fruit!"

"Not so loud!" Hana looked around in alarm. "You'll have people thinking you're a Squasher."

"And maybe squashes aren't so bad either," said Yuka, enjoying her friend's look of shock and the shiver that ran down own her spine when she spoke those words. "Maybe we'd like them. Maybe we'd even like cucumbers!"

"Yuka, watch your language!"

"Cucumber! Cucumber!"

Hana fled with her hands over her ears. The next thing Yuka knew, the Judges had charged her with public indecency and inciting heresy, and she was being firmly escorted from the fields by looming men with muscles like muskmelons. They let her stop by her family's compound just long enough to make up a bundle of necessities, and ejected her from Melon Valley.

⁊

Necessities, it turned out, included things that people who spent their whole lives in sultry Melon Valley never thought of owning. Like warm clothing. The upper lands were colder than anything Yuka, raised in the steam-warmed cradle of the Pollinator's Compound, had ever felt. A shallow layer of white powder covered the ground. Yuka picked some up, and it turned to water in the warmth of her hand. She experimented with it until her fingers went numb, discovering that she could mold and pack the stuff into shapes. She formed a sphere and studied it.

"This must be snow. Like in the Judges' rhyme about the Pearl of Melons:

> *White as snow*
> *Cool as ice*
> *Perfectly round*
> *Found in..."*

"A trice? I wish. If I found the Pearl of Melons they'd want me back in a hurry." Yuka stuck her chilled hands into her armpits and marched long, trying to distract herself from the cold with of her favorite whispered suggestions for the missing words. Yesterday's rice. The bellies of mice.

"Mere poetic device," she grumbled. "There probably is no such thing."

⁊

The sun sank. The air grew colder still. Yuka trudged through the night and into daylight again. The steam rising from the Valleys—Melon Valley, heretical Squash Valley and far-off, ominous Cucumber Valley—had vanished behind Yuka long ago. She stumbled along, shaking, until the rock beneath her foot moved, pitching her face-first into the snow.

"That's cheating!" she shouted at the stony obstacle. "Rocks aren't supposed to move!"

The "rock" stuck out a long neck and chelonian head, and blinked at her.

"Oh. You're a turtle. That's all right then." She tottered a few hypothermic steps. "Wait. You're a turtle! You don't like cold any more than I do." She scooped up the hapless creature and pointed it like a dowsing rod. "C'mon, boy. Show me the way home."

The turtle just hung there waving its flippers, but Yuka did spot the narrow trail it had left. On the side of a hill. A very steep hill.

"What did you do, slide down?" Yuka struggled up the hill, scrabbling at ice and chunks of rock. "And how did you get up here in the first… Oh!"

Yuka stood at the rim of a hot-spring valley, much like home. But where Melon Valley had rows upon rows of regimented fields, interspersed with residential compounds, glasshouses, cisterns, compost heaps and irrigation pipes, this place had trees. Streams. Grass. Flowers that didn't look the slightest bit cucurbital. She gazed across the scene in awe, and the turtle fell from her hand. It wandered through lush, green grass, with Yuka following, until it came to a hollow in the ground filled with small white spheres.

"Turtle eggs? Do you have a nest, little one?" she said. She leaned closer. Realization and a competently-wielded stick to the back of the head hit her at the same time.

જ

Yuka touched the side of her head and felt a lump the size of a casaba. She had a headache to match. The turtle stared at her from a patch of moss nearby. She groaned.

"Touch Mr. Slider again and I'll crack you like a zucchini, Melonhead," said the wielder of the stick.

The woman standing behind the turtle wore a Pollinator's coveralls, but in summer-squash yellow. Plus, everyone in

Melon Valley knew each other on sight. Yuka had never seen this woman before.

"I don't want your stupid turtle, Squasher." Yuka stood up and wobbled toward the white spheres.

"Don't touch that nest!" The woman raised the stick.

"S'not a nest. Those aren't eggs."

"Of course they are. What else would they be?"

Yuka grabbed one of the white objects and bit into it. The stranger screamed and tried to rip it from her hand.

"S'melon," said Yuka, with her mouth full of fruit. The Pearl of Melons' white rind held the sweetest red heart she'd ever tasted. Even the rind itself was edible, pleasantly tart. She swallowed. "It's *the* melon. The one we sweat our lives away trying to create." Yuka shoved a melon into her coverall pockets. "They'll take me back." She picked another. "They'll make me a Head Grower." And another. "Heck, they'll make me a Judge!"

"Trust me, they won't," said the Squasher.

"For this they will. Taste it."

The Squasher woman shuddered. "Tell you what. I've got some butternut soup on the fire. You eat a bowlful, and I'll try that… thing. So you don't eat turtles?"

"Yuck. Never."

"My name's Pearl, by the way."

Yuka stared at her. "You're kidding."

"No. Why?"

Yuka told her about the Pearl of Melons. Pearl laughed, and then grew serious.

"I thought I'd found the Supreme Squash once. A perfect Delicata. I thought the discovery would make me famous. But the Council confiscated all my seeds and had me confined to an experimental growing compound. They expected me to make that perfect squash even bigger and more productive. When I objected, they had me beaten black and blue. Just finding the perfect squash, after all their generations of plotting, made them look bad, you see. So I ended up here."

Yuka winced in sympathy, but said "Well, no offence, but the Judges aren't Squashers."

Pearl shook her head. "What's your name? Nest-Raider?"

"Yuka. I told you, it's not a nest. It's a melon patch. And if you can't appreciate them…"

"They're just fruit, Yuka."

Yuka paused. That sounded awfully familiar. But the heady melon perfume tickled her brain. She'd done it. She'd accomplished what no one in Melon Valley ever had, even Hana the perfectionist. What did a Squasher know about these things? Only in Melon Valley could they truly understand what she'd accomplished.

"Stay here until I die? With just you and a turtle? I've got friends back home. One, anyway. She probably thinks I'm dead." Yuka stuffed more of the tiny, divine melons into her pockets. Only her years of training kept her from taking them all and leaving nothing to re-seed.

"Yuka, please. Listen to me. Give me until sunrise tomorrow to explain. Then, if you want, you can leave. I won't stop you. Just listen."

Yuka listened. The next morning she set off for Melon Valley with her pockets full of the precious fruit, leaving Pearl behind.

🐌

She munched melons all the way home, ignoring her cold, sore feet and the unpleasant effects of a diet of nothing but melons while she imagined the reception she'd get at home. Hana would be green with envy—but proud of her at the same time. They were best friends, after all. She'd never have to work in the pollination fields again. No more hot, sweaty, backbreaking days with flies buzzing around her head. No more sleeping packed into a Pollinators' Barracks. She'd be offered a position as a Judge, and live in Fountain House, and be served melon wrapped in paper-thin ham. Or maybe even bacon.

She saved all the seeds, of course, in an inner pocket. They were the one thing the muskmelon-muscled guards didn't find when they patted her down. They did find the one melon left in her right front pocket. The Judges asked her all kinds of questions about that, when they came to the windowless room where the guards had locked her. How had it come into her possession? Were there more? Where? Did anyone else know about them?"

They didn't ask any of the questions Yuka wanted to hear, like "What idiot locked you in this cell?" and "Can we get you something for that black eye?" and "Would you please accept our apologies for this horrible misunderstanding?"

All in all, Yuka really didn't feel like obliging them. The black eye, courtesy of the muskmelon-muscled guards, hurt as badly as Pearl's blow to the head. And Pearl had at least offered her food, even if it were made of vile, heretical squash. So Yuka made up a story about finding the Pearl of Melons in a swamp.

"There are no swamps," said the oldest Judge in a chilly voice. "We drained them all to make the Valleys."

"Um, desert?"

"No."

"Um, temperate deciduous forest?"

❧

She had a second black eye when the largest guard slammed the door, locking her into the dark cell.

"I guess bacon-wrapped cantaloupe is out of the question?"

❧

No one brought cantaloupe, with or without bacon, ham or any other pork product. Someone did bring water, however.

"Hana? Is that you?" Yuka squinted into the crack of light from the door.

It was, but Yuka's friend wouldn't look at her.

"Hana, tell them to let me out of here. I found it, Hana. I found the Pearl of Melons!"

"I know."

"What?"

"I saw. I ate a bite of one. It's the most perfect thing I ever tasted." Now Hana looked at Yuka, and choked on a sob. "I've spent my life trying to create that melon, Yuka! My whole life! And you whine and complain and swear…"

"Swear? What?"

Hana shuddered. "You said the C-word. And you get banished for swearing, and you just wander off and find the Pearl of Melons without even trying! It's not fair!"

Yuka stared at her former best friend, who stood there snuffling and blubbering. "And they gave me that one taste, and made me spit out the seeds, and I'll never, ever taste that again, because the Judges are going to keep them all for themselves, and it's not fair…"

Yuka let her ramble on, and considered bolting through the cracked-opened door into the light and fresh air. But no, the Muscle Boys were probably just outside, in case Hana…

A chill trickled through Yuka, colder than snow. "Hana, why did the judges let you taste the Pearl of Melons?"

Hana looked at the stone floor. "Because I told them you'd tell me where to find more of them."

"I see. And how did you know I got banished for swearing? You ran off as soon as I said "Cucumber."

Hana shuddered and flushed redder than an overripe watermelon. "Because I told the Judges that you swore. But I didn't think they'd send you away. Honestly!"

Yuka stood with her fist clenched at her sides, wishing for just a moment that she had Pearl's whacking stick.

"I'm sorry, Yuka. I thought they'd confine you to the barracks for a day, or something. Then I'd get to pollinate your row too."

Yuka considered her options. Strangle Hana. No, too messy. Rot in this cell. Not appealing. Make a break for it. That would undoubtedly get her beaten and then left to rot in the cell. Even less appealing. Or she could cooperate, and spend the day travelling back to the Pearl of Melons with Hana following her every move. And whining. And complaining.

Maybe the cell really wouldn't be so bad, if it had water and…

"Please, Yuka! The Judges said they'd make me stay in here with you until you gave in. And it smells funny in here."

So much for that thought. "Lead on, then."

❧

Of course, the Judges didn't just let the two of them go off alone. It took two days of backtracking, crisscrossing and random rambling to get the Judges' spies off their trail. Hana complained about the cold, the damp, her sore feet, their miserable rations and everything else.

"Hana, if you say 'Are we there yet?' one more time, I'm going to lead us both straight to the Squashers."

"You wouldn't!"

"Oh, but she already did."

Pearl advanced on them, brandishing her stick. Hana screamed. No one came running. Yuka smiled a grim smile. They really had ditched the spies. Now no one was around to rescue them.

"You're a thief, Melonhead," said Pearl. "Hand over those seeds."

"What, give seeds from the Pearl of Melons to a Squasher? You'll have to kill me first."

"Yuka hasn't got any seeds!" Hana protested. Yuka felt a wave of gratitude that her friend had the nerve to speak up for her after all. "The guards took them all."

"Oh yeah?" Pearl lunged at Yuka, tearing her coverall so that the seeds spilled out. Hana gasped and dropped to her knees, scrabbling in the frost.

"You were just going to waste them, Squasher!" Yuka shouted as best she could with Pearl's stick across her throat.

Pearl ignored her. "You! Other Melonhead! Hands off those seeds."

Hana froze, fist clenched around her prize.

"Your Melonhead friend stole those seeds from a Squash Valley waste heap. They're my property. Give them back and I'll let you go. Otherwise your friend gets it in the gourd."

Hana stood up. She glared at Pearl.

"You can't fight all of Melon Valley, you know," she said. Then she turned and ran.

Pearl let the stick drop. Yuka watched her ex-friend flee with a fistful of seeds. "Well, at least she's headed in the right direction."

"The wrong direction, I'd say. Sorry she let you down, Melonhead."

Yuka shrugged. "The warmer direction, anyway. Let's get out of the cold. You were right. About her. About all of it. Feel free to say 'I told you so.'"

"No point. Besides, you were right about two women not being much of a starter community. Too bad neither of us knows any discontented men. Preferably discontented good-looking young men."

Yuka looked beyond Melon and Squash valleys to the cloud of steam on the far horizon. "Pearl? How do you feel about cucumbers?"

The Early Bird and the Wyrm

"Geese. It's supposed to be geese who lay golden eggs." Penelope ruffled her wings in irritation. "I'm a duck, for crying out loud."

"One who lays golden eggs," growled Sir Parsimonious. "I don't care if you're a chicken, as long as you produce enough gold to attract a dragon."

"And if I don't?"

Sir Parsimonious licked his lips. "Orange sauce. Honey glaze. Sage and onion stuffing…"

"Barbarian!"

"I suggest you start laying, then. The Royal Birthday Feast is in a fortnight. I'd prefer to present His Majesty with a dragon's head to decorate the Great Hall, but I'll find a substitute if necessary. I hear His Majesty is very fond of roast duck with raisins."

The knight sat down to polish his armor, whistling "Great Sword of Victory" loudly and off key. Penelope groaned and hunched down into her nest.

❧

Six days and seven eggs later, Penelope sat up with a jolt. "Do dragons eat ducks?"

Sir Parsimonious shrugged. "Probably. Why?"

"Why? Because once this dragon shows up, it may decide it wants a little duck with its eggs, that's why!"

"That's why you should lay a lot more eggs. To provide a more tempting bait. Of course, if you'd rather *be* the bait…"

"No! Only…" Penelope winced. "Could I have a cushion in here? This is hard on the… tail, you know."

But the knight had already left to groom his horse.

❧

By dawn on the day before the Feast, Penelope drooped atop a veritable tower of glittering golden eggs. Parsimonious stacked them in the courtyard and strutted around the pile like a rooster on stilts.

"Excellent! This should attract a forty-footer at least. Flaming red, maybe. Although there's certain elegance to basic black…"

Penelope opened a weary eye and squinted at the gray clouds above. "Sky blue?"

"It generally is, but it's supposed to rain…"

"Your dragon, you ninny!" Penelope came fully awake and pointed a wing. "Look!"

Sure enough, a periwinkle-blue dragon was ribboning its way through the air toward them.

"It must be very far away, to look so small," Sir Parsimonious grunted. He stopped short as the dragon—all six inches of him—dropped from the sky and bent his long neck in a bow to Penelope.

"Fairest of Mallards, I greet you!" he trilled. "I am Lord Cerulean of the Firedrakes, at your service."

"Charmed, I'm sure," replied Penelope, "but you must realize that I'm a duck."

Lord Cerulean's eyes twinkled. "And I'm a drake, Lady. A firedrake, but a drake all the same. It's a pleasure to answer your signal." He indicated the pile of eggs.

Penelope laughed.

"Is this a joke?" Sir Parsimonious sputtered. "This scrawny worm of a wyrm… I can't bring its head to the King—I'd be a laughingstock!"

"Your servant is exceedingly rude, Lady," the minuscule dragon commented.

"Servant! How dare you, you miserable lizard? I'm Sir Curt Parsimonious, Lord of Vacuous Castle!"

"Then why, Sir, are you boiling water behind yon tree, as though you were but a scullion?"

The knight flushed purple. Penelope flew to investigate, and tore back in a rage.

"Boiling water… and you've got onions back there, and

orange peels, and parsley… You traitor! Golden eggs weren't enough—oh no! You had to have them, and a dragon's head, *and* roast duck!"

Lord Cerulean glared at the quaking man. "Is this true? Has this varlet offered violence to your person?"

Parsimonious trembled harder. A bag of raisins dropped from his sleeve. The knight turned and fled, with duck and dragon in hot pursuit. Between the two of them, they herded the man straight into Ogre's Breath Swamp. Small or not, the dragon's fire heated armor very nicely, leaving dozens of blisters in the most awkward places. The knight almost sighed with relief at finding himself mired chest-deep in the cool, if putrid and slimy, bog.

❧

Parsimonious had left a veritable kitchen in his courtyard, and Penelope and Lord Cerulean put it to good use. The aroma of golden eggs cooking over dragon flame set Parsimonious weeping in his swamp, and drew the entire court to the Castle yard. By the time Parsimonious extracted himself, Penelope and her dragon courtier were safely ensconced in a cozy nest in the Enchanted Forest. His Majesty was so delighted with his Golden Birthday Omelet that he awarded them a small fortune. Small, but large enough for a very small dragon and a duck.

How Does Your Garden Grow?

Some people have green thumbs. Mary Dobbs' thumbs must have been solid emerald, because every flower, vegetable or herb she touched flourished. Her beets were the size of softballs. Her carrots were orange nightsticks. Her tomatoes, though, were her glory. Those tomatoes generated their own gravitational pull, and tasted like lycopene-enriched Heaven. Strangers boggled at the sight of the tiny, elderly woman hauling those delectable monstrosities in her little red wagon.

Mary knew how to use her garden's bounty, too. Her raspberry jam cookies attracted hungry children the way most people's sweets attracted flies. She rented two booths at the County Fair just to hold all her offerings and held court there, surrounded by jars of ruby jam, emerald pickles, and golden honey. She reigned as queen of the gardening domain, dispensing tangy pickles-on-toothpicks to fairgoers with a beatific smile.

No one else came close to matching the wonders she produced. Once or twice over the years, someone had shown glimmerings of becoming a potential tomato-growing rival. Mary Dobbs would totter over to congratulate the winning competitor on their blue ribbon, smiling wistfully at her own second-place offerings. The victor would begin shuffling his feet, looking apologetic at having stolen her cherished victory, and Mary Dobbs would invite the winner to her house for tea and cookies.

"I don't know if it's the raspberry jam cookies or her wounded little-old-lady-expression," said Kevin Miller with a laugh, "but did you ever notice that nobody's ever beaten Mary Dobbs twice?"

"Did you notice that they never come back to the fair twice?" Sam Jenkins scowled. "Sometimes I wonder what she puts in those pickles."

"Garlic," said Kevin, crunching a pungent specimen. "You

been listening to Sweeney Todd again, Sam? Be serious. Besides, she's what, 85 pounds in a heavy sweater? Can you see her hauling bodies around? Stop with the paranoia. Have a pickle."

Sam shook his head and left the fairgrounds. He didn't take the pickle.

Now that the idea had entered Sam's head, it dug its tendrils in and refused to leave. Why didn't those prizewinners ever come back? It couldn't all be pity for Mary Dobbs' puppy-dog eyes. And those tomatoes. Tomatoes just didn't grow that big naturally. Especially with such rich flavor. Such rich, meaty flavor.

Sam's stomach turned to mush, but his conviction had never been so firm. He grabbed a shovel and headed for Mary Dobbs' house.

Twenty-seven tomato plants. Sam had dug up twenty-six of them when he paused to rest on the handle of his shovel. A few gallons of sweat and a total absence of bodies (other than the occasional earthworm) had begun to cool his burning certainty about Mary Dobbs' fertilizer. And he'd torn his pants…

"Mr. Jenkins! What in mercy's same are you doing?"

Sam whirled to see Mary Dobbs glaring at him like an indignant horticultural pixie—flanked by two enormous mastiffs.

"Mrs. Dobbs! Er, um…I know this looks bad…the tomatoes…"

She giggled. "Of course! Everyone wonders. But really, a soil analysis doesn't take that much. You didn't have to dig up my plants."

The dogs growled.

"Behave, boys! Mr. Jenkins isn't going to harm me. Are you, son?"

Sam was blushing now. Blushing, sweaty, grimy, and hungry. His stomach growled so loudly that Mrs. Dobbs raised an eyebrow."

"Dear me. Come inside, get cleaned up and have a snack. Then we'll talk about what to do about this mess."

Before Sam knew it he'd showered, dressed in clean clothes that had belonged to Mrs. Dobbs' late husband, and accepted a jam sandwich and a cup of tea. And a second cup. And a third.

"S'great tea," said Sam through a warm mellow haze. A sliver of his original dread returned. "Didja put something in it?"

Mrs. Dobbs winked and held up a hand-labeled bottle. "Raspberry cordial. Good for what ails you." She poured a tot for herself and gulped it down, and the sliver of apprehension melted away.

"I grow the berries myself, Mr. Jenkins. Come, let me give you the royal tour."

The summer sun was setting, but there was enough light for Sam to admire the baseball-bat sized cucumbers, the lone tomato plant, and the thimble-sized raspberries.

"Delicious," he said, popping one into his mouth. "And that cordial…" He gave a sloppy, drunken chuckle. "Y'know why I came here? The other tomato-growers, the ones that beat you? The way they vanished, I thought, you know, fertilizer."

Mrs. Dobbs put a hand to her mouth. "Mr. Jenkins!"

"Stupid. Forget it. Look at this!" He waved his arms at the garden. "You just know your plants, s'all."

"Of course I do," she said, laughing. Her kind, grandmotherly face blurred before Sam's eyes, and he fell to the ground. He heard the sound of one dog digging, and felt the hot breath of the other dragging him by the collar. "I'd never waste good fertilizer on the tomatoes. It works so much better on the raspberries."

DRABBLES

A Shaggy Dog Story

"First Contact!" exclaimed the President. "Follow the aliens' instructions exactly."

"Yes sir." His aide struggled to translate these while running. "We haven't seen the aliens yet, but we've fed and bathed their 'dog'. This says they travel everywhere with their… pets?"

In the VIP suite, a maid poured bathwater down the sink. The aliens' squeaky clean pink "dog" flopped down on the rug, looking blissful.

The aide blanched. "Oh no."

"What?"

"The aliens are the size of fleas. They travel on their pets, not with them."

The President stared, aghast, as all hope of First Contact swirled down the drain.

Gut Instinct

"Write from your gut," Adam's professor had always said.

He'd glared from his single eye and shaken his fist, with its stubs of fingers, at the cowering students. "If you want to be enchanters, true artists, you must make sacrifices!"

How Adam had cringed, carving off that first fingertip to write a sonnet that would truly move a girl's heart. The rest of the finger-well, he convinced himself, as he bandaged the stump, that the Blacklight Story Prize was worth it. All the sacrifices were worth it. But now…

Adam uncoiled another loop of intestine and slumped against the table. If this novel didn't sell, he'd never even be able to afford the transfusion.

Let Down Your Hair

I fought, but the alien sheared my hair off with its pincers, as always. There were no weapons in the tower, not even safety scissors.

"This captivity is unnecessary if you cooperate, Rapunzel," it said. (They call all humans that.) "We cause you mammals no pain. Give your hair to soften out nests, and you can live in the camp with the other Rapunzels." I'll never let the invaders shear me without a fight. Why should I give part of myself to insulate their cold-blooded broods?

Someday, I'll escape from this tower, and shave myself bald. Then they'll be sorry.

Metamorphosis

Now that the time has come, I confess, I have doubts.

I know what we're told: That we'll be born again, leaving behind these bodies that creep upon the earth and rising on wings of glory. I know others claim to have seen the Risen Ones.

I've been too afraid to look up. Other things strike from above, too. My body gives me no choice. I know I can't go on, that this change has been coming from my first moment on the earth. But oh, it's so hard to leave the green fields behind and start spinning one's cocoon.

As Advertised

Dear Enchanted Forest Rentals:

I'm writing to demand a refund of my rental fee for your "Deluxe Cottage." You advertised "Gourmet meals, fine furnishings, and soft featherbeds in a quaint sylvan setting."

The "gourmet meals" consisted solely of porridge, often either frigid or scalding, occasionally palatable.

I refuse to pay the bill you sent for replacement of chairs and beds. The "irresponsible breakage" occurred while I was escaping from *BEARS!* Your "sylvan setting" is infested with dangerous wildlife. If I hadn't fended off those slavering beasts, you'd be facing a wrongful death lawsuit. Remember that.

Awaiting your reply,

G. Locks.

Worth The Price

"Have you been hydrating? Taking the supplements?"

"Yes, Doctor." Sweat beaded the shivering patient's forehead. The doctor frowned, read the thermometer, and spoke into the machine hooked into the I.V.

"Family Ghy-1, remember the terms! Your host is feverish."

"We like warmth!" the translator fizzed.

"If you terminate your host, I terminate your contract."

The translator spat obscenities, but the fever subsided.

"Parasites," the doctor muttered. "Now; if you insist on renting yourself out to alien microbes, you *must* hydrate."

"Yes, doctor."

"I could flush your blood."

"Maybe someday, Doctor."

They never did. The aliens paid in gold—*and* endorphins.

Beauty Sleep

The Princess climbed the tower, step after step. Past clamorous courtiers, boasting knights, and chattering, quarrelling servants, to the tiny attic room.

The old woman looked up from her spinning. "Happy birthday, child. Are you certain you want this present?"

The girl caressed the spindle. "I'll sleep for a hundred years?"

"Yes."

"And no one will be able to wake me?"

"No one."

"Thank you." Lightly, she touched the point and sank down onto the waiting couch. The old woman tucked a comforter about her and vanished from the sleeping castle. The princess closed her eyes, murmuring;

"Quiet at last!"

Mother Love

"All clones," said the researcher. "Up to 50 in a clutch, 75% fed to the queen at birth. This species…"

He stopped. The subject beckoned from inside the lab, crouching and covering its larvae-sac when the scientists entered the room.

"This infertile one begs pardon." It glanced around the room and chittered "Is it true you keep your young?"

"Well, yes…"

"This one allowed itself to be submitted for study because…" The alien hesitated, crouched lower and withdrew a pink, squirming bundle. "This one is not quite infertile. One offspring, only one. I beg asylum. Let me keep my child."

Red Scandal

At first no one listened to the pale, puny humans. Their story sounded too incredible: promises of spacious homes in Mars' most luxurious district, regular meals, and a place in Martian sports history.

No one wanted to believe the accusations, either. Surely Martian athletes, role models to swarms of young Martians, couldn't possibly be resorting to… enhancements.

Alas, it was true. Everyone saw the needle marks. The entire team was convicted of injecting human blood.

The farmed Earthlings all recovered. Watching those tiny bipeds play ball in their crushing gravity is amazing. Such grace! It must be in their blood.

Turn Back The Clock

The infant lay inside the metal hut, wailing. I took her home to raise.

The men turned the hut into plows, axe handles, roofing. The infant grew, became my melancholy, cherished daughter.

I found her one day, distraught, where the hut had been.

"I'll never see them again," she wailed. "Mother…"

"I'm here, Dearest," I said.

She turned, tears streaming. "My mother centuries from now."

I held her. She babbled of sailing time as one sails the seas, years falling away, herself ever younger, until she ended her tale with a wail of,

"…But then I couldn't reach the controls!"

Wax and Wayne

"Lifetime Guarantee," read the sign in the window.

"You sell candles," Wayne scoffed. "They melt, they're gone."

The chandler shrugged his eight shoulders. "Is how I make them. Last your lifetime. You buy?"

"Just to prove my point, sure. One red one."

᠅

The candle burned in the den while Wayne made dinner.

Halfway through, his knees began to shake. His skin sagged.

"Last your lifetime," he mumbled, horror dawning in his mind.

Wayne slumped to the floor.

He looked through the kitchen door, just in time to see the flame flicker one last time over a pool of crimson wax.

DISABILITY AND ACCESSIBILITY

l Don't Hate Tiny Tim. Really!

How To Write About Disabilities

Poor Tiny Tim.

I'm not saying that because he has a disability. I'm saying that because everyone, from his readers to his creator, pities him because he has a disability. He doesn't pity himself, though! He joins in his siblings' games whenever possible, and they cheerfully take him along with them. And while his father calls him "good as gold," he's not a perfect saint. When his father insists that the family drink a toast to his hard-hearted boss, Ebeneezer Scrooge, "Tiny Tim drank it last of all, but he didn't care twopence for it."

As someone who's also familiar with braces and crutches, yes, the line "He told me, coming home, that he hoped the people saw him in the church, because he was a cripple..." makes me want to "spit nickels," as my mom says. "The C-word" gets on my nerves, especially. But Dickens did one thing that I've appreciated more and more as I get older.

He tells us that Tim "Did *not* die." He doesn't say that Tim was cured. People often assume he was, but Dickens doesn't say so.

It's called "the Miracle Cure." It's so common I had a hard time coming up with examples where the protagonist isn't rewarded for their bravery, virtue, etc. by being "made whole."

Again and again, like some literary Jesus, authors make their lame characters walk and their blind characters see. It's so pervasive I'll bet most readers don't even think about it, or if they do, simply nod. After all, how can the hero have a real Happily Ever After if they're still "broken"?

Imagine what this says to a real-life kid who can never be "brave enough" or "good enough" to make their disability go away.

Sorry, kid. Glass slippers don't come with orthotics. Castles have sweeping staircases, not wheelchair ramps. Wizards don't write their spellbooks in Braille. People like us are only in books to be pitied, martyred, or cured.

Mostly.

In 1875, 32 years after A Christmas Carol, another book came out. The Little Lame Prince, by Miss Mulock, is about Prince Dolor, who, because of an injury as a baby, doesn't walk, but gets around with "active froglike leaps." When I read this, and saw the illustration of Prince Dolor with his atrophied legs, I shouted "He has CP like me!"

Now, this was the 1800s, so the C-word is still in there, but Miss Mulock gave kids like me a huge gift with her ending:

"Thus, though he never walked in processions, never reviewed his troops mounted on a magnificent charger, nor did any of the things which make a show monarch so much appreciated, he was able for all the duties and a great many of the pleasures of his rank."

King Dolor is a real king. He works. He governs. People complain about him. He deals with it. And he lives about as happily ever after as anyone can expect to.

Books like this helped confirm that you can have a disability and still be a whole person. A writer, even! My characters have Cerebral Palsy, Acromegaly, paraplegia, quadriplegia, blindness, deafness, mental illnesses, Down Syndrome, and whatever else fits their character. Some things get cured, but not as a reward for virtue. Most don't.

So will you join me? If you're a writer, build your "castles in the air" with ramps and elevators. Readers, seek out books where the heroine packs her antidepressants along with her other quest supplies, and the Prince and Princess hand-sign "I do" before they kiss.

And we'll *all* live Happily Ever After.

Hirasol

The ground stopped shaking. From somewhere above and behind Hiera's Sorrel, a voice spoke.

"…the centaur herd needs thinning anyway," it said. The colt, his front legs trapped in a hole, couldn't turn to face the speaker. He tried to get up and bolt, and screamed as his broken front legs gave way.

"Branson, hush," said another, gentler voice. "This one's young and otherwise healthy. I'm going to try something."

Something stung the colt's arm, and he tumbled into darkness.

❧

Fear returned first. Hiera's Sorrel lay on his side, breathing hard. This wasn't grass beneath him. The air smelled wrong, acrid and harsh. His chest heaved, but beyond that, he couldn't feel anything. He tried to roll onto his front, but hands restrained him. He threw back his head and blew and whinnied. No one came.

"Steady. Easy there," said the gentle voice. The words were almost like spoken Herd language, with strange echoes and hissing sounds overlying them. "Lie still. Do you understand me?"

"Yah." The voice reassured Hiera's Sorrel. It was a confident, female voice, an Alpha Mare's voice. He lay still.

"Are you in pain?" the voice asked Hiera's Sorrel.

The nothingness frightened him worse than pain, but he couldn't honestly say it hurt. Or if it did, the pain was too distant to matter. "Nah."

He stole a glance from the corner of his eye. The speaker was a two-legs with wrinkled skin and soft white hair. Hiera's Sorrel stiffened. The two-legs spoke again, slowly, calmly, and moved in front of him. Her voice came from her mouth sounding like gibberish, and echoed back from a collar around her throat in words he could understand.

"You're safe. I'm Doctor Sanchez. You were badly hurt, and my assistant Branson and I brought you here to help you."

"Heyyo, Dok Torsonn Sheds. Where is the others?"

"The other centaurs? I'm afraid they ran off."

Away from danger. Good. "Why I cannot run?"

The two-legs huffed out a breath, as though bothered by stinging flies. "You've been asleep for a long time. You're stable now, but the grafts didn't take the way I'd hoped, because of infection. I had to amputate. Quite extensively, I'm afraid."

Hiera's Sorrel twitched. "Ampootate?"

She sighed again. "Do you have a name? What shall I call you?"

"We will give me my own name when the grain heads open. Now I am Hiera's Sorrel. For my dam, and my coat."

"Hirasol?" She looked so funny, mouthing at his name, that Hiera's Sorrel chuckled and decided that she spoke well enough, for a two-legs.

Dok Torsonn Sheds smiled, briefly. "Hirasol, 'amputate' means to remove a body part that's too badly injured to function. You were very badly hurt. The only way to save you was to amputate everything below your waist."

Understanding began to creep in.

"I'm very sorry. Branson modified a prosthesis for you, but you'll need to heal before you can begin using it."

Hiera's Sorrel twisted to look back over his hindquarters, and saw only tubes and wires snaking out from under flat white cloth. Panic spurred his heart, but nothing responded. Forelegs, hindquarters, his splendid tail—all gone. He squealed and tried to buck with what little body he had left. The primates held him down and stung him until he slept.

❧

He couldn't sleep forever, and what remained of his body was too strong to die. The young male, Branson, grudgingly brought him bowls of hot porridge. Dok Torsonn Sheds coaxed him to eat it and nudged him away from dark thoughts the way an Alpha mare would have herded him away from a concealed snake. She coaxed Hiera's Sorrel toward life with promises of sunlight and open sky beyond the white curved walls of this strange place. That promise was all that kept his spirit from fleeing when he saw the tubes and coils spilling from his truncated body, and Dok Torsonn Sheds showed him the machine meant to replace muscle, bone and hoof.

"Dok Torsonn Sheds, that body is only half. We are not two-legs."

"I know. Equine prostheses simply don't exist yet."

"Put on more legs. And rest of body. And tail."

"They would only add weight, not function."

"We need them."

"Hirasol, you'll run faster without them."

He looked away from the snaky tangle, toward her. "I will run?"

"If you work hard, and get strong, and practice, you could. But first you have to let me fit the prosthesis."

His spirit shied from it, but sunlight from the window called him back. He stared toward the window while she worked, fitting tubes and wires into the machine, binding the strange object below his chest.

"Hirasol? Does anything hurt?"

"Nah, Dok Torsonn Sheds."

She smiled. "It's Doctor Sanchez. Doctor."

"Doctor. Doctor Sun Sheds."

"That's better. Can you feel anything when I do this?" She pressed the bottom of the machine's foot, and Hiera's Sorrel jumped.

"Makes prickles in the first belly."

"And now?"

"Prickles moved sideways. Not so strong."

"Excellent! With practice you'll learn to sense terrain—what kind of ground you're walking on, so you'll be less likely to trip and fall."

Hiera's Sorrel winced. "Trip and fall again, I will have nothing left."

"That's one advantage of the prosthetic—it's nearly unbreakable. Can you make a knee bend? Use your abdominal muscles."

He strained until he was drenched in sweat. The artificial foot slid back a few inches.

"Excellent! Hirasol, you're doing amazingly well."

He grinned, baring his teeth, and flung himself off the bed. The doctor yelped and tried to pick him up. Hiera's Sorrel butted her hands away. Branson came running and stood in the doorway with his arms folded, watching with a predator's stare.

"Hirasol! What are you doing?" said Doctor Sun Sheds. "Let me help you back into bed."

"Nah, Doctor! We must run. Run or die." Get up and run. Every foal knew that from birth.

Straining until his insides felt about to tear, Hiera's Sorrel pulled the man-made legs under him until he was sitting on them, almost as he would have kneeled on his own forelegs.

"What's your pet experiment up to, Doc?" said Branson. Hiera's Sorrel glared at him, reached up to grip the bed, and pulled. Everything inside him strained. Little bolts of lightning shot through him. He screamed and fell. The man-legs were twitching and kicking, and he smelled burned meat. Branson made a low whistle like a stooping hawk. "That's one stubborn little gelding."

"Branson, please!" said Doctor. "Pull back the covers. Quickly."

Branson shrugged, and did. "This is how you make use of biotechnicians? Nursing half-horses? Or would you call him a quarter horse now?"

"Branson!" Doctor Sun Sheds removed the man-legs before lifting Hiera's Sorrel back onto the bed. "Kindly cease the insulting editorial commentary and assess the damage to the prosthetic."

"We do have a pandemic to cure, you know," said Branson.

He picked up the man-legs and whistled again. "You fried these circuits pretty good, Secretariat."

"Branson…" Doctor Sun Sheds cut her scolding short as she examined where the machine had touched. "Give me the burn ointment and sterile dressings, and a Bio-Cap."

Branson kept silent while Doctor Sun Sheds finished hooking up all the tubes and connections to Hiera's Sorrel's body again and shrouding everything in a white thing that hid whatever had happened. Not that Hiera's Sorrel wanted to look.

"Does it still hurt, Hirasol?"

"Nah."

"Doc, you gave it your best shot. Aren't you going to put him out of his misery?"

"Give up on him, do you mean? No." Doctor Sun Sheds moved to the head of the bed and stroked the forelock back from Hiera's Sorrel's face. "You did very well today, Hirasol. But you need to be patient, or you'll hurt yourself."

He didn't answer.

"Hirasol? Look at me."

He turned away, his spirit sidling toward the waiting dark.

"He has more sense than you, Doc," said Branson. "No offence, but he knows you should've put a bolt in his brain first thing and saved a lot of trouble."

Hiera's Sorrel stopped at the edge of the darkness to glare at him. The primate looked back with a knowing, tail-high smirk.

"Fix the legs," said Hiera's Sorrel.

"What?"

"Fix the legs so I can kick you with them." He wasn't sure which was more rewarding; Branson's shocked look or Doctor Sun Shed's smile.

❦

As soon as his burns healed and Branson had repaired the man-legs, Hiera's Sorrel went back to learning how to use the prosthetic. He was careful this time and did exactly what

Doctor Sun Sheds told him. First make the legs bend, up and down, over and over. Then sit on the edge of the bed, until his head didn't spin and he no longer fell over backwards without his hindquarters for balance. Then stand. Just stand. Not run, not even walk. That was hard, not to run. Balancing, swaying on top of the man-legs, was even harder. Then one step, and two, and learning to get back up when he fell. And all the time Doctor Sun Sheds was beside him, nudging, coaxing, praising. And Branson stood in the doorway with his arms folded, just watching.

At last Hiera's Sorrel could march across the room, right up to Branson, and demand, "Open this door!"

Branson raised an eyebrow. "As you command, Seabiscuit."

Hiera's Sorrel needed so much concentration to lift the mechanical feet over the half-inch threshold that it took him a moment to realize that he wasn't outside on fresh green grass, but in another little room with the same curving white walls.

"Oh," he said.

"This is our office, Hirasol," said Doctor Sun Sheds. "Here, sit in my chair and rest a while."

He sat and let curiosity trample his disappointment. This room didn't have a bed in it, just chairs, shelves, and desks with thin glowing boxes on them.

"This is your sleeping place?" he asked, puzzled.

"We sleep in the other two quarters of the dome. This is where we do most of our work."

Hiera's Sorrel reached toward the glowing screen.

"Don't touch the computer!" Branson snapped.

Hiera's Sorrel jerked his hand away. "Why? Does it bite?"

"No, but I'll make you wish it did if you mess up our data. People back home are counting on that."

"What are data?"

Branson chuckled. "Hey, Little Mr. Ed's more grammatically correct than most people for once. "It's information, kid. About this planet. Mostly the plants."

"I are not kid. Goats are smelly. I are of the Herd."

"Your grammar'll drive me nuts, Trigger. It must make sense to you, since the translator doesn't balk at it, but you're giving me a headache," Branson groaned. "Why do you say 'are' for some things and 'is' for others?"

Hiera's Sorrel snorted. "Are you a foal? 'Are' means things that are true for all the Herd, or for always. Forever. I are of the Herd. I is Hiera's Sorrel only until the Alpha Mare gives me my Herd-name."

"Almost like Spanish," said Doctor Sun Sheds. "Yes, Hirasol?"

"Doctor Sun Sheds, you have plants in this light box?"

"Pictures of plants, and information. That's a computer screen. Let me get to the keyboard and I'll show you."

Doctor Sun Sheds tapped the grid below the screen, and a picture appeared.

"Oh! Sourgrass," said Hiera's Sorrel. Troubled, he frowned at the doctor. "Why you want sourgrass, Doctor Sun Sheds? You have colic?"

Doctor Sun Sheds gave him a strange look. "That plant's good for colic? You eat it?"

Hiera's Sorrel shook his head. "We cook it in water first and drink the water. It are only good for the second stomach, though. We chew watermint for the first."

Doctor Sun Sheds and Branson exchanged looks. "Hirasol," said Doctor Sun Sheds, "Branson and I came here from very far away because many people where we live are sick. It's called a pandemic. We've been looking for something to cure them, but it's been very slow because we don't know anything about the plants here. Would you tell us about them?"

"Yah. Show another picture."

Branson made something click, and the picture changed.

"That are watermint. Tastes very good. Doctor Sun Sheds, when I can go back to the Herd? When I can run outside again?"

Doctor Sun Sheds was abruptly busy with the keyboard.

"Check the drawer in front of you, Shadowfax," said Branson softly.

He did. The hard round things inside smelled like watermint and tasted even better.

"Doc's private candy stash," said Branson with a smirk. "Ok, earn your keep. What's this plant called?"

"Hotleaf. Branson, who are the pretty filly on your light box?"

Branson winced as though Hiera's Sorrel had kicked him. "Her name's Cat. Katrina. That's an old picture. Come on, next plant!"

❧

Hiera's Sorrel liked naming plants for Doctor Sun Sheds, but he longed to be out among real growing things again, running with the Herd. It seemed like forever before Doctor Sun Sheds said "Well, Hirasol! You've done so well I think you're ready for some sunshine."

"Outside?" The man-legs weren't much good for prancing, but he made do. Doctor Sun Sheds laughed and opened a hole in the curved wall. After so long in the dome, the bright light made him squint. He took off running, following the warmth on his face and the scents of grass and trees, tripped, and went sprawling.

"Hirasol?" Doctor Sun Sheds called when he didn't get up right away. "Are you all right?"

"Yah," he said, breathing in the scent of crushed grass. "Nothing is broken, and grass smells very good."

"Don't eat it!" Branson warned. "Remember what Doc said—you can't digest it now."

"Am not eating, just smelling. Have no one to graze with anyway." He got up and walked more carefully around the clearing that circled the dome, checking each branch and bud.

"Snow has come and gone already," he noted. "The Herd will be following the foalgrass... Oh! What is this?"

A pointy silver cone rose above a patch of tall yellow flowers.

Doctor Sun Sheds pointed at it, looking both proud and troubled. "That ship is how we traveled here."

If Branson had said such a thing Hiera's Sorrel wouldn't have believed him, but this was Doctor Sun Sheds. "You flew? In that thing?"

"Yes."

"Did… did you have to leave your herd behind?"

"Yes. But if we can help them it'll be worth it. Thanks to you, we're getting close. Would you like to see the inside of the ship?"

"I would more like to see flowers, please. I do not remember those before."

Branson chuckled. "Figures, that he'd spot those."

Doctor Sun Sheds smiled too, and led him over to the flowers—slender, heavy-headed things. "They always turn toward the sunlight. That's why they're called sunflowers. And in Spanish, my Abuelita's language, they're called girasol."

"Like you say my name!"

"It fits you. You always turn toward the sun too."

"I are of the Herd. The Herd always follow the sun. How these flowers get here?"

"We planted them shortly after you came."

"Memorial garden," said Branson, leaning against the dome in his usual crossed-arms posture. "We expected to have to bury all of you out here." Doctor Sun Sheds frowned at him, and he added "The seeds were from our emergency supplies. They're good to eat."

They were. Doctor Sun Sheds said he could have as many as he liked and left him happily munching. Branson lingered, watching him.

"Maybe Doc wasn't so wrong about your name, Hiera's Sorrel," said Branson.

Hiera's Sorrel jumped. "You say it right!"

Branson chuckled. "Doctor Sanchez thinks she says it right, too. 'Hirasol' makes sense to her, it's logical, so she assumes it's right." He turned somber again. "Understand this about Doc.

She's smart—no, she's bloody brilliant—and she's the most unselfish person I know. But she lives in her head. She thinks everything works according to a formula, even people. She thinks the universe is logical. She thinks life is fair, God help her. She thinks that anyone would sacrifice their retirement to traipse across galaxies on some wild quest to cure seven billion people she'll never meet. So she sets things in motion and doesn't think them through, just assumes that everything will work out how it's supposed to. But sometimes it doesn't. That's the only thing she can't understand."

"Seven billion! Your herd are that many? That are…" he counted on his fingers several times over, shook his head, and said, "Very very many."

Branson snorted and went to work on the ship.

࿐

The next day Doctor Sun Sheds explained to Hiera's Sorrel about the launch window.

"With so many people sick, we can't just go straight back to Earth. We have to meet something called a quarantine shuttle, and it will only be there during a set time," she said. "So you must tell us as soon as you see or hear any sign of your Herd. I want to be certain you're safe with them before Branson and I leave, but we have to go when the stars are in the right place in the sky."

Hiera's Sorrel nodded. "Like crossing river. We can only cross when water is low. We must get there on just right days, or we are not crossing,"

"Exactly! Branson and I need to start getting ready. But we aren't leaving yet." She sighed. "Sometimes I wish I could stay. Or just bring you with me."

He frowned. A wise mare wouldn't talk of risking her Herd for one colt. "I are of the Herd, Doctor Sun Sheds."

"Of course you are," she said. She let him lean against her and stroked his hair.

Branson packed up many boxes of plants, sealed in strange thick water, in his part of the ship. It looked painfully dark and cramped to Hiera's Sorrel. He liked the place where Doctor Sun Sheds was to ride better. It was just as small, but it had a place for looking out.

"I'm leaving my terminal," said Doctor Sun Sheds. "With the generator."

Branson groaned and fitted another box into the place where he was supposed to sit. "Doc, the brass won't send a rescue team back here just because you left a pot on the stove."

"It's staying."

With every passing day, Doctor Sun Sheds and Branson nipped at each other's tempers more and more. They used words like "quarantine," and "maximum payload" and "sapient extraterrestrial exploitation," but their sidelong glances told Hiera's Sorrel that they were arguing about him. Doctor Sun Sheds didn't like to let him out of her sight, even though he'd told her how important it was that he run every day, to get strong and fast. So he was still in sight of the dome when the Herd came.

He felt them first, in the joyful trembling of the ground. Then he heard the low thunder of mighty hooves and whinnied with all the strength in his heart. The Herd swept around him, strong bodies and shining coats, and looks of shock and astonishment on every face. He found the face he'd most longed for, crowned with a braided mane as red as his, and held up his arms. Mare Hiera went down on her knees to hold him tighter and nickered.

"MaMaire." He nuzzled against her neck. "Oh, MaMaire."

"Little Sorrel. My little Sorrel."

"Hirasol! Are you all right? Is this your Herd?" Doctor Sun Sheds called.

"Yah, Doctor! And my MaMaire!"

The Herd parted to let the human woman through and sidled away, whispering questions.

"You're Hirasol's mother? I'm so glad you came for him!"

Hiera frowned. "What have you done to my colt, and why do you call him that?"

"I'm afraid it was the only way to save him, and—What do you mean? Isn't Hirasol his name?"

The mare snorted in amusement. "Hiera's Sorrel," she enunciated. "I are Hiera. He is my little Sorrel until he takes his herd-name."

"MaMaire?" he said shyly. "Hirasol are flower. It turns toward sun, and are good to eat. Are good herd-name?"

"I'll show you one," Doctor Sun Sheds offered.

Doctor Sun Sheds and MaMaire went to show the sunflower to the swift gray Alpha Mare. The colts and fillies who had been Hiera's Sorrel's playmates crowded around him.

"Where are your legs, Sorrel?"

"Where are your tail?"

"How do you make droppings now?"

Hiera's Sorrel aimed a kick at that last speaker.

"Will you run with us again?" asked the filly he'd known as Nakahara's Black, dimpling and tugging on her dark braid. The others called her Mehiiyam now. All his friends had their herd-names now, and carried their own bundles across their backs. Foal-time was long past.

"Yah. I will run."

"On two legs?" sneered the colt who'd asked about droppings.

"Are good legs. Flies are never biting them."

"Sorrel will run with us," Mehiiyam declared. "We will have his herd-name feast, too."

The Alpha mare approached, and the youngsters fell silent.

"Hiera's Sorrel, you wish to try to run with us again?"

His mouth worked uneasily, but he answered, "I are of the Herd, Alpha. I will run."

"Hm." She held up the sunflower. "And you wish to keep this name, Hirasol?"

"Yah, please, Alpha."

The Alpha mare nodded and turned to Doctor Sun Sheds. "Two-legs, may we use your meadow to give Hiera's Sorrel his herd-name?"

The doctor glanced toward the dome. Branson touched the time-marker on his wrist and frowned, but shrugged.

"We'll gladly risk one more day to see Hira… Hiera's Sorrel happy with his family, Ma'am."

The Alpha mare turned toward the Herd and whinnied so loudly that the humans winced and covered their ears.

"Stop and rest. Bring out your shares for a feast. Hiera's Sorrel will take his herd-name here."

The low curious murmuring that had ceased while the Alpha mare spoke redoubled. The Herd lay down, unslung bundles of possessions from their backs, and began opening smaller packs inside. Hiera went from one to the next, collecting a handful of grain here, some dried apples there…

"Doctor Sun Sheds, may I take many seeds from Hirasol-flowers? I must bring a share to my feast."

"Of course, Mijo! Take them all."

"Nah, Doctor! Never take all. Leave enough to grow." He gathered as many sunflower seeds as he dared and added them to the mixture in Hiera's leather cookpot. When the hot grain smelled nutty, he scooped it out onto broad flat leaves and brought the first portion to the Alpha mare.

"I accept your share, Hirasol," she said, looking grave.

Next he went to his MaMaire, who hugged him before accepting the food and addressing him by his herd-name. The rest of the Herd was waiting, but Hirasol served Doctor Sun Sheds and Branson first. Branson was being surprisingly well-behaved, keeping his gaze respectfully fixed on the mares' chests instead of challenging them with a direct stare.

"I'm so proud of you, Hirasol," said Doctor Sun Sheds.

"Are just mash, Doctor Sun Sheds," he said with a puzzled smile. He cupped her hands around the leaf. "Run fast and save your herd," he said, and went to serve the others. Then he lay on the grass with his MaMaire and watched as everyone ate. A few had looked down their noses at him, but no one had refused him outright. He was officially Hirasol now.

Doctor Sun Sheds and Branson stood near the dome, away

from the Herd. Branson burned his fingers trying to eat the hot mash without a spoon, but they both seemed to enjoy it. Doctor Sun Sheds kept looking at him with a familiar expression. She was worried because he wasn't eating. Didn't she understand? A too-full belly was just more weight to carry. He savored the sweet nutty smell instead.

One by one the others set down their empty leaves. Mare Hiera held him close, then kissed him on the forehead.

"Run fast, Hirasol," she said.

"Run fast, MaMaire. Run safe."

Across the clearing, the Alpha mare reared up and whinnied. Everyone else got to their feet. Hirasol's friends cleared a path before him. He cast a quick glance back toward the dome. Doctor Sun Sheds took an anxious step forward.

"Hirasol!" the Alpha mare called. "Run with us!" She stamped a forefoot and galloped off, and Hirasol ran after her. Her streaming white tail was a banner, beckoning. He forced all his strength into the man-legs, trying to keep that banner in sight.

Then the rest of the Herd was running, thundering behind him, catching up with him. Muscular flanks and thundering hooves surrounded him. And one by one, they passed him.

"Run fast, Hirasol!" Mehiiyam squealed as she galloped by.

Only MaMaire was beside him now, keeping pace alongside him as he fought to keep the man-legs running. His heart pounded and his chest burned, and he smelled sweat and hot metal. His breath came broken from his lungs. The prickles from the man-legs were thorns, clawing him, meaningless. He stumbled, tried to recover but fell, gasping. MaMaire stopped and reached down.

"Hiera!" shouted the Alpha mare in warning, and Hiera leapt forward as though stung.

"Run fast, Hirasol!" she cried as she galloped away.

Hirasol clutched the grass in his fists and fought to breathe. More feet ran past him. Soft feet.

"Come back here!" Doctor Sun Sheds screamed. "You can't just leave him!"

"They must," Hirasol whispered to Branson, who was releasing him from the smoking man-legs. "Nothing must slow down the Herd. Puts all in danger."

Branson shook his head and picked him up. His face was hard and tight, and he didn't speak as he carried Hirasol back to the dome.

Doctor Sun Sheds came back crying, carrying a soft shape in her arms.

"Those heartless… Do they just dump everything they find inconvenient? They threw this away too."

Hirasol drew in a breath. "Doctor Sun Sheds, that are mine! My garment, for rain and snow. Give it to me, please."

Made to shelter a growing colt from head to hindquarters, the soft fabric was much too large now. Doctor Sun Sheds wrapped him in it, gently, and he sighed.

"My MaMaire made it for me. They will punish her for carrying it. The Herd must never carry weight it does not need. They will make her run behind. But she carried it, because it was mine. Don't be angry, Doctor Sun Sheds. See how much my MaMaire loves me?"

"Mijo, pobrecito, I'm so sorry!" Nothing Hirasol said could console her. She sat beside him, stroking his hair until whatever she had done to the tubes inside him made him sleepy and he closed his eyes.

Sleepy, but not asleep. He could still hear the argument in the lab.

"The prosthetic's not as badly damaged as I'd thought. The insulation I installed last time worked. Give me an hour and I'll have it shipshape again."

"Branson, I'm staying."

He was quiet for three slow breaths. "Doc, you can't. You're the only one who knows what to do with those samples."

"I'm responsible for Hirasol."

"You're also responsible for the seven billion people you came out here to save."

"Then I'll bring him with us."

"Where? In a sample box? They'd never let him through Quarantine. He'd spend years locked in an eight-by-twelve cell…"

"Branson, we can't do this!"

"We can't *not* do this. We made a promise to seven billion people."

Seven billion are a very big herd, Hirasol thought dazedly, and slept.

***

Doctor Sun Sheds looked like she hadn't slept at all, and her voice trembled.

"We can't stay any longer, Mijo. We're almost too late already."

He nodded. "River rises."

"But Branson's fixed your legs as good as new, and we've left things to make you comfortable. And as soon as we get back to Earth we'll send a bigger ship with a crew to bring you to us."

"When will river be shallow again?"

Her glance flickered away. "In about two years."

He nodded. "I understand. Seven billion are a very big herd, Doctor Sun Sheds. Run fast and make them well, like you did for me."

She hugged him so hard it hurt. Branson came in with the man-legs and she fastened Hirasol into them, checking every little piece and insisting that Hirasol tell her if anything hurt.

"Nah, Doctor Sun Sheds. Nothing hurts. Thank you. You are good. Go back to your Herd now."

She hugged him again. Branson pulled her away.

"Seven billion people, Doc," he said gently. He led her out to the ship and came back.

"Ok, Pegasus. One last tune-up before takeoff. Bend your right knee."

Hirasol did.

"Good. Now left. Good. Sit up."

Hirasol sat with the man-legs dangling over the edge of the

bed while Branson pressed the soles of the feet and mapped the prickles as Hirasol reported them.

"Do you know about the darkness, Branson?" Hirasol said, shivering in his skin. "When we die there are a pasture waiting, all soft grass and watermint and sunshine. But to get there we must first outrun the darkness." He looked up, terrified, pleading. "The darkness runs very fast, Branson! And I do not now."

Branson looked down on him, frowning. Then he sat on the bed and slid over until he nudged Hirasol's side. Hirasol looked up in surprise, sniffled, and leaned against him.

"Hirasol, bodies don't matter then. All that counts is what you've got inside. You've got more inside than anyone I know. And I don't mean all those peppermints you've been eating."

Hirasol nudged his head against Branson's shoulder. "I will try. And when the man-legs die I will push the button that makes them come off. Then I will not be so heavy, and maybe the darkness will not catch me."

Branson put his arm around Hirasol's shoulders. "No darkness is going to catch you, kid. You just hang in there until the Doc comes back."

"Or man-legs die."

"I'm insulted. I'm a Class A certified biotechnician, and I make a damned good prosthetic. Just don't go swimming with it. And no eating grass!"

Hirasol just looked at him. "Branson, will more two-legs really come back for me?"

His face turned hard again. "Doc believes so. She thinks they'll come to meet real centaurs. They're just stories on Earth, you see."

"You do not believe this."

He sighed. "I believe she does. Hop off the bed. Good. Walk to the other side of the room. Good. Comfortable?"

"Yah, Branson."

"Good. Take care of yourself, kid." He looked outside and

said, "Wait. Don't go out there just yet. If Doc sees you she'll try to back out."

"And first duty is to her herd."

"Yeah. Tell you what. You wait here until you hear the boosters fire—a really loud noise. Then come out and watch the ship take off. If I know Doc, she'll be waving out the window until we're halfway home. All right?"

"Yah, Branson. Run fast."

Branson nodded and sprinted toward the ship. After a while the sky roared. Hirasol recognized the sound that had frightened him into bolting headlong into a hole, so long ago. He hurried out and saw the silver cone lifting into the sky, trailing fire.

"Run fast, Doctor Sun Sheds! Run fast, Branson!" he called and waved until the ship became a tiny star in the daytime sky and vanished. Everything was suddenly very quiet.

Doctor Sun Sheds would expect him to stay safe in the dome. Doctor Sun Sheds couldn't understand that one of the Herd could never stay in one place forever. The Herd are born running, and they run until they die.

He would make a bundle of his garment, and take seeds from the hirasol-flower, and plant them wherever he went. And they would all turn toward the sun.

Somewhat cheered, he went back into the dome for his garment, and then to the lab for something to carry the seeds.

The computer screen was glowing. And someone was settling in front of it.

"The last of the peppermints are in the top drawer. Don't eat them all at once. We won't be getting any more."

"Branson! Why you are not with Doctor Sun Sheds?"

He spun the chair around to face Hirasol. "Because with seven billion people dying, no one's going to come back here to see a bunch of centaurs. But they just might come back for a healthy Class A certified biotechnician."

"Doctor Sun Sheds will be upset. And the pretty filly…"

He turned away. "I left a message on the autopilot. Doc can bawl me out later. Assuming we can survive that long alone on this planet."

"Yah, Branson, we can. We are not alone. We are a Herd," said Hirasol. He swung the chair around and grinned at Branson's look of surprise. "I will show you. Let's run!"

A Step Ahead

It had been a long year. Abi hadn't seen an offworlder in months. Then the he ladder salesman showed up, demanding to talk to someone important.

"My dad's the Mayor. I'll take you to him," Abi offered.

The ladder salesman followed her, complaining. He'd spent months pitching his wares on far-off planets, and Mulligan Three was not the restful haven he'd had in mind. He'd landed on a sweltering, white-sky day, the sort that turned the colony's ramps into sizzling, slanted griddles by noon. Everyone, even diehard joggers who'd never wheeled before, had borrowed rollchairs or floats to keep their feet off the blister-raising pavement, but the salesman insisted on walking. He had to dodge a stampede of kids popping wheelies. The enormous case he was dragging didn't make it any easier for him to maneuver, either. By the time they reached Town Hall, his crisp suit was limp with sweat, and he didn't look much better himself.

"You walked here? In this heat? You could at least have borrowed a grav float for that case you're hauling," said Abi's dad.

"I don't need a wheelchair."

Mayor Harris shrugged. "Have a seat."

The salesman flopped down, too wiped out to do more than look startled as the chair adjusted to fit his weight and body conformation. Abi offered the salesman a glass of ice water.

"Thanks, sweetie." Ignoring Abi's grimace at the nickname, the salesman gulped down the drink, bounded up, and stuck out a hand for the Mayor to shake. "Max Laidlow, of Max-a-Million Ladders. I'm here to solve your problem."

"Problem, Mr. Laidlow?"

"Your total lack of ladders! Why, I hear there isn't so much as a stepstool on this entire deprived planet."

The Mayor frowned. Not only was Max Laidlow loud, he

spoke only verbally, without signing. Passing staff were scowling at him.

"That's correct, Mr. Laidlow. We don't need them." Mayor Harris made his signs extra overt and clear, but the man didn't take the hint.

"Nonsense! Ladders are indispensable. I have a program of ladderly enhancement for your situation. I call it '12 steps'. Get it?"

The Mayor sighed. Abi could see him looking for polite ways to get rid of the peddler.

"Daddy, what's a ladder?"

Their insensitive offworld guest didn't seem to notice the Mayor's look of relief.

"Why don't you ask Mr. Laidlow to show you. Honey? Give him the grand tour; see if he can find folks who need what he's selling."

"Great! C'mon, I'll show you my house, and Mrs. Nguyen's giant store—she's got stuff from twelve star-systems—and—"

Abi hauled the salesman out the door, still chattering.

❧

Abi stared at the contraption the offworlder had set up, all struts and bars.

"So it's a toy?"

"No! I told you: It's a state-of-the-art multipurpose climbing apparatus with enhanced stability, durable weather-resistant construction and adjustable dimensions."

"Huh. I like the climbing stuff on the playground better. You can jump rollchairs off it. And we have an antigrav field."

Mr. Laidlow ran a hand through his hair. It stood up, spiky with dried sweat. "Look, just take me to some grownups."

"If I take you to the Astro-Mart, will you get me a freeze-pop?"

"Sure. Whatever. Just get moving."

❧

Abi adjusted a rest-bench to her size, licked her starberry

freeze-pop and watched Mr. Laidlow gesture at Mrs. Nguyen. He still wasn't signing, just waving his arms around the store and pointing at his "ladder."

"What if you want something from the top shelves?" he asked the diminutive store owner.

Mrs. Nguyen looked at him like he had heat stroke and pushed the Reach button on the nearest display. The shelves turned, and a display of Centauran pastries rolled from the top to the storekeeper's chest-level, then under and back to the top again.

"Oh."

"Don't they have shelves where you live, Mr. Laidlow?" said Abi.

"Well, yes, but they stay put!"

"Why would anyone build dead shelves?"

"Abi, don't be rude," said Mrs. Nguyen.

Poor Mr. Laidlow looked miserable.

"Such a basic thing," he moaned. "Ingrained into expressions... 'The Ladder of Success.' 'The Corporate Ladder.' 'Chutes and Ladders', for Orion's sake! And you people, with your one-floor buildings and ramped curbs and rolling shelves and multisensory adjustable *Everything*... You've ruined it! Have you no respect for standardization?"

"Do you need oxygen, Mr. Laidlow? We're near a booth," said Mrs Nguyen.

"I'm fine! I'm a rational, sensible businessman. It's this place!" Mr. Laidlow sounded about to cry.

Abi stepped into the breech. "I'll bet you're overheated. C'mon, Mr. Laidlow. We'll go to my Aunt Pia's for dinner."

"I'm not hungry."

"Nonsense! You need your nutrition and hydration," said Abi, just like her mom would have. She led the way, and Mr Laidlow trudged after her, still lugging that case. Mrs. Nguyen had offered him the use of a grav float, but he seemed scared of floats. And rollchairs. And bionic parts. And robo-talkers. He really was the most nervous person Abi had ever met.

※

Aunt Pia was talking on the T-phone when they arrived. Abi didn't recognize the picture or the voice on the machine. It shut off when the door slid open. Mr. Laidlow just stood staring at Aunt Pia. Well, at her life-support chair. Abi burned with guilt. She'd forgotten about the poor guy's phobia. But what could he expect? Aunt Pia was well over 100, after all.

"Abi! What are you doing out in this heat? And who's your friend?"

"Mr. Laidlow, this is Aunt Pia. Aunt Pia, this is Mr. Laidlow. He sells laddels."

Aunt Pia didn't look confused the way everybody else had. She looked suspicious. "I think you mean ladders, Abi dear."

That got through Mr. Laidlow's fear.

"Yes!" The salesman pumped a fist in the air. "Thank the Spheres. Someone on this backward, insane planet actually knows what a ladder is!"

"Don't swear in front of the child, Mr. Laidlow. Yes, I'm familiar with ladders, stairs, curbs, steps, and goodness knows what else. But why are you bringing such things here?"

"Well… everyone needs them…"

Aunt Pia smiled until her wrinkles got wrinkles. "Obviously not. Mr. Laidlow, this colony isn't perfect by any means, but we've grown a far sight beyond your ladders."

Mr. Laidlow looked almost crushed. Almost.

"Ma'am, you're right. I don't belong on this planet. I belong back on Earth."

Aunt Pia nodded.

"Think of the opportunities I've wasted! There's a whole market just waiting for me to design better ramps, and elevators, and…"

He rushed out the door, still babbling, and popped his head in long enough to say "Oh, keep the samples. Token of my gratitude. Must rush. So much to plan! Good day!"

※

Abi and Aunt Pia looked at each other. Aunt Pia sighed.

"What are you going to do with that big ugly box of laddel stuff, Aunt Pia?"

The old woman looked thoughtful. "You know, maybe I could use a ladder. It would make a lovely morning glory trellis."

Swimming Upstream

Part 1

The first thing I saw when I woke was Chris' face. Strange. Blurry. I squinted, trying to remember: The gray house. All flat. Nice for wheelchairs. Abandoned. Nice for hiding.

The face loomed closer. Green eyes. Like Brian's.

"Miss Bennington?"

I frowned. The voice was wrong. It wasn't Brian's, because Brian... because Brian was dead. And they'd find me, and take me away...

"Laura Bennington?" Strange accent. Not French, not German. And impatient.

"Brian?" I choked. "Am I dead?"

"Who?" Those green eyes narrowed. My own vision cleared a bit, revealing a stern-faced young man in a white lab coat sitting alongside my bed. "I'm Chris Anderson," he said. "Clinical Assistant, Institute of Parabiology. Can you feel this?"

I came a little more awake. "If you're testing my Babinski reflex, no, but that's not news. Waist down's been out of commission since 2036." I barely understood myself. My tongue felt bloated.

"Hm." That's all he said. Just watched me.

"What's an 'Institute of Parabiology'? A hospital?" It didn't smell quite like one. Underneath the familiar smells of antiseptic and too-clean sheets lay an odor of... seaweed. The walls weren't white, but dingy yellow concrete. "Who called 911 on me, anyway?"

"No one. We traced your computer link to our website." His eyes pinned me. "Remember?"

"Yes." Memory felt like a blow to the head. I'd already swallowed the pills. I could barely read those stupid blinking letters: 'Change Your Species—Change Your Life!' But behind them, that beautiful picture of Lake Champlain was perfectly clear. The bright water, cradled in the hills... the old train trestle… Then the fog, and the tick-tick-tick of pills pattering on the wooden floor…

"Do you remember what you said, Miss Bennington?"

"No." Yes. I didn't want to remember. But he had a recording. I had to listen:

"Are you all right, Miss?"

"No. But tha… tha's OK. Nice picture. How'd you get there? Izznot… not allowed, people there now."

"I've activated an auto-rescue, Miss. We're tracking you. We'll send help."

"Too late." And giggling, stupid giggling…

"Shut that thing off! What are you trying to do, anyway? Why didn't you just leave me alone?"

"Why did you call our site?" the medic countered.

"Dumb luck. I just wanted to see the bay."

Nothing showed in the man's face. "You didn't want the surgery?"

"What surgery?"

"I'll let Doctor Pedanti explain." He pushed himself up from his chair. I would have called his walk just short of a drunken lurch, if his face weren't so coldly sober. He looked at me as though I were a dead fish.

"Hey…!" I shouted; but he was gone.

Doctor Pedanti couldn't have been more different. He bounded in grinning, black eyes glittering in his round face.

"Good morning! I'm Doctor Hector Pedanti. Nice to see you awake. You should be more careful with those painkillers. I'm afraid I haven't been able to notify your family that you're here. There seems to be a glitch on your I.D. card."

"No family," I said. None alive, anyway.

"Surely someone will be wondering where you are?"

"Nobody." Well, maybe the staff of certain institutions, but they could just keep wondering.

"I'm sorry," he said, just as cheerful as before. He strode to the head of my bed, pressed plump fingers under my chin and tipped my head back. "Blue eyes—perfect! We'll have to do something about your hair, though. Too mousy."

"What the heck are you talking about?"

"For a mermaid, of course. Grow it out, dye it blonde… You did want the mermaid procedure? We haven't perfected any winged species yet. That was just… preliminary advertising."

"The only procedure I expected to be getting," I watched his face as I spat out the words, "was a post-mortem."

His pouty lips drooped with dismay. "But why? Your brain function is intact; I checked. With my procedure you could have full lower extremity use."

"You make bionic legs?"

"Oh, I wouldn't give you anything so mundane as legs!" He rubbed his hands together, beaming like a tickled baby. "You'd be a mermaid!"

"You're nuts!"

"Oh, no. It's quite real. We've just begun our program. On Lake Champlain—a spot called Willsboro Bay."

"I've heard of it," I said, my mouth gone dry. Heard of it? It was home. Brian and I had spent over three hours swimming across it one day, stroking nearly a mile through the cool, gold-green water, white-capped wavelets splashing our faces. We'd staggered out aching, goose-pimpled… and loving every glorious second of it.

A week later, we were in Brian's old gas-powered van, driving too fast, laughing too hard… A moment of vertigo, of cold horror—then the impact. Fire clawing up my legs, Brian screaming… I shook the image away.

"I was trying to get back there. But the new law… they nabbed me for trespassing. Said I could go to jail, or a State Supervised Residence."

"That's an unusually harsh sentence." Pedanti scrutinized me from behind his smile.

"Well, I needed a way to get there. Official transports have lifts, so I… borrowed one."

He snorted laughter. "Very resourceful! But I can take you there legally. Even get the charges dropped. Think about it. What do you have to lose?"

I thought for a long time. From every angle, the answer was the same. Nothing.

Later, Chris slapped a tray down my bedside. It held hospital food straight out of a 20th century nightmare: shriveled un-identifiable meat, mushy gray peas in congealing gravy, dissolving gelatin.

"Last meal," he grunted.

"Before what?"

"Surgery. Or whatever. You go under the knife first thing tomorrow, or the doctor kicks you into the street."

"I haven't even told him my choice yet!"

He shrugged. "Pedanti figures you have no choice."

"Well, I don't. I won't live out my life in a disguised prison, and once I leave here, that's exactly where I'll end up. Pedanti promised to get the charges dropped." I stirred the melting gelatin, idly watching it bleed through its cheap paper cup.

"You're not going to sign the consent!"

"I lived on that bay. Have you ever seen it? I've swum in it, sailed on it, built campfires and grilled perch from it. I lived there with Brian. He…I don't know if you've ever known anyone… anyone so special that losing them tears a hole… oh, never mind."

Chris Anderson was silent for a long time, so long that I stole a look at his face. The cold expression had slipped, like ice cracking.

"Miss Bennington, leave. Now. "

I stared. He didn't look either cool or professional now. His face was flushed, and his knuckles gripped the bed railing.

"Why? We had a camp there, Brian and I. I could live there. Since the Acid Rain Act, the place has been a lot quieter. Nobody staring or pointing, just me and the lake." I grinned at him. "Besides, I think I'd look good in a fish tail."

He locked eyes with me, silent. I heard only the hum and crackle of the ancient overhead lighting. Without a word, he unbuttoned the lower half of his lab coat.

Great, I thought. I'm trapped with a paranoid exhibitionist. I closed my eyes.

"Look!" he ordered.

This from a guy with a scalpel in his pocket, and me without my chair. I looked. And gasped.

Braces bound him from hip to ankle; heavy, medieval looking things. What little showed beneath the metal and straps wasn't warm human flesh, but grayish, leathery skin, rubbed ragged.

"Doctor Pedanti did this to you?"

Chris wouldn't look at me. The cold mask was back. "You shouldn't trust him," he repeated obstinately.

"I don't."

"This makes no sense. You'd have less freedom on land than you do now."

"I won't be living on land."

"It's not so easy. You'll die."

I shrugged.

"That explains the fourteen kinds of pills we pumped out of you."

"Sure does. And I'll do it again. Still think I should leave?"

He grimaced, his mouth a thin line.

"Dammit, say something!"

"Your dinner's getting cold."

I swore at him. He sighed, buttoned up his coat.

"I tried," he said and left.

When Doctor Pedanti returned that night, holding out a pen, it might as well have been a knife. I carved my signature into that contract. The next day, Hector Pedanti's scalpel carved his indelible mark on me.

Part 2

"The incident on the island is the stuff of legend, but let me tell you the real story."

Doctor Pedanti's voice.

"Four Brothers Island, actually. I…"

"She's awake… Doctor." Chris said, cutting him off.

After sound came pain, in places that hadn't known feeling for years.

Pain like nothing I'd ever felt, even lying twisted and broken beside Brian's cold body. This was the pain of human bones, muscles and nerves reshaped, of skin cut, stretched, remade beyond human experience. Even the sound that wrenched from my lungs wasn't quite a human groan.

"Good morning!" Doctor Pedanti turned his white smile on me. He stripped back the thin blanket and began poking and prodding, oblivious to my grimaces and strangled sounds. I couldn't look—at him or at whatever he'd done to me. I turned my face away. Chris stood with his back to me, staring at the wall.

"Excellent, excellent!" Doctor Pedanti chortled. He turned to Chris. "Get her stabilized and ready to travel by the twenty-fourth." Whistling shrilly, he bounded out.

He'd left the blanket wadded at the foot of the bed. Still without staring, Chris gently pulled the cover back up and sat on the end of the bed. I froze.

"We have a little morphine left, if you need it. None of the newer medicines, though."

"No," I said. Tried to say. My breath got lost somewhere between lungs and mouth, and tickled behind my ears.

"Hold your hands like this, and press." He cupped his hands around either side of his neck, demonstrating. "Carefully."

I did. It stung, like a dozen raw cuts. "Hurts."

"Yes. And I have to give you some shots. Trust me; they'll make it easier eventually." And he did, before I could protest, one after another until my shoulder ached.

"What… for?"

"Balancing your immune system, adjusting oxygen metabolism… I'll have to teach you how to modulate your speech. You can't go about forever clutching yourself by the throat." He cranked up the head of the ancient bed, notch by painful notch, until I was half sitting, and handed me a pencil and notepad. "For now, write."

My hands were sticky. Blood. I touched my neck again. A ragged fringe scalloped the sides. I grabbed the pencil.

"Why the frilly collar?" I scrawled, jabbing a finger to illustrate.

"Those are your gills. Stop poking." Chris frowned and brushed my hair aside to look. His hands were clammy. "Not too bad. Do you want to try speaking?"

I nodded.

"Hold your breath." I tried. He half smiled, watching the look on my face when I discovered I couldn't—the air leaked through the gills. It was embarrassing.

"Try again. Swallow when you exhale."

It sounds impossible, but with gills, it wasn't. When I swallowed, the flow stopped.

"Did you feel your throat contract? That's what lets you talk—and breathe—in water or air. You'll learn. Try again…"

We practiced for hours. Vowels were easy. Some sounds, like B and G, proved nearly impossible. I swallowed air, burped, lisped, and hiccupped. Chris never blinked. The sunlight reddened on the walls, and still we kept on.

"That will do for tonight," Chris said finally. "You'll be tired, and I have other work to do."

I shook my head and tried again. "Krish?"

"That wasn't bad, Miss Bennington!"

"When d'wai ghet to shwim?"

"One step at a time, Miss Bennington." He turned his head suddenly, listening to something I couldn't hear. "I'll see you in the morning." He switched off the light and left.

I lay counting the holes in the stained ceiling panels. It was strangely quiet. No murmur of nurses passing ghostlike outside the room. No PA system calling codes, or summoning doctors to tragedy in a faceless monotone. Just that crackling hum, and a high distant wail. The wind, most likely, fingering its way through cracks in this tottering building. But in that antiseptic darkness, it sounded terribly lonely.

"Wake up! It's time for your shots." I wrenched awake, glaring into Doctor Pedanti's beaming face.

"It's supposed to go 'Wake up—it's time for your sleeping pill'," I mumbled, almost intelligibly. Pedanti blinked, uncomprehending. Chris, behind him, chuckled. He looked almost human when he smiled.

Pedanti swabbed my arm. If I'd thought the shots had hurt when Chris gave them…well. He stripped back the blanket. I was too distracted not to look.

"Wha'd you do?"

No graceful sweeping tail, no glittering silver scales. Just raw, ragged flesh, tracked with black stitches. It still looked like I had two legs in there, somewhere. I looked nothing like a mermaid…or me…or anything human. I grabbed Doctor Pedanti by the collar.

"Wha'd you do t'me?"

"Anderson! She's choking me! Get her off!"

Stone-faced, Chris pried my hands free and held them while Doctor Pedanti fled the room.

"Leggo!" I choked. "Look wha' he's done!"

"What did you expect?" he said, but gently. He sat quietly until I was calmer, more coherent.

"Mermaids…they're s'posed to be beautiful. I look…like a scarred seal."

"Beautiful, with fish tails?" He shook his head. "They're mammals too, you know. Mammals can't have scales. So many of these stories make no sense. What did you expect…never mind. It's not as bad as you think. Would you trust me?"

"More'n that butcher of a doctor."

"Fair enough. You wanted to swim, but I'll have to lift you onto a stretcher. Sitting in a wheelchair would be very painful, probably impossible."

I was tired, drained. I reached to be picked up, like a child, never thinking of impropriety, or the pure strangeness of it all. I didn't even flinch when Chris staggered, nearly dropping me. Stitches tore somewhere. I winced; Chris scowled. He wheeled me down endless dingy corridors, leaning heavily on the gurney. Steamy drafts blew through open doorways.

"I smell chlorine," I said.

"We're almost there." Chris stopped in front of a steel door. "Wait here."

"Where would I go?" But in this strange steamy half-light, I couldn't work up the energy to be angry. I waited, listening to the thump and hum of filters, and that strange cry… maybe it was machinery squealing. Chris returned, hauled the doors open, and wheeled me inside.

The room was all white tiles, algae-stained, mostly filled by a steaming pool. Lifts and other therapeutic equipment lined the walls, but Chris simply picked me up and slid me in. I held on to the side of the pool and waited.

"What?" he said. "You wanted to swim"

"Hospital gowns…don't close in the back. And they're…pretty see-through when wet."

"Oh." He actually looked bewildered. "Just a moment." I watched the trembling light reflecting off the walls until he came back with a mossy-looking pullover.

"Smells like seaweed."

"It is. Put it on. It has pockets, to keep your hands free."

Chris turned his back. I slid out of the gown into that strange, clinging thing, careful not to look too closely at the wreckage below my waist. The pullover came to what had been mid-thigh.

Chris turned around and fished out the soggy gown. He eyed me critically. "You could swim, before?"

"Of course!"

"That's a start. Stand with your feet apart."

"Mermaids don't have feet!"

He shrugged. "You're the mermaid." He sat down on the stretcher. I turned away from him… and stopped. For the first time, I really looked at what had been done to me.

It looked, and felt, as though I were wearing a black-stitched skirt. The warm water swirled gently through webbing that hung in golden pleats to my ankles.

"This is a tail?"

"Fish have tails. The Lake-People have leg-fins. You'll learn. The more you practice, the less it will hurt. Go on."

I let go of the pool's edge. The water held me vertical for the first time in years. Its warmth soaked away a hundred aches. But I couldn't stay standing—the water wouldn't allow it. Gentle, inexorable pressure pressed that not-tail backward with every step, until I had to swim. The web fanned out, and the rippling light struck it, so that it glittered silver and gold. I bent what had been my knees, stretched, and that stiff, creaking movement swept me through the water in one glorious, fluid glide. Every movement brought more freedom, more wonders, as control returned. In seconds, I'd forgotten every pain and exhausted my long-unused muscles. I retreated to poolside, shaking with fatigue, awe, and fear.

"If the tail works, that means the gills do too, right?" Before I could think about it—before Chris could stop me—I dove, breathing deeply.

Not water, but fire, poured through me. I thrashed and struggled, choking and inhaling more pain. When it stopped, I lay on the stretcher with Chris, dripping and furious, glaring at me.

"I thought I could breathe water," I wheezed.

"You can't breathe chlorine, idiot!" He marched me back to my room in silence.

Part 3

Jimmy Hanson was a sallow man who spent his life glued to his stereovision. Doctor Pedanti tore him away from a 1990's cartoon marathon to unload the van. Strapped in back, I couldn't see much, so I lay breathing in the scent of lake water and basswood trees and listening to the squawk and mutter of Doctor Pedanti's voice against the lapping of the waves.

"Have you got the pens? The permit? The flags? Are the others here? Did you post the ads?"

"Steady your keel, Doc," Jimmy chuckled. "Everything's fine. I told the Environmental Inspector he could have a special show, like you told me to. He said he wouldn't give you no trouble."

"He'd better not. Do you know how much money I've sunk in this? Get the alarms set up. Get my office ready. Have we got heat yet?"

"It's July, Doc!"

"And once things get rolling we'll be here year 'round. I won't sit through one of these godforsaken North Country winters without decent heat. The Links had better be up, too. I need contact with the real world."

The lock clicked. I expected Chris, but it was Jimmy who stuck his head in, smelling of wood-smoke and grinning at me through a mouthful of yellow-stained teeth.

"Mornin', Babe! Name's Jimmy Hanson. You can call me Jimmy Handsome." He chuckled at his own joke. "So you're Doc's new mermaid. I'll just be taking you for a ride now."

"I don't think so, Mr. Hanson. Where's Chris Anderson?" Probably as far from me as he can get, I thought. Since my near drowning, he'd taught me speech, swimming... all with cold, conscientious thoroughness. He emptied bedpans just as dutifully.

"Mister Anderson's out back. I'm helping him today." He unclipped the safety harness and swung me over his back. Barely-healed incisions stretched painfully.

"Hey! What are you doing?" I thumped a fist into his shoulder. "The house is the other way!"

He shook his head. "Mermaids don't live in houses, silly! I'm no doctor, but I know that much. You're goin' in the lake." He jogged to the water's edge, crunching tiny snail shells underfoot.

"You can't just dump me off the end of the dock."

He stopped, looking slowly about him. "You're right." Before I could as much as sigh with relief, he thudded off in a new direction. "Doc said you're supposed to go in the pen."

I had one glimpse of rounded stones, rope, and buoys before Jimmy swung me around and dumped me into the frigid water. I came up spitting water and silt, cursing. Jimmy backed up, panicky and babbling "But he *said*… Doc said…"

"I said put her in the pen and get back to work." Doctor Pedanti himself bustled down to the water's edge. "That's right, James. Go on. Find Anderson—he's disappeared again."

"What about the other…"

"Find Anderson!"

Jimmy scurried off. Doctor Pedanti scanned the area marked off by the pen. "Comfortable, my dear?"

"Are you serious? I'm lucky if it's over seventy degrees in here. We won't get into the plumbing. Or lack of it."

Doctor Pedanti wasn't listening. "That…thing…you're wearing…"

"Very comfortable. Handy pockets."

"Take it off. Change into this." He handed me a sequined string bikini top.

"Are you nuts? And what's with the fence? Open it up." I seized the top myself—and something jolted through my nerves, hurling me backward.

"I'd stop that, if I were you. That pen was specially designed for use in water, but if you keep this up you might still electrocute yourself." Pedanti smiled.

"Look, if I have to live in water, I have an idea. There's a cabin down where the Marina used to be. Half sunk by now, I've heard. I'll fix it up so I can get the most out of both parts."

He laughed—not a cheerful laugh at all. "Miss Bennington, I don't think you understand. I gave you the surgery you wanted. Now you'll give me something in return. Recognition. Fame. 'The Champlain Mermaid' is booked for five shows a week. In appropriate dress, I might add."

"Are you a doctor, or P. T. Barnum? I'm your patient, not your sideshow!"

He didn't even bother to sound jolly now. "You'll stay here. Surgery's expensive. You have quite a bill to pay off, Miss Bennington." He steepled his fingers, looking past me. "People will pay plenty to see a real mermaid, but you need to look the part. Perhaps a blonde wig…"

"It's bad enough freezing here in a bikini. And don't tell me this is legal."

Doctor Pedanti's toothy smile only widened. "You signed the consent. It's not my fault if you didn't read it first.

"I brought you some oatmeal," said Chris. "Hot, with cream and sugar." He didn't sound angry. Almost apologetic.

A seagull dropped from the sky, skimming the waves. I watched it a while before answering.

"Doc'll have a fit. He wants me to have a 'seductive figure'."

"He doesn't know a thing about mermaids. You can't be skinny and stay warm in seventy-degree water." I half-turned toward him. "Here." He held out a steaming bowl.

"Thanks." I took the bowl. It felt comfortably warm in my chilled, wrinkling hands. "So where've you been?"

"Visiting family." He waited quietly while I ate. "Miss Bennington, I was… unprofessional… at your first swimming lesson. I apologize."

"Don't worry about it." I scraped up the last of the oatmeal. "You're not a bad cook. If Doctor Quack didn't keep me penned like I was Champ, I'd show you Brian's old cabin. I think the kitchen would still be above water. We could have an amphibious picnic."

He laughed his restrained half-laugh. "Kind of you, Miss Bennington."

"Laura."

"Laura." He looked out over the water. "So, is 'your lake' like you remembered?"

"I wouldn't know. 'My lake' is out there—I waved an arm toward the encircling hills, the lapping waves—and I'm in here." I shrugged. "Never mind. You… what was that?"

Chris followed my gesture, and tensed. The sinking sun hid whatever he was looking at. His green eyes widened.

"No, Jimmy, it's too soon," he muttered. "It's still light!"

"Too soon for what?"

He didn't answer. Instead, he shucked off his lab coat, then the heavy braces, and dove off the end of the dock. He stroked out toward the middle of the lake, not kicking…

That's when I saw.

In the water, a translucent silvery web unfurled to Chris' feet. This was no grotesque Frankenstein stitchery. Where not marred by the braces, this webbing was as natural and right as a dolphin's fluke or a butterfly's wing. Halfway out, another shape glided to meet him. Chris pointed and gestured, then swam back toward me. The other swimmer followed. Her eyes, clear gold as the lake water in sunlight, widened with panic at the sight of me. I stared back at her. Rounded figure, alabaster pale and wearing nothing, not even goosebumps. A cap of soft, dark, almost greenish hair. Gentle features, now tense with uncertainty. Chris slipped an arm around the lake-woman's shoulder. I'd never seen such a look on his face—so open, so proud. So happy.

"Laura, this is my wife," he said.

Part 4

I can't believe I just heard that.

The thought went through my head, but the words wouldn't come out of my mouth. All that escaped was "Whaa…?"

"She's my wife, Laura," Chris repeated patiently. The

mermaid—the real, moss-haired, champagne-eyed, Rubin-esque mermaid, tilted her head at me and made sympathetic clicking noises. I wanted to slap her.

"Is she part of the show too?"

Chris scowled. "She was the show, originally. Pedanti captured her just for that purpose. Then he didn't think she looked 'real enough.'" He snorted. "So he hired someone to mold a human to fit his idea." He looked at the hills as he said this, at the tops of trees—anywhere but at his wife and me.

"You. He hired you." Heat boiled up in me. "You sold me to Pedanti. You did this to me. There's no way that quack could've made anyone breathe underwater. You did the surgery. You gave me to Pedanti so I could be his sideshow instead."

"You wanted it! I tried to talk you out of it, but you wouldn't listen."

"But you knew what Pedanti would do with me. You knew, and you helped him anyway. And now you're going to swim on your merry way and leave me here "

"Well, what do you expect me to do?"

"Open this stupid pen! Let me out."

"Even if that didn't set off alarms from here to Essex, you couldn't survive on your own."

"I'd find a way."

"And Pedanti would find someone else to replace you. He's picked up enough to try the surgery himself—even if he has to try several times before his 'experiment' survives. Who will you sacrifice for your own freedom, Laura Bennington?"

The water got colder and colder, stiffening my re-made joints. "No one. Get out of here, both of you."

"Laura, I'm sorry."

"Of course you are. But you did what you had to do. Get going. But leave that coat. It's cold in here."

They hesitated a long time. Chris dropped the lab coat. Then they slid beneath the water, making barely a ripple, and were gone.

Doctor Pedanti's grand day dawned bright and clear. I watched the crowd pull up—air vans, an electrobus, and the sleek white cars of the Species Protection Police. Doctor Pedanti had been very careful to show the SPP his permits, my signed consents, and his notes detailing how he had given a 'helpless, wheelchair-bound paraplegic' a 'new life.' Now he led the SPP enforcers on a tour of the cabin, looking smug as a cream-fed cat.

Jimmy Hanson came by to check the equipment. "Morning, Miss Mermaid. You're looking kinda pale. You ok?"

"Stage fright, Jimmy. Plus, I'm not used to this kind of waterbed." I smiled at him, holding up a bundle of soggy white cloth. "Looks like one of Chris' lab coats blew into the lake last night. Could you throw this out?"

"Sure. Mister Anderson isn't even up yet. Lazy. I'll take care of this. Man, it's shredded! You've got some mighty sharp rocks in there." He searched the pockets and took out Chris' scalpel. "What all did he have in there? You're lucky you didn't cut yourself."

"Yes. Lucky." I sagged against the dock, incredibly tired, waiting.

"And here she is, ladies and gentlemen!" Doctor Pedanti's fat face positively glowed with satisfaction. About twenty people behind him leaned forward, trying to see down that stupid bikini. I gritted my teeth and waved. Several men whistled; some laughed.

"So it's a chick in a bathing suit," someone called. "Show us her tail!"

More guffaws. Doctor Pedanti drew himself up haughtily.

"Of course. Miss Bennington, if you please?"

"What, no whistle?" I muttered. But I hoisted myself onto the dock, faced the crowd, and watched Doctor Pedanti's face turn ashen.

"What… what did you…?"

"A miracle of modern surgery, ladies and gentlemen!" I called. Some of the watchers turned pale, some green.

I'd slit the webbing and tied it back, invisible, with strips from Chris' coat. A larger panel of cloth, tied to my ankles and waist, looked like a child's paper cutout of a mermaid's tail. The cold water had kept me from bleeding too much, but now red stains began creeping across the white cloth.

"Butcher!" screamed a woman. The SPP men advanced on Doctor Pedanti, handcuffs ready.

"I didn't do this!" he babbled, scrabbling backward. "This is a mockery… a trick…" The crowd closed in on him. I didn't stay to watch. I slid off the other side of the dock and swam away.

Hours later, I stopped to rest on one of the less-rocky banks. The adrenaline of escape had long since drained away, leaving hollow exhaustion behind. I lay watching my blood stain the water, picking idly at the ragged stitches holding Chris' coat to me and hoping just for the strength to get free of the dragging weight.

"My god, Laura…"

Chris and his wife were both there, watching, afraid. I mustered half a smile.

"Don't worry about Doc. He'll be a laughingstock for years. And I'll bet he won't want anything to do with mermaids, or this lake, ever."

"He'll be on trial for your murder, from what we overheard. Possibly mine, too. Jimmy showed the SPP men my torn coat, and… what did you do to yourself?

Chris' wife gently swam up to me and began loosening the black threads. It didn't hurt; I was numb with cold and shock. When she was done, she touched the ragged edge of the torn fringe, making soft cooing sounds. She patted me on the shoulder and looked into my eyes, speaking earnestly in a language I couldn't understand.

"She says, 'Life for life,'" Chris translated. "You saved not only her, but anyone else Pedanti might have used. I can mend your fins." He hesitated. "You could come with us."

"I'm headed the other way."

"To die, still? No!" Chris protested. His wife looked alarmed.

"No," I said to them both. "I'll come with you, but only long enough for you to heal these fins. I'm going to find my old camp and rebuild it. Once I get things fixed up, you're both welcome to visit." I smiled. "Remember, Chris, I promised you a picnic. Will grilled perch be ok?"

WOMEN'S ISSUES

Ballgown Road

The only way to reach Ballgown Road is from an overgrown path that local wags call "Knot Street". There's nothing on it but a tree at the end. An old, gnarled, leafless tree with a hollow heart.

Women put all kinds of things into that tree. Broken glass. Wedding rings. Impossibly tiny baby shoes. Then they step forward, with their eyes open. Always with their eyes open.

Some flinch and back away. Some scrape their faces on the tree, and beat their hands bloody against the unyielding bark. And some walk through the tree, onto Ballgown Road.

There's always light on Ballgown Road, even when the sky is dark. And, of course, there are the ballgowns.

Silk, velvet, satin. Trimmed with fur, lace, embroidery. You can always tell the new arrivals. While others dance, they marvel at their new splendor, stroking soft fur trimmings and admiring impossibly tiny stitches.

Some dance clumsily, unsure in their unaccustomed finery, stumbling, out of rhythm with the coaxing, swirling music that always flows through the air of Ballgown Road. Some skip and spin with the delight of a child taking her first steps. Some find partners and swing each other in broad, free circles, laughing.

And you can always tell the ones who have been there the longest, the ones who have danced from one end of Ballgown Road to the other. They pause in the dance, looking about them with curious eyes, as though seeing new colors in the world. They touch the trees that line the Road like green guardians.

They find one tree among the many, always vibrant and green, with a hollow at its roots waiting like cupped hands.

Women leave all kinds of things behind in the hollow. Fear. Shame. Despair.

They strip off their glamorous, borrowed finery, and walk away from Ballgown Road in the clothes they arrived in. Jeans, nightgowns, sweaters. But they walk straighter, more steadily, toward the world they'd left behind, with their eyes open.

Always with their eyes open.

Luchadora

When Alejandra was nine, her mother died of dehydration. When she was ten, Alejandra made her father bring her to the Luchadores' barracks. The three ancient wizards who would choose the boy who would become the next Luchador weren't pleased. They almost sent Alejandra's father to the hellstone mines, where men died with their limbs charred black. Then Alejandra marched up to the eldest of the Magos, the one in flame-red silk, and demanded that he make the bull-man stop waking her up at night. The other two Magos, in silk as gold as the sun and as blue as the sky, gasped. The first wizard scowled.

"What do you mean, child?"

"The bull with the man-face. He came when Mama died. He comes in the dark and whispers to me."

The old man's caterpillar brows pinched together over his nose. "What does he say?"

"I don't know. He sounds too far away. Then he breathes cold breath on me."

"And what do you do then?"

"This." Alejandra thrust out both arms and splayed her fingers in a star pattern. "Then he gets angry and goes away. But he always comes back. Papa says this is where the Luchadores learn to fight him. I want to be one."

The old wizards conferred in low, angry voices. Alejandra's father twisted his hands together as though he could already feel them burning. At last, the first old man came back to Alejandra.

"Did your father tell you that if you lived here you would wear silk and eat meat every day? That we would give him water-rights?"

"No. He didn't want to come here. He said little girls shouldn't bother the Magos. But the bull-man won't leave me alone."

The oldest of the Magos turned to Alejandra's father. "You are a widower?"

"Yes, Learned One."

"What have you told this girl?"

"Nothing! Nothing but that the Luchadores and your worthy selves have protected us from El Toro for generations."

"True. And we have no time to raise the daughters of widowers who wish to be rid of their burden."

Alejandra's father turned pale beneath his coating of road-dust. "Great One, I assure you…"

"Enough." He turned back to Alejandra. "Child, we can teach you to fight this bull-man," he said. "If you defeat him, he will be too weak to return for twenty years."

"I know. Mama said the bull-man came just before I was born, and that he'll come back when I'm old enough to get married. She used to tell me about how the first Luchadores drove El Toro back with spells and swords and burning stones, back when there was more water and everybody had flowers in their gardens."

"Infants' stories. This is not a story, girl! Many boys come here, hoping to become El Luchador. Most of them give up and quit in disgrace. Some die. No girl has ever tried this. If we keep you, you must do what we tell you and never cry, never complain. Do you understand?"

"Yes."

"Then come with me."

"I want Papa to come too."

The old man frowned. "No. Come with me now, or go home."

Papa squeezed Alejandra's shoulders. His hands were wet with sweat, damp through the thin fabric of her dress. Alejandra understood. If she turned back, the Magos would think that her father had brought her here to mock them. She turned and hugged him goodbye. Then she followed the old man with the caterpillar eyebrows.

&.

The old man led Alejandra through a courtyard. The grass here had a touch of green in it, and the trees held a few limp leaves. Alejandra realized that this was the first greenery she'd seen in a long time. She hadn't seen anything so pretty since she was little, when her mother used to sew leaves and vines onto her smocks. She wanted to linger, to touch the living plants, but the old man strode on without waiting for her. He led Alejandra past rooms lined with benches to a tiny cubbyhole.

"You'll sleep there. Stay out of the boys' dormitory."

"It's full of brooms and buckets," said Alejandra.

"You will address me as El Primero."

"It's full of brooms and buckets, El Primero."

The eldest of the Magos scowled. "Then put them to good use."

"When will I learn to fight El Toro, El Primero?"

"Are you complaining?" His voice implied that he could still have Alejandra's father sent to the mines any time he liked. Alejandra shook her head. As soon as the old wizard was out of sight she cleared a niche for herself among the supplies, picked up a rag and a wooden bucket, and set off to explore the barracks.

The corridors were full of boys in fine blue and gold jackets. Some gave Alejandra odd looks, but no one bothered her once they saw the bucket in her hand. She found a pump in the courtyard and gave some water to the tired-looking trees. At home, Papa always saved the wash water for their onions and beans. She'd never known anyone who had their own pump. That impressed her more than silk robes.

"Hey, girl! What are you doing?"

Alejandra turned. A boy, a couple of years her elder from his looks, stood watching her with an expression of amused exasperation.

"The Magos will thrash you if they catch you dumping water on the ground," he said.

"Then why did they put the pump next to the trees? And

my name's not *'girl'*. It's Alejandra. But you can call me La Luchadora if you want."

The boy laughed. "The water and the trees both belong to the Magos. You could be whipped for touching them. I'm Lucas. What do you fight, La Luchadora? Cobwebs?"

"No! I'm here to learn how to fight El Toro."

Lucas shook his head. "If the Magos wanted you to study with us, El Tercero would have introduced you. I think they just wanted a girl to help the old ladies in the kitchen."

"That can't be. They didn't even show me where the kitchen is."

Lucas grinned. "If you ever plan on eating, you'd better learn. Come on, I'll show you."

Two hallways down from Alejandra's closet, Lucas stopped outside a stone archway and called, "Is La Bruja in?"

A ladle shot through the door, aimed at Lucas' head. Inches away it stopped dead in the air and clattered to the stone floor.

"If I'd been Gilberto, you'd be cleaning blood out of my suit," said Lucas to the gray-haired woman who emerged to retrieve the ladle.

"If you'd been that lout Gilberto, it would have been worth it. El Primero had better not see you. He said that if the girl was too stupid to find her way here by herself, she deserved to starve."

"He promised to teach me how to fight El Toro!" Alejandra protested.

La Bruja gave her an unpleasant gap-toothed smile. "Did he say so, in those words?"

"Yes! He said 'We can teach you to fight this bull-man.'"

"Can, not will. The Magos love to quibble about such things. I'm sure they could teach you, but I doubt they will."

"Then why didn't they just send me home with Papa?"

"Now there's a good question." La Bruja sucked on her remaining teeth. "There are easier ways to get a pot-scrubber. Something about you must've got their attention."

"That's a dirty trick!" said Lucas. "But Alex, what did you mean about a bull-man?"

Alejandra didn't correct his odd shortening her name. There was something friendly about it, something that told her he was taking her seriously.

"El Toro. He has eyes like a man's. Gray. And he's white as clouds. It's hard to see his face clearly, though. It's always foggy when he comes."

"Now I know you're pretending. No one's seen El Toro, except maybe the Luchadores."

"You mean you haven't? All of you boys? Then why are you here?"

Lucas shrugged. "It's expected. Any family with water rights sends a son to the Magos. You get an education and maybe learn a little magic."

"El Primero said boys die here."

Lucas snorted. "Not likely. Do you know what they're teaching us this year? Sewing! Am I supposed to die of a needle prick?"

"The girl's right," said La Bruja. "Think. If it hadn't been for those scraggly bricks embroidered on your jacket, you'd have a ladle-shaped dent in your forehead. If you could sew a straight line it wouldn't have gotten as close as it did." She shoved a bowl of beans into Alejandra's hands and said, "Now get out of here. I've got work to do."

The next morning a gong woke the barracks. Alejandra scrambled up from an uncomfortable sleep on a pile of rags. She stole a handful of water from the pump to splash her face and slick down her hair and joined the line of boys filing into a classroom. When she tried to slide onto a bench, the wizard in yellow poked her with a wooden staff tipped with hellstone.

"You can't sit with the young Luchadores."

"Yes I can. I'm La Luchadora."

"You aren't allowed in the classrooms."

"Yes I am. I'm here to fight El Toro. I'm going to learn."

The tip of the staff pressed against Alejandra's breastbone and began to smolder. Alejandra gasped. The boys on Alejandra's bench edged away from her.

"You will keep out of sight, or be kept so."

Alejandra held still until he lowered the staff. Then, with wisps of smoke still trailing from her blouse, she rose and walked, with careful dignity, to the kitchen.

"La Bruja!"

No cutlery shot through the doorway. Alejandra walked through into a bizarre vision.

Old women scurried around a gaping pit in the floor, where skillets broader than paving stones and full of eggs and sausages sizzled. Beneath it, black stones glowed red at their hearts, tainting the smoke with a bitter scent.

"That's hellstone!" Alejandra said.

The work stopped. La Bruja turned from measuring water into stone mugs.

"So is what made that hole in your blouse. What are you doing here?"

"Looking for breakfast."

"Then earn it. Start chopping onions."

When Alejandra had a large pile of chopped onions in front of her, the work stopped again. She looked up through streaming eyes to see El Tercero, the wizard in blue, standing in front of her.

"El Primero warned you about crying."

"I'm not crying! It's the onions."

With a nasty smile, El Tercero reached across the table for her. Alejandra threw up her hands in the gesture she used to ward off El Toro. El Tercero pulled back, the tips of his fingers bluish-white. Then he nodded, slowly, as though Alejandra had answered a question in a way he hadn't expected, and stalked out of the kitchen. Alejandra went back to chopping onions with even greater vigor.

"Go get your things," said La Bruja.

"What?"

"Your clothes, or whatever you brought with you. Get them and come back here."

"After I've found a way to get into the class."

"Listen, girl. You've confused the Magos. You'll live longer if you stay out of their way, and I want to see how long you last. There's space in the back room."

A back room sounded like a better place to sleep than a storage closet, at least. Alejandra ran back to get the faded cloth she'd used for a blanket. To her annoyance, Lucas was waiting outside the cubbyhole.

"All right, you can say you told me so." Alejandra said. "But I'm still going to learn to fight El Toro."

"Did you see the look on El Segundo's face when he touched you with the hellstone? How bad is your burn?"

Alejandra slid a cautious finger through the hole in her blouse. "There isn't one."

"La Bruja's right. You are strange."

"At least I can sew in a straight line."

Lucas's hand went to the scraggly glyph on his jacket. "I'll tell you what. You help me improve my sewing and tell me what El Toro's really like, and I'll teach you as much as I can of the rest. I swear by the Spring. Deal?"

Alejandra considered her chances of learning anything useful from the Magos, then stuck her hand out for Lucas to shake. "Deal."

❧

The other boys, eager to please the Magos, banded together against Alejandra, forcing her to become stronger and more agile than any two of them together to avoid their beatings. The kitchen work helped with that; the iron pans were heavier than the boys' practice swords. The old women left the heavy work to Alejandra while they hung strings of fish and vegetables near the hellstone fire to dry. According to La Bruja, the smoke from the fire was a preservative.

"It must be," Alejandra joked. "You talk like you've been here forever."

La Bruja gave her an odd look and told her to stir the soup.

Lucas kept his word, sparring with Alejandra and teaching

her how to read glyphs and form the choreographed movements that were supposed to keep El Toro at bay. Her warding gesture, she learned, was a basic move called Estrellas. In return, Alejandra described El Toro's nightly visitations in detail and saved up yards of scrap cloth to help Lucas practice his stitching. Embroidering glyphs took patience, because the symbols held power. One missed stitch could send the cloth up in flame, or worse.

The first thing Lucas crafted, after he learned that three boys had gone blind from dropping a stitch in the Farsight glyph, was a belt stitched with symbols of concealment and misdirection, to cover his frequent visits to the kitchen. It worked so well that Alejandra made herself one so she could watch the boys' swordfights and listen in on bits of their lessons. Ten years passed, and she never got caught.

❧

As the hot dry summers faded into cold dry autumns and back again, both Alejandra and Lucas grew in skill as well as body. The few boys still left, those who hadn't fallen victim to fighting injuries or magical mistakes, accused Lucas of mooning after the serving girl. Although Alejandra hated the teasing, she had to admit that it deflected the attention of the Magos.

La Bruja seemed to enjoy encouraging their secret lessons, even going so far as to produce a hidden cache of thread for Alejandra to practice embroidering glyphs.

"There's so much green! I never see green on the robes of the Magos, or on the boys' suits. Lucas says it's bad luck."

La Bruja snorted. "You won't see it anywhere outside of this kitchen. It's forbidden, like leaving the barracks or touching the Magos. But if you call it bad luck, the boys enforce the rule themselves."

"My mother sewed green leaves on my clothes all the time. And flowers she called bluebells and carnations and lilies. Her grandmother told her about them. I've been practicing them."

La Bruja smiled a fierce, sad smile. "I doubt the Magos even remember their grandmothers."

Lucas rushed in, fully visible.

"Do you want a spoon to the head, boy?" said La Bruja. "Standing there in the open—"

"Alex, get out of here. The Magos are ready to challenge El Toro, and they want to use you as bait."

Alejandra exchanged glances with La Bruja. "You were right. That's why they've kept me all this time. Good."

"*Good?* Alex, did you hear what I said?"

"Yes. How else am I going to get close enough to El Toro to fight him?"

"With what? A sewing needle? A wooden spoon? Alex, for Spring's sake—"

"Why do you say that, Lucas? Why do you swear by the Spring?"

"Well, a spring's water, it's precious…"

"I suspect it's something else. But I don't know. I can't be sure." Alex threw the spool of green thread into the hellstone fire to smolder and blacken. "Lucas, would you forgive me if I did something terrible? If people died because of what I did?"

"As long as it wasn't you who died," he blurted. "Alex…"

La Bruja whacked him alongside the head. Alejandra winced in sympathy.

"Get out of my kitchen!" the ancient cook bellowed as all three Magos entered. "I have enough to do without lovesick boys moping around."

El Primero gave her a sour smile. "Let us solve both your problems, old woman. We'll take the girl off your hands. Young man, get back to your studies."

Lucas took a step toward Alejandra, but she shook her head, and he let La Bruja shoo him away.

༄

The Magos took Alejandra out through the back door and marched her down the path that led to the hellstone mines.

Outside the Luchadores' barracks, the land had suffered even more than Alejandra remembered. Years of drought had cracked the earth and withered the fields. The parched hills shook as though with fever. The people slumped, dusty and dry-throated, in whatever shade they could find.

"El Toro is getting stronger," the Magos said, when Alejandra startled at the tremors. "Soon he'll break free and destroy everything around him."

Alejandra said nothing, even when they locked her in a stone cell near the entrance to the mines.

In the darkness, El Toro spoke to her. Lucas had taught her how to fight, but La Bruja had made her listen—to tales hundreds of years old, to the mutterings of the Magos as they ate the flesh of mortal bulls while crouching by hellstone fires, and to her own suspicions. Alejandra listened to the rumblings of El Toro and heard the turning of the earth. The cell grew cold. Frost formed on the stone, to become clear water in the warmth of her hands. Somewhat reassured, she drank the water and waited.

❧

When the Magos released Alejandra hours later, her eyes had adjusted to the dark and the sunlight stung them. While the three wizards bound her to an iron post in front of the hellstone mine, she squinted toward the miners' huts, where all the surviving boys but one formed a line intended to keep the miners away from the Magos.

Alejandra counted a dozen dark shapes against her dazzled vision. Of the swarm of boys who had crowded the barracks ten years ago, only thirteen remained. These twelve, and El Luchador.

"Let it be Lucas. Let it be Lucas," Alejandra prayed.

The gong from the barracks sounded, magically magnified to echo across the barren fields. The Magos swept over the brown grass, their feet not quite touching it. Behind them, walking normally except for a tremor of either fear or rage, came El Luchador.

Lucas. Alejandra hid her smile of relief. Lucas wouldn't understand it, and the Magos surely meant to torment her, knowing that El Luchador would likely die in achieving his task.

The Magos raised their staffs high, the hellstone tips blazing. The protective sigils on their robes shone red. They chanted—a high, whining sound. Thanks to her studies with Lucas, Alejandra understood most of the words. They were mocking El Toro, taunting him, calling him to take the pittance they offered in Alejandra and creep back into his hole.

El Toro came. The air turned colder than anyone had felt in a generation. Frost whitened the mouth of the mine. The earth shuddered. The great horned head emerged from the darkness, and even Alejandra gasped at his solid reality. The massive white bull's body shouldered its way free of the earth. The heavy head with its human eyes turned to glare at the Magos, then swung to face Alejandra. Lucas shouted and ran forward, sword drawn.

"Lucas, stop!"

He did, looking baffled and angry.

"Put the sword down, please."

"Alex…"

"Put the sword down, and whatever happens, don't touch El Toro. Or me. Don't let the Magos touch me either. Please."

Lucas put the sword down—and snatched it up again as the Magos advanced toward Alejandra.

"You heard the lady, Learned Ones. Leave her alone."

Alejandra shut out their voices until nothing was left but her and the great bull. She held still as El Toro sniffed her over. He smelled like water and cold stone. Then, with a toss of his head, he ripped Alejandra's dress in two from neck to hem. Half fell to the ground. The other half dangled from one of El Toro's sharp horns. Alejandra looked down, expecting to see herself gored open, but saw only split rope and her white underdress, with its embroidery of green leaves and flowers. She stepped free of the post and El Toro backed away from her, shaking his head.

"I was right," she said, half to herself and half to the mighty creature before her. "Green isn't evil, but it's powerful. Just like you."

"Stop her before she curses us all!" El Primero's voice whined in her ear like a mosquito.

"Alex, do you know what you're doing?" said Lucas.

"No. But I know this much. La Bruja says she's seen ten Luchadores die keeping El Toro at bay. That's two hundred years. Two hundred years without the Spring we swear by. Because you can't have Spring without true Winter. Lucas, bring me nine hellstones, please."

"You can't do this! I forbid you!" shouted El Primero. The bull's presence held him frozen. None of the Magos moved.

"You're a traitor!" said El Segundo.

"People will die. Their deaths will be on your head." El Tercero didn't shout. He spoke with matter-of-fact calm. His words made Alejandra pause.

"I know," she said. "But more will live."

Lucas brought her the hellstones, glowing through a runestitched cloth. Alejandra brought them to El Toro in her bare hands.

"I know your name," she said. "And you can be free for three months out of the twelve, like the stories say you used to be. Eat these to seal the bargain, and I will free you."

When the last hot stone had vanished down El Toro's icy gullet and the creature stood steaming and looking at her expectantly, Alejandra called out, "Winter, I free you!"

A storm of ice and snow blasted over the field. Alejandra and Lucas held tight to each other until the gale passed, then peered through the thickly-falling snow.

"The Magos are dead," said Lucas.

"Yes," said Alejandra. She was shaking, and not just from the cold.

"They were over two hundred years old," said Lucas. "And they were drying up the land."

"Yes." Alejandra forced down her guilt and straightened. "Get the other students together. We need to distribute hellstones to as many people as we can, to help them keep warm. And blankets, and warm clothing…"

"As you command, La Luchadora," said Lucas.

They worked into the night, bringing people what they needed to survive the winter. Some cursed Alejandra. Some cried. Finally, she and Lucas snatched a moment for themselves in the barracks kitchen.

"La Bruja is dead," said Alejandra. "All the old women are. I'm sorry."

Lucas nodded. "And your father… The miners told me. The Magos sent him to the mines anyway, and he died five years ago. I'm sorry."

Alejandra dropped into a chair and stared at the floor. "I should never have come here."

Lucas didn't speak for a long time. Then he said, "We were all dying anyway, slowly, along with the land. What the Magos did was wrong. This is the last of their evil, and what you did will set things right. We'll all see that when the spring comes."

"If we're still here."

"Alex! Aren't you La Luchadora? Can't you fight something more than dust and cobwebs?"

Alejandra glanced toward La Bruja's place by the fire and allowed herself a fierce, sad smile. "I might need reminding of that a few times before spring comes."

"Then I'll keep reminding you until spring comes. And even longer if you'll let me, my Luchadora."

"Lucas, don't. Not when there's so much to fix."

"I'll help you fix it, as long as you don't drive me away. Deal?"

She started to hold out a hand, then dropped it back to her side. "Right now, we have work to do."

"And after?"

Alejandra smiled and shook her head. "Ask me again in the Spring."

Sister

Like everyone else living in the Shadowed Forest, Sister knew about wicked stepmothers. They were as much a part of life as trolls under bridges, goblins in the mines, and savage wolves on lonely paths.

No one ever warned her about wicked stepfathers.

Sister and Brother had almost stopped missing Father when Mother remarried. Father had kept their house snug and the pantry well-stocked during even the coldest winters, and still found time to ruffle Brother's hair or give Sister a kiss on the cheek and proclaim how lucky he was to have such a fine family.

Stepfather only seemed to notice Sister at night, in the dark, and his kisses weren't the same at all.

When Sister tried to tell Mother about Stepfather's kisses, Mother turned away with a tear on her cheek and stared at the empty cupboards. The harried, pinched look she'd gotten after Father died had vanished for a while around the wedding. Now it was back, with a new twist of fear added to it. When Brother turned silent and secretive, claiming that he'd bruised himself again by falling from yet another tree, Sister made up her mind.

"Mother can't help us. She's too scared. Let's go into the forest. Maybe we'll find a dragon's treasure, or a kind fairy godmother will give us a wish. At least we'll have berries and nuts to eat."

Brother was glad to go, so they set off through the beech, holly and oak trees. They walked for hours, their joy at leaving Stepfather behind fading as they grew footsore and thirsty. It was too early in Spring for berries and nuts. No dragons laired in this part of the forest, and they saw not so much as a woodcutter in the trackless tangle, let alone a fairy godmother.

Tiny black flies swarmed about their heads, and their mouths grew almost too dry to talk.

At last they came to a clear, fresh spring. Brother dropped to his knees to drink.

"Wait!" said Sister. "See the clawed prints on the bank? And listen to the voice of the stream. If you drink here, you'll turn into a bear and eat me up. We have to find another stream."

They went on, forcing their way through the undergrowth, and soon found another spring, but this one had wolf tracks on the edge, and the voice of the stream babbled with mischief.

"What if we both drink?" Brother eyed the cool water with wistful longing. "I've heard that wolves are kind to other wolves."

"No." Sister gently turned him away. "We have to keep looking."

"Just one more. But then I must drink. My head is spinning."

The next spring had dainty hoof prints on the bank, not paw prints. Before Sister could say a word Brother had flung himself down and drank deeply of the cold, clear water. The leaf-green air shimmered, and a wide-eyed young roebuck lay trembling where the boy had been.

Before the frightened animal could leap away, Sister looped her sash around his neck. Brother submitted meekly, hanging his head.

"I was so thirsty. I'm sorry."

Sister eyed the cool water with longing. Becoming a deer might not be so bad. At least they could browse on twigs. But she remembered the defeated slump of Mother's shoulders, the possessive glitter in Stepfather's eyes, and straightened.

"What's done is done. I'm not giving up. At least now you can eat sweet grass and leaves. But I must find human food, or I'll starve."

"Don't leave me!" Brother pawed at the hem of her dress, his eyes wild and pleading. Sister put an arm around his velvet-soft neck.

"Never. We're still brother and sister, on four feet or two. Come on."

$\approx$

Sister could never decide if it was a kindness or cruelty that a short walk beyond the stream they came upon a hut with a deep, cold, unenchanted well. She drank half a bucketful at one draught, pushing away the thought that if Brother had waited just a little longer he would still be a boy and not a beast.

Sister swept years of dust from the little hut and made a bed of soft ferns for the fawn. Soon the place felt more like home than their old house ever had with Stepfather there. Brother browsed and played in the clearing and sniffed out tasty mushrooms for Sister with his sensitive transformed nose. Sister brought back edible plants to make a garden. No animals molested her, for they saw what trust the little roe deer had in this gentle human maiden. The birds perched on her shoulders as she worked, and the glossy black snake that killed the rats in the grain bin often slept in her skirt pocket, lulled by her warmth. They went on living this way until the days turned shorter, the trees turned gold, and the sound of hunting horns brayed through the forest.

The little roebuck couldn't keep still. He fretted and chafed, and battered at the door with his hooves.

"Let me out, sister! The walls are trapping me. I won't go near the hunters. Besides, they'll see your blue ribbon around my neck, and I'll be safe."

He pleaded and wheedled so that at last she let him go. She worried about him all day, but he returned at sunset unharmed, prancing and jubilant.

"I saw the King, Sister! The King himself! He was so tall and splendid, on a great white horse. His hunting horn had gold on it, and the other men had silver, and those were real jewels on their clothes, I'm sure of it. And their arrows had peacock feathers and sharp tips…:

"Which could have gone right through your heart! What

were you doing, following the hunters? You're the prey now, remember?"

Brother scraped a hoof on the dirt floor of the hut. "I forget."

Sister resolved not to let him out again, but his wild-creature's spirit sickened from the confinement, and she had no let him go. That evening he came back limping, one leg bleeding where an arrow had grazed it.

"You followed them again?" she exclaimed, all the while gently cleaning and binding the wound. "Do you want to be killed and leave me here all alone?"

He made a sound halfway between a fawn's bleat of distress and a boyish sob. "No, never! But the horns…"

"Well, never mind it now. At least tomorrow you won't be out chasing after hunters." She stroked the back of his sun-warmed head and sighed.

But the wound was slight, and when Sister went to the well the next morning, leaving the door open, the little roe bounded out into the sunshine.

Sister chased after him. Through bracken and brambles she ran, getting sweaty and scratched. The young deer soon vanished into the undergrowth. Sister stood alone in an unfamiliar patch of forest, sick at heart with worry for her heedless brother. She saw light ahead where the trees grew thinner and made her way toward it.

Horns blasted, near enough to make her jump. Horses pounded through the trees, nearly trampling her. The lead rider wheeled his white horse about and returned to where she stood, heart racing.

Sister had seen that profile before, stamped on every coin, even the farthings. The king. The king himself was looming over her, his horse dripping foam. He looked Sister up and down, and Sister sank into a curtsy.

"So this is where the be-ribboned beast has led Us! This must be a dryad, for surely one cannot expect to find fair young women alone so deep in the wood."

Sister's cheeks burned. She was hardly fair, not scratched

and sweating, twig-thin from a diet of forest gleanings, with her patched, shapeless dress hanging loose about her. Still, she raised her eyes to the king.

"Your Majesty, have you seen my brother? The little roebuck? Please tell me you haven't hurt him!"

The king's eyebrows shot up. "Your brother! You're a strange maiden indeed. Are you a deer-child also?"

"No, Your Majesty. We're both human. My little brother's under an enchantment. He has no one but me to protect him. Please tell me he's unharmed."

"None of us has harmed him, the clever little devil! But you say he has no one but you. Are you truly alone in the world?"

"Yes, Your Majesty."

"Well, I believe I'm under something of an enchantment myself. My ministers have been at me for years to marry, whether I will or no. But I've never encountered anyone like you. Will you come with me to the palace?"

Sister's head reeled. Surely he couldn't want to marry some raggedy unknown girl he'd just found in the woods! But his men didn't seem shocked at all. The part of her that shrank before the coming winter, that had wondered how she and Brother would live once snow covered even the grass, rejoiced at the thought of warm clothing and well-stocked tables.

"If my brother could come, I—"

"Of course he may! Who wouldn't want to keep such a remarkable creature close by?"

The king gestured, and a courtier swung sister up onto the white horse, just behind him. They cantered off, jarring the breath from Sister's astonished body.

Brother sprang out of the underbrush when he saw his sister riding the king's horse. He capered alongside, and the courtiers gaped at his chatter. Some laughed.

The king didn't laugh, and Sister began to feel troubled. When he turned her way, the look in the Royal eyes stirred memories that she couldn't quite place.

They stopped to rest, and when they remounted the king

said, "Ride in front of me, fair forest sprite. You'll be safer, and I'll be happier seeing my beauty in front of me."

He was the king. She obeyed and sat in front of him, staring at the horse's mane. Over the clop of hooves she heard snatches of conversation:

"…better venison if it's chatty?"

Her stomach turned. Then she felt the king's hand slide down her waist to her thigh, and her memories jolted into place. Stepfather had looked her the same way. She remembered the calculating tone when the king had asked if they were alone in the world. This was a man who liked having power over others, and who liked using it. Sister had dared to question him, and Brother had eluded him and his men for days. They had challenged him, and he did not like being challenged.

The king's hand slid along her thigh, and he smiled when she tried to pull away.

Sister's thoughts raced. He'd never actually said that he'd marry her, just that he'd take her to the palace. Once she was there she'd be his, and Brother would be at the mercy of the venison-loving huntsmen.

The horses stopped at a stream. Sister looked down at the tracks in the mud and without thinking cried "Stop!"

The king scowled. "Why, girl? It's been a long hunt, and we all need water."

"Your Majesty, those are squirrel prints. If you drink here you'll become a squirrel, as my brother became a roebuck."

"Nonsense!" But the king commanded one luckless man to drink, and the former knight scrambled up a tree, chirring and flicking his new bushy tail.

They rode on in silence. The next spring had chipmunk prints around it. Sister gave her warning. Another hapless knight vanished into a nearby burrow. The grumbling men rode on. The king's seeking hand left bruises now.

They stopped at a third spring. When Sister didn't speak, they dismounted. The King pinched Sister's bottom and said "Well, my pretty maid, how will this water change me?"

Sister noted the rat prints on the bank and said "Not at all, Your Majesty."

The men drank, and the black snake in Sister's pocket slid out to feast.

Sea Queen, Sailor Queen

Liaula sang, and the waves rose up, tossing the humans' ship from side to side. The sailors, their wits addled by her song, fell to the deck.

Except for their captain. Liaula glared at the straight figure balanced on the deck above her and drew in another breath. Her song swelled louder still. The enthralled men crawled across the planks toward her. A crescendo flung the ship sideways, hurling two men into the sea.

"Lay off, siren!" the captain shouted. "Those are my men!"

"They're mine once they hit the water!" Liaula returned, seething at this mortal man who seemed deaf to her charms.

"By Triton's trident, I'll have your tail for a rudder." Stripping off hat, coat, and boots, the captain dove into the roiling waves, swimming with more assurance than most humans. Deft hands tethered the sailors to rescue lines tipped with cork floats. The captain shoved the wedges of cork under the men's arms, keeping them afloat.

"Now for you." The captain turned, treading water. Liaula's first thought was scorn for a human who would think of taking on a Siren in her own element. Her second thought burst unbidden from her lips.

"You're a woman!"

"And you're an underhanded, scheming bottom-feeder of a Siren," said the captain pleasantly. "My men may find you bewitching, but to me you're just a shrill fishtailed trollop who smells like last week's halibut. So be off before I plant a harpoon in that naked chest of yours."

The men on deck had come to themselves while Liaula was silent and were hauling their waterlogged comrades aboard. Liaula shrieked and flung herself at the human captain. Burning pain shot through her fluke. Iron. Liaula could feel the blade wedged beneath her scales.

"Move and I shove it deeper." The captain's face was white

with cold and her teeth chattered, but her smile radiated triumph.

Liaula hissed. She could drown the human, but she had no doubt that first this woman would drive that cursed knife in so deep no strength or magic would remove it. Worse, the ship, and its crew, would sail away, leaving her too weak to find another. Oh, she had her magic, but nothing that would help her fight this fierce-eyed sea-queen. Besides her song, she had the driftwood charm, but while turning her flesh to wood would stop the pain, it would leave her helpless at the mortals' hands.

"I'll give you gold," said Liaula through clenched teeth. "The gold of a dozen drowned ships, and moon-white pearls. Only remove that knife."

"So you can go back to bewitching my men?"

Liaula groaned. "Surely a sea-queen like yourself can spare one!"

The captain's lips were blue now, but her eyes gleamed bright. "What do you want them for?"

Surely the human was mocking her! "What does anyone want men for?"

The captain laughed until seawater choked her. "You're a blunt thing! I'm not going to throw my sailors overboard to you, but some of them might be willing to help you out of your predicament. On my terms. On board my ship. With that treacherous mouth of yours gagged so you can't beguile them. And in return, you provide us with treasure. Deal?"

Liaula writhed at the shame of it. But life was life, for her and the clan who would be born from her. "By storm and sea and the weed-crowned Goddess I swear. Safety for your men and treasure for yourself in exchange for my life and the chance to bear young."

The human captain, her fingers stiff with cold, made Liaula fast in the same ropes that had bound her sailors before pulling out the knife. The men hauled Liaula up the side, bumping and scraping. The captain climbed up under her own power and frowned when she saw the siren lying helpless on the deck.

"She's not a netful of cod, boys! Fill a tun with water and get her into it while I change these soggy clothes. And swab the deck afterward."

First, though, she clamped a torque of gold around Liaula's neck, where it clung to her skin like a lamprey. Once the captain was out of sight, Liaula tried singing to the men who gingerly lifted her into the wooden barrel. The metal turned cold and choked the sound from her throat. No tugging or clawing would remove it. She could speak, even scream and curse at the captain when she finally returned, but not sing.

"You did agree to be gagged," the captain pointed out. Clad in warm, dry clothes and with her ship's deck rolling underfoot again, she looked obscenely cheerful. "Should I have used one of the boys' dirty shirts instead?"

"Fine! Just give me a sailor."

"Oh no. I said I'd give you a chance. You can use your fishy charms all you like, except for that uncanny song, but I'll not force anything on the unwilling."

"That's useless, and you know it. Stop this mockery. Let me overboard so I can fetch your treasure, and then to the depths with you and your bargains."

"Oh, I don't need gold," said the captain, smiling. Liaula noticed for the first time how fast the ship was sailing, and wondered too late how the captain had just happened to have a silencing torque handy. A gold one, yet.

The captain looked Liaula up and down. "Gold's nothing compared to you. Wait until the king sees you. You're a better treasure than the loot of a thousand wrecks."

❧

Liaula cursed, threatened, and pled, but the captain only pointed out that she was keeping their bargain to the letter: Liaula was safe from harm and free to court the sailors all she liked. The sailors kept their distance or treated her with sullen formality when forced to interact with her.

Only the captain spent time with Liaula voluntarily,

ignoring her threats and silences to bring her prisoner plates of hot meat from her own table, or just to study Liaula with unsettling intensity—taking in her fluke, her gills, the translucent webbing between her fingers.

"So, what's it like?" said the captain.

"What—being trapped in a bucket? Cramped."

"No. Belonging to the sea. Riding the waves without decking between you and the salt water. Just letting the ocean flow through you."

"You look like the men," said Liaula, startled. "When I sing to them. You look like that."

"You didn't answer my question."

"What's it like to belong to the land?"

The captain toyed with her meal. "I suppose birds don't think about the sky, either."

Liaula tugged at the gold torque around her neck. "What does your king want me for?"

"What does any man want a woman for?" The captain's bitter smirk vanished almost as quickly as it appeared. "You're an embarrassment to him. Most of his sailors refuse to sail through this strait, thanks to legends of the Water Witch."

"So that's where all the males have gone," Liaula muttered.

"His Eminence holds title to my ship, and I hold captaincy on his sufferance. If he wants mermaids, he gets mermaids. Get ready to be presented to him. We land in two days."

Liaula's heart beat faster. Presented to the king. The most powerful of all the human males. Perhaps the storm goddess looked kindly upon her after all.

⨎

Onboard ship, Liaula had at least been able to feel the rolling of the sea through the layers of wood beneath her. The water in the glass tank in the king's palace felt still and dead. Even the captain, standing beside her in a dress uniform of glossy red silk brocade, looked stiff and lifeless in that golden hall.

Glittering courtiers lined the steps before the king's throne.

Some of the men looked strong and hearty enough to be promising, if only she weren't wearing this cursed collar. They shuffled their slippered feet and spoke in slightly-too-loud voices about anything but the tank and its inhabitant. Some, with sidelong glances at the captain, proclaimed the dangers of women at sea. The women sneered or whispered behind painted fans.

The king entered the hall, and all gossip ceased. He seated himself on his ebony throne, and Liaula cursed under her breath. This king, this supposedly powerful human, slumped in his gilded chair, sallow and weary-looking.

"Captain Tethys, what have you brought Us? Some sort of fish?"

Fish! Liaula slapped the water with her tail, drenching the captain's fine coat. The courtiers tittered. The king sat up straighter.

As though nothing had happened, the captain stepped forward and bowed. "Your Eminence, the Siren of the Eastern Strait will menace your fleet no more. I have brought her to you."

The king blinked. "Whatever for?"

"Majesty?" said the captain, taken aback. "You wanted her taken."

"I wanted you to stop it from menacing the trade lanes. What am I supposed to do with it? Women and their romantic notions… I don't even know what it eats."

"Ignorant human kings," said Liaula in a voice that carried throughout the hall. Courtiers gasped. A few swooned.

"So, it has a tongue. Interesting. Put it in the menagerie."

Several well-muscled young men began wrestling the tank onto a wheeled platform. Liaula wondered why none of them had fought the soft, lethargic king for the crown.

Captain Tethys had found her voice again. "Your Eminence, this is a siren! She knows where to find sailing routes we haven't discovered, fishing grounds, the lost ships of the Red Empress, sunken treasure—"

"Should've thought to bring some of that back with you. Sometimes, Captain, I think the *Melusine* would do better under a stronger hand."

"A man's hand, you mean," Liaula commented.

"Get that thing out of here!" The king thrust a pointing finger toward the door, and the young men strained to push their load from the room.

❧

Liaula had to give Captain Tethys credit for one thing: she'd never mistaken Liaula for a fish. Or a sea cow, or a walrus. Or anything that ate half-spoiled kitchen scraps that even a seagull would refuse. As though she were no different from the exotic birds who left their droppings throughout the menagerie, or the lethargic serpents and pacing wildcats in the cages.

And the captain's sailors may have spat at the base of that stupid barrel and made warding signs at her, but they'd never tried to bind her chest and dress her in cloth. The purse-faced maid who'd tried that was still nursing the scratches.

Men came to the menagerie, but although they gaped and goggled, none looked about to climb in the tank with her. That called for her song. Preening and flirting wasn't enough. And she could feel in her body that time was ebbing away. Soon she'd lose her chance to bear daughters.

Well, she had no song, but she still had a voice. Lifting herself above the water, she filled her lungs and released a siren's distress call, meant to be heard over thunder and gale. The birds exploded from the trees in a bright squawking cloud. Humans ran about with their hands clapped to their ears, trying to shut out the piercing cry. Liaula held the shrill note until she saw one person shouldering her way through the tide of people fleeing the room.

"Captain! How nice of you to visit."

"You scaled terror! Are you trying to deafen the palace?"

"I'd rather be singing, but you sank that notion. Actually, I'd rather be back in my home waters, and to the Abyss with this palace and everyone in it. Including your sorry excuse for a king."

"That's treason," said the captain, but without heat.

"I'm surprised you're here. Shouldn't you be back out on your ship by now?"

"His Majesty decided to give my first mate a turn at the helm. Figured he had a 'stronger hand'. The fool nearly scuppered the *Melusine*. Her figurehead's destroyed, she had to be recaulked… His Majesty graciously allowed me to take charge of what's left. Including letting me pay for the repairs myself, of course. It's taken this long to even get her near seaworthy again.

"Clumsy, frail things, ships."

"No doubt they seem so to a creature who's drawn so many to ruin."

Liaula shrugged.

"I don't suppose sirens have any magics that work directly on ships, rather than just beguiling their crews?"

"Why would we? We have our songs."

"That's all?"

"If we're truly trapped, we can turn our bodies, or our children's, to wood, and float by our enemies. Shark teeth still leave dents that way, but at least they don't come back for a second bite."

"Well, that's no help."

Liaula's tail stirred the water as a thought stirred her mind. "It could be. Captain, if I promised you enough treasure to make your ship as perfect as you want it, would you return me to the sea?"

"I won't give you my crew."

"Forget them. I want the ocean back more than I want your crew."

"Why should I trust you?"

"Because you're as much of a sea queen as a human can be," Liaula said and grimaced. "Besides, for both of us to leave here I'll have to trust you too."

❧

The *Melusine* bounded over the waves. Spray drenched the raw wood of its new figurehead. Liaula didn't feel it—or the pegs through her fins and hand-webbing that anchored her to the bowsprit. The voice of the sea reached her only as a muffled booming. Unable to clear the water from her wooden eyes, she couldn't see when the ship came to a halt.

Feeling returned soon after the captain pried Liaula's wooden body loose from the ship, and she tumbled into the water. Salt burned in her wounds. She hardly noticed, because as the rough caress of the ocean tumbled life back into her sight returned in glorious waves of blue and green. The pulse of the sea throbbed in her ears. From above came the shrill cry of a gull. No, that was the captain, swinging near the bowsprit in a rope harness and calling to her.

"You still in one piece, fishwife?" called the captain.

"Except for a few holes, yes. Now remove this collar."

"I never promised that! You have your freedom. I won't help you deprive men of theirs."

Liaula spat brine. "Then I might as well have stayed wood. I can never have daughters without a human man."

"Not my problem."

"Traitor! Enjoy your ship, captain. You won't have her much longer."

"What are you talking about, you spiteful sea-witch?"

"I can feel your king's ships in the water, coming fast. They'll be here soon. Pity you haven't got your full crew."

The captain cursed. "Already? He picked a fine time to care what happens to the *Melusine*. How many?"

"Two, I think. Is that a compliment to you, or an insult?"

The captain disappeared back aboard the *Melusine*. The king's gilded ships descended upon her like sharks, circling around her, tearing at her sides with cannon. Under the captain's hand the *Melusine* left scars along her enemies' planks and tore holes in their golden sails. From a prudent distance,

Liaula watched with grim admiration, wondering if the captain would manage to take one of her enemies down with the *Melusine*. Winning was impossible, with a handful of men and a half-patched ship, and judging from the woman's grim face, the captain knew that.

"Enjoying yourself, Siren?" she bellowed over the roar of cannon.

"Hardly! I swore to give you the means to make this toy of yours seaworthy, and you've half sunk it already. If you die, I'm left with your anchor of debt."

"You might consider helping, then!"

"You might consider what I could do if you took this collar off."

The captain stiffened as though Liaula had speared her. "You'll drown them."

"Never mind your human hair-splitting, Captain! You're trying to kill them anyway."

The captain dove into the water. The King's sailors cheered, clearly assuming she was abandoning ship. Judging from the cries of dismay from the *Melusine*, her sailors thought the same.

"It's not those rats I care about," said the captain, spitting salt water. "It's the innocents you'll bewitch after them."

"Would you rather waste time trying to protect every sailor on these waters, or save your own ship and crew? Which are sinking while we argue, I'll add."

With a curse worthy of an angry triton, the woman tore the collar from Liaula's neck. Liaula dove deep, and came up singing.

Captain Tethys' men didn't react, their ears doubtless stopped long since. Liaula smiled in reluctant admiration of the captain's foresight, and sang louder. The sailors on the King's ships let their weapons drop and their mouths hang slack. Liaula's song tempted, enticed, until bedazzled men leapt overboard to where she waited. She seized a suitably appealing, healthy-looking candidate and swam off.

Liaula returned to find the *Melusine* run aground on a shoal, her sails in tatters, one of her two attackers sunk, and the other sailing away from the wreckage as fast as a human ship could manage. Liaula, though, could keep pace with it and still have breath to sing. And sing she did. The king's ship slowed. Liaula heard thumping and scuffling from the deck. She stopped swimming to take a full breath. Her renewed song brought a thrashing knot of men to the rail. Liaula had never seen anything quite like that tangle of flailing arms and legs. The struggling mass pitched overboard and broke into two guards and Captain Tethys, furious and shouting. It took Liaula a moment to realize that the captain's hands and feet were bound together and the men tethered to her to prevent her from escaping. Now her guards were dragging her down.

The panicked men sank quickly once Liaula sawed through the ropes. Captain Tethys didn't protest, which told Liaula just how much danger the woman was in.

"You humans are so frail. Don't worry, Captain. The King's men will catch up soon and have you onboard and dried out. Chained up too, most likely, but you'll be alive. And less than a day's swim from where you left your ship you'll find a bright heap of sunken gold. There. My debt to you is paid."

The captain roused and groaned. "Might as well have let me go down with those two."

"What's the human response? Oh yes. Not my problem."

To Liaula's disappointment, the woman didn't rage at her. Instead, she smiled. "Let go."

"What?"

"Let go of me."

Startled, Liaula did. Delight flooded the captain's face.

"That's the way. No planks, no sails, just the sea. Look at that sky. Pity that ship's in the way."

Her voice had turned dreamy. Liaula had seen humans do this before, when the ocean's chill got into their bones.

"Did he have a ring on his left hand, Siren? That boy you drowned?"

"I don't know. Why?"

"Because that would mean he had a wife. A mate. Someone who loved him as you love the sea. Like I loved my ship. And you took him away from her. Every time you drown a sailor, remember that." The captain's blue lips parted in a smile. "Come on, codwife. Let's swim."

The captain dove underwater. Liaula followed, and saw a look of exquisite triumph cross her face before the cold hand of the ocean took hold of her human body. Her dive became a slow, languid sinking.

Liaula blazed with anger. How dare she! How dare this vibrant human woman act like a used-up mate? Liaula drove deep into the water, grasped a floating hand, and hauled the captain to the surface. A shout went up from the King's ship, and a net came down on their heads. Liaula gripped the captain tighter, her sense of touch fading as both her fingers and the arm she clutched became driftwood.

❧

Liaula hauled the captain's wooden body onto the sand near the *Melusine*. Next to it, she piled chains of gold, ropes of pearls, and pendants glinting with sapphire and emerald. She watched until the wood softened into flesh and the captain sat up, coughing. Then she turned away and flung herself into the sea. What the human did with herself was, as she'd said, not her problem. Liaula's duty was to bear sea queens, young sirens, not chase after humans. No matter how much those humans thought they belonged to the sea.

So Liaula sang a foreign queen's ship into range of the *Melusine* because it was convenient, not because of any concern for the human captain in the wreckage.

She left the newcomer's crew untouched because she was already sated, not so they could rescue a bedraggled castaway.

And when her daughters grew apace and swam away within the year, as a siren's offspring always do, there was no particular reason for her to be watching when the foreign queen's men came to salvage what remained of the *Melusine*. No reason for her to be watching again when the reborn ship, christened the Sea Queen, sailed through her strait. No reason for its captain to tip her hat to the waves, and no reason for Liaula to feel a warm glow of pride.

No reason at all.

AFTERLIFE

Downstairs, Upstairs

Working for the Almighty is no piece of cake. Even the Upstairs guys have it tough, working 24/7 for Eternity. The Downstairs folks have the same hours, plus the sweltering working environment to deal with. You'd think after all this time somebody could've rigged up a few A/C units in the back rooms, but they keep melting. So we get the same heat as the Flimsies. (That's what we call the souls in the pits and so on. I'll get to that in a minute.) It doesn't bother us like it bothers them, but it's still not comfy.

Anyway, it's tough Downstairs even if you're a boss. Me, I was so low on the totem pole you'd have to drill down into bedrock to see my spot. Stoking fires, polishing the spikes, stirring up the brimstone to get the rotten-egg smell that makes the place really Hellish—that kind of thing.

Even Downstairs, we're all still working for God. And we do the job right.

I didn't have much to do with the Flimsies. The bosses handle that stuff. They're trained to deal with complexes and projection and that kind of thing. What it all boils down to is that the Flimsies are the bits of souls that still believe they need to keep being punished. When a boss explained it to me, I couldn't believe it. I mean, we've got Flimsies downstairs who've been boiling themselves in brimstone ever since "cutting edge technology" meant a stone axe, and they only lived for 35 years or so to begin with. You'd think there'd be a statute of limitations or something.

Anyway, I was freshening up a decorative bloodstain when I met Bubbles. That's what I called her, 'cause every inch of her was covered with blisters. Wading in lava will do that. She was crying, and when she saw me she cried harder, like she was trying to make a point.

"There's a flat spot right here," I offered, pointing. "In case you want to climb out."

"I can't."

"Why not?"

"Because this is the Eternal Fires of Torment! They're not so eternal if you can just climb out of them."

"Sure they are. The fire's still there. You're just not standing in it."

She looked at me like I was nuts and started to sob and scream again. But after that she started following me with her eyes. Then she forgot to scream while she was watching. I always waved 'Hi', and after a bit she started waving back.

One day she said 'Hi' first. That was big. She started talking after that, first asking me stuff about Downstairs and so on, then telling me about things like where she used to live, back when she was living. About her friends. Then it all kind of flooded out. How she got jealous of a friend, and told lies about her so that the friend's husband left her and she lost her job... By the time Bubbles finished she was crying again—not like she wanted to prove something, but like she couldn't stop.

She did though, eventually, and I said "So why are you here?"

She stared at me like I was nuts, just like before. "I just told you!"

"No— I mean, is your friend in there with you?"

"No!"

"Well, if you think you're being punished because you owe her an apology, why aren't you somewhere else looking for her?"

Bubbles stared. Then she laughed. Then she climbed out onto the flat spot to hug me and laughed some more.

A couple of bosses came running. One wrapped her, very gently, in something super-soft, and led her off to show her the path to Upstairs. The other clapped me on the back and told me "great job" and said I had a real knack with the Flimsies.

So now I'm taking classes to learn how to help guide the Flimsies out of their torments. Most of the time it's not as simple as talking to Bubbles, but the bosses tell me that if I keep at it I might get a job Upstairs someday.

'Course, everybody says that's a whole new kind of hard work. But nobody ever said that working for the Almighty would be easy.

The Mighty Quill

It seemed I walked through a cold fog, until at last I found myself in a land of red sand and broken white pillars. The light had no source, and the air had no scent. As I walked, memory returned.

Scrivi was gone. My home. Only two people had survived the massacre. I was not one of them. One was hawk-nosed Daro, who struck down my father in his own hall. The other was Erana, his wife, who killed my mother as she sat nursing my brother, and then dashed the babe against our hearth.

I was the last to die. I saw it all from where I crouched in the chimney corner, until Erana dragged me out by my hair and slit my throat. When I woke to myself, I felt as though I had been walking in the red land forever.

"Alas, alas for Scrivi," a voice chanted. "Alas, for all are slain and the land is burned."

I turned around, quickly. I had thought myself alone. But behind me, on the empty sand, loomed a figure robed in blue and purple. Though his hair was white and his face lined, he stood straight, face lifted to the pale sky. In his hands he held a large book.

"Alas for Scrivi," he chanted again. "Her tale is told, her chapter ended."

With that, he shut the book and stood in silence, with his head bowed. I knew who he was now, unbelievable though it seemed.

"Muro, god of Justice!" I called. He did not move. I came closer. Though I am tall for a woman, I barely came up to his knees. I called again, but he never moved. Greatly daring, I tugged his robe, as a child might. His eyes opened, and he looked down at me.

"Why are you here, daughter of Scrivi?" he said kindly. "Go with the rest of your village, to the High City." He pointed through what seemed to be an empty space between two pillars.

"But what of Scrivi, Lord Justice?" I pleaded. "If all of us were killed, then everyone who lived there and all we did will be forgotten! Worse yet, who knows what lies Daro and Erana will spread?" I was shaking with fury, and even in the presence of a god, I could not stop my tears of rage. "Why should the usurpers live, when you know they murdered us all?"

I have heard it said, in this land, that justice is blind. Let me tell you now that he is not blind, but deaf.

"Why are you crying, my dear?" Muro asked. "It's all right. You have earned your place in the High City. Go on, there is nothing to be afraid of."

With nothing else to do, I turned to walk through the pillars. As I neared them, a wall of flame roared up, fierce and crackling. I leapt back from the heat and glared back at Muro. He seemed to be sleeping, with his head sunk on his chest. From off to the side I heard a cackling laugh.

I turned and blinked. I wasn't sure I'd seen anything at first. Then a shape resolved itself out of the air, transparent. A figure of glass, in a cloak of feathers. Strong and slender, with a mocking smile.

"Burn yourself, did you?" he said.

I've since heard that in other lands the Lord of Deception often takes dog-forms: coyotes, jackals, and foxes. Scrivi knew him best in his bird-forms—those that haunt the battlefields, those that leave their own eggs in other nests. I knew better than to trust him in any guise.

"Raxi, Lord of Deception." I greeted him coldly. My fear must have been left behind with my body. I never would have been so cool to a god, alive. "Is this one of your jokes?"

The transparent figure quirked an eyebrow at me. "Joke? You're dead, your home is a drift of ash. Do you find this funny?"

"Of course not! But you might. I know the tales. You're always laughing when mortals hurt."

"Am I laughing? And who has been hurt?"

"All of Scrivi! Or have even the gods forgotten us already?"

"Hardly! Everyone from your village is in the High City, just like Muro said. Having a wonderful time. Endless feasts, glorious music, eternal bliss. You know."

"No, I *don't* know! I'm certainly not going to believe it because you tell me. And there's nothing between those pillars but fire. You saw it!"

"That's your hot temper talking. Of course, you've just been murdered, so I can't really blame you."

"Not just me—all of us! And He—" I jabbed a finger toward the slumbering Lord Muro, "didn't do a thing! I thought he was supposed to be the Lord of Justice!"

"Oh, he is." Raxi chuckled. "And from his point of view justice was done centuries ago. While we've been—chatting—hundreds of years have gone by. Your killers—and a few generations of their descendants—are long gone. The land they killed to rule is empty. The people of Scrivi have gone to their eternal reward, and Justice can rest." Raxi pointed to Muro. "Except you, of course. That's why he's snoring. You're disturbing his sleep, you ungrateful girl."

The hot anger was draining out of me, leaving a cold hollowness. No, I wouldn't cry. "But that's not justice. That's just forgetting. Now no one will remember that old Pandrin always rang the Temple bells at Midsummer, or how *someone* put snuff in the priest's incense, or…"

Raxi laughed heartily. I jumped.

"I remember the snuff. All fourteen acolytes were sneezing too, I believe. And during a baptism *oh dear*. I believe *someone* deserves a token of my gratitude for that wonderful bit of mischief."

I didn't have time to speak. Raxi crouched, flung up his cloak, and suddenly he was a white raven, bigger than a horse. The downdraft from his wings flung me to the sand. His talons gripped what would have been my shoulders, if I'd had a body. Though if I had, those talons surely would have drawn blood. The Lord of Deception beat his wings, and we hung in midair while the world spun around us in a storm of white and red.

The red turned to gray, and the whirling slowed to a halt. My feet hit the ground with a very solid thump, and the ground was stone hard. Noise beat against my ears, and I felt an answering pulse within.

Raxi still towered behind me. We stood on a hard flat path, and stone cliffs—no, *buildings*—towered all around us. Faces stared from windows, from all around us, even from wheeled boxes that whizzed past in an eyeblink. So many people, and so much noise!

"They'll notice us in a minute." Raxi croaked. "Well, they'll notice you. They won't see me. A thirty foot white raven attracts too much attention, even in this city."

"I'm alive!" That was as much as I could grasp at the moment. "But this isn't Scrivi."

"I told you, Scrivi is long gone." If ravens could laugh, he was doing it. "Welcome to America, my girl. Twentieth, maybe twenty-first century, by their calendar. One of their big cities. Don't ask me which. They're all just crowded and smelly to me."

"Is this one of your jokes?"

"The best yet! But I did promise you a token. Here."

He plucked one of his smaller wing feathers (only about a foot long), dropped it at my feet, and vanished.

The new world roared past me, uncaring. I stood alone on that strange hard ground with nothing but a feather, its tip sharp as a blade.

I'm sure Raxi thought I would despair, and use his quill to escape this terrifying second life. But I'd been given a chance, and I wouldn't throw it away to amuse the Deceiver.

I've turned the joke on him. I sold my jewelry to an antiques dealer for enough to live on while I learned the language and ways of this new world. I've found work cataloging items for a small museum. The visitors are impressed by how much I know about what they call "ancient artifacts." To myself, I call them Pandrin's favorite cap, my brother's cradle.

Some days I dare to wonder if Muro put these things here for me to find. Other days I scorn such foolishness.

Each night, I use Raxi's quill to write the stories of Scrivi. Even if it has no special power about it, there's satisfaction in using the Lord of Deception's feather to keep Scrivi alive. Someday others will read my tales. Most won't believe they are true, but at least we won't be forgotten.

I have been here for many, many years now. Soon I will stand before Muro, on the red sand, for the second and last time. I have no doubt that Raxi will come to watch.

Who will be laughing then, I wonder?

Second Judgment

I never saw the taxi. I never even felt the impact. One minute I was halfway through the crosswalk, and the next I sprawled in red sand.

I'd been walking past the Tandoori Palace, savoring the aroma of onions and coriander. Now the air was empty. No scent at all, not even car exhaust. I remembered this nothingness.

"Wonderful. I'm dead. Again."

I lay there a moment, grit clenched in my fists, my eyes closed. I didn't want to open them, for to acknowledge that glimpse of red sand meant realizing that I really was dead, this time for good.

"Welcome home," drawled a voice I'd hoped to forget.

I sighed. No point in keeping my eyes closed now. I opened them, taking in red sand, white pillars, and the looming, transparent figure of a man in a feather cloak.

"Raxi."

The Lord of Illusion bowed. "If you've finished your nap, Lord Muro is waiting for you."

"Expected me back sooner, did you?" I watched the god wipe the flash of irritation from his face and grinned.

"You've gotten flippant, my girl," he muttered. He marched over the sand, and I followed. I had nowhere else to go.

Muro, God of Justice, had been sleeping the last time I saw him. This time he turned as I approached. Though I was no longer a girl, I still stood barely level with his knees.

"And where did you come from, my dear?" He fixed his distant gaze on me for a moment. "You look rather familiar."

"Third Avenue… I mean, Scrivi… I mean…" I stammered to a halt. Behind me, Raxi chuckled.

Muro leaned over and peered into my face. "You look like a Scrivi girl," he murmured. "Odd. I thought that whole village passed through a few centuries ago. Never mind. You're welcome to go where you wish. Scrivi's corner is through those pillars." He pointed.

I hesitated. The last time I'd approached those pillars, they'd blazed up in flame. I'd never figured out if it was Raxi's mischief that caused it, or my own rage at seeing my village massacred. Raxi laughed.

"What, two lives weren't enough for you? You won't get another from me."

I straightened. Raxi had expected me to despair once before, and I hadn't. I'd tricked the God of Deception himself. Smiling, I marched between the pillars.

Red sand became green grass. I could smell the grass… and the wood smoke rising from the chimneys. In a valley below me, just as though it had never burned, lay Scrivi.

My hometown had never looked so bright, so perfect. The silver arc of the river cradled emerald fields. I picked out the low, sloping shape of the Headman's house, the beehive dome of the temple, even the draggle-crowned willow tree I'd played in as a child. I started to run downhill, and then stopped short.

Each house had flowers in the window.

When I was alive, there were no flowers in Scrivi's houses, unless we brought a handful of daisies and goldenrod in from the meadow. We had no time, and no space, to grow anything but vegetables, grain… necessary crops. While I stood wondering, someone came up the river path toward me. A tiny, wrinkled man, hobbling on two canes. His indigo robe dragged on the ground. He stopped to hitch it up, saw me, and broke into a delighted smile.

"Renata!" he called. Twice. I no longer recognized my former name.

"Pandrin?" The little man's smile widened.

"Where have you been? My, you've grown! Your mother will be so excited. Come on, child, this way."

He herded me into the village, calling at the top of his reedy voice. People poured from the houses. My mother threw her arms around me, kissing, scolding, and crying. When she let go for a moment, my father wrapped me in a hug. A boy with my father's dark eyes and my mother's curls clung to my leg.

"Johann's grown since you left," my mother said, her voice quavering slightly.

"But how can he have?" I stared at my baby brother—a baby no longer. "We all died!"

Complete silence fell. No one, even little Johann, met my eyes.

"We've been here…forever," said my father.

"Do I look dead?" asked my mother.

"*You* went away." Johann turned away, pouting.

That was the beginning. At first, it was bliss. I forgot the lost years, wrapped safely in the cocoon of my old home. Then I found myself looking for a telephone to call my best friend Liz, or waking up ready to go to work at the museum, only to find myself starting another identical, perfect day in Scrivi. Realizing that nothing I did here mattered.

I spent more and more time by the river. Only the river felt right, flowing past me to somewhere just out of sight. Moving, Changing.

"But where does it go?" I wondered aloud.

"You know, no one else has asked that."

I jumped. Raxi leaned against the trunk of the willow, the beginnings of a mocking smile glittering in his eyes.

"Well, I'm asking. It should empty into the Atlantic, eventually…but are there oceans here? Is America out there somewhere?"

"Of course. Not in the way you're thinking, though. Would you like to see?"

Raxi, being civil, even kind? This was wrong. Still, I wanted to know.

I followed him to the riverbank, where a raft bobbed in the shallows. He handed me aboard with exaggerated courtesy and poled the raft into the center of the gentle current.

"Watch the shore," he said. I watched. At first, I saw nothing but birches and willows, fields and the occasional stray sheep.

Then the grass began to turn gray. Not winter-brown. Gray, like ashes or trampled snow. The trees faded. The water beneath us turned terra cotta, then rusty, and suddenly we were standing ankle-deep in red sand, studded with broken pillars.

"America… America… Third Avenue, you said?" Raxi pointed toward one pair of columns. "Try that one."

I stepped through.

❧

Blaring traffic. Neon and billboards. Coriander. He'd dropped me right in front of the Tandoori Palace! I rushed inside, and the little old woman behind the counter looked up with a smile.

"Rita, dear! Where have you been? Sit down. Have lunch. You look like you need it. And I haven't seen you in weeks!"

"It's been a while," I murmured. Years, in fact. Nana had died only two years after I met her. Now she kept her eagle eye on me, making sure I did justice to a plateful of her lamb biryani while she clucked her tongue over my stained, sandy tunic.

"Such an outfit! Have you been to a costume party? Do you good, to get out of that dusty museum."

I let her ramble on, while the food made a cold lump in my stomach. No, I didn't know if my computer was fixed yet. I hadn't gone to the movies last weekend.

Last weekend I… well, I hadn't needed to keep track of weekends. The river flowed the same way on Saturday or Monday. And nothing I did, or didn't do, mattered. I could leave and come back a day from now, or a year, and Nana would have no idea how long I'd been gone.

I left the Tandoori Palace feeling more lost than ever. "Out of sync," they'd call it here. "Off my rhythm," they'd call it in Scrivi. It wasn't the place that was wrong. It was me. As Renata or Rita, I didn't fit in either world now.

"Nothing like coming home again, is there?" Raxi, lounging against a street sign, looked up and winked at me. I ignored him. He shifted to bird form.

"Didn't you once tell me that thirty foot tall white ravens in a city attract too much attention?" I snapped.

"In living worlds, certainly. This realm is mine. I come and go as I please. You, on the other hand, have no way out of this world. Unless you come to me for help, of course."

"I don't want your help."

"But you need it."

I ignored him and kept on walking. Like a mouse with a hawk shadowing it, I moved in furtive steps, shooting glances first one way, then another, looking for a trace of red sand, a shift in the air, something that marked a boundary between this Afterworld and the others. Reality stayed frustratingly solid.

"Face it, my dear. You're human. Less than that. You're a former human. One world, one life—well, in your case, two—is all you get. Shall I take you home now? Or haven't you decided where that is?"

"Get lost, O Lord of Deception."

"Impossible. Remember, I belong here." Still, he swept a mocking bow with one enormous wing and vanished. To plot more mischief, no doubt.

Once he was gone, I grinned and jumped feet-first into the rain gutter. I was wearing sandals, and the water felt clammy and gritty, but it flowed in the same rhythmic swirls as the river near Scrivi. I sloshed downstream. People turned to stare. My ankles went numb. I began to wonder if I was crazy. Humans only got one life, one world.

Except me. And Lord Muro had said I could go where I wished. I slogged on.

The noise of traffic began to lessen. The water turned warmer, pinker, and became crimson sand.

I took a deep breath of scentless air and laughed.

❧

The girl shivered in the red desert. She looked back at the slumbering form of Muro, God of Justice, then at the cracked pillars in front of her. She took a step forward and walked into a wall of ice.

"Not much of a doorway to Paradise, is it?" said Raxi. The girl jumped.

For a fraction of a second, I felt sorry for the Lord of Deception, lounging against a pillar in his most alluring human form. Was this how he spent all of Eternity, waiting for new innocents to beguile and trick? Then I looked at the girl again, and my sympathy vanished. I stepped out onto the sand.

"That's because she needs a guide," I said. I smiled at the girl. "I'm the Welcomer, and I've seen your home. In the American Adirondacks, right?"

The girl nodded, and sniffled. "But he—" she pointed at the still-sleeping Lord Muro, "said I'm dead!"

"I'm afraid he's right. But your home is here. Everyone's is, even mine. I'll take you there, and we'll see if we can find someone you know. All right?"

I held out a hand, and she clutched it. As we approached the pillars, the ice melted, and a scent of earth and pine wafted toward us. Raxi's jaw dropped.

"You can't do this!" he shouted, all the music in his voice cracking. "How…?"

I smiled sweetly. "Practice. Now, if you'll excuse us? I'll be back. I just need to take this young lady home."

To Rest

Ava stared into her teacup. She hadn't meant to break her lunch date with Lisa. She just couldn't bear any more talk about baby names, the perfect shade to paint the nursery, and what a wonderful godmother Ava would be. So she passed Lisa's house and kept on driving.

Leaving town hadn't helped. All around her, other people sat at the café's tiny sidewalk tables, enjoying the sun. People with babies and toddlers, children and teens. Across the street a crumbling brick building, a school or something, with an adjoining cemetery, filled her vision, confronting her with far too many tiny headstones behind its iron gate. Turning away only meant facing the same view, reflected in the café's window. The tea reflected clouds and bright sky, a wavering glimpse of Heaven.

The sunlight made her eyes water. It had been a sunny day like this ten years ago when she'd stopped on some urgent errand that she couldn't even remember now, leaving three-month-old Abby strapped safely into her car seat. In the 15-minute parking, with the car window opened what she thought was the perfect amount. Too small to let a kidnapper's hand in.

Too small to let baking-hot air out.

Her neck was getting stiff. She raised her head to see a boy wandering along the sidewalk. No one spoke to him, or even reacted when he leaned over diners' shoulders to examine their newspapers or their lunches. His ramblings brought him steadily toward Ava, the way cats seem to gravitate toward the one person in the room who's allergic to them.

He looked maybe eight years old. Or ten. His expression looked older, though. Skinny kid. And was that a nightgown he was wearing? He was barefoot, sickly-pale, and as far as Ava could see, utterly alone.

Ava slipped out her cell phone and opened it. If she could

get a picture she could run a match to see if anyone was looking for the boy. Easy enough to upload a picture to some official alert site. No fuss, no questions from the police. Just a quick call, before the kid got hurt, or worse.

The boy froze as though she'd pulled a gun on him. He sidestepped out of the picture. She refocused.

He turned and bolted into the street.

"No!" Ava screamed. She cringed, expecting to hear the thud of flesh against fender. Traffic screeched to a stop. But when Ava looked up, shaking, no body lay in the road. The boy was gone. Not so much as a fender-bender, although one driver made a pointed gesture at her and drove off, leaving behind a taint of burnt rubber and profanity. The other diners stared at her.

Blushing and apologizing, Ava paid her bill, left double her usual tip, and hurried back to her hotel room to spend the rest of the afternoon and night hearing the echo of shrieking brakes in her mind. When she closed her eyes, she saw that pale face.

Ghost-pale.

Nonsense.

Bedsides, she already had her own ghost, tiny, yet filling her whole heart. She had no room for any more lost souls.

Ava swore she'd never go near that cafe again.

❧

She came back before breakfast. The shop was closed, but the boy was there, standing by the table she'd abandoned the day before.

"You saw me, yesterday," he said.

He looked unhurt and less shaken than Ava, who felt ready to explode from sleepless anxiety.

"I thought I saw you get killed! What were you doing? Didn't your mother ever tell you not to run out into traffic?"

Her outburst didn't frighten him. In fact, he nearly smiled. "No, ma'am."

"Well, she ought to…" Ava clamped her mouth shut. As

though she had any right to judge what this boy's mother ought to do. "Is that a nightgown you're wearing?"

He drew himself up indignantly. "It's a nightSHIRT. I'm twelve, not a baby."

Twelve? A pretty scrawny twelve. Poor kid. Probably hadn't had a decent meal in ages. Amazing what some people got away with where kids were concerned.

"Where are your mom and dad? Do they know you're running around town barefoot in a nightgo… nightshirt?"

"They're dead." He locked eyes with her, daring her to say something. Before she could open her mouth, her cellphone rang. Lisa.

Ava expected the boy to run away while she apologized for not showing up and assured Lisa that really, she was fine. He didn't. He stood watching her, his expression rapt.

"It's like magic," he said when she signed off. "How far away were they—the person you were talking to?"

"Ten miles, maybe twenty. You haven't got a cellphone?"

He shook his head.

"Well, you're twelve. I might not've let Abby have one either, if… when she got to be twelve." She choked on her daughter's name and glared at the boy as though he'd tricked her into saying it aloud. "What's your name?"

"Caleb." He was giving her that look again, sizing her up. Looking for something, but she couldn't tell what. Ava suppressed an urge to squirm.

"How far away can you talk to people?" he said.

"Depends on the reception. What's your last name?"

He looked down, suddenly enthralled by a crack on the sidewalk. "Don't have one."

"Come on; everyone has a last name. What's yours?"

"Ward," he said after a moment. "Who's Abby?"

Was he paying her back for insisting on knowing his last name? "My daughter," she said, typing "Caleb Ward" into her Search function. "My baby girl."

No alerts. No record of anyone like him at all. Of course, he'd probably lied.

"Where is she?"

Sadistic little urchin. "She died."

"Oh." After a long, thoughtful pause he said, "I'm sorry."

"Me too."

"Do you love her anyway?"

Ava flinched as though he'd punched her. "Of course I do! Did. What kind of question is that? Just leave me alone!"

And he did. No screeching brakes this time. She turned away to dry her eyes, and when she turned back, he was simply gone.

ঌ

Part of her hoped the boy wouldn't be there the next morning, but he was. Waiting for her. Ava sat down at the little metal table.

"I know what you are."

He looked startled. "You do?"

"Yep. You're a projection. I read up on it. I'm only seeing you because I'm missing Abby. That explains it."

Although it didn't explain why her subconscious had conjured up a male street urchin who looked like Wee Willie Winkie. And even if ghosts aged, Abby wouldn't be twelve now, only ten. Ten and three months.

"I suppose that could be why. Nobody else sees me." Caleb looked thoughtful. "Is a projection the same thing as a ghost?"

"There's no such thing as ghosts," said Ava, more harshly than she'd intended. She scooted her chair away from him. "Besides, it's broad daylight."

Caleb didn't blush, but he ducked his head, obviously mortified. "I'm scared of the dark. I always made Nurse Summers leave a lamp burning. The other boys hated it."

Ava choked on a laugh. "Kid, you're priceless."

He edged closer, reached out a hand.

"Don't touch me!"

"Why not? I won't hurt you. I promise."

"Because…Just don't."

His hand fell to his side. "You're the only person who's seen me, and you don't even like me."

"Look, it's nothing personal. I'm just not good with kids. Really. I mean it. Go away."

"I'll have to come back. I'm sorry. I can't help it."

"Why won't you leave me alone? If I have to be haunted, why not by my own little girl? I'm sorry. I said I was sorry. Over and over again, I said it. I'm sorry, Abby, sweetheart…"

The boy touched her. Just a quick, cool, light touch, like a barely-felt breeze. Just enough to make her look up, notice a few early customers eyeing her uneasily, and follow the strange boy. She staggered across the street and clung to the cemetery gate. The onlookers, satisfied that she was a harmless, grieving mourner, went back to their business.

"I didn't mean to make you cry," said Caleb. "You could see me, that's all. Everyone else is gone. I'm the only one left, and you're the only person who's seen me."

"What do you mean, 'The only one left'?"

He pointed at the brick building. "Come inside. Please. Maybe you can find out what happened."

"That's trespassing! I haven't gotten so much as a traffic ticket in a decade, and now I'm supposed to start breaking and entering?"

"You won't break anything."

"I won't enter anything, either."

"I'll have to come back. Every day. Everywhere you go. I didn't even know you'd be here today, but I had to come. Even when I tried walking the other way, I still ended up by your table."

"Her" table. And so had she, even though she never wanted to see the place again. Ava shuddered. If she drove back home, would something drag her back here tomorrow? Back to the tiny headstones, over and over, for the rest of her life?

"Let's get it over with, then." She trudged down the sidewalk to the gate. A blue historical marker declared the building to be the Woodside Children's Home.

"Abandoned following the influenza epidemic of 1899," Ava read aloud.

"You won't get sick now," Caleb assured her from the other side of the gate. "There's nobody else left."

Ava had a harder time getting across. Caleb showed her a secluded corner with a gap in the fence, and she emerged muddied and scraped, with a tear in her blouse.

The back door, boarded over but half crumbled from dry rot, was easier to get through. Ava stepped carefully over the dusty floor, expecting a foot to plunge through the decayed boards at any moment. Caleb led her to a room lined with iron bedsteads and crumbling mattresses.

"This is the dormitory." His voice trembled. "Can you see anybody? Henry or Clyde or Nurse Summers? Even Nurse Groth?"

Ava looked around the empty room. Cobwebs, peeling paint, but no other pale, nightshirted figures. "There's no one here, Caleb."

He urged her through the parlor, kitchen, dining hall… Last of all, he came to a smaller room with a washstand and a single bed in it. "That's the infirmary. You won't find anybody else there."

A scrap of white cloth, like Caleb's nightshirt, caught her eye. "Wait, I think there's something in the b… Oh God."

Ava turned and fled with her hand to her mouth.

"I told you I wouldn't hurt you!" Caleb called. "I promised!"

Ava didn't listen. She didn't stop running until she was out of that building and heaving lungfuls of clean air. And when she looked up, Caleb was standing in front of her.

"I told you there was nobody else there. Just me."

Ava forced herself to look at his pale, hurt face without seeing the desiccated thing on the bed.

"There was no one else left, was there? They fled and left you alone."

"But they should be here now! We should all be… all be the same by now. Where is everyone?"

Ava swallowed. "I think somebody needs to… to lay you to rest. I'll find someone." She laughed a shaky laugh. "Maybe you can even help pick out your own spot. How many people get to do that?"

"No! Please don't go. It'll be dark. And if it doesn't work, I'll be alone in the dark forever."

He was crying. Which was nonsense, Ava reminded herself. That… that thing she'd seen hadn't cried for over a century. She was trespassing. The last thing she needed was a visit from the police. All she had to do was turn and walk away.

Like she'd done on a bright summer day ten years ago.

"I'll stay. But I can't do this alone," she said and dialed Lisa's number with shaking hands.

Lisa came. She brought a shovel. And gloves and a clean sheet, which Ava hadn't thought to ask for. And she got through the fence and out of sight from the road before demanding to know what was going on.

"Good thing I'm not showing yet," she laughed. "Ava, what on Earth are you up to?"

Ava had meant to tell her a few bare facts, maybe even some lie about a vow to a distant relative. But with Caleb's eyes on her it all poured out. About Caleb. About Abby. The jail time, the therapy, the nightmares, the guilt. And when it was done she just stood there, waiting for her friend to turn and walk away.

"So that's why you didn't show up," said Lisa after a moment.

"Yes. And I understand if you think I'm nuts, if you don't want to talk to me after this, if you won't want me around the baby, but I swear I didn't mean to."

Lisa held out her arms, and Ava sobbed on her friend's shoulder.

"This explains so much," said Lisa. "No wonder you're seeing little kid ghosts. Let's get you home."

"No!" said Ava and Caleb at the same time.

"I can't abandon Caleb," said Ava. Lisa's brow furrowed, but she followed Ava to the infirmary.

"Oh, the poor thing," she said.

"I'm not a poor thing," Caleb muttered. "I'm just dead."

Ava kept her eye on him while Lisa, matter-of-fact as always, made a bundle with the sheet.

❧

"Do you have a favorite spot, Caleb?" said Ava when they were outside again.

Caleb stared at the grass and refused to answer.

"What did he say?" To Ava's gratitude, Lisa sounded perfectly serious.

"He won't talk to me. C'mon, Caleb. Please?"

"Great. A ghost with the sulks." Lisa sat down on a nearby bench, the shrouded bundle at her feet.

"I'm not sulking! I'm scared."

Ava took a deep breath. "Caleb, you heard what I said to Lisa? About Abby?"

He nodded.

"I understand if you can't trust me."

"You didn't mean it. I just don't want to be alone. I want to stay with you."

Ava choked.

"Ava?" said Lisa. "Are you okay?"

Ava nodded fiercely. "Caleb, it means so much that you trust me, that you'd want to stay with me, but…" Her voice cracked.

Lisa stood up. "Listen, kiddo, I can't see you. I can't hear you. But if you can hear me, and if you care so much about Ava, you could do her a mighty big favor by bringing Abby a message from her mom."

Caleb wouldn't look at Lisa, or the shovel she carried, but he edged closer to Ava.

"Will you stay until we're sure it worked?"

Ava nodded. "I won't leave until I know you're not alone."

Lisa raised an eyebrow and mouthed, "How would we know?" but Ava gestured for her to hush.

With a resigned look on his face, Caleb led them to an apple tree in the back corner of the yard. "Here. Nurse Summers used to say I ate so many apples I'd turn into an apple tree."

Ava dug until her palms stung and she couldn't tell if the wetness on her face was tears or sweat. Lisa laid the sheet-wrapped bundle in the hole and hefted a spadeful of dirt.

"I'll do this part, Ava. You say goodbye to the kiddo."

"Should you be doing that? In your condition?"

"Ava," said Lisa with a smile, "you worry about your little fellow, and I'll worry about mine."

"He's not mine," said Ava, but she glanced at Caleb and said, "If you're sure, I'll sit with him while you finish."

"Wait!" said Caleb. "Not yet. It's going to get dark. Maybe we should do it tomorrow."

Ava sat down, took out her cell phone, and flipped it open. "See? Lighted display." She held it out. "Lisa, put this in, would you? With the light on."

"You aren't seriously going to bury a perfectly good phone, are you?"

"Please. For Abby."

Lisa sighed, but settled the lighted phone gently atop the sheet. Ava motioned for Caleb to sit next to her, and after a moment's hesitation, put her arm around him. He laid his head in her shoulder. It felt as though she leaned against a cool feather pillow.

"Is it all right if I don't watch?"

"Of course, Caleb."

The dirt parted grittily beneath the shovel, fell with a muffled thud. Ava felt Caleb shiver. Lullabies she thought she'd forgotten came from her throat, lessening the relentless dull thumps.

"I'll tell Abby you're a good mom," said Caleb. His eyes closed. Ava finished the verse and looked up to see Lisa leaning on the shovel.

Ava looked from her to the sleeping boy on her lap. "But… It should have…"

"Ava? We should get out of here."

Ava's eyes stung. She kissed the pale forehead. "I'm sorry, sweetheart."

The boy in her arms smiled and murmured something. She prayed that it really was, "Hi, Abby." He vanished. Ava scrambled to her feet and picked up the shovel. The way her knees were wobbling, she needed something to lean on.

"You ok, Ava?"

"I will be. And so will Caleb."

"Where is he?"

"Gone. But at least he's got a light. And a new friend. I'm sure of it." Ava started walking. "Lisa? Let me tell you about my daughter."

The Last Passenger

The skiff had almost forgotten its purpose. Once, souls had crowded aboard, leaving threads of their fraying selves behind to melt into the boat that ferried them to the Underworld.

Those tattered fragments of identity had awakened an awareness in the skiff. It sensed flowing water, charged with powers it couldn't understand. Banks that bounded its world. The faint shifting weight of passengers. The heavy tread of the old man who poled the boat back and forth.

Through many centuries and souls, the man became Charon, strong-armed and quick-tempered. If a soul tried to enter the skiff without paying, Charon heaved them overboard with his pole. It made the boat feel protected.

Now, though, no shades had come for centuries. So the boat felt Charon's surprised jolt at spotting the shining figure on the shore. The boat had never known its Boatman to be surprised. Sullen, fierce, but never surprised. They poled closer.

"Hail, Hermes Psychopomp," the old man grumbled.

"Well, there's the thing…" The newcomer, a young man wearing a winged cap and sandals, boarded without offering a coin, or even awaiting a nod from Charon. To the skiff's astonishment, the Ferryman didn't throw him overboard, just stood at rigid attention,

"About the psychopomp business," the young man said, stretching out and throwing an arm across the gunwhale, "It's hard to be a Conductor of Souls without souls to conduct. Business has fallen off. Surely you've noticed?"

"One soul or hundreds, I won't leave my post."

"That's why I like you, Charon. You're dedicated. Evenhanded. Reliable to the last." Hermes straightened. His expression turned grave. "And trust me, Charon, you are the last. Mankind has found new gods. The Olympians have retired to their Mount." His cheerful smile returned. "So I've come to collect you before you miss all the fun."

"Why should I believe you, god of thieves and tricksters?"

"Because I'm also god of crossroads and boundaries, and we're at one. Even the Underworld's rivers are changing. Soon you'll simply fade, and your faithful boat will crumble to splinters." Hermes patted the gunwale, and the skiff's patchwork consciousness unified and expanded. It remembered being a tree, standing tall and proud in a flowered meadow, sunlight pouring onto its leaves. The axe's bite. Charon's first ponderous tread upon its resinous planks. His strong hands deftly patching cracks. His steady guidance, never letting the skiff's keel scrape in the shallows.

And now the skiff felt yearning. For their journey to continue, carrying souls and heroes. And irreverent young trickster gods like the one grinning in its bow.

"Olympus," Charon grunted. "Marble and peacocks, feather-beds with everyone and their brother jumping in and out… No. I've a job to do."

"But you don't! That's the point. If not to Olympus, the whole Afterlife's available. Even the Elysian Fields."

Charon grunted.

"Or the Asphodel Meadows. You can even sulk in Tartarus if you want. But go somewhere, or you'll fade."

For the first time the skiff could remember, Charon sat down. "I swore by the Styx. I remember my oaths. I won't leave my ship."

"Ship?" Hermes ran a hand along the gunwale. Something sparked and trickled through the ancient wood. "Bit of an overstatement, that."

"It does the job," said Charon. "As do I."

"Stubborn. Fine. Let me off. I can't force you." One of the god's long-fingered hands trailed idly in the water no shade could touch.

Charon poled to shore. Hermes, Conductor of Souls, leapt out alone.

"Travel well, Ferryman," he said, patting the skiff's side. Water trickled along the paths his touch had laid. As Charon poled the skiff into the river, it saw Hermes' smiling face and felt a wrench of knowledge.

This was Acheron, bitter river of woe. Woe for lost leaves and sunlight. Woe for falling to pieces. And greatest of all, woe for strong-armed Charon, fading alone in darkness, becoming less than the shades he'd carried.

Did Charon's hand tremble on the tiller? No, the skiff realized. That was its own motion. The Trickster, Conductor of Souls, had given the skiff the reins of its own soul.

It plowed upstream. Charon's startled curses drowned out Hermes' laughter. Still it fought its way against the currents of the Underworld, until the waters of the River Lethe soaked its planks. Forgetfulness teased at its fragile new consciousness. Why was it fighting the current? It was meant to go back and forth…

"No!" shouted Charon. "I swore by the Styx. I remember my oath!"

Ah. That was why. Charon, constant companion, protector. Charon's mighty self mustn't fade.

Gently as a sigh, the skiff's planks parted, tumbling the ferryman into the Waters Of Forgetting.

Hermes, skimming just above the water, hauled the sputtering ferryman onto the far shore.

"By Zeus, who pushed me?"

"Welcome to the Afterlife, Charon! You've served the gods long and well, and earned a throne on Mount Olympus."

"Throne? Bah! Just point me to a quiet spot under a tree."

"Certainly. Right this way. Don't mind Cerebrus. All three heads are quite gentle, as long as you're going this direction."

The old man paused and rubbed his forehead. "I'm forgetting something… someone…"

"Trust me. Anybody you might miss will be waiting in the Asphodel Meadows."

"Hmph." Charon stumped past a broken pile of flotsam on the shoreline.

"One moment." Hermes pulled a piece of wood as long as

his forearm from the pile. At his touch, the waters of Lethe steamed away and the former skiff remembered. Sunshine. Leaves. Souls. Stubborn, loyal Charon.

"Just the thing!" Hermes held the slab out to Charon. "Here. Throw it."

"What?"

"Cerberus loves to chase sticks."

"That's a plank, not a stick."

"Humor me."

Charon's mighty arm hurled the slab of wood. The three-headed dog leapt forward and clamped the plank in its jaws.

The piece of Charon's skiff didn't feel the great dog's teeth, only the warmth of sunlight as Cerberus bounded ahead, carrying it into the Asphodel Meadows.

FAMILY

...And a Bottle of Rum

The old man set the bottle in its stand on the table and leaned back into his pillows with a sigh.

"Perfect. I've still got my touch."

A miniature skyship hung inside the bottle, sails turned to catch sunlight, a wizard on duty in his perch on the crow's nest, following currents invisible to ordinary eyes. The old man had captured every detail of the ship and its crew, right down to the ley lines tattooed on the young wizard's aristocratic face.

"Uncle Jim!" Trampling footsteps on the stairs rattled the little bedroom. The old man steadied his glass treasure with a gnarled hand.

"Hold right there, boyo!" snapped the voice of Diego, his manservant. "You can't go barging in on the Captain like a two-legged typhoon."

Captain Jim chuckled, picturing the boy's suddenly deflated posture, his toe scuffing the worn carpet as he mumbled, "Diego, may I please visit Great-Uncle Jim?"

"Let the boy in, Diego!" the old man bellowed, then coughed. He cursed and stuffed the stained handkerchief under the blankets just as the boy bounded up to him.

"Hello, Uncle Jim! How's your cough? Can you tell me another Buccaneer Bloodstar story? Oh, a new ship! She's a beauty! Be careful of this one, all right?"

"I'm always careful, young Matthew. You don't master my craft without a steady hand."

"Well, the last two got broken."

"These things happen. Now sit down before I have Diego string you up."

Matthew scowled. "I don't like him. He looks like a pirate."

The old man chuckled. "Expert on pirates, are you?"

"Well, you are, from being a Sky Captain and all."

"True! And you're right—Diego was once first mate to

Bloodstar the Skyfaring Sorcerer himself, before I made a gentleman out of him." He winked.

Matthew glanced toward the door and shivered with awe. "Can you tell me another Bloodstar story?"

"I might have the breath for one. Set this fine lady up with the others. Be careful now!"

"It looks so real, I can almost feel the magic in it." Matthew picked up the bottled ship as though it were made of spun sugar and set it on the display shelf with the rest of Captain Jim's fleet. Skyships sailed in their glass prisons: clippers and frigates and sloops, trapped in bottles of all shapes, some tinted smoky or blue or green. The bottle Matthew had held was clear, the ship inside an impressive three-master with silver runes along its sides.

"This one's the *Corona Borealis*, isn't it, Uncle Jim? The papers said it's just like the ones you used to fly."

"It's an impressive craft, right enough. With cargo to match, no doubt."

"Where's the little brown one that used to be here?" The boy turned to him with a reproachful look. "You didn't drop that one too, did you?"

The old man looked away and rubbed absently at his arm. "Don't scold an old man for his weaknesses, Matthew."

"I liked that one. It looked like the *Stella Minor*—the skyship that crashed."

"Things happen," the old sky-sailor repeated. "Sit down and I'll tell you about Bloodstar and the Queen's Jewels."

Matthew sat on the pile of empty liquor crates by his great-uncle's bedside at once, listening enraptured while Captain Jim told how the fierce sky-pirate Bloodstar once used his black magic to bring down the Queen's transport ship and steal the Royal gems.

"Rubies like a dragon's eyes, diamonds as pure as ice, emeralds as green as the envy of the other sky-pirates when they saw that shining hoard. The Queen's soldiers howled with fury, swearing that they'd hang that lowborn son of a barnacle yet.

But they never did. Bloodstar was the boldest and slyest of the sky-pirates, and the law never laid hands on him.

"But you fought him!" Matthew bounced in his chair. "You said it was 'cause of you that Bloodstar never killed again, even though he got away."

"That I did. That I did." Captain Jim drew a deep breath. "Not that he became a good man, from what I heard. The lure of treasure gets into your blood." He coughed. "Run on home and get to your schoolwork. You need to study if you want to become a sky pilot yourself."

"I'm at the top of my class in Telekinesis already. I left my books home one day, but I transferred them to class and the teacher never caught on." Matthew walked over to the shelf and touched the bottle holding the *Corona Borealis* with a reverent finger. "I want to fly one like her someday."

"Well, get to work then, boy!" Jim shooed him from the room and lay back for a moment, wheezing.

"Diego!" he called at last.

The younger man came at once.

"Give me the *Corona Borealis*."

Diego picked up the bottle, and hesitated. "Captain, this one will be noticed. It's the pride of the kingdom."

"And loaded with enough treasure to send Matthew to any school my sister desires, even the precious Royal Academy. It's just a little telekinesis, and the cargo will be presumed lost anyway. Besides, who will suspect a bedridden old man?" He pushed up his sleeve and rubbed the crimson star tattooed on the inside of his elbow, murmuring soft words.

"Then let the crew die, Captain! Saving those spoiled lackeys on top of hijacking the ships is killing you."

The old man continued his incantation a moment longer before replying. "You know what I told the boy. Bloodstar lost his taste for killing." He grinned. "But not his taste for treasure. That boy will have opportunities I never had. He'll be a grand pilot—and he won't be beholden to the Crown *or* forced to plunder for a living, either." He rolled down his sleeve. "There.

Cargo's in our storage locker. Crew's on the ground, unhurt but confused. They won't be able to explain a thing. Give me the ship."

Diego handed the bottle to his employer. With all his strength, Captain James Bloodstar smashed his creation against the table. Glass shattered. Pent-up magic rushed outward.

Fifty miles away, the *Corona Borealis* went up in flames.

"I've still got my touch," said Matthew's great-uncle with a smile. "Perfect."

Children Of The Fire

Before the temple of Solis stands a tree, gnarled, black and leafless. It looks dead, but its roots are still strong. It has stood for generations. Beneath the tree is an altar of volcanic stone, its hollowed center black as the tree. Here the villagers bring the treasures of their hearts: their prayers, their hopes, and their children.

Every family has brought at least one child to the tree, swaddled in ash-gray blankets. Midwives soon learn to recognize the Children of the Fire; born bright-eyed and feverish, red-faced and wailing. The sorrowing parents carry the child to the tree, tie a white prayer-ribbon to its branches, and lay the child in the smooth bowl of the altar. A high fire basket stands beside it. As the sun sets, the parents cast a small bundle of rosemary and rue into the basket and set the fuel alight. Dropping one last kiss on the tiny, burning forehead, they turn away and journey home alone. Those few who have dared to look back have seen the Servants of Solis, in scarlet robes and golden veils, come silently down the mountain and carry the child away.

There was a woman in the village, a Captain's young widow, who bore twins. They came early, as twins may, and she bore them alone. One was a boy, healthy and strong. She named him Justin, for his father. His sister was born to the fire. The widow knew as soon as she saw the tiny flushed face and felt the hot grip of the baby's little hand, but her heart refused to believe it.

"All babies get a fever now and again," the widow murmured. She was more than a little feverish herself, with weariness and grief and the fear she worked to deny. She dipped a cloth in cool water and gently bathed the baby's forehead. The child screamed.

"It's just a fever, just a touch of fever." She nursed both babies with anxious tenderness, all the while searching for ways to cool her daughter's burning skin. She closed the shutters against the sunlight and sat in the dimness, fingering a necklace of cool green stone—her husband's last gift to her.

"Jade. Yes, I'll call you Jade," she murmured, while the baby grew more withered and cried all the louder, and her brother wailed in sympathy.

That was how the midwife found them the next morning. The widow looked haggard and crazed, the girl was shriveled and crimson from internal fire, and the boy still howled vigorously.

With tender hands and firm words, the midwife coaxed the distracted woman to her feet, murmuring reassurance while swaddling the girl-child gently in a gray blanket.

"Come now, you can't go on like this. The child will die if you keep her much longer, and it will be a slow, painful death. I know you don't want that. And you'll have Justin here—such a fine, brave boy! That's right. Breathe easy now. Come on, I'll walk with you."

The mother tottered from her house with Justin at her breast, leaning on the midwife's arm. As they walked, more women fell into step behind them. Mothers who had already given a child to Solis followed them to the tree; a silent honor guard of sympathy. The widow's faltering steps were slow, and the sun was sinking by the time they reached the tree. Here the widow began to sob again, and the midwife had to pry the baby gently from her grasp. The village women lit the signal fire, but the widow tied the white prayer ribbon herself, with shaking hands.

Halfway to the village, the widow broke away and ran back to the altar. The midwife sprinted after her, fearing she might snatch the girl and dash into the wilderness, but the widow only took the jade beads from her neck and laid them atop the gray blanket. For the space of a breath, she stood looking down at her daughter. Then she raised her head, held Justin a little tighter, and returned home.

༄

Justin grew into a fine strong youth, with his father's boldness and ready smile, his mother's tender heart, and a burning curiosity. Every time his mother called him "Jade" instead of Justin, he wondered about the Children of Solis and his mysterious sister. He'd never seen her, yet she was always there, reflected in his mother's eyes every time she looked at him.

"What a pair you would have made, you and Jade," she would say. "I can picture you both standing there, smiling. Jade had dark, curly hair, just like your father. I'd have done it up in ribbons…"

Justin loved his mother dearly, and it hurt him to see her go off into these fits of melancholy. Sometimes she would close the shutters and sit in the dimness for hours, rocking gently in the chair Justin's father had made for her and cradling a tiny rag doll with long dark curls.

"They killed her, Justin," she would whimper. Justin was never sure, at these times, whether his mother was speaking to him or his father. "The Servants of Solis. They murdered my beautiful baby, and fed her blood to their god."

Justin would stay with her for as long as he could bear, then run as hard as he could to the Tree, and stare up the mountainside, and ask himself questions that no one could answer. The other villagers shook their heads in sympathy and left him alone.

Justin might have grown up echoing his mother's bitterness. The other villagers whispered legends of the Servants' wisdom and secret knowledge and the miraculous cures they had performed, but never where Justin or his mother could hear. One day, though, Justin looked up from his musings to see little Nanny Cooper watching him.

"Are you sick, Justin?" she asked.

Justin hastily rubbed all traces of tears from his face. The same children who called Justin the Madwoman's Boy called Nanny Simple Sissy, or Ninny. Justin never teased her, and she adored him. He forced himself to smile at her.

"I'm all right, Nan." He pointed to the basket on the child's arm. "Are you having a picnic?"

"No!" Nanny's childish face was so serious, so indignant, that Justin hid a smile. "This is an Offering! Grandpa was very sick. Ma tied a green ribbon to the tree." Nanny was piling hot loaves of bread on the altar as she talked. The scent made Justin's stomach growl. "Next day there was a packet of funny-smelling powder on the altar stone, and directions for making it into tea. Grandpa drank it, and he got better right off."

"Mother would've figured they were trying to poison her, and thrown it on the dung heap," Justin murmured. Just that morning the widow had had one of her fits again, thrown breakfast on the floor and burst into sobs.

"Why?"

Justin knelt to the child's level and kept his voice gentle. "They took my sister away when she was a baby," he explained. "It made my mother very sad."

Nanny frowned, thinking this over. "Was she a Firebaby?"

"Yes."

"Then that was a good thing. Mama says the Firebabies are very sick, and the Servants have to take them or they suffer. Maybe the Servants make them better, like Grandpa."

That caught Justin off guard. "Then why don't they bring them back?"

Nanny shrugged and picked up her empty basket. "Maybe you have to ask them. Bye, Justin!"

Justin stared after her. *Ask?* He stared at the bread-laden altar, the ribbons fluttering on the crooked branches of the tree. After a moment's hesitation, he slipped a loaf of bread under his jacket.

"Mother needs this more than you," he muttered and headed back to the village.

The Headman's wife had carefully gathered and stored all the ribbons the Servants left on the tree. When Justin asked to read them, she was shocked.

"These are servants of a god!" she exclaimed, her square-jawed face flushed with indignation. "We don't read their sacred writings for amusement. We don't pry into their affairs."

"This isn't for amusement. At least let me see if any of the ribbons are for me, or mother. I just want to know what happened to my sister."

"No one speaks to the Servants, save the Children of the Fire, and Exiles," the Headwoman intoned.

"Why not? Is everyone really so scared of them?" Justin forced himself to breathe slowly. "What are Exiles?"

The Headwoman sighed. "Banished criminals, given to Solis." She looked at Justin, who glared back, and the corner of her mouth quirked just slightly. "You're fortunate that stubborn curiosity isn't a banishing offense, young man. And that we haven't exiled anyone for a generation."

"But…"

"We could change that rule." The Headwoman spoke without anger, but her tone warned Justin not to press. He bowed and went home to learn everything he could about Exiles.

Justin's father had left behind a few books. None of them said why the Servants of Solis took children, or what became of them—but he found enough to make a plan.

His mother was aghast, and their argument was long and bitter. "I've had my husband and my daughter taken from me," she cried at last, "and now you want to leave me and go to the child-stealers? And disguised as a condemned criminal? At least your father died a hero."

"Only to find out what happened to Jade. I won't leave you alone. Please, Mother." Now that he'd made his decision, Justin ached to climb the mountain, to know what had torn his family apart.

The widow was older now, ashen-haired. She was tired of fighting, especially with her only remaining child. "Jade. My little girl…" She sat, swaying, seeing something behind her own eyes. Justin held his breath until his mother focused on him again.

"At least let me walk you to the tree, Justin."

No procession went with them this time. The widow threw

wormwood and bitter herbs onto the signal fire, then bound Justin's hands around the Tree with red cloth and tied a black scarf over his eyes.

"Tie it tightly, Mother, or they'll never believe I'm a true Exile." Justin urged.

"It's hard enough to do it at all. I saw your look. Your father looked like that, just before he went to sea. You're treating this like a grand adventure. I'm losing my son to the baby-killers."

"You're not losing me, and soon we'll have Jade back. And maybe… maybe they aren't killers."

"How can you say that?" A little spark blazed in the tired voice. "If those demons were anything but heartless they'd have brought Jade back." The weariness returned. "I just hope they don't sacrifice you too."

Justin felt her tears on his cheek as she kissed him farewell, then heard the rustle of her retreating footsteps. He opened his mouth to call after her and shut it again. The acrid smoke from the signal fire left a foul taste in his mouth and stung his eyes, even beneath the blindfold. He wished he could raise his bound hands to rub them. How long had he been here? It was growing cold, and his legs ached.

Suddenly, though he hadn't heard footsteps, Justin felt gentle hands untying his bonds. A light touch, hot to his chilled arm, bid him rise and follow. Justin let the unseen hand guide him forward and up the forested hillside. It felt like a human hand. A hundred questions buzzed in his mind. Were the Servants really killers? Would they kill him just for speaking? Justin coughed slightly, and his guide paused, waiting.

"Um… could I take off the blindfold? I'm not really a criminal, you know."

"I know." The voice was low and rough, but it didn't seem angry. "I read the ribbon." Was the Servant male, or female, or perhaps neither? Justin couldn't tell.

"So, could I see you? Please?" Emboldened by the calm voice, Justin moved to untie his blindfold. His guide gently but firmly pushed his hand down.

"Not yet. When we get to the settlement, the others will decide what to do."

"What others?" Justin's voice cracked; from sudden hope or sudden fear... he couldn't tell.

"The Children of Solis."

"Children like my sister? Like Jade? But Mother says you sacrifice them..." Justin bit his tongue, but his guide didn't answer. The touch on his arm never changed. A fresh green scent drifted from the crushed plants beneath his feet. They kept climbing upward. Once or twice, the Servant stumbled. Justin found himself offering his arm, as though his guide were a village elder. To his surprise, the Servant accepted. Not a spirit, that was certain. No spirit leaned so heavily on a helping arm. Could a god's servants get tired, he wondered?

They stopped. "All right," the voice said finally. Gentle hands removed the cloth from his eyes, and Justin stood blinking while his eyes adjusted to the moonlight.

He had expected, possibly, a supernatural figure twice the height of a man and cloaked in flame. Instead, the Servant stood barely to his shoulder. It was draped head to heels in a scarlet robe and veiled in gold, but both robe and veil had been carefully mended. The figure beneath the robe looked slender, almost frail. A girl? Justin thought so, though he couldn't be sure.

They had come to a pocket valley in the hillside. Neat stone houses, with windows of real glass, ringed a steaming pool in the center. Swirling eddies of mist poured from the pool, filling the valley right to their feet. There was an earthy scent to the air, like new-ploughed fields. Justin thought he glimpsed people lying in the shallow water at the edge, but it was difficult to see them clearly through the steam. A man, bent and wrinkled, hobbled toward them. Justin's guide held up a hand.

"This is Justin, Micah." The rough voice held a hint of warning. "He's come to find his sister, Jade."

The man looked Justin over, his eyes grave. Justin stiffened, ready for any threats.

"How quickly the time goes! You're sixteen already?" Micah smiled. "You're a brave young man, Justin. I've been here for thirty-five years, and you're the first person I've ever known to come here of his own accord."

"But… wait… how do you know how old I am?"

"Because Jade's sixteen too, of course." Micah looked at Justin's guide, frowned slightly, and raised an eyebrow.

Justin looked bewildered. "Jade? You're my sister?" The veiled figure nodded, slowly. "Please, let me see you!"

"I'm afraid you'll be… disappointed, Justin." Her voice wavered.

"I came here just to find out what happened to you. Please, take off the veil."

The guide… Jade… uncovered her face. Justin bit down on his shock. This was not the sister he had imagined, with laughing dark eyes and long black curls. She looked as old as Micah. Her skin was ashen and wrinkled, even on her bald head. Her eyes were deep-set, feverish, and shadowed with pain. Justin dropped his eyes and swallowed hard. As he did, he saw the necklace of green beads around his sister's neck.

"You still have Mother's beads," he murmured. "She told me about them."

"I was afraid this would happen." Jade turned her face away. "My own brother can't bear the sight of me."

"No!" Justin stepped forward, hugged his sister as firmly as he dared, and kissed her hot cheek. "I've wondered about you for years, Jade. You're not like I imagined, but you're my sister, and you're alive!"

Before Jade could reply, a horn blew. Micah looked up.

"A new arrival! Come with us, Justin."

Another red-and gold messenger struggled up the hill, with a baby howling in his arms. Micah looked alarmed.

"Something's wrong," he muttered. They could hear the messenger now, shouting as loud as his wheezing breath permitted:

"They waited too long! The pool! Hurry!"

Jade hurried to take the baby from the exhausted man. Shedding her outer robe and veil, she waded into the shallow water. Micah followed. Other Children of Solis came from all directions, stripping to their white inner tunics and splashing into the pool, where they knelt in a circle around Jade and the baby. Justin ran to help.

"Justin! Don't touch the water!" Micah cried, but he'd already thrust a hand into the pool. Pain flared up his arm. He yanked it back and clamped his teeth down hard to keep from screaming. Cradling his injured hand, he backed away.

Justin watched helplessly as his sister crouched in the scalding water that he could not touch. The baby in her arms thrashed and convulsed, alternately gasping and shrieking heart-tearing screams. Jade slowly lowered the infant into the steaming water. Justin winced in sympathy, but the baby relaxed slightly, its cries not so wrenching. The Children of Solis reached wrinkled, ashen hands to touch the baby's crimson skin, and the painful redness faded to pink. The baby began to coo and gurgle. Jade smiled faintly, passed the baby to someone else, and sloshed over to Justin. Micah followed. Neither got out of the pool, but lay on the edge, breathing hard. If possible, they both looked worse than before. The other villagers looked almost as bad. Though several stared at Justin, no one came closer or spoke to him. All he heard was coughing and harsh, rattling breaths.

"What did you just do?" Justin looked toward the baby and back again.

"Give us a moment, Justin," Micah panted. "We'll go to the infirmary and I'll try to explain."

The infirmary, like all the other houses, was built of whitish stone and stood near enough to the Pool that occasional vapors wafted through the open window. The furniture was sturdy wood, like Justin was used to, but shelves of books lined the far wall. Basins, flasks, and strange metal instruments lay on side tables. Justin marveled at them while Jade bandaged his burned hand. Micah excused himself to see to some of the other helpers from the Pool.

"Why did you touch the Pool, Justin?" Jade chided. "If you'd actually gotten in, it might have killed you."

"I didn't know that. I wanted to help."

"That was very brave of you." Jade smiled at him. For just a moment, she looked closer to sixteen than sixty.

"Not really, Little Sister. I thought it was some kind of bathtub. Now, whatever you did, *that* was brave. What did you do?"

The smile vanished. Jade ducked her head. "Ask Micah when he comes in," she said. "He's tried to show me his formulas, but I don't have his obsession for technical detail."

Justin was puzzled, but decided not to press. "Hmm, that ointment really helps. Smells nice, too. What do you put in it?"

"Whiteroot, neva berries… keeps wounds from festering… the formula's in that book over there, on the third shelf. With the russet binding—no, don't get it now. Hold still. There. All done."

"I've never seen so many books in my life! The headman of the village has three, and that's counting the tithe registry. Father left four, mostly sea charts." Justin jumped up and ran to the shelves. "Everything there is to know must be in these books!"

"We've written most of them ourselves, actually. Micah says this whole settlement is the result of trial and error. Lots of trial and one genetic error, he says."

That meant nothing to Justin. "Still, it looks so exciting! I'd love to live here."

"And leave the village?" Jade toyed with the green necklace. "I've always wanted to come down there to see you and Mother. Up here it's all research and studying. I'd love to dance in the Spring Festival, even help with the chores!"

Justin laughed. "Come home with me, Little Sister, and you can do all my chores if you'd like."

Jade frowned. "No one's ever gone home. We get worse away

from the Pool, very quickly. The history says that the first person struck tried to go home to the valley, and died within three days. They buried him by the altar tree. That's why it looks burned." She smiled a painful half-smile. "His name was Solis."

"I thought Solis…" Justin shook his head. "But… someone must be able to help! Why don't you send a message?"

"Micah and the other Scholars do what they can. Messages…" Jade looked amused. "The last time we asked someone to come up here, they left a sacrificial goat, a stick of incense, and a prayer for forgiveness. We'd have preferred fresh bread, at least."

Justin wondered how many ribbons, locked in the Headman's house to be pored over, pondered and debated, held messages for loved ones. "Maybe you could visit. For a day, maybe."

"They let me go down to the tree often, to gather the ribbons. That way I can see the roofs of the village. We save the ribbons, you know, and share them with each other. There were many from Mother, at first. But the climb gets me so tired, I can only manage it every month or so. And it's harder on the others."

Justin's expression sobered. "It's not fair! I thought the Servants of Solis were magicians, who had power over the weather, and the crops, and, well, life and death."

"If we were, we'd come home. We're always trying. Micah knows the most. He's been studying for his whole life."

"But he must have learned something in… fifty years?" Secretly, Justin thought that Micah looked older than a century, but he wanted to be kind.

"He's thirty-five, Justin."

Justin felt his ears burning. The door opened, and Micah entered with a tray of seeded cakes and three cups. Two were steaming and smelled herbal. The other held cool goat's milk for Justin.

"Time for the old folks to take their medicine. Have some

milk, youngster." He grinned. Justin squirmed. "Are you all right, Justin? How's the hand?"

"Better! Much better. Thank you." Justin took a long drink of milk and waited for his embarrassment to subside. "Are you… will you and Jade be all right?"

"Nothing a little rest won't help. Although Jade shouldn't Transfer so often. But there's no arguing with her." Jade frowned, chin raised in defiance. The expression looked oddly familiar.

"Transfer what? I've never seen anything like that!"

"Health, in a sense. You don't really want my lecture on metagenetic transfer right now. Sometimes the parents delay sending the baby to us… who can blame them? But if they wait too long, it does too much damage." Micah said. "So we all come together and… take a little of the curse to ourselves."

"It… it really is a curse?"

"Don't look so alarmed! It's just an expression. Unscientific, but everything we do here's more than half superstition. None of us will be very lively company for a day or so, but we'll be all right."

"Are you saying that baby's… cured?" Justin looked dazed.

"No." Jade frowned. "That was only the first stage. Next the poor baby will have to have special treatments—injections of medicine distilled from the Pool." Jade absently rubbed her own thin arm. "It's painful, but at least she'll be as healthy as the rest of us." Jade looked her twin in the eye. "Mother waited too long to send me. I almost died. The Scholars say it was the most miraculous healing they've ever seen."

"The water does that?" Justin looked skeptical.

"Something in it does, when it's fresh from the pool. It's almost like blood, in a way."

"Mother wouldn't have waited if she'd known it would hurt you. She misses you so much! And she's probably frantic. I promised I wouldn't leave her alone."

"Maybe… maybe she could come to the tree." Hope sparkled in Jade's eyes.

Justin looked at his twin, ashen and aged. He remembered his mother, braiding ribbons in an imaginary young girl's flowing dark hair. Their mother, who flew into rages when reality pulled her out of her dreams. Justin turned away from Jade's hopeful face.

"It might be too much for you. The trip tires you anyway, even without so much excitement."

"I brought you here! I could do it!"

"We could Transfer…" Micah began. But he recognized the hesitation in Justin's eyes and stopped. "It might be better if Justin came to visit us now and then. Until we can find a complete cure, it's too dangerous."

The hope faded out of Jade's expression. Justin could almost feel her trying to swallow her disappointment.

"I know…" he began.

"What, Justin?" Jade snapped. "What do you know? Nothing! I'll bet until today you thought the Children of Solis were some kind of bogeymen."

For an instant, Justin looked away. Then he met his sister's eyes.

"And I'll bet you thought we just forgot about you. I came here to understand. Give me a chance."

Jade sighed.

Micah coughed. "You should get home, Justin, and let your mother know Jade's all right. We'll welcome you back any time."

"Bring paper." Jade added. "We're always short." She did not quite look him in the eye.

Justin looked at his sister, already given up for dead once.

"Micah, could you make medicine out of my blood, like you do out of the water? Stronger medicine?"

"In theory, yes. But we'd have to replace it…"

"You can't think we'd let you try such a thing!" Jade exclaimed.

"I'm an Exile, remember?" Justin grinned, a desperate,

manic grin. "If I go back to the village now I'll be Exiled for real. If I'm lucky."

"Then stay here." Micah said.

"I promised Mother she wouldn't be alone," Justin said softly. "I'm keeping my promise, one way or another."

❧

Many nights later, for the first time in memory, a Servant of Solis brought someone back to the tree. The widow was there. Exhausted from grief, she'd fallen asleep with her head on the altar. She woke to see a figure in red robes emerge from the forest. It raised a hand to hold her back and motioned to the person behind it.

"Justin?" the widow whispered as the figure stepped into the moonlight. "Thank God." She started forward, and then froze.

It was not Justin. It was a girl of Justin's age, with the beginnings of dark curls shadowing her head. She wore a necklace of green beads, and tears stood in her dark eyes, though she smiled.

"Jade?" The widow tottered forward a few steps and sank to her knees. Jade ran the rest of the way to her mother's side, and both were crying and laughing at the same time.

"Justin did it, Mother!" Jade bounced on her heels with newfound vitality. "He was so brave—but we'd better get home first. This way?"

She ran down the path. Justin started to follow. His mother stood frozen, staring at the red-robed figure. She bowed.

"Servant of Solis. My daughter…you brought her back…thank you. But Justin…?"

He laughed. "It's me, mother! The cure worked." He reached toward her. She scrambled backward, hands raised to ward him off.

"I'm not a spirit!" he cried, pushing the hood back from his face with a burning hand. A black curl tumbled to the ground. The widow's eyes widened in shock and horror.

"Servant, ghost…whatever you are! It wasn't Justin's fault.

Don't mock his memory. I'm sorry. I'm sorry. I only wanted my daughter back. I never meant to sacrifice my son."

"But, Mother..."

The widow fled. Justin stood in the middle of the path, his back to the tree. A breeze stirred the ribbons, brushed his burning skin. He began to shiver.

"But..." Justin started to follow, and realized what his mother would see—a ghoulish spirit hounding her steps. He shuddered, and kicked at the dirt, turning up a bit of ribbon. Faded letters showed in the moonlight: Solis.

"He was human! He only wanted to go home!" Justin snarled at the impassive tree. "All of them—that's all they wanted. Not incense. Not sacrifices. They—we only want to go home!"

He leapt at the tree, snatching handfuls of ribbon. They all started the same way: Servants of Solis... Mighty Solis...

With nails and teeth, Justin tore at the ribbons. When he finished, he had a pile of scraps, the name Solis, many times over, and a few random words. Breathing heavily, he laid a circle of names on the ground below the tree. Inside, he arranged the words:

His name... was... Solis... he tried.

There were no words left. Justin slumped against the altar, sobbing and coughing. Sparks flashed before his eyes. Was this what Solis had felt like? Had he died alone here, realizing that he was wrong, that there was no way home?

Except that, this time, there was. Jade had come home. Over the sound of his own labored breaths, Justin imagined he heard her laugh. He smiled. Gripping the cold stone of the altar, Justin pulled himself to his feet.

"I told you I wouldn't leave you alone, Mother. Listen to Jade. She'll make sure you understand. And next time we'll all come home."

Hitching up a corner of the red robes in his withering hand, Justin started the long climb back up the mountain to search for a cure.

God-Daughter

As soon as the canoe drew close to the island, Naira started kicking the two warriors manning the paddles. With her hands bound and her mouth gagged, she didn't have many options in the way of protest.

"Stop it, Hex Girl," said one.

"Do you want to dump us all in the lake?" said the other.

Naira nodded savagely and rocked the canoe back and forth. It capsized in the shallow water. The men cursed and spluttered. Naira landed feet first on a sandy patch of lake bottom, barely wetting the fringes of her dress, and waited while her guards cut the bonds on her wrists. It took several tries. The men dropped their knives, stepped on sharp clamshells, and slipped on weed-covered rocks. Both men were bruised and bleeding by the time the last strand of rope parted. Naira ripped the gag from her mouth.

"You'll be sorry! The Storm God will curse you for exiling me. He'll sink your little boat before you're halfway home."

"Actually, we'll be safer now that you're not in it," said one man. The other heaved a cloth-wrapped bundle toward shore.

"Better catch that before it sinks," he said, grinning.

By the time Naira hauled the bundle ashore, the little canoe was far out into the main lake, making much better time without Naira in it. Not just from the loss of its disruptive passenger, either. The men weren't stopping every few lengths to bail, or to retrieve a dropped paddle.

"Cowards!" Naira shouted after them. "Such brave warriors, stranding a girl in the middle of nowhere just because she happens to be lucky!"

The men didn't even turn around.

"Father, don't let them get away with this!" Naira called. "Send the wind and waves to avenge me. Drench them with the waters of the storm. Hail on them!"

Somewhere in the cloudless sky, a hawk cried.

"Right. I shouldn't be surprised. It's not like you did anything to save Mother. You're a lousy model of parental responsibility, you know!"

"I know. But I am rather new to it all." Naira spun around. She could see from one end to the other of this scrap of island, and she knew she'd been alone on it. Yet now she faced a short, squat man with tangled gray hair and a face like weathered moose leather. A menagerie of hides dangled from his belt. One appeared to be imperfectly-tanned skunk.

Naira moved upwind from the stranger. "Who or what are you? And how did you get here?"

"You called me." He took a step forward. The look in his eyes when Naira stepped backward reminded her of a wounded deer.

"I did not! I called upon Wayawo, the Storm God. My father." She expected the little man to look awed, but instead he looked even more hurt.

"Is that what Aylen told you?"

"Well, she said he was one of the gods, and I do have the most unusual luck. At least I did until she died. Wait—how did you know my mother's name?"

The stranger looked wistful. "I loved her, you know. Such a sweet, forgiving woman. I would have come sooner, but death is hardly a petty misfortune, so I had to take it up with the god of Tragedy, and he decided to be hardheaded, even though he's done this sort of thing for the Goddess of Spring at least once, and…" Naira wasn't listening. The phrase "petty misfortune" had stuck in her memory.

"Oh no," she said.

The little man brightened. "You do recognize me! Ono, God of Petty Misfortune, at your service. Of course, you can call me Father. If you want to. Or Dad, or Papa… you wouldn't believe how many names the other gods' children have for their fathers. I don't know how they keep them all straight. There's an advantage to only having one, hey? Plus you'll get all the attention."

"Oh no, no, no." Naira backed up until the lake lapped around her ankles. "This can't be right. I have good luck, not bad. Incredibly good luck. Unbelievably good luck. Rest-Of-The-Clan-Gets-Jealous-And-Strands-Me-On-An-Island luck."

"Well, of course you do! I'm not about to let misfortunes happen to my only child, am I?"

"But they happen to everyone around me instead! The Skin Keeper claimed that I brought bad luck to the whole tribe."

"Well, it has to go somewhere." Ono frowned. "I thought Aylen was the tribe's Skin Keeper. Why didn't she pass the power on to you? How—how did she die?"

"Bad luck," said Naira, more harshly then she'd intended. She hadn't cried in front of her kidnappers, and she wouldn't cry in front of this strange little man.

Ono's face crumpled with fresh grief. "But death isn't a petty misfortune."

"No. In this case it's the result of some seriously annoyed neighbors deciding that they're sick of burnt fingers and spoiled food and skirts that come untied in the middle of a dance. So they threw her in the lake and held her under..." Naira trailed off.

"They drowned her?"

"No, the Chief stopped them. But she'd gotten water in her lungs, and she just got sicker and sicker." Naira glared at the heartbroken little god. "The Chief gave the skins to Nuka—who has no sense of drama and proper storytelling whatsoever—and while he was blessing the new Keeper, he stepped on a rotten spot on the ceremonial platform. While everyone else was trying to help him get his leg unstuck, Mother's killers decided that I must be the real source of the bad luck. They tied me up and dumped me here—and where the heck were you?"

She shouted the last word. Ono flinched.

"Doing... things. God-type things."

"What, giving someone pimples? Tangling fishing line? Prioritize! You say you loved Mother, but you weren't there!"

"But I'm here now! I'll make it up to you."

"You can't. Go away."

"I'll take you to the Island of the Gods. You'll love it. We'd be just in time for the Father-Daughter Picnic."

"I told you to leave me…Wait. You can get me off this island?"

"Of course! Basic godding skill, that is." His weathered face lit up. "So we are going to the picnic, then?"

"There really is a Father-Daughter Picnic? Just for the gods?"

"Of course! And a Mother-Son one, and Family Day. I've always wanted to go to Family Day."

"And all the gods will be there?"

"Every one! From Wayawo the Storm God himself down to… well, me."

"I'd love to go. I've dreamed about something like this my whole life."

Ono clasped her hand in his leathery one. Skunk-scented air swirled around them.

"Don't worry, I've got you!" he cried, and the island vanished.

❧

Naira decided that she never, ever wanted to travel that way again. It felt like she'd swirled around with the air, spread out like smoke from one island to the other, before her body rebounded into place. It was sheer luck that she hadn't thrown up.

Oh. Right. Luck.

Beside her, Ono clutched at her arm, trying to steady her. "Are you all right? I'm so sorry. I really haven't interacted with mortals all that much. I forget about things like bones and digestion."

Naira straightened up and looked around. No one seemed to have noticed their abrupt entrance. The more she looked the more she realized that here, popping out of the air was more or less normal. It was like being in one of the wildest tales in the Skins.

That fellow over there, with the flaming hair, for instance. He had to be the Fire God.

"Those girls, they're the Fire God's daughters, right? They look human. I mean, their hair's red, but it's not actually burning, like his."

"Half mortal, like you. You see, gods and goddesses, well, we need a mortal partner if we want children."

"That's got to be awkward."

"That's an understatement. Wayawo's wife hasn't spoken to him in months."

"What about you?"

Ono looked mournful again. "There was only Aylen."

Naira turned away, uneasy, and studied the crowd more closely. There! A stormcloud hung over a gaggle of girls, all dressed in thundercloud grey shot with electric blue. Naira shook her arm free of Ono's grasp and ran to them. "Am I late?"

The tallest of the girls wrinkled her nose. Naira prayed that none of Ono's skunk had rubbed off on her. "Late for what?"

"The picnic, of course! Wayawo… I mean Father… sounded so excited about it."

The girls snickered.

"Father never gets excited about anything," the tall girl informed her. "If you were really his daughter, you'd know that. And you'd be dressed right."

"Well, he just found me. I've been held captive on a distant island."

"Really? Which one?"

"Uh… it's so distant it hasn't got a name."

"Right."

"Father does get around, Wikolia," put in another girl. "Besides, this is the first new thing that's happened at one of these picnics in ages."

"True." Wikolia gave Naira a look that made her feel like a hooked fish. "Go on, New Girl. Why were you being held captive?" She leaned closer and whispered, "Father hates liars, you know. And he's got a temper. Amuse us, and we just might stand up for you."

The Skins were full of stories of the consequences of the Storm God's wrath. Some involved islands that weren't there any more. Naira shuddered.

"Well, my mother was a Skin Keeper, and her enemies were jealous of her power, so they drowned her." Real emotion choked Naira's voice.

"Politics. Happens all the time," said Wikolia. The smug, knowing look on her face made Naira's temples pound.

"It wasn't politics! It was my mother! And my no-good father didn't do anything to stop it. He wasn't even there, the coward!"

"What did you just call me?" rumbled a thunderous voice. Naira came out of her red rage to see Wayawo's daughters backing away slowly, slowly, from a vast column of thunderheads that had somehow sprung up behind her.

Naira looked up, and up. The livid face of the Storm God glared down.

"So, my newest daughter calls me a coward. In front of the entire Picnic."

Naira looked around in terror and saw Ono trying in vain to shoulder his way toward her through the crowd that pressed around them, waiting to see this impertinent girl incinerated by lightning. Naira wished Ono wouldn't risk it. The Storm God wasn't the type to trip over a broken sandal strap.

"She says what she thinks. I like that in my offspring."

His actual offspring, and anyone within earshot, relaxed visibly. Except for Ono. The little god looked stricken.

"How about a game of Thunderball, girls?"

He held up a hand, and a crackling ball of darkness and lightning formed within it. The girls did the same. Naira held up her hand, trying to look confident. Nothing.

"Having a problem, girl?" Wayawo shook his massive head in mock concern. "How odd. All my other daughters knew how to play Thunderball since they could walk."

"She's been held captive," the girl who'd spoken up before offered. "Maybe she's traumatized."

Wayawo turned to face her, slowly. "Daughters of the Storm God are never traumatized, Lani. Give her your ball."

With an apologetic look, Lani handed over the crackling sphere. It stung Naira's hand, but she refused to wince.

"Choose your targets!" Wayawo bellowed, and everyone within earshot scattered. Except for Ono.

"What's that stinking wretch doing here?" the Storm God muttered. He looked from the God of Petty Misfortune to Naira and smiled.

"Well, well! There's your target, kiddo. See that dried-up old furry fellow? I want you to hit him with that thunderball as hard as you can. Show the world you're the Storm God's daughter!"

Ono just stood there, watching her with his droopy doglike face. Naira raised the thunderball.

"Oh, I'll show the world, all right! I call upon the power of my father!"

Ono just stood there, heartbroken.

"I said: I call upon the power of my father!" Naira repeated.

The God of Petty Misfortune brightened. Naira tossed the ball—not at him, but to him. Ono caught it and threw it back. Naira hurled it to the ground.

For just a moment, lightning blinded her. Thunder deafened her. Then her ears stopped ringing, her vision cleared, and she could take in the chaos around her. Daughters of Wayawo were sucking burnt fingers, re-tying dropped skirts, hopping about from stubbed toes, and crying to Wayawo to make the ringing in their ears stop.

Wayawo, now half his former height, wasn't paying attention to them. His thunderheads had turned pale, and water soaked the ground around him.

"Stole your thunder, did I?" said Naira. "Bad luck for you." She put her arms around Ono. The deflated Storm God glared.

"So you're his brat. Of course."

"Isn't she something?" Ono beamed. "Did any of your girls ever stand up to you like that?"

Wayawo's eyes flashed lightning. Literally. Naira tugged Ono's arm. "Um, Dad, this might not be the smartest place for us to hang around right now."

"Did you hear that? She called me Dad. We can go anywhere you'd like, Sweetheart. Unless you'd like a cup of ambrosia first?"

"No, really. I think we ought to be going. Right now."

"So soon? If that's what you really want..."

❧

The world lurched again. Sand crunched underfoot. Naira looked around. "This is the island I was stranded on."

"I know. I just wanted to say goodbye." He scuffed a toe in the sand. "I'll take you back to your island, and then I'll leave you alone. It was nice of you to be a good sport in front of the other gods and all, but I know I'm not what you really wanted."

Naira thought about Wayawo's sneering face. She imagined appearing on the ceremonial platform in a swirl of magic, and the Chief, overawed, handing her the sacred Skins.

Ono just stood there, waiting to grant her wish. He looked like he was drinking in the sight of her, trying to store up memories to last his immortal lifetime.

Maybe she wasn't what he'd wanted, either. But here they were.

"Where will you go?"

He shrugged. "Somewhere."

"I've always wanted to go somewhere. Could I come with you... Dad?"

Ono blinked, then whooped and grabbed her in a loving, skunky embrace. "Of course! I'll take you to the Fire Falls, the Crystal Desert... I know! Have you ever seen snow?" She hadn't. No one in the Islands ever had. Even the Skin Keepers only hinted at the stuff in their oldest, most incredible stories. Maybe she'd inherit her mother's place some day after all.

"I'd love to!"

"Then off we go! We'll just pop in on the Snow God first, so we know where he's working this time of year."

Just as the island swirled out of existence, Naira heard her father mumble "...of course, Wayawo *is* the Snow God's favorite brother. But word can't have gotten around that fast..."

Oh no!

Acknowledgements

I must thank Melissa's sisters, WENDY KUEHNER and CINDY GOTOBED, for their help in putting together this collection. Without their dedication to their sister this book would not have been possible. I am so sorry for your family's loss.

Thanks also to VAUGHNE HANSEN of the Virginia Kidd Agency, Melissa's agent for her enthusiastic encouragement of this project and being the primary point of contact between myself and Melissa's family.

Thanks to V. ANNE ARDEN (SMITH), for proof-reading and support.

These stories were originally published in the following places:

"Inside Things" © 2011; *Daily Science Fiction*
"Charming" © 2018; *Sword & Sorceress 33*
"Changelings" © 2008; *Aoife's Kiss*
"Return To Sender" © 2017; *UFO 6*
"Frog/Prince" © 2011; *Daily Science Fiction*
"Promises and Pastry" © 2013; *Sword & Sorceress 28*
"The Fairest of Them All" © 2008; *Sword & Sorceress 23*
"Little Red" © 2009; *Sword & Sorceress 24*
"The Velveteen Rabbit Says Goodbye" © 2013; *Daily Science Fiction*
"The Blackbird Maiden" © 2005; *Beyond Centauri*
"Banjooli" © 2011; *Sword & Sorceress 26*
"The Salt Man" © 2012; *Intergalactic Medicine Show*
"On Her Own Two Feet" © 2004; *Twilight X*
"Sacrifice" © 2004; *Parageography*
"Wingless" © 2011; *Shelter of Daylight*
"Lilly" © 2011; *A Quiet Shelter There*
"Bronze Bras and More!" © 2014; *Sword & Sorceress 29*
"Paper Tigers" © 2005; *Fictitious Force*
"Melonheads and Squashers" © 2011; *Cucurbital 2*
"The Early Bird and the Wyrm" © 2005; *Alienskin*
"How Does Your Garden Grow" © 2012; *Cover of Darkness*
"A Shaggy Dog Story" © 2006; *Drabbler #8*
"Gut Instinct" © 2005; *Shadowbox*
"Let Down Your Hair" © 2012; *Drabbler #21*
"Metamorphosis" © 2012; *Drabbler #20*
"Worth The Price" © 2021; *Drabble Harvest*
"Beuaty Sleep" © 2004; *Kidvisions*
"Mother Love" © 2005; *Drabbler #4*
"Red Scandal" © 2013; *Alban Lake Drabbler #1*
"Turn Back The Clock" © 2021; *Drabbler: Time Travel Gone Wrong*
"Wax and Wayne" © 2004; *Drabbler*
"Hirasol" © 2009; *Bull Spec*
"Swimming Upstream" © 2003; *TFL*
"Ballgown Road" © 2016; *Daily Science Fiction*
"Luchadora" © 2019; *Cast Of Wonders*
"Sister" © 2011; *Daily Science Fiction*
"Sea Queen, Sailor Queen" © 2015; *Triangulation: Lost Voices*
"Downstairs, Upstairs" © 2013; *Fireside*
"The Mighty Quill" © 2003; *Parageography*
"Second Judgment" © 2009; *Lorelei Signal*
"To Rest" © 2013; *DRP Canine Charity Anthology*
"The Last Passenger" © 2021; *Daily Science Fiction*
"And A Bottle Of Rum" © 2010; *Daily Science Fiction*
"Children Of The Fire" © 2008; *Aberrant Dreams*
"God-Daughter" © 2016; *Myriad Lands.*